THE HOLLYWOOD HIGH CHRONICLES

book 5

Aftershock

by **Melissa Velasco**

ISBN 978-1-960378-25-5   (paperback)
ISBN 978-1-960378-26-2   (eBook)

1st Edition

Models contracted through DMe Talent Agency:
Deidre Michelle (Agent) @dmetalentagency11

Front Cover Models: Maddie Dawn Cordero, Julian Gopal, Shylo Molina, Winslow Trullinger, Abby Max, Leah Grace Franco, Gabrielle Chevalier

Back Cover Models: Maddie Dawn Cordero, Julian Gopal, Winslow Trullinger

Makeup and Hair: Nathaniel Garcia
Costume Concept: Melissa Velasco
Cover Concept: Melissa Velasco
Photography: Tino Duvick @brokenchainphotography
Photo Shoot Directors Assistant: Sharon Daily
Front Cover Design: Tino Duvick and Anna Hall
Editor: Kyle Fager
Typeset: Anna Hall
Proofreader: Doris Nehrbass

Dedicated to Steve Harden, a dad who always had a video camera on his shoulder, never missed a chance to visit a toy store with his kids, and loved a family vacation more than anyone I've ever met. You worked like a demon, never pulled a punch, and you stayed true to your conviction every single moment. Thank you for teaching me that, "If you tell them everything you know, they know twice as much as you." You were the calm voice of reason, except when you weren't. That fire lives on in me.

You are missed, but never forgotten. We all hear your laughter in our minds still.

AFTERSHOCK

CHAPTER 1

I sigh. Sauntering aimlessly alone through the outdoor mall has proven as joyless as I imagined it would be. You see, I'm friendless. This summer has been a lonely misery. At least I chose Fourth Street Promenade, so I'm not a complete douche-cicle.

Striding my way, wearing a shit-eating grin, is quarterback extraordinaire Drew Hutchins. He crows, "Melanie Slate," as he cuts a trail across the outdoor shopping center full of people.

I chuckle to myself. *Well, at least not everyone hates me.*

Drew scoops me up in a boisterous hug before plunking me down. He looks me over, taking in my tight black leggings, Cherry Bomb black-and-red crop top, and heeled ass-kicking motorcycle boots. "Why do you always look like a wet dream and my worst fears all rolled into one?"

I grin back at him. "What's up, superstar? I heard you're on scholarship with UCLA."

Drew nods. "I've been at practice all summer. They've got me as second string, but I'll make it to the first string by midseason, if I have any say in the matter."

"I'm proud of you. They'll see the light."

Drew quirks his mouth after surveying me. "Shot in the dark, but hear me out. I'd love for you to come to my homecoming game in a few weeks."

I feel someone hovering and look over my shoulder. Zane Drell and his buddy Rocco Rutelle are indeed hovering. I squeal and hug Rocco, followed by Zane. We'll get to them in a second. First, I need to get rid of Drew.

I turn back to the quarterback, who's gaping at Zane. "That's quite an offer. I'd be a disappointment though. I know less about football than I know about flying to the moon."

Drew throws his head back, belting laughter. "You'd love it. They have a snaaaaack bar. You love snacks. I'd put you in the wives' and girlfriends' box. It's full of catty simpletons you could throw dirty looks at the whole game."

I crack up. "Well, *that* actually is tempting."

Some of the other football players from Hollywood High exit the PacSun store. A jerk named Brad Davis barks, "Get away from the Queen of the Damned, Drew!"

I sigh. "Your social reputation bell just got rung. Scurry along now."

Drew winces. "I'm sorry about them, Melanie."

"You *know* I'm the Bermuda Triangle," I say with a shrug. "Best not fly into my airspace, or you'll become a social ghost. Go be popular now."

Drew jogs over to his idiot friends, who throw dirty looks my way, loudly talking smack while they razz Drew.

I roll my eyes, muttering, "What happened to that hostage situation comradery?" When Hollywood High was held hostage last school year, the football team was on my side. Turns out I was just a means to their survival ends. When the fear dissolved—and when we wound up all over the news with fresh drama—the social niceties went out the window.

I exhale hard and turn to Zane and Rocco.

"Ouch," Rocco says.

"It's the norm. Everyone at school either hates or fears me." I brighten. "Hi, you two. Long time, no see. Whatcha up to?"

We're interrupted by another uninvited miscreant. "Melanieeee! What's uuup, duuude?"

I turn and internally wince. *Not Surfer Guy Tad.*

"Hi, Tad," I politely reply.

"Wanna surf with me?" Tad drawls out in his wannabe surfer way. "I'm headed to the pier."

I glance down at my outfit. "I don't think I'm surf ready, but what a sweet offer."

"Wanna mack under the pier then?"

"Pardon?" I rattle my head. "Have we ever . . . macked?" I grimace at the word. It gives me the willies.

Surfer Guy Tad's face splits with a dopey grin. "You made out with Adam under the bleachers."

My expression scrunches with sarcasm. "Adam is Adam. I don't just slather about with any available guy."

Tad chuckles, and his red, hooded eyes droop a little. "Wanna smoke weed and eat hot dogs then?"

I fight not to laugh as Zane and Rocco rudely spurt chuckles.

"I believe I'll pass. But thank you."

Tad looks Rocco and Zane up and down before drawling out, "Whoooa, you guys are raaad."

Exuberantly, I point to Rocco. "Not only does he like hot dogs, but he also fancies a solid macking under the pier."

Tad claps an amused Rocco on the shoulder. "Thanks for the offer, my man, but I'm straight and looking for a date."

He gestures at Rocco with a friendly head tip. "But you're a friend and a confidant." Tad ambles off while whistling the theme song to *The Golden Girls*.

My face bunches as I study Tad's retreat. "I have to get out of Hollywood High," I mutter disgustedly.

"And here we were with nothing to do," Zane teases. "You passed on a heck of an offer there, Rocco."

Rocco chuckles. "We're continuing to do nothing, I assure you. What are *you* doing, Melanie?" He looks around. "Where's your misfit posse?"

I sigh. "MIA all summer."

Rocco and Zane exchange a look. "Why didn't you come to the Beach Bar?" Rocco asks. "The Surfrider crew's been there all summer."

My gaze drops to the pavement. "I've been avoiding the Riptide reminders." Pierre Riptide Strader was my boyfriend, briefly turned husband, who was murdered in a bomb blast at a competition in Hawaii. Yeah, I know. I'm sixteen. Just go with it. Nothing about my life is normal. Anyhow, it was horrific, and I can't deal with it. The person who murdered him, I murdered in turn—but he earned it. To the police and media, Jet Trippley was known as the Boulevard Butcher, a necrophiliac freak who'd eluded the Keystone Cops of Hollywood long enough to become a serial killer. That whole debacle is why my friends have backed off. You see, teenagers want to have fun, and my life isn't fun.

As if the universe hates me, and I wasn't already aware, I hear a squealed, "Melanie!" I turn and watch as my entire former friend group from Hollywood High approaches. Finley Ferrell bounces to me and hugs me tight.

"Hi," I say, halfheartedly returning the hug.

"Where have you been?" Finley asks.

My eyebrows rise.

With a vapid expression, Victoria Garcia cocks a hip. She's wearing the equivalent of a pair of denim panties. "The Black Widow ditched us for her new crew. Duh."

My gaze shifts to her, hardening. I can't stand this snake. "Victoria, if you ever so much as *allude* to me being a widow again, I'll put you through the floor. Don't speak to me. Don't speak about me."

Victoria's eyebrows rise in challenge, but Demitri Cantrell, my former best friend and Victoria's boyfriend, puts a hand on her arm, halting her attack.

"Where have you been?" Arch Terani asks.

"Excuse you?" I retort.

Presley Verelle, my other former best friend, clears her throat. "I love your Cherry Bomb shirt." She compliments me hesitantly.

"Thanks," I reply with a hand flick her way. "I got it for you for your birthday last week, but I wasn't invited to the party. So . . ." I flourish my hands over the shirt I chose to keep.

"I'm confused," Darren Whipple says. Darren is the quiet poet of the group. "Are we salty at Mel?"

Demitri exhales hard. "Melanie, I know you thought you were being ostracized. I talked to a few of these guys at the start of summer, and they have no idea what you were talking about."

"You called to tell me that when, exactly?" I bite back.

Demitri grimaces and flicks his eyes Victoria's way. No clue what he's stealthily attempting to communicate to me, and I don't care.

I land a look on Trey Valdez, my permanently pensive former boyfriend, who winces. "I let Melanie know that we needed a break from her this summer."

"Excuse the *fuck* out of all of you?" Zane spits out ferociously.

"You haven't been inviting her?" Bear barks at Trey.

Trey's mouth drops open as he stares at Bear. "*You* were the one who said we needed a break!"

Bear's face scrunches. "I meant at first. Melanie had just gotten out of the hospital, and she needed downtime. Then Adam and Valerie's wedding happened, and Adam said he needed some space from Mel."

"Adam stopped hanging out with us a month into summer when Valerie became a pain in the ass!" Demitri yelps.

"Right." Bear nods. "And none of you invited Melanie?"

"Why didn't *you* invite her?" Demitri asks. "You and Adam were the ones who requested the damn break!"

Bear looks to Trey. "She's *your* girlfriend. I thought you were inviting her."

"He is *not* my boyfriend," I exclaim. "I haven't seen Trey since the wedding!"

"WHAT?" Bear bellows.

Trey swallows. "I needed a break also."

"That's weak, man," Tanner Devick scolds. Tanner is Trey's best friend, and they're close enough that he often puts Trey in his place. "I don't appreciate this, Trey. Finley and I spent all summer trying to call Melanie. She kept blowing us off."

"I did too," Presley informs.

"I'm not talking to people who need a break from me," I say quietly.

"*WE* didn't want a break from you!" Tanner squawks. "We missed you!"

Presley holds up her hands in a peace gesture. "This is fixable. We still have two more weeks of summer. We're headed to Sound Waves to buy tickets for the Cherry Bomb show." She gestures to my shirt. "You're already dressed for the occasion. I would love for you to join us. We're going to the show for my birthday." She cuts hard eyes Trey's way. "I asked you to invite Melanie."

"Cherry Bomb, huh?" Zane says. He gets a mischievous look as he dials a number on his cell phone. Someone answers, and he puts the call on speaker while smirking at Presley. "Craig?"

"What's up, Zaney Mania?"

"I need to host a VIP party tonight," Zane says. "How many tickets do you have left for the Cherry Bomb show?"

"A hundred and ninety-two," Craig replies dejectedly.

"How many did you sell?"

"Eight." Craig groans. "I'm about to lose my ass on this thing, man."

Zane grins. "I'm buying all the remaining tickets." He narrows his eyes at Presley. "How much merch do you have for this event?"

"Two hundred shirts and CDs."

Zane's mouth drops open. "You bought TWO HUNDRED shirts and CDs for a show with two hundred tickets?"

"Yeah, I screwed this up," Craig admits. "I'm still learning. I bought the club three months ago, and this is the first big group I've toured in."

Zane chuckles. "All right, how much are the tickets, shirts, and CDs?"

"Everything is ten each."

Zane rolls his eyes. "Sold. I'm buying all of it, but the band has to sign my girl's CD. She wants to see the show, and I don't do crowds. I'll fill the house with my people."

"Who wants to see the show?" I murmur at Rocco. I crunch up my face. "Is he talking about me or someone else?"

Rocco chuckles. "He's talking about you. Apparently, you want to see the show."

"Good to know," I muse.

"Are you serious?" Craig asks in disbelief.

"Yup," Zane says. "Is there food and a bar?"

"Bar yes, food no."

"Make it an open bar. I'll cover the tab. Figure out food."

"Like what?"

"Hell, I don't care if you serve barbecue weenies in crock pots, just make it happen."

"I like crock pot weenies," I chirp.

"My girl likes crock pot weenies," Zane says with a grin.

"You're doing all of this for some chick?" Craig says, sounding baffled.

"Yuuup," Zane fires off. "Consider the show sold-out. No more tickets that I don't approve. Rocco's going to call you with a list."

"You got it! Thank you, Zane. I owe you big."

"You're welcome." Zane hangs up and turns to Rocco. "Call Pepe and Luis. Have them call the Pier Boys. Also, call the Beach Bar and get some more people together."

Rocco steps away, making a call.

Zane dials another number and waits for the answer. I'm both surprised and unsurprised to hear my stepfather, Rich, answer.

"How's my favorite future father-in-law?" Zane asks.

Rich cracks up. "Hey, Zane. To what do I owe the pleasure?"

My mother giggles out, "Hi, Helicopter Hottie!"

"Hello, Mom," Zane replies with a soft look. He loves my mother.

Trey struts up. "Are you seriously allowing Zane to greet you like that?" he demands into the phone.

Rich's tone drops. "That man can call me anything he wants to. How dare you question him after everything he did."

"Trey doesn't know," I say softly, as I'm turning a blazing shade of humiliated red at the reminder.

Zane wraps an arm around me and squeezes a little. "I know we haven't talked about it, but you're okay," he assures me.

"What happened?" Trey demands.

Zane ignores him and returns to talking to my parents. He explains the situation and how he's organizing a party at Sound Waves for Presley's birthday. "Wanna come to my 'some of us still love Melanie' party?"

Rich howls laughter. "Hell, yes, we do. Melanie's cried all damn summer. How many spots are you looking to fill?"

Zane side-eyes Rocco, who informs, "We've got a hundred and seven left. Beach Bar is closing, and everyone is going to head that way."

"How's it hanging, Roc?" Rich crows.

"A little to the left," Rocco jokes.

"I'm calling the Hellhounds," Rich says. "I guarantee they'll want to come. They keep asking about Melanie. Put me down for sixty of those tickets."

"Kick ass. Only forty-seven left."

We say goodbye to my parents, and Zane ends the call while Rocco keeps working on expanding the guest list. He gets the number down to thirty, and then, while he's holding on his latest call, he asks, "Who the hell are Cherry Bomb?"

Zane shrugs. "No clue, but any band that creates *that* crop top, on *that* girl—" he points to me—"is a godsend."

Trey's jaw tightens. "Back off, Zane."

Zane gives him a baffled look. "Well, Trey, why would I do that? You aren't dating her." He points at Demitri. "He's apparently slogging around at the bottom of the sludge pond."

Victoria blinks blankly, having no clue she's being insulted.

"Wow, bro," Zane says with a judgmental look for Demitri. "And Adam's so pussy-whipped by his wife that he's controlling all of *you*." He smirks at Trey. "I'd like to thank you for ignoring Pierre's request."

"Oh lord, not this again," Rocco groans. He gives Zane a pointed look. "You get one night partying with Melanie, and then you're going radio silent again."

After our most recent brush with death, Zane made Rocco promise to talk sense into him if he ever developed a woohoo thing for me. There's definitely a woohoo thing between us, but he's attempting to avoid his reputation—and his career as an A-list Hollywood actor—going up in statutory flames.

"Nice," Zane crows. "I'll take it." He hugs me tight, and I giggle.

Trey closes his eyes. "I'll reconnect with Melanie again, per Pierre's request."

"When?" Zane chirps. "When fun summer is over?" He cocks his head. "Once shitty school resumes, so does shitty relationship?"

"You're twenty-one," Trey reminds, clipped.

Zane nods slowly. "Indeed, I am." He waggles the phone in his hand. "Rich and Carol didn't seem as excited to hear from you as they were to hear from me."

Trey rolls his eyes. "Melanie, can we talk?"

"Nope. I'm gearing up for Zane's crock pot wiener offering." I grin up at Zane, who spurts laughter. "So romantic!" I purr jokingly.

Rocco claps Zane on the shoulder. "Good old Crock Pot Wiener! We can always count on him." He grins at Zane. "Melanie's given you the best freaking nicknames!"

"I'll be Crock Pot Weiner," Zane says appreciatively, "and Helicopter Hottie, as long as she's happy."

"Anyway, back to your question, Rocco. Cherry Bomb is an alternative ska grunge fusion band out of Santa Cruz." I shrug.

"They're super popular in northern California, but apparently only eight-ticket popular in Los Angeles."

Zane waggles his hand about. "The band isn't the point. Reminding your friends that they suck *is*."

"The Crock Pot Weiner has spoken!" Rocco chortles. "And so it is!" He holds up a finger, apparently having been taken off hold on the call. He wanders a few steps away, happily chatting about tickets. A few seconds later, he calls out, "Thirteen left."

"I need to shop for jeans," Zane says, smiling down at me. "Shall we?"

"Can we get ice cream?" I ask.

"Absolutely!"

Victoria stomps her foot. "You have thirteen tickets left. There are . . ." She looks around, counting. She has to start over twice.

Finally, Trey huffs, "There are sixteen of us."

Zane scrunches his mouth. "When Victoria called Melanie the Black Widow, none of you said anything."

Heads hang.

"And you spent the whole summer ignoring Melanie?"

Everyone winces.

Zane hits Trey and Demitri with scathing glances. "You two didn't show up ONCE when she was in the hospital."

"How do you know that?" Trey asks.

"Because I'm the one who stayed with her," Zane bites back. His jaw tightens and the color drains from his face.

Everyone surveys the usually cool and collected Zane with alarm.

"What happened at the hospital?" Bear demands.

My chin shakes as I start to tear up. Zane and I are frozen in a distraught state.

"What happened, Melanie?" Finley asks compassionately.

I just shake my head as I start to step away from Zane.

"No, you don't," Zane says while pulling me back into his arms. "You aren't running from this." He looks down at me. "Are you still having issues?"

I shake my head slightly, wanting to die.

"Then we did good," Zane says. "You and me."

Those words became our mantra through everything that happened. I put my head on his chest and whisper, "You and me."

"What happened while she was in the hospital?" Bear asks again, concern rolling from him that I pick up on with my empathic gift.

Zane shakes his head while staring at me intensely.

"Please tell us," Finley breathes out on a wave of worry.

"I don't hang with scallywags, cheats, sluts, or assholes," Zane exclaims, getting back on topic. He points around at the Hollywood group as he pulls it together. "That eliminates many of you. Raise your hand if you're a cheat."

Trey rolls his eyes and raises his hand. He had a tacky affair with a girl named Tiffany Savoy. Apparently, now he's ready to openly admit it without excuse. Points for him.

Zane flicks his hand. "Then you're over there."

Trey makes no move to separate from the group, so I send out a little energy push, forcing him to his new spot.

"Now, who's a scallywag?" Zane asks.

"Define," Bear says.

"A person who behaves badly," I announce, "but in an amusing way."

Tanner Devick and Marcus Vinsky raise their hands with grins.

"Oh, well, when you put it that way, I guess I do hang with scallywags, almost exclusively." Zane grins at the two. "You're over there." He points to the other side of the group from Trey.

"Now, who are sluts?" He surveys the group. "Come on, come on! Raise your hand, Victoria."

Victoria huffs and crosses to Trey without being told.

"Now for the assholes," Zane requests.

Demitri sighs. "That'd be me. Victoria asked me to cut off communication with Melanie all summer, and I did." He crosses to Victoria and Trey while I give him a look.

"Me too," Bear says. "I didn't clarify or call Melanie to rectify her being MIA." He heads to the asshole group.

Darren wanders over to Marcus and Tanner's side. "I had not a damn thing to do with this, and I have no issue with Melanie."

Finley heads to the nice group. "Me either. I've missed her."

Zane watches as Deb Johnson, Drake Santi, and Jayla Bethel head to the nice group. He gives me a look and I shrug.

"I guarantee those three don't want to hang with Victoria and Trey over me," I explain. "Neither do they," I add as I point toward Arch, Hiram Friedman, and Susan Cranz.

The three of them join the good group.

Arch cuts mean eyes toward the assholes. "I don't appreciate this drama."

Kelsey Valdez sighs. "I knew about all of this and kept my mouth shut." She dejectedly joins her brother, Trey, in the asshole squad.

Presley is left alone in the center. She groans. "I didn't personally invite Melanie today. I trusted Trey too." She starts to head toward the assholes.

"Wait," I call out.

Presley slides a hopeful gaze my way.

I waggle my hand her way. "This is her favorite band, she intended to invite me, and—" I leer teasingly toward Marcus— "she likes teeny weenies."

Marcus gives a good-natured grin.

Presley bounces adorably. "I love me a teeny weenie!"

"She can join us," I huff.

Zane counts the collection of nice friends. "Eleven." He grins at Rocco. "Only two to go!"

I frown and survey the rejected assholes. "Ugh. There's five of them. Make tickets happen. They might be assholes, but I'm not."

A call comes through, and Zane answers. He listens, nodding brightly. "Say it ain't so! Thirteen? What a kawinky-dink. Have them meet at Sound Waves at eight." He hangs up and gestures to the divided Hollywood kids. "You can all gather up again. You're all assholes, and I'm out of tickets."

"Who was that?" Presley bashfully asks.

"That," Zane says, "was a friend who came through for me. Remember how that works?" He offers his winning smile. "Have a terrible day," he adds politely.

He wheels me around, but I put a hand on his arm. "I don't want to be mean to them. Please let them come to the party."

Zane glares at my former friends. "You ostracized her all summer, yet she wants you there tonight. You should all be ashamed of yourselves." He tips my chin up to look in my eyes. "You deserve better. You aren't doing this to them. They did it to themselves. If that doesn't work for you, then *I'm* doing it to them."

"Damn it!" Tanner belts. "I made this shirt for the show." I survey his sequined Cherry Bomb shirt, and it really is nice.

"Come on, Melanie." Zane leads me into the Nordstrom department store, with Rocco in tow.

CHAPTER 2

Zanc is occupied on a call with his agent, Chelsea Alice. We just finished watching a warm-up rehearsal by the band. Cherry Bomb seems to have pleasantly surprised him. I take the opportunity of his distraction to head to the table at the front of the club.

Craig, the club owner, smiles at me. "Thank you for doing this, Melanie."

I shrug a little. "Zane gets all the credit on this miracle." I gesture to the list. "Any chance I can add sixteen people? It may put us over capacity if everyone on the list shows up."

"No problem. We have a three-hundred-person fire capacity."

I lean over the list and write the names of my asshole friends before taking my cell phone from my pocket. I ponder which of the jerks to call, settling on Tanner. I dial the number and wait.

"Hey, Mel," Tanner says bashfully.

I can hear people shooshing each other in the background. "Hey. You're all on the list."

"Seriously?" Tanner says, his voice rising with hope.

"Yeah," I reply, clipped. "See you later."

"Thank you, Melanie," Tanner says enthusiastically. "We'll pay you for our tickets."

"Whatever, Tanner." I hang up.

———

Zane slides through the crowd, devastatingly handsome in his new jeans and Cherry Bomb T-shirt. He's stopped by people here and there, but since everyone is part of our collective crew, he seems much more relaxed than he would be if they were random fans. Zane can rarely go anywhere without being accosted. I watch as he pauses with my parents for a few seconds, all smiles and laughter, before making his way past a few faces I recognize from the Hellhounds.

Finally, he gets to me and hugs me tight. "You good?"

I nod happily. I've caught up with everyone, and it's been nice.

Well, it was *nice.* I watch as the Hollywood group crush into the entryway of the tight club, and my happiness takes a dip.

"Why are they here?" Zane asks.

"I couldn't do it."

Zane smiles softly down at me. "You're a good person, Melanie."

"I wish I wasn't," I say while staring at my feet.

The Hollywood crew walk up and start putting their free shirts on over their outfits. Craig is giving a shirt to everyone who walks through the door, per Zane's directive.

Presley squeezes my hand. "Thank you, Melanie."

I nod and wander off, uninterested in a discussion. They can be here, but they aren't entitled to my time.

Through my soulmate connection with Trey, I hear Zane inform the group, "She was really happy until you all got here." Apparently, Trey forgot that he needs to shield off my access to what he can see and hear. It's been long enough since we've seen each other that he's out of practice.

"I'm so sorry," Bear insists. "I didn't intend for any of this to happen." I watch through Trey's eyes as Bear hits him with an honest look. "You've been a pouting mess all summer, Trey. Now we know why."

Trey's eyes close for a moment. "You guys have no clue what we went through."

Zane glares daggers into Trey.

"So, the solution is to abandon her?" Bear asks.

"You should have called me, Trey," Zane insists. "She shouldn't be alone. After *everything* she went through with being stalked, Riptide being murdered, her killing Jet, and spending six weeks in thc hospital." Zane shakes his head. "I would have been there for her all summer. But I left her be so she could get back to her normal life."

"Then why was she with you today?" Trey demands.

Zane shrugs. "We just ran into each other. She came to Promenade by herself."

"Has she really been alone all summer?" Trey asks Demitri.

Dejected, Demitri stares at the floor. "No clue. I haven't called her since . . ."

"*You* haven't even called her?" Trey snaps.

"I promised Victoria I wouldn't. It caused a big fight when my dad mentioned that Melanie came over with a package from Caroline. The package had a scrapbook from Melanie's Hawaii trip in it, and Melanie didn't want to open it alone."

"I don't like you hanging with Melanie," Victoria snarks. "Is that a crime?"

Demitri levels her with a pleading look. "She's my best friend, Vic."

"Now she's not." Victoria smirks. "Problem solved." She slides her smirk Trey's way. "You're both better off."

Zane gives Demitri a sad look. "Your girlfriend's attitude sucks. I respect that Melanie invited you, but Victoria needs to go."

Demitri seems to agree. Victoria starts to argue, but Demitri wraps an arm around her shoulders and guides her toward the door. He takes the CD Victoria is holding, stacking it with his own, and sets them on the check-in table. Victoria starts bellowing, but Demitri doesn't relent. They leave, and I exhale hard. That's when Trey figures out that I've been listening.

"I'm sorry, Melanie," he sends through our soulmate connection. It's close to impossible to lie mind-to-mind, and his sentiment is so sincere. *"I thought you were spending time with Demitri. I had no idea you were alone."* He snorts a little. *"He's certainly never left you alone before."*

I close my eyes while my heart hurts. *"Demitri and I found out after Pierre died that he and I had a spirit-guide connection that went deeper than a soulmate connection. That's why we couldn't seem to distance ourselves. Without knowing it, Demitri abandoned our connection in lieu of a soulmate bond with Victoria."*

Alarm shoots down the connection from Trey before he shields off hard. *"I didn't know that."*

"I told you that Pierre said Adam and I are done, and I'm meant to be with you."

"You didn't tell me Demitri is out," Trey insists.

"Well, he is. He's Victoria's guy." I shake my head. *"Just do your thing, Trey. I told Pierre that I didn't want a soulmate connection with you, and I meant it. This route is for the best."*

"Wait, Melanie." Trey panics a little. *"I want a connection with you. I . . ."* He falters before finishing with, *"I miss you."*

I shut down my connection with Trey just as Zane strides my way.

"Demitri and Victoria are leaving," he says. "I asked them to go."

"Thank you," I reply with big eyes.

Zane seems to get a little lost in them. He runs a thumb along my cheekbone. The soft look in his eyes speaks volumes.

"Reel it in, Zane," Rocco murmurs.

After rattling his head a little, Zane seems to come back to his senses.

"Media is here," Rocco reminds.

"Yeah, I know, but they're *my* media. They won't paparazzi me." Zane quirks his mouth while he looks at me again. "Sorry. I get a little lost."

"If it helps, I do also."

"Let's get this show on the road," Zane says. "Come on, gorgeous." He takes my hand and leads me to the stage. I hop on the little stage and stand with Zane as he announces to the crowd, "I'd like to thank you all for coming out this evening." He raises his beer bottle. "I hope you're all enjoying the crock pot weenies."

I crack up as plates are happily raised and exuberant cheers ring out. Everyone is grinning. This is the most easygoing crowd of people.

"Tonight is special for many reasons," Zane continues. "Not only did Melanie survive a vicious attack that nearly left her paralyzed . . ." Everyone in my Hollywood High group exchanges looks because none of them were aware of the extent of my injuries. " . . .but it's also Presley's birthday."

Another cheer lifts from the crowd. Most don't know Presley, but they're all clearly up for a celebration. Presley is beside herself.

"Now," Zane continues, "without further ado, I present Cherry Bomb!"

The band fires up as Zane and I hop off the stage, joining the suddenly dancing crowd. He whips and swings, dips and turns me, and I love every second of it. I'm more impressed with the band in person than I was with their CD that I picked up at the swap meet a few weeks back.

When Ms. Alice strides up, we stop dancing for a second. "I want to sign them," she says to Zane over the music. "Hook me up."

Zane waits until the band's second song wraps to hop on the stage. He strides to the lead singer, Mystery Morecox. I have no idea what her actual name is, but her stage name kicks ass. He leans into the microphone and asks the crowd, "Do you like Cherry Bomb?"

The crowd lets loose an explosive roar. Presley's on Marcus's shoulders and holds up a double set of devil horns. She's loving this, and I'm glad I got her on the list. My friends are grinning from ear to ear. Arch yanks me to them and hugs me tight.

Zane nods. "That's good news because I'm going to need your help spreading the word. It's time for Cherry Bomb to get signed."

The ladies in the band appear stunned as they drift toward Zane with their mouths open. Mystery Morecox bashfully says, "What?" She looks to her bandmates. "Is Zane *Drell* seriously even standing here? This is wild."

Zane nods. "Chelsea Alice of the Alice Agency, everyone." He flourishes a hand, and Ms. Alice makes her way onto the little stage.

The Cherry Bomb gals seem well versed in the industry, because they instantly know who Chelsea is. They exuberantly greet her before trying to play it cool. They fail, but it's so charming that it doesn't matter.

"You've got a solid sound, a good look, and I'd like to sign you to the agency," Ms. Alice says into the mic. "I'll get your album in with every music producer in my Rolodex."

After a little conferring with her bandmates, Mystery Morecox squeals, "You've got yourself a DEAL!"

"There's one caveat," Ms. Alice says mischievously. She waves me forward, and I join her onstage. "I'm considering Melanie Slate for my agency."

A roar from the crowd of my people interrupts her while I blink in stunned wonder.

"That's my kid," Rich yells, and everyone chuckles while he receives back slaps from several of the Hellhounds.

Ms. Alice chuckles. "As I was saying, I need to test Melanie for commercial print modeling. I'd like for her and Zane to take some pictures for band promos while you do your thing."

Mystery Morecox high-fives me.

I grin up at Zane, and we clear the stage after the band is congratulated with another raucous yell from the audience.

As the band fires up, Zane and I take our positions in a spot chosen by a photographer who works for Ms. Alice. We pose as the band plays their cover of "I Love Rock and Roll" in the background. Demitri must have rejoined the party during the announcements because he's grinning like a nut while he watches the photo shoot, along with the rest of the Hollywood crew. Apparently, when Victoria isn't around, Demitri's still great with me. I choose not to get caught up in that. Instead, I focus on Zane's arm, slung around my chest and gripping my side. Always the pro, he's careful not to block the band's logo on my shirt. I cock a hip and stare intensely at the camera. After an unreal number of shots, the photographer nods his approval.

"We got 'em," he informs Ms. Alice over the driving beat of the music.

She gestures for him to get pictures of the band.

I squeal and hug Zane tight after Ms. Alice walks away. "Think I have a shot?"

"Hell yes, you do, gorgeous." Zane scoops me up and plunks me on his shoulders as the party rages.

CHAPTER 3

Zane exhales hard while he wraps me up in his arms. We're standing by my car in the parking garage. We closed the show out, the last to leave after Zane paid the monumental tab. He promised he'd see me to my car. Mom and Rich left us to ourselves with no issue, but my Hollywood crew had a harder time skedaddling. They all wanted to talk, and Trey was beside himself about wanting to walk me to my car. I declined.

"Thank you for letting me walk you," Zane says, his voice thick with emotion.

I put my forehead on his chest. "We needed to say goodbye."

Zane's hand lands on the back of my head. "It's difficult."

I look up at him. "Think it'll get easier?"

Zane shakes his head. "No." He kisses me on the forehead. "What does your schedule look like?"

Rocco clears his throat pointedly while he leans on the back of my car.

"Don't start, Rocco," Zane says.

"Zane, you were screwed up for a month the last time," Rocco says quietly.

"I'm aware," Zane replies.

"I didn't know that." I look up at him with big eyes.

Zane quirks his mouth. "I took care of you in the hospital for a long time, Melanie."

My expression melts. "I feel terrible you were stuck there for so long."

"It was a lot better after you woke up." Zane smiles softly.

I swallow hard. "No, it wasn't. What we went through was terrible. I'm so sorry."

He shakes his head. "You did great."

"Will you fill me in now that it's just us?" Rocco asks.

We look his way, and Zane informs, "Melanie had to relearn a lot. She broke her neck and had severe issues from a concussion. The wreck rattled her brain badly. She could move her arms and legs while she lay down. Once they got her on her feet, she couldn't walk at first." He gazes down at me. "We got her rewired though."

My blush is so deep, it must be fuchsia.

"Don't spin out about any of it, Melanie."

Rocco looks curious. Zane shakes his head as if to say he shouldn't ask for more details.

I wince and decide to explain. "The lower half of my body didn't cooperate for the first few weeks after I woke up. It got messy. The hospital staff moved slowly, and then Zane took over. I begged him not to, but he wouldn't listen once the rashes started. The hospital staff left me a mess for so long each time. If it weren't for him, I . . ."

Zane hugs me tighter.

"Seriously?" Rocco asks, but there's no judgment in it, only compassion.

"We got through it," Zane says quietly.

"Why didn't her parents help her?" Rocco asks.

"I was between projects, so I had more time," Zane says. "It just all hit at once for her parents. Carol had to go to Texas to help her dad through an emergency surgery, and Rich was in the middle of a big production. He showed up every single minute he could be there, but I refused to leave even when he was around. Rich had to sleep at some point, and he quickly trusted me with Melanie."

"You're a good guy," Rocco says.

"He really is," I whisper, mortified about how I hadn't seen Zane since he left the hospital. Now that I'm clearheaded and back to a sense of normalcy, the horror of what went on is humiliating.

"Don't do this, Melanie," Zane insists as he studies my expression.

My eyes flutter closed. "I didn't think about it when I first saw the two of you. I'm sorry I acted so normal when I ran into you earlier today."

"I was relieved when you were so normal with me." Zane smiles. "I've worried about how you'd handle seeing me again."

I wince. "Shouldn't I be worried about how you'd handle seeing *me* again?"

"Everything's fine," Zane says. "We got through it one day at a time."

"Damn, Zane!" Rocco appears stunned. "Now I understand why you lost it when you got home." He meets my concerned gaze as he explains, "I stayed with him for a week. He was sick to his stomach worried about you not having help. He was so upset he couldn't eat or sleep."

Zane closes his eyes and wraps me up tighter. "Carol got back, and you were right to make me leave, but damn, it was difficult to walk out of that room."

I laugh a little, but it holds no humor. "I was past the worst of it at that point. All my muscles fired again, and Mom got the easy part

of that deal. Except for all the guilt she had about not being there."
I gulp down my own guilt and look up at Zane. "It would have
been a lot better if she'd been able to deal with it instead of you."

Zane shakes his head. "No, it wouldn't. If Pierre were alive, he
would have handled everything. I stepped in." He takes my hands.
"You trusted me. I was honored. I've never been through anything
like that with a woman, and it taught me a lot."

"Thank you for helping me," I whisper while I stare at my feet.
"You didn't bail when things got rough. Trey thinks his trials with
me were bad?" I scoff.

"He said, 'You have no idea how bad it got,'" Zane says, "and
I almost slugged him." When I grimace, Zane shakes his head.
"Nope. No regrets. We got it figured out."

I roll my eyes. "The physical therapist I was assigned was useless.
If it weren't for your dance training and kinesiology knowledge,
I'd still be in trouble."

"What did Zane do?" Rocco asks softly.

"He knew how to retrain muscles to fire. It was one thing when
my quads wouldn't engage. It was another when my bowels had a
clear path with no resistance."

Rocco's head drops back, and he rubs his face hard. "I'm so
sorry, Melanie. No sixteen-year-old girl needs those issues on her
résumé."

"You're still good now?" Zane asks.

I nod. "I was released from physical therapy appointments a
week ago."

"Good. It's been hell not calling you." He hugs me tight.

"Thank you for dropping a fortune on us tonight. You didn't
have to do any of this." I smile up at him with my chin resting
on his chest.

Zane shrugs. "I got to party with you. Plus, I usually never go to concerts because I get mobbed at them." He grins. "I also got to help Craig, piss off your friends, get Ms. Alice a new client, help Cherry Bomb, and get you a step closer to being signed. I'd say it was a big win."

"It was an *expensive* win," I remind.

Zane shrugs. "Eh. It was worth it." He kisses me hard on the forehead. "Love you, gorgeous."

"Love you too," I reply.

Rocco steps next to Zane. "This seems deeper than I thought."

The color drains from Zane's face. "I worry about her."

"He really does," Rocco tells me.

"I'm okay."

Zane snorts, informing, "I own that magazine now. I sued the shit out of them for running that article."

"I didn't know you retaliated." I blush deeply again. A magazine ran a story about how Zane was helping his invalid girlfriend who suffered incontinence upon being rendered a paraplegic. "That caused so much heat for you with Ms. Alice because of the girlfriend mention."

"I don't care what she thought. We were dealing with reality. That's the thing about show business. People lose track of what matters. I refuse to do that."

"Of all people, a millionaire movie star helped me," I say with a wince. "You've earned your way out of facing filthy reality."

"I'm still a human being, Melanie," Zane scolds gently. "Sure, I could have hired someone to deal with it. A hired nurse couldn't have helped the right way though. I was there to deal with your psychological state. The body issues were the least of my concerns. I had to make sure you didn't give up or fall victim to humiliation."

Rocco puts his hand on Zane's arm. "The moment she's eighteen, I'll never drag you away again," he promises.

Zane's expression is pained as he looks to Rocco.

"I know, man." Rocco hugs me. "Love you, Mel."

"Love you too, Rocco."

I hug Zane one more time. "Call me next time there's something exciting."

He opens my car door for me. "I will," he barely manages to choke out.

The door closes behind me after I slide in. I start my car and pull out of my parking spot. A glance in the rearview mirror as I drive away reveals Zane's hands over his face, with Rocco talking to him. Tears slide down my cheeks.

CHAPTER 4

I make my way into the new state-of-the-art auditorium at the school. Hiram strides up to me with a wide grin.

Awestruck, I say, "I can't believe the job Stubbs and his company did rebuilding this place."

The theater is a monument of modern engineering. Wood-paneled walls, perfect in their acoustics, tower tall. Above us, red metallic acoustic panels grace the ceiling.

"Honestly!" Hiram exclaims. "If Jet wasn't dead, I'd thank him for burning the old theater down. This place is incredible. We've got all the latest equipment. The insurance payout was quick, and the amount was impressive. Stubbs should be done with the finishing touches just before school starts again."

"How do you know all that?"

"Stubbs hired all of us for the rebuild," Hiram informs.

Hurt bubbles up in my chest. "Yet again, I'm ostracized," I mutter.

Stubbs, a Hellhound and the illustrious construction business owner in question, comes up the center aisle. "You kids holding up okay?"

A handful of my friends emerge from the booth. Trey is among them, and I get distracted by his six-pack as he pulls up his shirt to wipe his forehead.

"Melanie!" Stubbs says. "Wake up."

I laugh bashfully, surprised by myself. "Sorry. Trey can be distracting."

Trey appears pleased as he sends a love pulse down our connection.

Stubbs grins. "Mr. Isley's waiting for you onstage, Mel." He turns to the guys and asks, "Can I keep the rest of you for another couple hours? We need to get the technical booth set up and test the new equipment."

Trey, Arch, and Hiram all agree to stay.

"I need to run and check on Valerie," Adam says apologetically. "Can I take a lunch hour and be back at one?"

My relationship with Adam Stone has been beyond complicated. Long story short, he's a tall, stunning, blond-haired-and-blue-eyed pain in my ass who was finally tamed by his wife, Valerie. Adam and I have a sordid history that involves similar fiery energies and a soulmate connection that's now blocked with the help of Bear's and Darren's energy work.

"How's she holding up?" Stubbs asks.

Adam shakes his head, his expression pensive. "She has good days and bad days. She's measuring a lot bigger than she should be. We have another doctor's appointment tomorrow."

"It's going to be okay," I assure in response to his worried expression.

He nods but doesn't respond. My wedding present to Adam and Valerie was agreeing to let Bear and Darren help shut down the soulmate connection I once shared with Adam, but ever since, it's seemed like both a good and bad decision. On one hand, only having one defunct soulmate connection running through my psyche has certainly made things easier. Adam's also said that things with him and Valerie are better now that he's not splitting his attention between her and me. On the other hand, Adam and I no longer know what the other is dealing with. We used to communicate so well mind-to-mind that we could reach each other even from across town. In that regard, our connection was stronger than the one Trey and I have, but two soulmate connections in one girl is rare and incredibly complicated, and that's before we even get into the tangled connection I shared with my departed husband, Pierre.

Adam looks down at me, and his eyes narrow a touch. I know he's testing the walled-off connection. I also know that Darren and Bear were thorough in their work. He's not going to get through.

Trey's watching Adam. Everyone else walks away as Trey quietly asks, "Testing it again?"

Adam nods. "I worry about her because I don't know if she's okay."

He never even talks to me anymore, I ponder skeptically.

Trey looks at me as he says to Adam, "I'll make you the same promise Valerie made to Melanie." Trey makes eye contact with Adam. "I've got Melanie covered. No matter what happens, I'll keep her safe. She can reach me from long distances easier now. We don't have the range you two did just yet, but it's getting better all the time."

My eyebrows rise because some of what he just said isn't true. Trey certainly hasn't been checking on me. I let it go because Adam needs to feel better.

Adam nods and leans down, kissing my forehead. "I'll be back." He makes his way briskly up the aisle. His shoulders are slumped, and he's clearly weighed down by a whole lot of heavy issues.

I sigh and head to the stage.

As I approach, Mr. Isley motions me over. "Kendra's out," he explains, referring to Kendra Poth, one of the most talented dancers in school. "She twisted an ankle and has a severe sprain. I called you in because I need you to replace her."

My eyes fly wide, but Demitri beats me to the argument. "Melanie broke her neck in April! She had surgery. She also broke her wrist and several ribs. Dancing socially at a concert is one thing, but performing would be crazy."

Mr. Isley surveys my wrist. My cast is long gone. "She looks healed to me."

"Broken NECK," Demitri insists.

Mr. Isley rolls his eyes. "She's Melanie, Demitri."

I turn and bellow to Stubbs, "Apparently, I can crash course a dance piece, but I don't get the luxury of a summer job?" I look to the guys in the booth. The window is open, and I yell, "Got the Hellhounds on your side, also, I see."

"Whoa, whoa, whoa," Stubbs calls out. "No one is anti-Melanie." He looks to Mr. Isley. "Rich told me what happened. She has *zero* business dancing in this show!"

Demitri's jaw tightens angrily. "Kendra sprained an ankle, and that was grounds for you to give her a break. *How* is a broken neck less severe than a sprained ankle?"

"Melanie's had months to heal." Mr. Isley looks my way. "Give it a shot. If you can't handle it, I'll pull the piece."

My stomach bubbles. I'm not ready for this, but Mr. Isley is a mountain of personality with a no-nonsense attitude and soaring expectations. His resume is staggering, and arguing with him is always fruitless. He would only hold it against me, and I don't want to lose my spot on the Allstar dance team.

Stubbs attempts to argue again, but Mr. Isley just ignores him.

"Melanie, I'm very sorry I left you out of the crew assignments,"

Stubbs calls out. "I did it out of respect for your stepfather's wishes, not because I was trying to disrespect you."

I glare at Trey, Hiram, and Stubbs. "I spent the whole summer being left out. I don't care, Stubbs. Hire those you deem worthwhile."

Stubbs heads into the booth, where a heated discussion with Trey and Hiram seems to fire up.

Resigned to this, I go to the spot Mr. Isley indicates, and he starts working me through the choreography.

CHAPTER 5

Mr. Isley bellows from the back of the audience seating area, "Damn it, Melanie! You can do this!"

I huff, close to tears. My entire body quakes with exhaustion, and we haven't even made it through a run of the first minute of this song. I have the group piece down, but this duet is kicking my ass.

With a glance Demitri's way, I shake my head. Demitri is hands down the best dancer at this school. Luckily, he hasn't blown up yet. We've danced together before, but this is the first piece I've had a lead in with Mr. Isley's Allstar team. It's also the first time I've danced since I was injured in April. I'm rusty, and quickly discovering that my body isn't even close to ready for this.

Demitri hollers to Mr. Isley, "She's doing great, but we're asking a lot. This piece is tough."

"Trial by fire. Nothing works better. You can lead her, and I know what Melanie can do, even if she's doubting herself." Mr. Isley turns toward the booth and yells, "AGAIN!"

I drop my head and sigh before making eye contact with Trey

across the expansive theater. He radiates that he wants to say something to Mr. Isley. He can feel my exhaustion through our connection.

Mind-to-mind, I pulse to him, "*I'm going to try again. Don't say anything. I just need to get through this.*"

The past few hours have served as a good bonding moment for Trey and me. He's been in my head, surveying my body pain, and talking shit about Mr. Isley. He's pissed, which is usually when Trey is at his best.

Demitri and I go to our opening positions for the duet, and Demitri encourages, "Focus, Meley. You've got this."

Javier Hernandez and his partner Jayla Bethel step up to the edge of the stage. They're two of the best dancers at the school, and Jayla's partnered with Demitri a lot. Javier is Demitri's best friend. He generally dislikes me, but his concern for my condition has taken over for his usual catty bullshit.

"Hold your weight, Melanie," Jayla instructs. "And remember that this piece has a slinky Tango vibe, even though the music's a pop song."

"You can do this, Mel." Javier looks to Demitri. "*Please* be careful of her neck."

The song, Janet Jackson's "This Time," has become my arch nemesis. The music hums through the speakers ominously as Demitri jazz walks my way. I hit him with a sexy sneer. My sensuality and performance commitment seems to be all that I've done right in this rehearsal.

As if to confirm, Mr. Isley's voice booms through the cordless microphone he's holding, "Good, Melanie! Carry that vibe from your face into your body."

Demitri pulls me into a firm Tango stance. The vocals croon through the speakers, and we're off. We start the complicated foot rhythm, weaving and whipping around each other to the franti-cally fast drum hits that pound briefly through the song.

As the music wafts into a high soprano crooning, Demitri instructs, "Watch my left hand. I'll always lead with that hand. Your opposite foot will always follow. This piece has a cross-body dynamic."

I shift my gaze and study his hand. It tenses every time just before he pushes.

When I finally get the feel of the piece, Mr. Isley yells into the microphone, "YES, YES, YES! That's it, Mel!"

Demitri pushes back, and we circle in opposite directions, turn-ing and drifting away from each other. I look over my shoulder, and our eyes meet with a seductive glance.

We step back together and weave and grind around each other. Demitri grips my waist and rolls me through a backbend, snapping me up to his right. My neck pain flares terribly. I try to ignore it while Trey growls irritably in my mind. With my head on Demitri's shoulder, I slide my left leg up his side. He expertly pitches me right, across his body, and I secretly struggle to hold my weight.

"Yes, Melanie!" Jayla exclaims. "That's it!"

Demitri pulls me upright and rolls me down his side. I shake with the effort not to collapse. I can barely do this, but we push through the first half of the piece, making it to the half we've yet to run successfully.

This "effortless" piece is grueling, I think to myself.

Nervous energy makes my hands shake as Demitri and I jazz walk away from each other. *"Here we go,"* I send to Trey. *"This is the lift that scares me."*

Demitri and I stop opposite each other. I prep a leap, racing across the stage before pliéing and launching toward Demitri. I push off his bent knee as he flips me, rotating me onto my stomach on his shoulder. He gets hold of my arms, and I stretch into a bluebird lift. He spins twice to the right.

Out of the corner of my eye, I notice Victoria strut to the edge of the stage. I can feel her glaring at us. "Demitri!" she bellows angrily.

Distracted by his girlfriend, Demitri flips me two counts early, before I've prepped the weight shift, and I start to fall. He squawks and slides under me, breaking at least some of my fall with an extended leg. Despite his best efforts, I bounce off his leg, and my tush thumps the floor hard. I wince as pain reverberates up my spine.

Frantically, Demitri reaches for me. "Melanie!"

I shy away. The music cuts, and everyone waits nervously to see if I'm okay.

"I'm fine," I announce while Demitri stands and hefts me off the floor. My right knee collapses, and Demitri grabs hold of me. He stares at my quaking leg. I manage to get my feet under me, but tears fill my eyes. Fear that my muscles are about to quit firing fills me with dread. If that happens, and my bladder and bowels give, I'll be in a humiliating sort of trouble.

I rush offstage at a hobbled limp and head down the hall. Demitri follows. I close myself in a bathroom stall in the closest dressing room and wait to see what's about to happen.

"Melanie, talk to me," Demitri insists.

"I really don't want to discuss this," I manage through tears. "Give me a minute." I use the facilities, and my muscles that matter to my social reputation prove worthwhile. Discovering that I still have control causes my fear to dissipate. I unlock the stall, and Demitri's standing there. I glare at him.

"I wasn't going to leave just because you had to pee," he says. Demitri leans against the counter while I wash my hands. "Please tell me why you ran away."

"I can't handle this dance show right now." I swallow hard, deciding to trust Demitri. Considering how many lifetimes we've apparently spent together, it's worth a shot. "I had brain damage from the crash. That's not the words they used, but I can't remember the technical term." In the mirror, I catch how my cheeks blaze a humiliated crimson. "I was incontinent most of my hospital stay."

Demitri appears confused. "Incontinent?"

"The doctors didn't think it would improve. It also started to look like I would never have full use of my right leg again. I was told I'd spend the rest of my life on a cane, wearing diapers."

Demitri's mouth falls open. "Why didn't you call me?"

I laugh scoffingly. "I figured you saw the damn trash rag article about it and cut ties with me."

"What article?"

"*The Prowler* paid a nurse for the story. Everyone was rather taken that Zane *Drell*," I say his name with weighted sarcasm, "was wiping my ass for me. So, she spilled my dirt."

"Oh shit. Zane stayed through your hospital time . . ." Demitri's eyes widen as he realizes what I went through with Zane.

"He played nursemaid through all of it."

"I didn't see the article," Demitri informs.

"If you didn't see it, maybe the others didn't either. I've been worried sick that word would get around school." I snort. "As if my reputation needs *that* added to it."

"I'm so sorry you went through that, Melanie."

"Zane was furious. He apparently sued the magazine, and now he owns it. I spoke with Ms. Alice, and she says they're revamping it into an entertainment promo magazine."

I shake my head. "Zane worked with me tirelessly to get my muscles to fire again. We got every one of them back in working order, but it was horrible. I've never hurt that bad, been that ashamed, or felt that hopeless. Thank God for him."

Demitri looks crestfallen, and I can sense why. Just before the accident, my departed husband, Pierre, came to me in a dream and revealed a lot about the uniqueness of my connection with Demitri. "That should have been my job," Demitri says. "I'm so sorry that I abandoned you."

"You abandoned me long before I was crapping my hospital bed," I quietly reply. My smile carries sadness. "Anyhow, when I fell during rehearsal, my quad wouldn't fire. I was scared that the rest of my muscles would betray me."

"Hence, why you ran to the bathroom?"

Dejectedly, I nod.

Demitri wraps his arms around me. "I'm so sorry I missed the dismount. I'd never intentionally drop you."

"I'm sorry you're stuck dancing with me."

"Melanie, I *love* dancing with you."

I extricate myself, putting some distance between us. "I'll do what I can," I promise before heading out the door.

We make our way back to the stage, where everyone has gathered, clearly concerned.

"What happened?" Mr. Isley demands.

"That was my fault," Demitri says. Exhausted, he looks at me. "I apologize, Meley. I've never dumped a partner on her ass before."

Trey asks through our connection, *"You okay?"*

"Sore, but I'm fine."

"Try it again," Mr. Isley orders.

I shake my head. "I'm done for the day. I can't handle any more."

"We have thirty more minutes of rehearsal," Mr. Isley demands harshly.

"*You* have thirty more minutes of rehearsal," I push back. "My neck is throbbing. My hip hurts. My legs are gelatin."

"Part of coming back from injuries is pushing through," Mr. Isley encourages.

Demitri holds up a hand to stop him. "She just filled me in on the extent of her medical issues, and this rehearsal is done. We need to take this slower."

Everyone looks at me curiously while I slide unsure eyes Demitri's way. My fear that he now thinks I'm repulsive is alleviated as he softly says, "Now that I know, I don't want you pushing until you start shaking. We need to give you time."

Mr. Isley tries to argue, but Trey cuts him off with a no-nonsense, "Enough. She's done." Trey holds a hand my way. I walk to the edge of the stage, and he lifts me off, setting my feet on the ground next to him. "How about you and I spend some time talking?"

"Yes, please," I say bashfully. "First, I'd like to rinse off."

Trey drapes an arm over my shoulders and guides me to the dressing room. When we're alone, he cups my cheeks. "Will you tell me everything?"

I nod. "I need to get ready first."

Trey leaves the dressing room, pulling the door closed behind him.

CHAPTER 6

Arm in arm, Trey and I descend the staircase outside the theater and head around the building and across the street to the student parking lot.

"Anything from your intuition about Val?" he asks.

I look inward and force my intuition to the surface with a fiery nudge, just like Bear taught me. I study it and shake my head. "Something's weird . . . , but . . ." I pause as my intuition image turns slowly, like a three-dimensional bubble, and I get to study the backside. My mouth drops open, and I look up at Trey.

"Oh God, what?" he asks.

"Well, it's not bad . . ." I study it again, hardly believing what I'm seeing.

"The suspense is killing me."

I laugh quietly. "She's so big already because they're having twin girls."

"Oh crap. Are you serious?"

"Do I tell Adam?"

Trey shakes his head. "Nope. Let them have that moment at the doctor's office tomorrow. They don't even know they're having *one* girl. They want it to be a surprise."

I laugh as Trey opens the passenger door for me. "It'll be a surprise, all right." I switch gears. "I can drive myself. My car is here."

"No, I'd like to spend time with you," Trey insists. "I'll bring you back to your car later." He rounds the front of his black muscle car and slides in. "Two babies. That's a lot."

He closes his door and starts the car with a rumbling growl. His gaze shifts seductive. He puts his fingertips lightly on my forehead before running them down to my chin. I close my eyes and sharply inhale. Guilt bubbles in me. I loved Pierre more than anything in this world. Pierre's been clear that I need to move on and reconnect with Trey, but that's easier said than done. My husband being dead doesn't stop the fact that my heart still belongs to him.

Trey senses my misgivings through our soulmate connection. "Melanie, I'm sorry I was so distant for so long."

I open my eyes, and they hold dead weight. "I'm not going to chase you, Trey."

"No, you're not. I'm done being distant."

His car rumbles out of the parking lot, headed toward the 101 freeway.

— —

As we pull into the Universal CityWalk parking garage, I squeal and clap my hands. I'm suddenly bubbling over with excitement. This tourist spot opened in May, but I haven't had a chance to check it out yet. It's turned out to be just as big a hit with locals as out-of-towners.

"We finally get to come here!" I say enthusiastically. "I'm so excited. I've heard it's really cool."

"It is. You're going to love it." I glance at him, confused, and he clarifies, "I came here with our friends."

"Another group outing I wasn't invited too, huh?"

Trey winces.

Suddenly feeling blazingly uncomfortable, I close my eyes. Being left out all summer while I struggled through my personal hell may not be something we can get past.

The car shuts off, and Trey sends a curious pulse through the hand he laces with mine.

Yet again, I feel like a stranger in my own soulmate bond.

My intuition blasts, and I gasp around the pain in my chest. My eyes snap wide as the glaring certainty that a big problem is about to unfold bubbles up. Suddenly, a massive new energy roils from the intuitive blast and quakes to the surface of the dark water in my mind. I study it and realize that it's a new ability. The potential magnitude of this ability causes me to freeze internally.

There's no way, I think to myself. *I can pull memories directly out of people's minds now?*

This was one of Pierre's abilities, so I know how it works, and it's definitely a burden I don't want.

To test the ability, I casually scan through Trey's mental memory timeline like a librarian riffling through a card catalog. I intended to find his trip to City Walk, but instead, the new ability settles on a memory of Trey hanging out at a party with the baseball team.

His thoughts are clear as day as a pretty redhead flirts with him. *"God, this would be so simple,"* he's telling himself in the memory. *"Things are so complicated with Melanie. Don't do this, though. The last thing you need is another call like the one you got from Tiffany."*

The mention of Tiffany makes my breath catch. Back at the start of the last school year, I had a mental breakdown and wound up in the hospital in a coma. Trey had an affair with Tiffany during the weeks when I was unconscious. As for what he meant by "another call," I have no idea.

I extricate myself from the memory. The desire to riffle through his memories and see what really happened with Tiffany is so strong that it doubles me over. I lean forward, putting my head on my knees and lacing my fingers on the back of my neck, covering my ears with my arms.

This is bad. Having this ability is a moral and ethical nightmare.

"Melanie, what's wrong?" Trey quietly asks again. "Talk to me."

I shake my head, unsure what to say. Finally, I go with, "A *lot's* wrong."

Trey looks beyond confused. "Whatever you're thinking about has you spun out. Fill me in."

When I don't respond, Trey gets out of the car and makes his way to my door. He opens it and kneels next to me. "Melanie, I don't know what's happening in your head. You're shielding hard on your side. You need to talk to me."

I stare into his eyes. The desire to riffle through his mind is overwhelmingly distracting. I make a hard choice and intentionally shutter our soulmate connection tighter than usual, completely walling it off on my side. Trey doesn't know how to take it down on his side. It might not be fair of me to make this decision without talking to him, but I need something standing between me and his open mind that's just waiting to be pilfered. Besides, with his actions all summer, he shut us down first.

He grabs my hands, squeezing a little too hard. When he gets nothing through our walled-off connection, he gasps out, "Melanie, what did you do?"

"We have some serious things to discuss."

"What does that mean?" Trey's expression holds an edge of panic.

I swing my legs out of the car and stand, forcing him to stand with me. With a hint of sadness, I smile. "Maybe some soulmate distance is good."

"Whoa, whoa, hang on a second. I'm aiming to fix things with this date."

"I need space." I give him a pointed look. "I also need honesty."

"What does that mean, Melanie?"

"We'll deal with it, but right now, I just want to see this place I've looked forward to visiting."

As CityWalk opens in front of us, my mouth falls open. It's magic from the very first glance. There are neon signs as far as the eye can see. A parade of lights, textures, and colors stretches out before us. Outlined in neon, a giant gorilla hangs from a building overhead. I turn in a circle, grinning as I take in the wonder of this new place.

Trey's watching me, his expression carefully caged, with tension around his eyes.

To avoid getting trampled by a family of rowdy kids rushing by, I step closer to him. "Our mind-to-mind connection just got more serious," I inform him. "I'm questioning whether I can handle it."

Trey holds my shoulders and says with conviction, "Whatever it is, just tell me. This is going to make me crazy."

"Can we please discuss my other issue first?"

In a rush, Trey pulls me across the courtyard to a quiet spot. Completely out of character, he faces a wall as he says, "This is the best I can do for privacy in this mad crush."

"If it helps your stress levels, at least I haven't been attacked since Jet finally died."

"Perfect," Trey says. "Then, yes, please tell me."

"I'd like for you to understand why Zane was so angry when you told him how hard what you went through with me was."

Trey seems to accept this, so I start to fill him in on the developments. Just as I get past the most graphically unpleasant part, a happy squeal pulls me from the humiliating tale.

"Umm, girls, let's wait!" Tanner's unmistakable voice warns.

I look over my shoulder just as Finley and Presley bounce up to me. Finley's engaged to Tanner, who smiles sadly at me. Tanner has an androgynous David Bowie-like sexiness to him. He's in one of his trademark over-the-top outfits, and I wonder how he keeps from burning up in the red leather pants and high heeled boots he's wearing.

Presley's green eyes sparkle as she hugs me. "Surprise!" She cocks a voluptuous hip. Pres has the body of Jessica Rabbit, and her crop top and hip-hugger jeans are particularly flattering today.

I pan a slow gaze Trey's way. The timing of this invasion couldn't possibly be any worse. "I thought you and I were going to have a serious you-and-I talk?"

Guilt pressed on his face, Trey looks down at his hands. "The group wanted to meet us. We made this plan when you were showering in the dressing room. When I invited them, I didn't realize how serious this was."

"Uh-oh," Finley says. "Bad timing for group fun?"

"Very," Trey replies, clearly forlorn by what my expression is revealing.

Panic boils in my gut. "I trusted you," I say to Trey. The emotion is irrational, given that he was so thoughtful to have invited everyone, but what I was discussing is incredibly private. "You didn't tell me about this."

"It was supposed to be a surprise," Trey admits. "I was so stunned by our talk that I didn't think to call Marcus and stop everyone from showing up."

"What's going on?" Bear asks as the whole group crowds around.

Dejectedly, I stare at Trey.

"We need a minute," Trey insists.

"Please talk to us, Melanie," Tanner begs.

"You can trust us," Presley insists.

"We've missed you," Finley piles on.

The panic redoubles. I'd made it my life's goal to keep the news that I was sharing with Trey out of circulation among the school's general population. "I don't want them to know," I whimper loudly enough that only Trey will hear. "They're all friends with Victoria."

"She won't find out," Trey murmurs back while he wraps me up tight. "Neither will they."

The moment Trey's arms are around me, a memory of his blasts into my mind. My eyes widen and my knee gives out. I can't stop the memory. I can't control it. All I can do is hang on tight as it plays in my head.

As the memory ends, I gape at Trey. "You got Tiffany *pregnant* during your fling?"

Everyone looks like they just got kicked in the teeth.

The color instantly drains from Trey's face. He blinks shocked eyes, and his hold on me loosens. I plummet to the ground, my shaking legs unable to hold me. Darren rushes to my side while Trey stares into space, frozen. Finley puts the stuff that fell out back into my purse.

Sense returns to Trey's eyes. "I need everyone to leave us alone."

"Let me stay and help you through this," Darren offers.

I grab Darren's arm, and Trey relents.

"It's not true, right, Trey?" Tanner says softly. When Trey swallows hard, Tanner's mouth falls open. "I'm your best friend, and you never told me that!"

My empathic gift allows me to sense the judgment that pours from our friends in waves. I rattle with the realization of what I just revealed about Trey and Tiffany.

"PLEASE, give us a minute," Trey insists.

Darren scoops me up, carrying me to the closest bench. He sits with me while Trey slowly makes his way over to join us.

Trey tells Darren, "Melanie was in the middle of explaining what happened to her at the hospital. It's horrific, and that's what we really needed to deal with."

"We'll get to that," Darren says. "First, we need to deal with this Tiffany issue."

"How did you know?" Trey asks as tears brim in his eyes.

"The memory jumped to me. I got a big intuition pulse in the car in the parking garage, before a new ability opened in me. I didn't know what was happening until after I'd accidently worked through one of your other memories. As soon as I figured it out, I shut down our connection. My control over seeing these things in your mind is literally zero. The only way I could protect your privacy was to wall off our connection." I swallow hard. "Unfortunately, our friends' rude, completely unwelcome invasion startled me enough that my wall crashed down again."

"We were invited," Darren insists.

"I did *not* invite you." My statement is harsh and rude enough that Darren winces.

"That was my fault," Trey rushes to say. "I should have never invited them. I had zero clue how bad the things were that you were going to discuss." He clears his throat. "What *I'm* about to discuss, I need to preface. I want you to understand how much I love you, how incredibly sorry I am, and that I didn't tell you because the whole thing was such a massive mistake. Hurting you further wouldn't help." Trey takes a deep breath. "Tiffany did end up pregnant during our fling."

My mouth drops open. I instantly feel sick. I'd already seen the memory, but hearing him admit it puts me in a state of shock.

Trey takes a breath and continues. "She found out after you confronted her at school, and she was terrified to tell me. She finally told me, and then she woke up bleeding. She called me, and I went to pick her up. It was a Saturday, so I took her to an urgent care doctor. They confirmed that she'd miscarried. I helped her through it and decided not to tell you."

My mind is sputtering, trying to grasp the news. "You *helped* her?"

"Of course I did." He winces. "But I should have been there to help you when you needed me after the car accident. I'm sorry. Me helping her, and not helping you, does NOT mean I care more about her."

"Back when Deb first met everyone at our lunch table, I noticed Tiffany standing nearby, grabbing her stomach." The pieces fall into place. "I thought it was odd at the time." I hit Trey with accusatory eyes. "You hid this from me?"

Trey and Darren exchange a glance.

"Is that the extent of what you're hiding?" Darren asks.

"That's it," Trey answers.

Darren turns to me. "Melanie, what do you need to ask about this? Now's the time."

I shake my head and pull my cell phone out of my pocket. Before anyone can object, I dial Zane's number. After four rings, his outgoing voicemail message picks up. I hang up, unsure what to do.

The sound of footsteps approach.

Demitri kneels by me. "Marcus filled me in."

Stunned tears roll down my cheeks. "I'll never be enough," I whisper.

"We're leaving, Melanie," Demitri insists. When Victoria starts blathering her protest, Demitri whips around and barks, "Shut up! I've had enough."

"Damn it!" Trey says. "I don't want you leaving with Demitri. *Please* talk to me!"

My emotions are raging, but I manage to calmly say, "I'm not okay with you having all these secrets about Tiffany. I'm sure everyone at school knows, and I'm the moron who's a joke, yet again."

"*No one* knows," Trey assures.

I stare into Demitri's eyes, unwilling to look at Trey. "I gave him a chance! I came here to reconnect with him. He invited everyone to listen to my nightmare that I didn't even get to finish discussing. Now, there's this?"

"I had NO idea how serious our discussion would be," Trey insists.

"We all know anyway, Melanie."

I slowly turn, and Marcus winces a little. "Tanner found the two of you first and heard what you were saying. He told us, but it's because we *need* to know. We can help you."

My mouth drops open as I look to Tanner. "I thought you were my friend!"

"I am," Tanner insists. "We all are. That's why I told them."

"Did you tell Victoria?" I demand.

Tanner slides guilty eyes Victoria's way.

She smirks. "I heard."

Tears fall, and my head drops. "How dare you," I whisper. I look from Tanner to Trey. "I can't believe the two of you!"

Demitri stalks over to Victoria. "Let me be abundantly clear. If you tell ANYONE what you know, I'll leave you."

Presley slides evil eyes to Victoria. "If you tell anyone, I'll fuck you up."

"So will I," rings out from Finley and Jayla.

Deb saunters up to Victoria and taps her finger on Victoria's cheek menacingly. "I'll end you."

Victoria's bravado leaks away, and she cowers. "I won't say anything."

"Yes, she will," I barely choke out. I slump on the bench. "I can't take any more of this."

I dial another number, waiting. Rocco answers.

"I need a ride," I inform him.

"What's wrong, Melanie?"

"Trey tricked me into telling him everything while my former friends eavesdropped."

"I didn't mean for them to hear any of it!" Trey barks. "I had ZERO clue Tanner was listening! He was behind us."

"Zane!" Rocco yells from the other end of the line. "Wrap it up! Melanie needs help." I hear muffled talking. Rocco's voice comes clear a moment later. "Honey, where are you?"

"CityWalk."

"Well, that's convenient. We're up the street at Ahh's."

There's a shuffling, and then Zane's voice comes over the line. "I'll be to the turnaround in a few minutes. Go to the silver globe. I'm going to pull up in a tan Honda Civic. I won't get out of the car because I'll be recognized there."

"I'll be waiting," I say through tears.

"Who's picking you up?" Trey asks the second I hang up.

I manage to stand, and my legs hold, but they feel like gelatin again. The more upset I get, the worse my issues flare. My mind and body still aren't right.

"Go to hell, Trey," I say with zero emotion.

When I start to walk away, Demitri grabs my arm. "I'll stay with you while you wait for your ride."

"You think I trust *you*?" I point to Victoria. "Did you know she was listening when Tanner spilled my dirt like the town crier?"

Demitri winces. "Yes. I was so shocked to learn you'd told Tanner. I just didn't think about it."

"I didn't share *anything* with Tanner. I told you and Trey. That was it. I wanted NONE of the rest of these people to know."

"Please, Melanie!" Demitri says. "I'm so sorry. I should have stopped Tanner. I didn't figure out that he'd overheard it until he was done spilling it."

I head down the walkway to the silver globe. Everyone follows, listening as Tanner begs for me to understand.

Trey grabs my arms, and I try to get away. He hangs on tight, pleading with me to please realize that he didn't intend to betray my confidence. The harder I try to get away, the harder Trey begs. I'm so distracted by the cacophony that I don't realize Zane and Rocco have arrived.

"Stop!" Rocco barks. "You can't do this! You'll end up on the damn news!"

It does no good because Zane is headed my way at a full-tilt run. Rocco races to catch up, and barely stops Zane before he punches Trey in the face.

Trey lets me go, seeming stunned instead of angry.

"I wasn't trying to hurt her!" Trey insists.

"Don't EVER touch her again!" Zane snarls.

Rocco grabs him. Zane attempts to shove him away, but Rocco tightens his hold around his massive friend. "Listen to me, Beastie Boy," Rocco says, just loud enough for us to hear. "You can NOT start a fistfight in the middle of CityWalk. People are staring at us. There's no hiding you. I need you to go back to the car, let me bring Melanie, and we'll leave."

Finally, Zane's muscles relax, and Rocco exhales hard. He slowly lets Zane's arms go. Zane levels me with a blistering look. "Who told them?" he demands.

"I told Trey. Tanner eavesdropped and spilled my dirt to everyone."

Zane slides a calculated gaze to Trey, followed by Tanner. "If any of this, and I mean any of it, gets out to one more person, you'll be hearing from my lawyer. I *own* the magazine that leaked this. I'll end you and your families."

"None of us are going to say anything," Tanner assures, but he makes the mistake of sliding unsure eyes Victoria's way.

Zane smirks at Victoria. "I know who you are, Victoria Garcia. I also know who your father is. I'll happily destroy Garcia Enterprises. You think your daddy has money?" Zane tips his head challengingly. "You ain't seen nothing yet. I'll take him for everything he's worth. Fuck with me. I dare you."

Victoria's mouth drops open. She rarely meets a bigger fish in her pathetic pond. "I won't say anything," she whispers.

Zane's eyes narrow.

Rocco puts his hand on Zane's arm, murmuring, "You're threatening children."

"Sometimes an adult must put children in their place. The best thing that happened to Melanie this summer was how these people disappeared." Zane gives my friends a reproachful look. "The moment Melanie let them back in, chaos abounds."

"I'm hated at that school," I say pitifully. "It's going to get out. I need to suck it up. Things can't get worse for me there."

Zane glares at Trey. "Do you have *any* idea how hard she cried when that story broke? Any clue what my lawyer, Ms. Alice, and I went through doing damage control? She made the choice to tell you, which I think was a massive mistake, but it was hers to make. WHY did you invite everyone to listen in?"

"They wanted to reconnect with Melanie," Trey says meekly. "Everyone felt like crap about how she was treated this summer."

"We've always been a unit," Tanner says. "We have each other's backs. I saw this as a moment where we really needed to back Melanie." He squints his eyes shut. "I never should have revealed this in front of Victoria, but we've gotten used to her being around."

"You put your fate in Victoria's hands," Zane informs Tanner. "Now that you know that, are you still as confident in her?"

"Not at all," Tanner says. He blinks, flustered. "My parents are in the middle of a horrible divorce. My family can't take any more upheaval. I'm asking you not to call your lawyer."

Zane shrugs. "You're asking the wrong person." He looks around at the group. "Hopefully this *unit* has your back."

Tanner slides fearful eyes Victoria's way. She takes an even breath, before informing, "I hate Melanie, but I'm not *that* sadistic. What we found out isn't good gossip material. It's sad, rather gross, and frankly, the fact that she's even able to walk again makes her a hero. I'll keep my mouth shut."

People have started to gather because of a celebrity sighting. Rocco puts a hand on my back and steers me to Zane's car.

We get in, leaving my group gaping at us. As soon as the door closes, Zane says, "You need to leave that school, Melanie."

My heart sinks. I used to love it there, but he's right.

CHAPTER 7

My bedroom phone rings, startling me. I rush to answer before it wakes up my parents. Midnight calls are frowned upon around here.

"Hello?"

"Melanie?"

"Yes." I take an unsure breath. I don't recognize the female voice.

"It's Tiffany. Trey told me you know about my miscarriage."

My eyes widen. I have zero clue what to say, but an idea occurs to me. "Hold on." I grab my cell phone from the nightstand and quickly dial Trey's cell number, hoping he has it by him and it doesn't wake his parents. When he answers, I whisper, "You need to hear this." I put both calls on speaker, setting the receivers next to each other.

"There's some things you should know," Tiffany continues. "Trey and I went on *dates*! I met his *parents*! I spent a lot of time with his sister, Kelsey. He took me skiing in Big Bear for the weekend! He TOLD ME HE LOVED ME!"

My mouth drops open.

"I thought he was my boyfriend, and then you popped up out of nowhere."

On the inside, I'm cratering. I drop all my shields and send down my connection with Trey, *"Are you going to let her talk about me like I'm no one?"*

The sudden opening of our connection leaves Trey battered with everything I'm feeling. He gasps.

Tiffany starts to speak again, and Trey says, "Tiffany. Please stop talking."

"Trey?" Tiffany asks in disbelief.

"Yeah, I'm listening," Trey informs. "I'm going to give it to you straight. I was playing a game to maintain my sanity. Melanie was in the hospital, and I was terrified she was going to die. It was all too much, and you flirted with me when I was vulnerable. I used you, and somehow convinced myself that it was a *thing* in the process."

"Did you mean it when you said you loved me?" Tiffany asks.

Jealousy floats through me as I shake my head.

"I'm sorry, Melanie," Trey says quietly, ignoring Tiffany's question.

My shoulders slump, and I put my head in my hands.

"Melanie needs to promise me she won't tell anyone," Tiffany demands.

I pick up the receiver resting on my dresser and hang it up gently.

Trey is just starting to speak when the phone rings. I push the ringer volume switch down to avoid the post-midnight call waking my parents. I pick up the receiver and hang it up again. A moment later, the phone rings again, quietly this time.

My answering machine picks up, and Tiffany's snotty voice growls, "If you tell anyone, you're going to deal with me *personally*."

This chick can't be serious.

The answering machine clicks off.

"Now I get to change my phone number because the love of your life is off her rocker," I say as I hit the delete button on the answering machine.

As if to punctuate the point, my phone rings again.

The answering machine clicks on, and Tiffany's voice blisters through the speaker again as Trey desperately implores, "She's not the love of my life, Melanie."

"Why is she calling me?" I demand.

Trey sighs. "I didn't want her blindsided if anything came out. So I told her you know what happened."

"I'm going to stop you right there," I snarl. "You had no issue blindsiding me with eavesdroppers."

Our connection still open, Trey winces in our minds. I slam my blockages up because we're still on the phone.

"Please don't shut me out," Trey pleads. "I'd rather have this conversation mind-to-mind."

"No thank you."

Trey sighs. "I swear to you I wasn't trying to blindside you. I'm furious with Tanner. We had it out after you left. Everyone's mortified. No one thought you'd want to shut them out, but they all understand why you do. This whole situation is a disaster."

"Instead of being on Team Melanie, you chose to have Tiffany's back?"

"Melanie, please," Trey begs.

"Who gives a damn if we know that she's a tramp?" I demand.

"I . . ." Trey falters. "I was trying to be upfront with her. I swear to you that I want to be upfront with you too. I'm so sorry Tanner told everyone, and I need you to understand that I'm honored that you trusted me with the story about what happened to you in the hospital after the accident."

"She's calling over and over," I gasp, panic boiling in my gut.

"I can hear it," Trey replies. "I had no idea she'd do this."

"I want nothing else to do with you, Trey."

"Please, Melanie. I've never been more relieved than I was when you decided you wanted to reconnect with me." Trey takes a gasping breath. "I never should have invited everyone. I should have made it a date night just between us. I also never should have told Tiffany that you know her secret."

I hang up my cell phone and stare at my bedroom phone as it continues to ring, followed every so often by crazed answering machine messages.

Trey pounds on the blockage in our connection. I finally drop it just in time for him to hear through my ears as Tiffany screeches, "His mother told me I was the best thing that ever happened to him!"

"Your mother hates me," I send.

"Melanie, I'm so sorry."

"I'm fully aware of what a sorry waste you are, Trey." My mental voice becomes tiny. *"Now even my bedroom isn't a sanctuary. How could you let her do this to me?"*

"I'll make her stop. I swear to you I'll fix it."

I block Trey off, and Tiffany doesn't stop.

CHAPTER 8

I wake late, having been kept up most of the night by maniacal ringing. I thought about unplugging it a thousand times, but every new message clued me in a little more to how much Trey isn't mine.

I heft myself up, and my leg and tush hurt. I cross to my full-length mirror hanging on the back of my door and survey my brand-new, footlong, eggplant-purple bruise. I sigh and shake my head. *It's going to be a blast at rehearsal today.*

My thoughts are interrupted by a tap at the window. I check the time, and it's ten-thirty in the morning. *Dang, I really did sleep in.* I need to get moving if I'm going to make my rehearsal at the studio. I cross to my window and pull back the curtains. There stands Bear, Darren, Trey, Presley, Demitri, and Trey's sister, Kelsey. I sigh and open my window. Without waiting for them to speak, I toss a pair of flip-flops out the window and hop through, wearing a sports bra and dolphin shorts.

Mercifully, no one speaks.

While I slip on my flip-flops, I ask Darren, "Can I have a smoke?"

He takes one out of his pack, hands it to me, and flicks his Zippo lighter, holding the flame to my cigarette.

Demitri surveys the bruise on my leg. He shakes his head and looks mortified.

Presley hits Trey with a death glare and says to me, "Trey called this morning and filled Bear in. Bear rallied the few of us he thought might be helpful. What happened?"

I gesture inside my room. "My answering machine was busy last night. Everything you need to know is a button push away. Have at it."

My friends start hopping in through the open window, but I stop Kelsey with a raised hand before she enters.

"Did you know about Trey and Tiffany?"

She looks uncomfortable and stammers a bit. "I knew. I didn't know what to say, so I chose to stay out of it."

I take a drag from my cigarette before leveling her with a heavy glare. "You were my friend."

She shakes her head frantically. "You're still my friend."

"So, as my friend, you told Tiffany all my dirt, but didn't tell me her dirt?"

Kelsey looks panicked. "I never mentioned you to her, or her to you. That was part of how I stayed out of it."

I gesture to the cars parked at the curb. "You're welcome to leave now."

Her mouth falls open, and she looks toward my open window. I glance that way and discover that all our friends are staring at us. Kelsey's eyes fill with tears.

"This isn't on my sister, Melanie," Trey says. "I put her in a terrible position."

I wave my hand dismissively in Kelsey's direction. "Leave, Kelsey. My house, my choice."

Darren hops out of the window. "You handle everything here," he says to Bear. "I'll drive Kelsey home."

Darren takes a tearful Kelsey to his car, and they drive away.

I lean my head back on the wall and listen as the answering machine button beeps. The answering machine's computerized voice says, "You have forty-three messages. Message one." Another beep, and Tiffany's voice screeches through the speaker, "HOW DARE YOU HANG UP ON ME! Who do you think you are? I'll tell you who you are! You're a loser who couldn't keep your man happy. THAT'S why he turned to me."

The answering machine beeps. "Message two."

Tiffany screams through the speaker, "And, let me tell you ANOTHER THING YOU MIGHT NOT KNOW. Twenty-two times in two weeks, Melanie! Twe—"

Having had the pleasure of hearing them all live and in color while she left them, I tune the messages out.

I'm so tired of sleepless nights full of drama. I don't think I can do this anymore.

The messages keep rolling, each one more bat-shit crazy than the last. Some are oddly desperate, some are angry, and others are full of tears and apologies for her previous messages.

The computerized voice finally says, "Message forty-three."

Now Tiffany's voice is hard and final. "At this point, it's you against me. Be ready, because I'm coming for you, *and* I'm getting Trey back. May the best woman win."

I turn and hop through my window. I scan my friends' shocked faces.

The machine clicks off.

"Tiffany is clearly unhinged," Bear says quietly.

I smirk his way. "Isn't it lovely that she's targeting *me* over this?" I glare at Trey, adding, "Last time I checked, I didn't tell her I loved her, break her heart, or get her pregnant, yet *I'm* the problem." I narrow my eyes. "Twenty-two times, Trey? Seriously? Aren't you

Mr. Wonder Dick when it comes to Tiffany!"

Trey closes his eyes. "It was new, Melanie."

"Shut up, Trey!"

"I'll help you beat her ass on Monday," Presley offers.

I smile at Presley. "I know you would, but that's not my plan. I'm going to ignore her."

Presley scrunches up her face. "I'm sorry, WHAT?"

"I'm going to ignore her. I have zero room left in my life for her drama."

Demitri nods. "Well played, Melanie."

"I'm proud of you," Bear says with a smile. "You're exactly right."

Trey just shakes his head, staring at the answering machine.

"Your bitches are aaall CRAZY," I quip.

Trey looks at me, radiating sincerity. "I'm so sorry, Melanie. I've never seen this side of her before."

"You're always sorry, Trey. You also always put your side girls' feelings before mine. That's your biggest flaw, Captain-Save-a-Ho!"

Trey starts to speak, but Bear interrupts him. "You should have NEVER discussed this with Tiffany." He gestures my way, adding pointedly, "You better hope Tiffany stops before Melanie's temper blows sky high. Your sidepiece is staring down the barrel of serious injury."

I can't help the sadistic smirk that slides up when Trey looks my way. I chuckle evilly. "I've killed, maimed, and rendered brainless. Since Tiffany's already brainless, that leaves me with killing or maiming her . . . If she doesn't leave me alone, that is." I gesture to the answering machine. "Good thing she's so stable. Nothing to worry about. She won't push me."

"Melanie," Demitri says, "you don't want to end up in prison."

I slide dead eyes Demitri's way and hit him with a blasé, "That's the interesting thing about my abilities. Police don't have a test for brain-melting energy attacks. I won't go to prison. And I won't feel bad about it."

I tip my head, shifting to stare at Trey. I know my lack of emotion is creeping him out because his eyes widen a touch.

"There's no more nice girl left in me," I add for good measure. "There's no more *rational*. My head isn't on straight. I'm in emotional survival mode and have been since my car accident. From now on, I'm just going to cut a swath through whatever hinders my path." I gesture to the phone. "Your side chick picked the wrong time. I was destroyed, and in self-mutilating 'why me' mode before her insanity last night." I grin sadistically. "NOW, I'm pissed."

Trey already looks like he's going to be sick, but just to screw with him, I drop the shield from our connection and put on full display how much I don't give a shit about what happens to Tiffany.

"It's one hundred percent her choice, Trey," I seethe. "If she's rational, I'm rational. If she pushes, I push."

Trey looks at the answering machine with huge eyes, knowing full well that Tiffany plans to push.

Demitri attempts to be the voice of reason. "Melanie, you can't set Tiffany up that way. She's a Normal girl. She has zero clue that she's stepped into the gladiator arena armed with a butter knife."

I scoff. "It's not my problem that Tiffany mistook me for a pushover. That's her problem."

"Pierre, I need your help," Demitri says desperately. "You have to stop Melanie." His eyes widen as he appears to listen to something in his head. After a long moment, he says to me, "Take the memory of what Pierre just said and pass it around." He looks Trey's way fearfully.

My heart pounding about the chance to hear Pierre's voice, I put my hand on Demitri's outstretched arm and take the memory.

I pass it to Trey through our connection, then stretch out my arm, and everyone grabs on to receive the memory. We all close our eyes.

The memory plays.

"Let Melanie kill her," Pierre says. *"Who gives a damn?"*

Demitri mentally replies, *"You have to do something, Pierre! You can't let Melanie hurt Tiffany. Where are your ethics?"*

Pierre snorts and says flippantly, *"Not only is Tiffany a Normal, but she's also a shallow waste of air. In the grand scheme of things, she's nothing but cannon fodder. I plan to watch the show."*

We all open our eyes, and I laugh a touch maniacally. "Thanks, love."

Pierre's disembodied voice wafts into the room. "I love you with every part of my soul, Melanie. Never forget where you're headed. It makes no difference that Trey's a confused waste."

Everyone appears stunned by the ghostly voice.

I study Trey distantly, and suddenly, he's less than interesting to me.

"Melanie, do what you will with Tiffany," Trey whispers, "but please don't look at me like I'm no one."

My expression shifts, and he shrinks under the scrutiny. I feel his blazing realization that he's not my equal. I nod slightly in agreement, and he blanches. "No one? I was no one all summer. I was also no one at the beginning of the last school year, when I was in a coma and you were in *Tiffany*. How does it feel to be no one, Trey?"

Trey fights back tears. "I'm going to talk to her. I *will* fix this."

"Oh, she'll be stopped." I pull the cassette tape with all the evidence from the answering machine, complete with her threatening to kill me, and grab my cell phone. I dial Zane's number. He picks up, and I put the call on speaker. "Love, we have a new layer."

"Ugh. You have to be kidding."

"Nope. The girl Trey had an affair with called me forty-three times last night, threatening to kill me, ruin me, etc. etc. I'm going to call the police."

"Do you have proof?" Zane asks.

"Yup. I'm holding the answering machine tape."

Zane chuckles harshly. "She left *messages?*"

"So many messages," I inform while smirking at Trey.

"How bad are they?"

"Bad enough that I'm positive hell's going to break loose when school starts on Monday."

Zane laughs evilly. "I need that tape. I'll make an appointment with my lawyer. Tiffany's going to receive a restraining order."

Presley snorts. "This school year is gonna be awesome!"

"Thank you," I say into the phone. "I have rehearsal at one. I'm going to shower, and then I'll rush it your way before heading to the studio."

"Rehearsal for what?" Zane asks suspiciously.

"Mr. Isley's forcing me into the dance show. Kendra sprained her ankle."

Zane scoffs. "She sprained her ankle? How logical. You just broke your neck. You can NOT do a show right now, Melanie. You had such a severe diffuse axonal brain injury that you were almost rendered paralyzed. Your brain stem was severely injured when your neck broke. Doctor Shaffer told me it was a medical miracle when we got your right leg to hold weight again."

Fear rips through me. "My right leg craters when I get emotionally overwhelmed."

"What about the other issues?" Zane asks softly.

"That was a problem last night when I got really upset halfway through Tiffany's calls," I reveal, my face burning red.

"Shit," Zane exclaims.

"Things seemed back to normal once I calmed down." I glare at Trey. "Naturally, Trey woke me up with all of my friends in tow, so I'm all worked up again."

"Kick them out. I'm headed your way for the tape. I want to check on you. I'll be there in thirty minutes."

Before I can argue, Zane hangs up.

I slide cold eyes Trey's way. "Please leave."

"I'm going to stay with her," Presley assures.

To my surprise, there's no further argument.

After everyone leaves, Presley quietly asks, "How much needs to be washed?"

Tears spill down my cheeks.

"I swear you can trust me, Melanie," Presley rushes to say.

"Three outfits, and two sets of sheets," I admit. I pull the unsoiled sheets currently on my bed aside, revealing a plastic tarp. "I finally admitted all of this to my mom. My parents are a worried mess."

"Are they here right now?" Presley asks compassionately.

I shake my head. "They had to go to a luncheon for Rich's work. They were leaving at ten."

Presley nods. "Okay. Where are the clothes and sheets that need to be washed?"

Mortified, I head to the closet, opening the door. I gesture to the full garbage bag I've stashed in there.

Presley hugs me tight. "You go get in the shower before Zane gets here. I'll get the washer loaded."

I shake my head. "You don't want to deal with this, Presley."

"Yes, I do. I'm in this with you."

CHAPTER 9

Mercifully, our rehearsal is finally done. I've had no further issues beyond the usual nasty looks I've always received at Hollywood High. I turn to the barre and take two steps back before bending down to stretch my back and sore legs.

Demitri sidles up to me. "Do you have plans after this?"

I glance his way curiously. "My plan was to go home and continue being pissed. Why?"

"I have something to reveal to you."

Part of me wants to tell him to leave me alone, but I hang by him while everyone makes their way out of the dance studio. When it's just the two of us, Mr. Isley waves us over.

He unfolds a tumbling mat, dropping it with a thump. "Full disclosure," Mr. Isley says. "Demitri filled me in before rehearsal." I start to turn red, but Mr. Isley holds up a hand. "I'm in no way judging you for any of this. I realize how humiliating your medical condition is, along with this Tiffany mess." He looks to Demitri. "I'm here to provide a safe space."

Demitri takes a deep breath and gestures to the mat. "Please sit."

It's almost surprising when I do. I'm hesitant to participate in anything more right now.

"I'm about to tell you something that only a few know," Demitri says as he sits down beside me. "Those few are my dad, Bear, Darren, and Mr. Isley. I don't share this because energy workers who can do what I can tend to be sought after."

"Sought after?" I ask, having no clue what he's talking about.

"By the government, enemy factions, and wealthy assholes," Demitri says. He takes a deep breath, nervous. "I'm a healer. As far as I know, I'm likely the strongest healer in the world."

"This sounds like cult shit," I say, unsure.

"I know, but I'm about to prove it to you."

Realization dawns, and I tear up desperately. "Do you think you can fix me?"

Demitri nods. "I rushed over here after I left your house. Mr. Isley and I looked up diffuse axonal brain injury in the school library. I think I understand it."

"How does this work?"

"Lie down on your stomach. What I'm going to do won't hurt, but it'll feel weird."

Without further hesitation, I lie down, and Demitri's hands land on my neck and lower back. I close my eyes and feel an odd searching within my body. He's right, though. It doesn't hurt.

"Got it," Demitri whispers. "Here we go, Melanie."

His hands heat up, and I slide a curious gaze his way from my prone position. Sweat starts pouring off Demitri's forehead in rivers. His shirt quickly soaks, and sweat droplets fall to my back. His head drops as his breathing becomes labored. The pain starts to dissipate in my neck, and then my legs regain full feeling after a long moment.

I gasp.

"You okay?" Demitri murmurs.

Not wanting to disturb him verbally, I nod under his hand.

Time stretches so long that I start to worry. Finally, Demitri sags as his hands drop to his sides. "Done," he says, sounding exhausted.

I sit up and take stock of my body. My eyes widen in disbelief. "My legs feel right again. I didn't realize how numb they were before you did that." I look to Demitri. "My neck doesn't ache now."

Demitri nods. "Your headache is also gone."

He's right. I've had a dull headache almost every minute of the day and night since the hospital first declared me recovered.

"Unbelievable," I whisper as I gaze at Demitri. "I had zero clue you could do that." I rush to add, "I'll never tell anyone!"

Softly, Demitri smiles. "You can tell Zane. He deserves to know you're healed after everything he went through with you. I also trust your parents with this information."

"Understood." My expression melts until I'm staring at him lovingly. "Thank you for helping me."

"You're welcome." Demitri looks to Mr. Isley and tears up. "She had permanent damage in her brain stem. This issue wasn't going to improve. It was starting to degenerate."

Mr. Isley kneels and puts a hand on Demitri's back. "I know it's difficult for you to reveal these things, but you did the right thing by helping her." He smiles at me. "Feel better?"

I nod in wonder. "I feel back to normal."

All at once, an epic posttraumatic meltdown hits. Tears roll down my cheeks, and I crawl the few feet to Demitri. He sits cross-legged and pulls me into his arms.

With a soft smile, Mr. Isley stands. "You kids work through things. I'll be in my office if you need me." He heads to his office on the other side of the dance studio and closes the door.

Demitri squeezes me tighter. "You know I love you, right?"

"I love you too, D."

He waits out my breakdown for a long while. When I finally calm, he says, "I'd like to take you on a date."

I rattle my head a little, stunned by the request. "Demitri, our spirit-guide future eternity bond is gone."

Demitri chuckles. "I'm aware." He gives me a gentle look. "I might be working on that." He gestures toward me pointedly. "Hence healing you."

"You talked to Pierre?" I ask in a rush. My eagerness reveals how desperate I am not to lose Demitri, and I blush.

Demitri smiles as if my reaction gives him confirmation that he's on the right track. "He and I have discussed this at length. Turns out there are options if I do my job with you. My job is taking care of you." He really studies me. "So much time away from you didn't help. I thought if I distanced myself and focused on the soulmate bond with Victoria, I'd be able to move forward." He shakes his head. "The moment I saw you again, it all came raging back."

My eyes widen. Demitri and I started off soulmates our first lifetime together two hundred and three lifetimes ago. We were so attached that we decided to forego our soulmate bond for a deeper eternal possibility. This was all revealed to us by Pierre, after he died. He explained that soulmate bonds dissolve after the course of a soul's lifetimes. This is when a soul moves on to its eternally bonded mate, and the pair achieves spirit-guide status. Pierre revealed that Demitri and I have twelve lifetimes left, but Demitri derailed from the path when his shallow desires for shallow women crept into his habitual process. He developed a soulmate bond with Victoria, which fizzled our deeper bond, but didn't know it at the time. Pierre then replaced Demitri as my eternally bonded mate. None of this went over well with Demitri. It's remarkable what happens when someone has all the pieces to the puzzle.

"I'm glad you tried with Victoria," I inform sincerely.

Demitri swallows hard. "It's awful."

I snort out a laugh. "I'm aware. My soulmate bonds with Adam and Trey are also awful."

"I'm wasting my time with Victoria. There's nothing there." He slides a mournful gaze my way. "You have no idea how sorry I am, Melanie. I know our eternal bond is a mess, but I promise I'm working on that." He smiles a little. "I thought we could also work a little on our actual bond."

My eyebrows rise curiously. "What's our actual bond?"

"D and Meley, who clearly have a thing for each other that D runs from while Meley cries and gets all caught up in trying to make it work with Trey."

When I giggle, Demitri chuckles a little. He scrunches his face. "What's happening between you and Zane?"

I sigh. "I'm positive he loves me. I'm also positive our age difference tortures him." I shake my head dejectedly. "That man is perfect. He never falters. He's always there when I need him. He deserves space."

"Are you sleeping with him?" Demitri asks.

"No. He hasn't even kissed me." Reflexively, I rub my forehead. "My forehead had a permanent bruise the whole time I was in the hospital though." My eyes flutter at Demitri. "He kisses my forehead so hard it hurts. It's all he's got."

"Oh, eeew. No. I don't like that. He really is perfect, isn't he?"

I nod with big eyes. "I love him. I think he might be my guy, but I'll have to wait to know, because he won't overstep while I'm underage."

Demitri rubs his face hard. "If you were eighteen?" he asks, clearly dreading the answer.

"It'd be over, and I'd never look back," I inform almost venomously. The power behind the statement surprises even me.

"That means I have a year and eight months to prove to you that he isn't your guy," Demitri says with just as much conviction.

I laugh a little. "You don't have to do this, Demitri. I appreciate you helping me more than you know, though. I'm okay being just your sidekick."

Demitri gazes at me intently. "No, I miss you and want to give us a shot. Come on a date with me today."

I find myself pleasantly surprised. "What about Victoria?"

"Don't you think it's time I ditched her?"

After the briefest contemplation, I look up at Demitri. "What did you have in mind?"

His lips part into a massive smile. "I have an idea. Go get changed."

— —

We round the corner, and I bounce happily as Demitri pulls me into the exit turnstile at the Alice in Wonderland ride at Disneyland. The attendant takes the pass Demitri pulls from a never-ending stream of them that he seems to have in his pocket.

We load into the cute purple caterpillar.

"How did you pull off all these front-of-the-line passes?" I ask.

"My uncle's a shift leader in Tomorrowland," Demitri says. "He hooked me up."

"Well played, sir. I'm impressed."

Demitri puts an arm around me, and I snuggle happily into his side as we go through my favorite ride.

When it ends, he asks, "Where to next?"

"We've made it through my favorites. You pick."

He laces his hand with mine, and we stroll over to Tomorrowland. We get to Space Mountain, where a man gestures us toward the exit corridor. He smiles at me as Demitri introduces us. Intrigued, I study the man as he chats with Demitri. He's Demitri's uncle but I'd never know if I wasn't told. Demitri and his dad are the ultimate chisel-jawed hotties, with piercing steel-blue eyes. Demitri's uncle is an ample man with a personality to match. His eyes are an oddly dull shade of light blue, but the way they twinkle makes me smile. He proves to have an infectious laugh that makes his gut jiggle.

"It's nice to finally meet you, Melanie," Demitri's uncle says. "You two, come on."

We go up a winding series of exit ramps, and he puts us on the front of the next roller coaster that pulls up.

It's warm tonight, and I'm leaning on a rail with Demitri's arms around me. The fireworks show starts. We have a front row view, thanks to Demitri's VIP access.

"This has been amazing," I tell him with a warm smile. "Thank you."

"You're welcome. Thank you for agreeing to come with me."

Something about the magic of the moment seems to sweep us both away, and the crowd disappears as the world narrows to just us. Demitri gently slides his fingers along either side of my jaw and leans in, delicately kissing me. My head spins. I find myself completely happy for the first time since Pierre died.

Demitri ends the kiss and seems shell-shocked. After he relearns how to speak, he gravels out, "You sure you and Trey are through?"

I smile shyly. "I'm sure. Trey's a never-ending downward spiral.

I've never been that connectedly disconnected with someone."

Demitri smiles and gathers me in his arms. We watch the finale of the fireworks show. He doesn't let me go until the massive crowd disperses. When we're alone, he asks, "Ready for dinner?" He leads me up a walkway to the Blue Bayou restaurant.

Excitedly, I bounce. "I love this place. I've only been here once."

It's usually impossible to get into this gorgeous place, but when Demitri gives his name, we discover that his uncle somehow managed to get us onto the reservations list.

We're guided to a quiet table by the rail. This restaurant is inside the Pirates of the Caribbean ride. I gaze around taking in the soft, moonlit-night feel, and pretty-colored paper lanterns strung overhead. I watch as a ride boat drifts by in the water.

After we finish perusing the menu and place our order, Demitri leans closer to quietly talk to me. "You need to know some things."

I huff. "Serious talk for a second, and then more fun."

Demitri's head drops. "I should have been the one to help you in the hospital. I flat couldn't do it. Because of my healing ability, it causes me a great deal of turmoil to be in hospitals. Knowing that I could heal so many people in those places nearly causes me to rattle out of my skin. With that said, I should have manned up and gotten my ass down there." He smiles wistfully. "My dad was furious with me for not going down there and healing you. Adam was the one who helped relieve Rich and Zane at first. He'd give me updates on your surgeries and broken bones." He swallows hard. "Then, Zane started discouraging Adam from coming to the hospital. Considering that Valerie was pissed about it anyway, Adam quit going. I've figured out that must have been when the more embarrassing stuff started after your medical coma was lifted, and Zane was protecting you from other people finding out."

I blush, thankful it won't be obvious in the dim restaurant. "I can't believe Zane still talks to me. You have NO idea how horrible it got."

"It's all fixed, Melanie. You don't have to worry about that happening again."

"Thank you. I've been sick worrying about going back to school."

"I'm sure. No one wants dropping deuce in the quad on their record."

Jokingly, I smack him on the arm.

He grins at me, but his expression slides toward thoughtful again. "I feel sorry for Trey about this Tiffany mess. We talked after you left CityWalk. He never wanted you to know, and guilt has apparently been eating him alive."

I furrow my brow. "I don't like secrets. I don't like affairs. I don't like Tiffany."

"That's all valid, but I can vouch that Trey's mortified." Demitri gives me a look. "We all know he knocked her up, and he's catching shit from everyone."

"Think she's going to continue coming at me?" I ask.

Demitri wobbles his head. "Everyone's decided that if she does, Tanner, Presley, and Deb are going to spread her dirt far and wide."

I wince. "Now that I'm feeling better, and not worried about fogging my drawers every time I get nervous, I'm a little more open to living and letting live."

Demitri shrugs. "Then we try that approach. I'll talk to her on Monday."

"I can't believe summer is almost over."

"We still have a few days." He smiles as he takes my hand. "I'll meet with Victoria and end things tomorrow afternoon. Can I pick you up at four and take you for a nice dinner?"

I smile softly at him. "I want it clear that I would normally never spend today with someone who's taken. It was one thing when we were friends, but a date is different."

Demitri smiles back. "I should have ended things with her before I took you out, but the date idea came to me during rehearsal, and I couldn't pass up one of our last days of summer. I apologize for the mixed-up order of things, though."

"Are you positive you're done with her?"

Demitri leans in and puts his forehead against mine. "I've never been more positive of anything." He kisses me, and my heart hammers with joy.

CHAPTER 10

I look at the clock and wonder if I'm an idiot. Demitri's nearly an hour late to pick me up for our date, but he isn't answering his cell phone.

When my doorbell finally rings, I take one last look in the mirror. I've outdone myself getting ready. I'm usually a frumpy mess around Demitri, between sweaty rehearsals and my habit of wearing grungies back when we used to get together and chill at his house. Today, I decided it was time to show him the side he's been hoping for.

I'm the only one home and need to answer the door. Nervously, I fidget with my curled chestnut hair one last time as I make my way down the hall. I open the front door, and there stands stunning Demitri in a dress shirt that brings out his gray-blue eyes. He looks a little bowled over as he takes in my fitted black dress with a slit to my hip, and my stiletto black heels. I've applied soft honey and light-pink makeup with just enough shimmer to give me an ethereal glow.

"You're beautiful, Melanie."

I smile softly. "I love when you wear grayish blue. It brings out your eyes."

Just when I reach out to take his hand, a voice in my head says, *"Stop, Melanie. Ask why he's late."*

My heart starts pounding, and dread creeps up in my gut. Pierre's on a spirit-guide ethereal plain that's unreachable, so it's a bad sign that he once again jumped through the hoops needed to communicate with me directly.

"What held you up?" I ask with manufactured innocence.

"Traffic."

Pierre says in my head, *"Wrong. Game over."*

My expression droops. "Not you too, Demitri."

"What is it, Meley?"

A memory pops into my mind, hand delivered by Pierre. I close my eyes and watch it. It's of Demitri, and he's in what I assume is Victoria's bedroom. He tells her it's over, and next thing I know, she's unbuttoning the dress shirt he's currently wearing. I get through enough of the memory to know precisely why Demitri's late but cut it off before I disgustedly yak from the tawdry happenings.

"Thank you, Pierre," I murmur. "I love you."

Demitri's eyes widen a touch. "What is it, Meley?"

I shake my head slowly at him while a surprisingly strong heartbreak makes me flush hot. "Cut the crap, Demitri. Why are you, of all people, playing me?"

He has no clue how to respond. I touch his arm long enough to send him the memory of Pierre telling me to stop and putting Demitri and Victoria's hump-fest in my noggin. Demitri watches the memory with his eyes closed, and he appears visibly ill as he realizes that I know he's lying to me.

When he's done watching the memory, he opens his eyes and hits me with a remorseful expression.

I cringe. "You're wearing the same clothes. You're *covered* with Victoria regret."

Demitri tips back his head. "I apologize. I didn't expect Victoria to come on to me. I got swept up in it before I came back to my senses." He holds out his hand. "Can I show you what happened when I realized the mistake I made?"

I wince. "Hell, no. I know where that hand's been."

Demitri groans. "Please let me make this up to you. I ended things with her as I rushed out the door."

"Go boil yourself in acid to sluff off the evil Victoria coating, Demitri."

"Melanie, please discuss this with me."

"This isn't up for discussion," I bark back. "How dare you. You kept me waiting for an hour while you were buried in Victoria! Leave, Demitri."

He stares at me with his mouth hanging open. It's like he's frozen in place with no intention of leaving.

"You have my dead husband living rent-free in your head," I remind him. "Did you really think Pierre wasn't watching to see what you'd do? The day before his ocean memorial, I told you how he said your actions would determine your fate. Well, now your fate is getting the fuck out of my house!"

Demitri squeezes his eyes closed before finally turning and stepping through the front door onto the porch. He turns back, starting to speak, but I close the door and engage every bolt and lock.

I lean with my back against the door, aware that he can see me through the pretty plate glass squares, but I can't muster up the ability to care. My shoulders slump as my lungs tighten. I collapse around them as tears stream down my face. I let down my guard with Demitri and got burned.

I know better.

My eyeliner and mascara run. Demitri loves polished, vampy girls, and I was aiming for sultry and mysterious when I got ready.

Now I look like precisely what I am: a pathetic mess.

I turn and look at him through the grided window on the door. He puts a hand over his mouth as he studies my distraught state. I'm sure my running mascara is *gorgeous*. I opt not to care. I'm never going to be good enough for him. Not when perfect Victoria's around.

I reach for the cord and pull down the blinds, cutting off Demitri's view.

Screw this.

I yank off my heels and stalk into my room, dumping them in my closet. When my phone rings, I'm so upset that I don't think to just let the answering machine pick up.

"Hello," I bark.

There's a throat clearing, followed by, "Hi, Melanie?"

I smile. "Zane."

"Um, it sounds like I've called at a bad time," Zane says, unsure.

"Not at all. It was a bad time made better because you called. What's up?" A smile creeps up. I love when Zane calls.

"All right, here it is," he says nervously. "There's this thing . . . an event. There will be dancing, and I hate doing the dance evenings alone."

"Okay," I say encouragingly.

"So, I wanted to see if there's any chance you have tonight free. I know it's last minute," he rushes to say. "I . . . well—"

"Zane," I interrupt, "I would love to."

"You don't have plans?" he asks incredulously.

"Plans fell through." I smile. "Now I'm glad they did. What's the dress code for this shindig?"

"Really formal. Like meeting with the queen formal."

"Umm . . ." I open my closet and wince. "Does the queen go to homecoming?"

"I'm sure whatever you have will be perfect," Zane says, and I can hear him smiling.

"Do I meet you there? I'm so excited!"

Zane laughs a little. "No, Seashell. I'd like to pick you up."

His use of Pierre's nickname for me throws me off for a second, but I quickly recover. "I'd love that. Thank you. Um . . ." I look to the closet again. "Can you hold on a second?"

"Sure," Zane says, sounding unsure again.

I hit the mute button on my cell phone and grab my bedroom phone. My heart racing, I quickly dial a number.

Mama Mabel answers.

"Emergency!" I squeak out.

"What's wrong?" Mabel asks. We've been through a lot recently, Mabel and I, and she sounds ready to jump into action.

"Zane's asking me on a . . . date? I think it's a date. I don't know." I flap my hand. "I need help! He says it's super fancy, and I only have homecoming fancy!"

"Girls," Mabel yells. There's a shuffling in the background before she asks me, "How long do we have?"

"Um . . . I don't know. Hang on." I unmute the other phone. "Hey, Zane. What time would you need to get me if I'm right off Hollywood Boulevard?"

"Seven."

"Seven," I hiss into the phone to Mabel.

"Hurry," she insists before hanging up.

"Hiii, Zane," I say, attempting casual. "Please pick me up from Mama Mabel's brothel."

"Brothel?" he barks. "Wait, I thought Mabel had an event center."

"Sex is an event."

"I suppose it is," Zane replies, sounding perplexed. "Mabel's at seven?"

"Yes, please." Already, I'm frantically tossing hair and makeup stuff into a duffel bag.

"Okay. I'll be there." Just before he hangs up, he adds, "Oh, and Melanie . . ."

"Yes, Zane?"

"Thank you for doing this."

I giggle. "No, no. Thank you. This sounds amazing." I hang up and make a mad dash for the door with my two formal dresses, and every bit of makeup and hair stuff I own, falling from my arms.

CHAPTER 11

"**A**re you sure?"

Mabel nods, a little misty-eyed. "I'm positive. You look so perfect."

I survey myself in the mirror in Mabel's guest room. I didn't need to change my hair, but my tear-streaked mascara face seems to have challenged Destiny's skills to the max. Somehow, she's accomplished a mysterious look, with gold hints. I'm in a show-stopping gold satin dress that Vs beautifully in the front. I turn, surveying the back over my shoulder. It plunges, leaving my back exposed, save for the slightest covering by the teeny spaghetti straps. My shoes are beautiful, strappy, jeweled stilettos that I'm positive are going to kill my feet by the end of the night, but it'll be worth it.

"I look twenty-five," I whimper.

"You look like a Hollywood-Golden-Age-of-Cinema starlet," Destiny assures.

I bubble with desperate excitement. "Thank you both so much. I don't know how you pulled this off."

Mama Mabel flourishes her hands. "Magic, my dear."

Unable to contain my delight, I squeal and bounce.

Destiny and Mabel laugh.

"I want you to spend the evening confident," Destiny says. "We'd stop you if we thought you weren't dressed for whatever this is."

"What do you think this is?" I ask Mabel. "Date? Weird friend thing? Maybe he needs someone to carry around his coat?"

"Doesn't matter what it started out as." Mabel gives me a knowing look. "You'll be in his head now, for sure."

"You approve, even though he's so much older than me?" I ask sheepishly.

"Sure do. Your mother approves too. So does your stepfather, despite himself. Zane is damn hard not to adore." Mabel's brow furrows. "What's happening with Trey and Demitri?"

I huff, filling them in on the latest series of disasters. I end my diatribe with, "Demitri stood me up tonight." I bite my lip and wiggle all over. "Thank goodness!"

Mabel giggles. "All right, Firebird. Your date will be here any minute."

My eyes widen from the reminder. "Firebird! Oh no. Should we cover my tattoo?" I look over my shoulder in the mirror and panic as I see the red-and-orange firebird tattoo on my shoulder—the one that's covering the scars from a gunshot wound.

"If he can't handle that tattoo, then he can't handle you," Mabel replies. "Now, you'll likely deal with paparazzi. Practice the poses again."

I cock a hip, letting my leg pour from the high slit on the left side of the dress.

There's a knock at the door, and Misty, the bartender, calls out, "Zane Drell says he's here for Melanie."

Mabel opens the door, and Misty looks like she's starstruck.

I take a frantic breath as Mabel grabs my arms. "You've got this," she says. "Be you, and you'll be fine. I'm a call away. Just say, 'Did my mother call?' and I'll know that I need to come rescue you."

"Did my mother call? Got it." I hug Mabel. "Thank you."

"You're welcome. I'll go greet Zane. Take a minute to get it together." Mabel rushes out the door, and I give Destiny a desperate look.

"Hold your arms up over your head and come with me," she says.

I rush to follow Destiny to the bathroom. She grabs the hairdryer and hits the cool setting, blowing the cold air on my sweat-stained armpits.

"Oh, no," I whimper.

Destiny cracks up. When my soggy state is remedied, she slathers another coat of antiperspirant on me before spritzing me with perfume that smells like jasmine and sugar.

I inhale and smile. "That's exactly how I want him to think of me."

"Perfect. Now get out there."

Destiny opens the door, then hands me a beautiful sequined purse as I step through. "Your phone, license, and money are in there."

"I didn't have any money in my wallet!"

Destiny smirks. "Mabel's got this. Money, tissues, the perfect lip gloss. You're set."

The moment I step through the door and into the parlor, Zane's conversation with Mabel falters. His eyes widen a touch as he stares at me. Mabel smirks and slides a knowing gaze my way.

"Hi," I say softly as I study how stunning he is in his classic black bow tie tuxedo. I've never seen anyone more handsome.

"Hey," he replies. Neither of us say anything else for a long stretch. Finally, he smiles, and his eyes twinkle a little. "You aren't even human, Melanie."

I blush a little, hoping it stops just as it hits the point of looking charmingly flushed. "Thank you for inviting me."

"Thank you for coming with. These things are more fun with a date."

"Now, there's no pressure, Zane," Mabel says, "but I have a bow tie that perfectly matches Melanie's dress."

"I would LOVE that," Zane says.

Mabel boings about happily while Destiny produces the bow tie. He takes off the one he arrived in, puts it in his pocket, and allows Mabel to do the honors of fastening the new one. As she straightens the gold bow tie, I notice how it's made of the same satin as my dress.

She smiles up at him. "Take care of my girl."

"I promise I will," Zane says. "Where should I deliver her after?"

Mabel looks to me, and I shrug. "My parents are gone all night for an event at Paramount. I don't know." I bite my lip, unsure.

"How about you bring her here after, and we'll have some girl time?" Mabel suggests.

Destiny grins.

"Done," Zane says.

Mabel requests details about where we're headed, and I'm nervous to hear that we're going to the Egyptian Theater.

"I've never been there," I admit.

Zane smiles fondly. "You'll love it, and you'll fit right in." He gestures to my dress. "First, though, we'll head to Musso & Frank. I made dinner reservations."

"I thought you just asked Melanie today?" Mabel says.

"I did, but I called after I got off the phone with her," Zane replies. Mabel gives him a quizzical look, and he chuckles. "They made it happen. There's a room set aside for when someone on their list calls."

Mabel nods approvingly. "I'm impressed. I'm on the same list."

"Would you like to come with us?" Zane offers.

Mabel breaks into a devious chuckle. "No. I'd like for you two to go, and then I plan to show up and spy on you like a self-respecting godmother."

"You're her godmother?" Zane asks curiously.

"I am now," Mabel says. She squeezes my hand. "Have fun, my Cinderella."

"Thank you."

Zane guides me out the foyer door, and there waiting for us is a Bentley.

My huge eyes settle on Zane's. "What happened to the Honda Civic?"

"That's for when I want to blend in," he explains. "This is for special occasions." Brian, a man I know as Zane's pilot, opens the backseat door with a professional flourish. "You're stunning, Melanie."

I blush and duck my head a little. "Thank you. I see you drive as well as fly."

"That I do," Brian muses.

I scoot into the car as Zane rounds the back and climbs in the other side. I try not to act like a complete idiot as I survey the inside of the car. I've never seen anything like it. When the car starts moving, we sit in silence for the short ride to the restaurant a couple of blocks away. Brian pulls into the Musso & Frank back parking lot.

"I haven't been here in years," I inform with a grin as Brian opens my door.

Zane comes around to my side, and I take his arm. "You've been here?"

"Rich had a production meeting in the back room when I was twelve. I read and ate while they hashed out a big show. He landed the producer spot at that meeting."

Zane guides me through the back door. The place hasn't changed since it was first built, and all these years, it has retained its luxurious 1920s feel. We head down the stairs, passing the dark-wood phone booths packed into a tight hall. We're stopped by a maître d', who greets Zane efficiently and by name.

People stare at us with open mouths as we pass tables on our way to a back room, where we're guided to a quiet private booth.

The maître d' places several leatherbound menus on the table before assuring, "Your waiter will be right with you."

Zane sits only after I do. He scoots around the rounded booth to sit next to me with his back to the restaurant.

"As usual, everyone seems to know you," I point out.

He sighs. "I was hoping this booth would help. We'll see." He hands me a menu.

"What are you getting?" I ask as I look it over. The prices are astronomical.

Zane smiles a little. "Your mother clearly taught you well. Don't worry about the formalities. You don't need to match your selection's price with mine. Get what you want."

"But we've never had dinner *dinner* together. I'm nervous. I don't know if I can eat much."

A stunned side-eye colors Zane's expression. "You usually eat a *healthy* meal, Melanie."

I turn stern eyes on him. "No judgy-wudgy, Zaney."

Zane grins. "Hi."

I giggle a little. "Hello."

"There's my girl. Now, quit being nervous. You're Melanie, and I'm Zane. Ignore the clothes, and that damn car, and settle in." He rolls his eyes. "Paparazzi are going to clamor, and I need the right car for the red-carpet pictures. When I tossed those keys at Brian, I didn't take into account how down to earth you are."

"Remind me . . . How do you know Brian?"

"He's my older brother."

I exhale hard. "Oh! That's easier, then. I didn't talk in the car because I didn't know if we could trust him."

Zane chuckles. "Good. I thought it was because you were having second thoughts about doing this."

I give him a baffled look. "If you knew what I went through to do this, you'd know better."

"Did you decide what you're eating?"

I nod, and Zane closes his menu book before taking mine from me. He sets mine up, blocking the view of the few tables that can see our faces. We duck down behind it, and I giggle.

The waiter strides up to take our order. Zane informs that we have to be at the Egyptian Theater at eight forty-five.

When the waiter leaves, Zane grins at me. "This place takes forever if you don't warn them you have a life to live."

I giggle.

"Tell me what you went through to make this night happen."

I wince. "Bad form, love. I can't discuss that right now."

Zane gives me a look. "I want to know."

"Okay. You asked for it. I was supposed to go on a date with Demitri, but he showed up an hour late. Pierre revealed that he'd been hunching Victoria while I cooled my heels. I was dressed up." I scrunch one eye. "Not this dressed up, but you get the idea. Anyhow, Pierre aired Demitri's dirty laundry, I cried like the kind of girl I look down on, and then you called. Seeing as how I only have my dresses from homecoming, and winter ball last year, I did a hundred on the 101 getting to Mabel's. Luckily, she has a massive wardrobe for her hookers, and was able to whip up this dandy delight."

As his eyes close, Zane looks almost mournful. "I didn't think about you rushing around, I had no idea you were mid-meltdown, and it never occurred to me that you didn't have a closet full of dress choices." He looks at me with extreme concern. "Hookers got you ready?"

"They really tried. Sapphire took in the dress. Destiny did my makeup. Mabel fluttered about, making the kind of fuss that was really flattering."

"Destiny and Sapphire?" Zane asks, unsure.

"They're so nice. You met Destiny. She brought out the bow tie for you."

Zane's face scrunches.

"I needed help," I say hesitantly. "I've never gotten ready for something like this by myself." I touch Zane's arm. "Is this okay for the event?"

Zane inhales hard. "Yes, of course," he rushes to assure.

I'm a nervous wreck inside. *Maybe getting put together by escorts isn't okay.* I certainly know it isn't normal, but I'd thought they did a really good job. My shoulders hunch. I suddenly feel like a vampy mess and wonder if I look like Victoria.

"You don't look like a hooker, Melanie. I apologize."

I purse my lips. "This is a custom Bob Mackie dress." I lean a bit toward Zane. "I have no idea what that means, but the point was made several times by Destiny and Sapphire. They seemed impressed by it."

Zane cracks up and rubs his face. "He's a designer. In fact, he designed the dance costumes in the movie we're about to see."

Zane grins. "That makes your dress all the more perfect."

"Well, woohoo," I say, perking a little. "Lucky me."

"What's about to happen is important for your career," Zane says. "I need you to trust me." He slouches a little. "I'm sorry that what I said came across the wrong way. It's just that every time I turn around, there's something newly shocking happening to or around you. Blasting Jet into the wall, marrying Pierre, stealing a car, getting arrested for assault, and now you're getting dressed up at a brothel."

I sigh. "That's why my friends run, Zane. This isn't new, and you aren't alone in feeling that way."

"Damn it," Zane says with a wince. "I'm sorry again. I'm not running."

Before I can reply, the waiter arrives to deposit our soups on the table. I wait until he leaves before saying, "If you do, I just ask that you get me back to Mabel's before you take off into the night in your fancy car."

"You really do look perfect," Zane says bashfully.

I take a bite of the best French onion soup I've ever eaten, moaning a little as I swallow it down. "Soup's good," I chirp, wanting to change the subject.

"The food here is always amazing."

"They have dessert?"

Zane scoffs out a little laugh. "Yes."

I gesture to the waiter, and he makes his way to us. "Yes, miss?"

"In light of the fact that we're in a hurry," I say with a grin, "I thought it best to add to the order now. Best dessert you have that's not chocolate?"

The waiter smiles back at me. "The cheesecake is life-changing."

"Yes, please. I'd like one of those. What else?"

The waiter chuckles. "We have key lime pie that's simply unreal."

"That too." I point to Zane. "He wants that one, but you can deliver his fork to me."

"Done," the waiter says. He winks at Zane. "I like her."

Zane laughs. "I do too."

"Would you like dessert?" he asks as he leans closer to Zane's shoulder. "One that your date doesn't plan to eat on your behalf?"

Zane shakes his head. "I'm not hungry enough. Thank you, though."

I give Zane a look. "Yes, you are. I'm not going to scarf down two desserts while you pout."

Zane chuckles. "The 1919 sundae, please."

"No problem," the waiter says as he leaves the table.

"There. Now we're even. Me racking up your bill with desserts is your punishment for being rude about my godmother who knows Bob Mackie."

Zane rubs his face hard. "I'll apologize to Mabel personally." When he opens his eyes, I'm holding his spoon by his face.

"Eat. This is amazing, and I plan to be a piggy. You be a piggy too. Besides, I have VERY exciting news to fill you in on."

With a curious expression, Zane accepts the spoon.

"So, Demitri helped me with something yesterday." I grin. "Guess who's not going to crap her pants anymore?"

Zane sprays wine out of his nose, choking as he cracks up.

CHAPTER 12

"So full." I'm groaning as I lie in the back of the Bentley in the restaurant parking lot.

Brian looks over his shoulder and busts up. I'm sprawled on the back seat with my leg hooked over Zane's knee. My dress is askew, and I don't care.

Zane throws his head back, howling laughter.

"I can NOT wear this," I moan. "I need sweatpants. I feel like a baked potato wrapped in gold tinfoil."

The guys howl louder.

"Oh my God, I love her," Brian gasps out around his laughter. "She's so much better than the fake fluff-heads we've had to drag around in the past."

Zane wipes laughter tears from his eyes. "Agreed on every level. When she's not pissed, she's hilarious."

I sit up and moan again. "Sapphire took this dress in with gusto. She didn't account for the steak swell."

"Or the baked potato, French onion soup, and two desserts," Zane teases.

"Uuugh. I can't eat like that when we're out in formal sausage casings."

"Where the hell did she put it all?" Brian asks as he surveys me.

"No clue, but she eats like I do," Zane informs.

As Brian puts the car in gear, he says, "Good, because it annoys you to no end when a girl orders food she doesn't touch."

"Ain't that the truth."

"Must be human," I say, scolding myself. "Hamster must waddle down red carpet." I take my lip gloss from my sequined purse and apply a layer. "Superpowers activated," I say as I screw the tube back together. I look to a chuckling Zane. "What's my role in this A-list charade? Date? Little sister? Escort?"

"You're my new partner at the Alice Agency," Zane replies as we pull up to a grand spectacle outside the Egyptian Theater.

"Wait . . . *What*?"

Zane's already stepping out of the Bentley as flashbulbs go off rapidly.

When he closes the door, I hiss at Brian, "What is happening?"

Brian grins at me in the rearview. "Showtime, gorgeous."

"Is he serious?" I ask in disbelief.

There's soft wonder alive on Brian's face. "Knock 'em dead, Melanie. Zane did it. You're in."

"I have a shot," I murmur, trying to wrap my head around the possibility.

I pull it together just as Zane opens my door, flashes a winning smile my way, and holds a hand out to me. I take it and manage to gracefully exit the Bentley while subtly situating my dress. I land a sparkly smile on Zane before we turn and pose by the car while more flashbulbs go off than I've ever seen before. I lean a little into Zane, nervous but covering it well.

The crowd is wide-eyed and starstruck by Zane. When I spot

a pair of familiar faces, my heart sinks. I grab the back of Zane's jacket, clenching it hard. He glances down at me before following my gaze. There, in the line of movie-watching hopefuls, are Demitri and Victoria. He's still in the bluish-gray dress shirt and slacks. She looks like the hooker I felt accused of being. She's in a black leather skintight club dress so snug and short that she best not bend even slightly. Her knee-high hooker boots look ridiculous.

"Wow," Zane murmurs. I look up at him to see if he's impressed by her. He's keeping his expression neutral, but murmurs, "What a train wreck."

"I can't believe Demitri gave up his eternal bond with me for her."

"What an idiot." Zane squeezes my waist a little and guides me forward. We strut up the red carpet.

As we pass, Victoria tactlessly hacks out, "Is that MELANIE?"

I look up at Zane, unsure, and he turns a snide glare on Victoria. We continue our aggressive sashay up the red carpet. Hips swaying, I fall into perfect step with Zane. He smiles down at me as I relax into the moment. Confident, I smile back.

We stop at the step-and-repeat background. Zane squeezes my hand before letting it go. I wait, watching while he takes photos by himself, and with another man. The man looks my way and asks, "Who is your date?"

"My new partner at the Alice Agency." Zane gestures me over. "This is Melanie Slate, dancer, singer, and actress."

I pose for a picture with Zane and the mystery man.

He offers me his hand. "Jack Griffin. Nice to meet you."

Immediately, I recognize the name. Jack Griffin is a huge movie director. I manage to wrestle my shock into a delightfully surprised look as I shake his hand. "It's so nice to meet you."

"I'll keep her in mind," Jack says before heading off into the building.

Zane poses with me. After the pictures, another man walks up. Zane shakes hands with him. "Melanie, you remember Ron Slater, chief photographer for the Alice Agency."

I smile. "Thank you so much for taking the pictures at the Cherry Bomb show."

"It's so good to see you again, Melanie," Ron says. "I've got an area cordoned off. Let's get some shots."

We follow him into the building, and my mouth falls open. I've never seen anything like this gold-adorned palace. It's breathtaking. He guides us to the landing, with theater seats and the stage in the background. We pass through the red velvet ropes and get into position.

"Series of couples shots," Ron instructs. He gets his camera ready, Zane wraps his arms around me, and I put a hand, and my cheek, on his chest. Ron grins. "Serious faces." He takes a few more shots and then says, "Babydoll eyes, Melanie. Hard jaw, Zane."

We do as requested.

Zane dips me low, and I drape over his arm. We both artfully extend our outside arms, and Ron's smiling from ear to ear as he snaps photos.

"Good," he encourages.

I notice that the spectators have moved inside. Demitri and Victoria are gaping at us, along with a whole lot of other people, as we work through our photo shoot.

"Solo shots, you two," Ron requests.

When I step aside, Zane quickly proves what made him a movie star in the first place. Ron motions me over and I take my spot. I dramatically cock a hip, letting my tanned leg pour from the aggressive slit in my dress, just like I practiced with Mabel. I switch to a mermaid pose, pulling my foot in, with my hands on my cocked hips.

"Damn, she's good," Ron announces.

"She's got a bright future ahead," Zane agrees as he crosses to me.

Director extraordinaire Jack Griffin joins us. He's studying me intensely. "Does she ever. She's spectacular." He smiles mischievously. "*Glitz* has a sequel called *Glamour* that I just started casting for." He raises his eyebrow. "I've got a dance role for a character named Char." He looks to Zane. "Can she dance?"

"Oh yeah," Zane assures.

Mr. Griffin gives me a penetrating look. "Pending a little audition, would you be interested?"

"Absolutely," I breathe out, dumbstruck.

"Done." Mr. Griffin looks to Zane. "I expect you both at the studio tomorrow at four. Can you make that happen? I need to test her out."

"We'll be there," Zane assures.

Mr. Griffin strides down the aisle, and I look up at Zane with my mouth hanging open.

"Did that just happen?" I gasp out.

"Welcome to my world, gorgeous."

"Yes," I breathe.

Zane laughs, hugging me and swinging me back and forth.

When I look out at the crowd, I spot Demitri. He's standing statue-still, watching me like his world is ending. Victoria makes quite the production of melting and mushing all over him. He noticeably winces, and I giggle a little. He chose her, after all.

Zane chuckles at Demitri's expense as he guides me past the ropes and down the aisle to a VIP section at the front of the theater. We take our seats just as the lights start to dim.

CHAPTER 13

The next morning, after a night full of A-list gossip with Destiny and Mabel, Zane picked me up at Mabel's and drove me to Hollywood High. We realized that we were both due at the same demonstration at the school. I have no idea why Zane is scheduled at my high school, and he was tight lipped about it. I just wanted to see him again, so I accepted the ride offer with gusto.

I strut into Mr. Isley's dance studio with Zane at my side. I've done my makeup in my old go-to style: harsh eyes and vampire-red lips. I'm blazingly insecure about whether I'll be able to get through this demonstration, so I'll have to fake it till I make it. I had zero time to choreograph a new solo, so I'm hoping an old one will suffice.

Zane is gaped at by everyone in the studio, but he's well-practiced at ignoring the fame scrutiny.

Ms. Alice approaches and hugs me. "Melanie, it's good to see you. Congratulations on last night. Zane filled me in."

"Thank you! We head to the audition right after this demonstration."

"You don't have to do a solo today," she says quietly. "I was ready to sign you the second I saw you dance in the surf competition show. I watched specifically to see if you had what it takes to be a member of my agency. Add to it the possible movie role, and I'd be insane not to sign you. You're already in." Her expression morphs sad. "I'm sorry to bring that up. You must still be mourning Pierre."

I fight to breathe around the reminder. "Thank you. It's hard, yes."

Zane wraps his arms around me, and I hear a hissed, "Zane *Drell* is hugging MELANIE?"

"We were told this was a demonstration," I say, trying to get back to business. "Mr. Isley didn't tell anyone they're auditioning for you."

Ms. Alice grins. "I know. I want to see their work ethic preparing for a random school demonstration. If we told them what it was for, they wouldn't show me what they're actually like."

Our conversation is cut short as Mr. Isley surveys the students who have showed up. Most of them, I'd expected, but I'm surprised to see Victoria and Justine here. Victoria is arrogant enough to show up, but I'm stunned to see Justine. She's my size, with brown hair my shade. That's where the similarities end though. The girl has zero personality and even less dance skill. Both girls are crappy dancers, but gorgeous, so who knows what will impress Chelsea.

"Welcome," Mr. Isley announces. "I'd like to introduce Chelsea Alice."

Chelsea steps forward, all business. "Good afternoon. I'm here from the Alice Agency, one of the leading dance agencies in Los Angeles. When Mr. Isley contacted me, I agreed to view a demonstration today."

Everyone looks at each other nervously. I catch Demitri's gaze from across the room. His eyes look haunted. Victoria leans confidently against the barre next to him. He subtly shifts away from her as she attempts to run her hand down his arm.

"I've brought two of my signed dancers today," Ms. Alice continues. "This is Zane Drell and Melanie Slate."

I hit Chelsea with huge eyes.

"Zane and Melanie will help judge your performances," Ms. Alice adds, to my horror.

Several of the catty female dancers start whispering gossip back and forth and giving me the stink eye.

"I . . ."

Zane puts a hand on my arm to stop me from speaking. I look up at him and swallow hard. He's watching the dancers, clearly unsure now that the dynamic is starting to unfold. The dance department is largely full of jealous snots, and I'm frequently the target of their social attacks.

Zane leans into Ms. Alice and quietly says, "I believe we have a problem."

I continue to stare straight ahead.

"Explain," Ms. Alice murmurs back while she stares at the floor.

"Four girls are already talking shit about Melanie after you introduced her as a judge."

"Which four?" Ms. Alice asks.

"Sports bra and booty short duo on the right, and baby pink and purple duo in the middle."

Ms. Alice takes a breath before looking to the sports bra and booty short duo. Their names are Natasha and Dell. Those two despise me, and I do my best to avoid them. Unfortunately, they're amazing dancers, and I guarantee the moment Ms. Alice sees what they can do, they'll get signed.

"You two," Ms. Alice calls out with a no-nonsense tone as she gestures their way. "Is there a problem?"

"No, ma'am," Natasha replies arrogantly.

"I believe there is," Ms. Alice bites back. "Don't waste my time. Leave."

My eyes snap wide, and I shift my gaze to the floor. I can see from my peripheral vision that everyone is stunned.

"Ma'am, please," Natasha says, shocked. "We'd like to audition."

Ms. Alice shakes her head. "I'm a firm believer in first impressions, and I'm not impressed. I invite you to leave." Before they can argue, she shifts her gaze to Tessa and Tana. They also hate me but tend to be a little less vicious than the other two. She gestures to Tessa. "Pink leotard, what were you smirking about?"

"Nothing," Tessa insists politely.

Ms. Alice raises her eyebrows. "There was something. You cut a dirty look at Melanie. Why?"

"No, ma'am. There's no problem."

"Do you want to be a professional dancer?"

"Yes. I've been working nonstop since I was three."

Ms. Alice nods. "Something tells me you've been gossiping since you were three also."

Tessa's mouth drops open, and she starts to tear up.

"Now," Ms. Alice barks, "what is your issue with Melanie?"

"I have none," Tessa replies quickly.

Ms. Alice gives Mr. Isley a disgusted look. "Is pink leotard any good?"

Mr. Isley nods. "Tessa's talented, but I agree that her attitude could use some adjustment."

"I have no interest in adjusting her attitude," Ms. Alice informs dismissively.

"I'm so incredibly sorry," Mr. Isley says, embarrassed.

Ms. Alice stares down Tessa. "Melanie booked a movie role at a red-carpet premiere last night." She smiles. "As her agent, that pleases me." It's an exaggeration, because I didn't book the role yet, but she's making a point. "What did you accomplish for your career this week?"

Tessa looks down. "I came to rehearsals here."

"How exciting." Ms. Alice looks my way. "Melanie, have you also been at rehearsals here this week?"

"Yes, ma'am," I reply quietly.

"Melanie, what's your opinion of pink leotard's dance skill?"

A little mortified about being put on the spot like this, I suck in a breath. "Turns are her specialty. She has excellent musicality. She partners well, and has incredible body connectivity."

Tessa's expression softens. "Thank you," she says to me. "I didn't know you felt that way."

I nod a little.

"Melanie, I'm sorry," Tessa says. She sounds sincere enough that I look her way.

Before I can decide on a response, Ms. Alice says, "Thank you for your time. You're dismissed, along with . . ." She points to Tana.

"They really are talented," I argue.

Ms. Alice smiles at me, but it has bite to it. "Los Angeles is full of talented people. I'm after professionalism. The last thing I need are reports from directors and choreographers that someone was difficult to work with." She looks to the dancers. "Auditioning for my agency is a privilege. Respect your opportunities."

"Yes, ma'am," is the reply from many.

It's clear that Chelsea isn't pleased. She gives Mr. Isley a caged look.

He passes a harsh stare at everyone remaining in the group. "Let's pull it together," Mr. Isley says. "I'd like to invite our intermediate dancers to perform first. You each get one minute."

He calls Justine up, and she forgets her choreography halfway through her piece. The pressure gets the best of her, but we all politely applaud.

"It's okay, Justine," Mr. Isley says. "Working through pressure is part of the process."

He calls Victoria up next. She starts to hump and gyrate through the equivalent of a stripper routine to "Nasty Girl" by the Vanity 6. It's mortifyingly inappropriate. Chelsea bites her lip and nearly expires with the effort not to laugh. I cover my mouth with my fist, my massive eyes betraying how funny I find this display.

"Where did Demitri find this floozie?" Zane murmurs to me.

I turn my back to avoid anyone seeing my laughter. Zane holds my shoulders tight while I fight not let them shake. He's radiating amusement. I glance to the side, and Demitri looks like he wants to die. He catches my gaze as I bury my face in Zane's shoulder, silently laughing harder.

Composed again, I turn just as Victoria hunches and wiggles past us.

When the torrid display is done, Mr. Isley does nothing to hide his bafflement as he says, "Well . . . all right."

The auditionees snort and erupt here and there with inappropriate bursts of laughter, but everyone quickly gathers themselves, attempting to be polite.

"Apparently it's striptease day at ye olde high school," I whisper to Zane.

Victoria gives me a nasty look. "Is there a reason Melanie doesn't have to audition?" she haughtily demands of Ms. Alice before sneering at me. "I'd like to see *you* do that."

Well, that does it. I feel my tact slide out my ear. "Someone rustle me up a sparkly thong. I'll recreate that magic, *stat*."

Zane howls laughter while Demitri covers his reaction with a fitful cough. Everyone else fights not to laugh, because Victoria is queen bee of this hellhole school. They finally lose the battle, and laughter starts to peel.

I mutter to a chuckling Ms. Alice, "So sorry." I give Demitri the look he deserves for choosing Victoria over me, and he grimaces so dramatically that even Victoria's stale brain catches on.

"What exactly are you making that face about?" she demands of him.

Demitri's eyes nearly pop out of his head.

Ms. Alice sighs heavily. "We're leaving. This isn't going to work, Mr. Isley. Zane doesn't offer his time flippantly, and I misunderstood the level of talent I was likely to find here."

"Wait," I rush to say. "Please, Ms. Alice. Four people should audition."

"All right," Ms. Alice says as she surveys me. "You're putting your reputation on the line. Are you positive you'd like to vouch for them?"

"Yes, ma'am," I reply as hopeful gazes survey me.

Clearly unsure about who I'm going to recommend, Mr. Isley narrows his eyes my way.

"Call the four forward," Ms. Alice orders. "I want you to run them through leaps before I witness their solos."

"Yes, ma'am." I turn to the dancers and awkwardly clear my throat. "Can I get Tanner, Jayla, Javier, and Demitri to join me?"

The expression on Javier's face is one of overwhelmed appreciation. Despite our personal strain, he's incredibly talented, and I'd like for him to have a shot at this.

The chosen four step to the center of the studio, and I take a CD from the case in my dance bag. I hand it to Mr. Isley. "Track one, please."

As I pass Demitri, I touch his arm subtly, giving him a little dark-water energy boost. He squeezes my shoulder, silently appreciative, as I settle into the back left corner of the studio. The chosen four get in line behind me as I make a quick plan.

"No Limit" by 2 Unlimited blasts from the speakers. I recall the best leaps for each of the dancers and put them all together in combination. I take off and hit a perfect set. Ms. Alice smiles up at Zane.

Jayla goes after me, and she bangs. It's perfect.

"Yes you did, Jaybird!" I crow.

She gets to me, and I high-five her.

Tanner is next, and I swear he flies. Jayla and I clap for him.

Javier hits a gracefully perfect set.

I take a deep breath and hold it in as Demitri steps up next. He preps and takes off. It's like he has springs in his feet. The height and extension he gets is unreal.

Ms. Alice breathes out, "Damn."

Inwardly, I smile. As much as I can't stand Demitri right now, he's wanted a professional dance career since he was a kid, and he deserves this.

Ms. Alice nods. "So far, so good. I'd like to invite each of you to perform your solos. You're guaranteed only a minute."

As Jayla hands over her CD, she looks so nervous that she almost can't function. She's shaking like a leaf. I settle next to Zane, and his brow furrows.

"Jaybird," I quietly say. When Jayla looks my way, I assure her, "You've got this."

Jayla seems to steel up a little. But when Bette Midler's "Wind Beneath My Wings" comes on, I wince. It's a great song, but not for this. Jayla gets through the first minute, and it's good but not stellar.

"Thank you," Ms. Alice says politely.

Javier takes his turn, followed by Tanner.

Finally, Demitri is invited to places. He works through a stunning solo to Bob Seger's "We've Got Tonight." Ms. Alice is clearly impressed because she doesn't stop him after the first minute. Every extension is breathtaking, and Demitri does a phenomenal job showcasing his talent. I'm fully aware that the piece is about me. I can't help a soft smile as he looks at me when the piece draws to a close. He quirks his mouth a little, and my heart clenches.

I really do adore him all the way down to my soul. I despise his player side, but he's got the biggest heart.

Chelsea nods her approval. "Excellent work. Here's my assessment. Jayla, you're almost there, but your nerves get the best of you. I need you to work on that, and I'd like to reassess in a year."

Jayla's incredible sweetness shines through. Her eyes light as she promises, "I'm going to work really hard. I'll prove myself to you." She looks my way. "Will you help me, Melanie?"

"Absolutely." I smile, realizing how beautiful she is.

Her long curly hair is down, perfectly framing her face. She has big brown eyes and a tiny frame.

Ms. Alice smiles. "That's the perfect attitude, Jayla. I appreciate how you recognize this as an opportunity instead of a slight." She turns her attention to the guys. "Tanner, I'd like to privately audition your dance skills, with Zane's assistance. In the meantime, I'd like to offer you a commercial modeling contract."

Tanner's expression breaks with glee. "You do *not*," he crows flamboyantly.

Ms. Alice laughs. "I do. You're different. You clearly aren't scared of a little makeup. I could use your unique vibe."

"Yes, *girl!*" Tanner caws. It would come off as offensive and unprofessional from anyone else, but he's Tanner.

Ms. Alice chuckles a little before she looks to Javier. "I'm offering you a dance contract. You're technically flawless, and you're light on your feet."

Javier's eyes widen. "Thank you so much," he breathes.

"You're very welcome. But you need to thank Melanie. You weren't on my radar before she pointed you out."

Javier slides a sincere gaze my way. "Thank you."

I smile and nod.

"Now, for the difficult choice." Ms. Alice looks to Demitri. "I'm signing you to the modeling division and putting you in my top ten file. I've never seen anyone who looks like you. You're Statue of David perfect."

Demitri blushes a touch. "Thank you."

"You're as good a dancer as Zane is."

Zane snorts, and Ms. Alice smirks at him.

"The question I have is what to do with Melanie," Ms. Alice says. "Zane is too tall for her, if we're getting down to it. Demitri, I need to see you dance with Melanie."

My eyes widen. I have zero interest in dancing with Demitri right now. I lean to Ms. Alice, quietly saying, "I'd rather not."

She gives me a baffled look.

"Demitri is uncomfortable having a sensual connection with me," I explain in a whisper. "He fights it in dance rehearsals. I have a giant bruise on my hip because of our lack of connection."

Chelsea appears concerned but undeterred. "Do me a solid, Melanie."

After an internal sigh, I rally. "Yes, ma'am."

"Melanie, please go to places."

Michael Jackson's "In the Closet," comes on, and we blaze through the blisteringly sensual piece. I put my all into it, unwilling to embarrass myself in front of my new agent.

Demitri lowers me from the torch lift, and I drape over him seductively on the final note of the song. The moment I can, I step away.

"She's right," Ms. Alice says. "Demitri, you have no heat with Melanie."

Demitri looks stunned.

"You hold back. You don't give in."

"You've got that right," Victoria interrupts rudely.

Gasps ripple through the room.

Ms. Alice's brow furrows as she looks to Victoria. "Explain."

Victoria cocks a voluptuous hip. "The number of times Demitri and I have fought about him dancing with Melanie is ridiculous. I told him that if he does sexy pieces with anyone but me, then we're through."

Ms. Alices lips purse. "I see. So, you control him?"

Victoria smirks.

"Good to know."

"Ms. Alice, please," Demitri rushes to say. He looks to Victoria, then to me. "May Melanie and I please try again?"

Chelsea shakes her head. "Now that I know you can only dance full out with Victoria, that puts me in a tough position. Considering that Victoria is an intermediate dancer at best, it means *you're* an intermediate dancer at best." She gestures to me. "What I just saw Melanie do was mediocre for her. Now, the question is, is Melanie mediocre, or are the two of you a bad pairing?"

Demitri's eyes widen. "I was holding back. I apologize. I made that promise to Victoria when there was nothing more than dance classes at stake."

Ms. Alice surveys me. "Isn't Melanie bruised because you dropped her?"

Demitri blushes fuchsia.

"He *what*?" Zane snarls.

"I'm okay," I assure him.

Zane glares at Ms. Alice. "Melanie is *my* partner."

"Do the two of you have a duet I haven't seen?" Ms. Alice asks Zane. "I'm now questioning whether Melanie should be signed to the dance division."

My eyes widen as I look to Demitri. He winces.

"I need something with some heat," Ms. Alice adds.

Zane scrunches up his mouth. "I need to teach her a section for her movie audition, but I planned to teach it after this demonstration."

"What song?" Ms. Alice asks.

"Santana's 'Your Touch.'"

Ms. Alice slowly smiles. "I want to see her learn it on the fly."

"May I confer with Zane briefly?" I ask.

"Of course," Ms. Alice replies congenially.

I take Zane's arm and pull him to the far side of the room. He bends so I can whisper in his ear.

"There's something that might help us here. I probably should have told you this already, but I can take and give memories now."

"Like Pierre's gift?" Zane asks.

"New metaphysical mess," I say with a nod. "But it's about to come in handy. Do you have a memory of the piece?"

"I'm the choreographer for the movie," Zane whispers back. "I've never done the piece with anyone. I choreographed it for you. Just know that it's not a duet for the role of Char. I'm trying to steer things at the audition. Get you a better part."

"Do you have a memory of you imagining what it would look like?" Zane nods, and I murmur, "Think of it. I can take it, and then we'll blow her away."

He winces. "My thoughts aren't good for you to see."

"I'll mute the memory and just watch the physical movement," I assure.

"Done." Zane closes his eyes, somehow managing to trust this craziness. He's a very rare Normal that way. I take the memory, careful to do as I promised, and mute the thoughts, only watching the physical movement.

Once I have it, I look up at Zane, and we mark through the piece with our hands while he explains it.

"I'm ready."

Looking unsure, he grabs a CD from the soft-sided case in his dance bag and hands it to Mr. Isley. We get into place. I lean back against him, and he wraps his arm around my chest as "Your Touch" pulls and sighs through the speakers. The piece has a sultry ease to it. It's unrushed, and I give in to the lifts and dips, trusting Zane.

He spins me twice to the right, and I plunge with my eyes closed. His hand lands on my back, and I open my eyes, dipped low. He pulls me to standing. I run my leg up his side as he grips my hip, lifting and turning us. He smiles at me with sultry mystery in his eyes. I can't help the seductive smile in return. This is the first time we've ever worked through anything with a vibe this sensual. I choose to enjoy it instead of feeling awkward. Yes, we have an audience, a majority of which don't like me, but I have no interest in being partnered with Demitri at the agency.

Knowing what's on the line, I slink and slither, drape and wrap around Zane. In turn, he grips and holds me with no concern for my age. He performs the piece exactly how he imagined it.

The song draws to a close as Zane pulls me to him and picks me up. I drape over him and close my eyes as my cheek lands on his shoulder. Our breathing syncs, and Zane drops his face to my shoulder. We hold for a long moment before applause rings out.

Zane lowers me to my feet but doesn't let me go.

"You two are magic," Ms. Alice says. "That was heated, mysterious, and everything about it was exactly right. Melanie, you just proved yourself to me. I'm partnering the two of you in the agency."

Zane beams. "Thank you, Chelsea."

It takes everything I've got not to squeal and bounce. Zane leads me to the side of the room, and only then does he squeeze me tight.

Mr. Isley beams from ear to ear and dismisses everyone with a thank-you. Ms. Alice offers her card to Tanner and Javier, giving them instructions. Then she calls Demitri over while everyone gathers their stuff. As Demitri gets to Ms. Alice, Victoria glazes herself on him, and he looks at her like she's insane.

"Head out, Victoria," Demitri says flatly. "I need to take care of business with Ms. Alice."

Victoria purrs, "I'll wait for you."

"Please leave. This isn't the time."

Victoria huffs off, loudly exclaiming to one of her snotty dance friends about how dramatic Demitri is as she exits the studio. I can't help but smirk.

After Victoria is gone, Demitri says quietly, "I apologize, Ms. Alice."

Chelsea gives him an appraising look. "You're gorgeous, talented, and completely whipped by her."

"That won't be a problem," Demitri assures nervously.

She stares at him for an uncomfortable moment, looking unsure. Finally, she says, "It's already a problem. Victoria is rude, tactless, and pushy. I flat don't do drama, and I've been down the problematic girlfriend road with some of my dancers before."

Demitri looks crestfallen.

I jump in on his behalf. "Ms. Alice, I promise Demitri's solid. I'm sure he can keep Victoria at bay."

Ms. Alice contemplates this for a time. Reaching a decision, she looks to Demitri and points toward the door Victoria just exited. "That girl will cannonball your career. You're stunning, and incredibly talented, but you clearly have bad judgment where your personal life is concerned." She exhales slowly, lost in thought while she studies Demitri. Finally, she says, "I'm sorry, Demitri, but I'm rescinding my offer. I can't trust that you'll commit to the work. Right now, your commitment is in placating Victoria's demands."

Demitri's eyes close, and his complexion runs pale. "Please reconsider," he quietly implores. "I *will* curb Victoria."

Ms. Alice shakes her head. "Your demonstration with Melanie was mediocre. She's injured because of your desire to please your girlfriend. I don't trust you." She holds her hand out. "It was lovely to see you again."

Looking stunned, Demitri shakes her hand.

Ms. Alice turns her attention to Zane and smiles. "Thank you for helping me today."

"You're welcome," Zane says. "I'll let you know how Melanie's movie audition goes."

Ms. Alice pats my arm. "Break a leg. I'll schedule a meeting with your parents so you can sign the agency paperwork."

"Thank you so much."

As Ms. Alice steps away to gather her stuff, Mr. Isley approaches.

"How do you know Ms. Alice?" he asks quietly.

"Chelsea was my dead husband's agent."

Mr. Isley is clearly baffled. "You were married? To whom?"

"Pierre Riptide Strader."

His mouth drops open. "The international champion surfer who died?"

"Correct," I say, trying to keep my emotions in check.

"Do your parents know about this?"

"Yes, sir. Riptide was my stepfather's godson."

"Did you know Riptide?" Mr. Isley asks Demitri.

"I knew him well," Demitri says bitterly. He doesn't elaborate.

"I'd like to talk with you for a minute, if I could."

Demitri sighs. "I'm not in a good place to discuss this right now. I need to talk to Melanie."

"No thank you," I whisper.

I have never seen my best friend so distraught.

CHAPTER *14*

Zane stares into my eyes and smiles the tiniest bit. There's mystery in the moment, and I melt into him. His hand lands lightly on my back as our audition song draws to a close. My eyes close on the final note.

"Wrong, Barry!" Jack Griffin barks. "I'm telling you I have a feeling about this!"

My eyes snap open as I realize that the director of the film is engaged in a heated debate with his casting director, Barry Yen.

"We hired Molly Horwitz!" the latter man argues.

"She hasn't signed her contract yet." Jack Griffin gestures loudly in my direction. "I don't give a damn if she's *ten*! Did you SEE that?"

Barry grimaces. "That vibe is hard to ignore, but she has no name. She's a complete unknown!"

My eyes widen, but I keep my mouth shut. Zane puts his arm around me, his hand tense on my back.

Jack continues to talk like I'm not there. "Layanette was *written* originally for a little brunette! It was *rewritten* to fit Molly." He tips his head condescendingly toward Barry. "Which would YOU pick? This whole series is a desperately broken fantasy!"

Barry gives Jack a look. "I'm highly unlikely to pick Melanie *or* Molly," he slathers out flamboyantly.

I subtly turn to Zane and stare at the front of his T-shirt as I attempt to turn myself into an inanimate object.

Jack Griffin tosses his hands. "You're the CASTING director! It's your *job* to figure out who will make someone cry. Who will piss someone off. Who someone wants to crank one out to when they get home from the theater."

My eyes widen. Zane fights amusement.

"Molly has fake sandbags!" Barry insists.

"But will the audience fall in love with her sandbags?" Jack Griffin huffs. "Layanette is supposed to be the irresistibly adorable, tortured, newlywed wife of Zane's character." He gestures fitfully my way. When he gets no response, he yells, "Screen test both of them. NOW!"

"Yes, sir," Barry snarls, while Zane's eyes widen.

"Molly's first," Jack barks back.

Barry strides over to me and harshly grabs my wrist. He yanks me with him. It's rude, abrasive, and he doesn't give a damn. I'm an object to him, but that's this business. They love you when they need you, and then they ditch you when they don't.

He opens a door, and there's Molly Horwitz sitting in a waiting room full of couches. She starred in one of my favorite movies, so seeing her in person is a little stunning, but I simply smile pleasantly as we pass. Barry hands me two pages that I take with a polite, "Thank you." I glance over my shoulder and watch Molly sashay through the door in a black skintight dress that immediately makes me positive that I don't have a shot in the world to land this part. Barry briskly closes the door, cutting off my view of the stunning woman. What I can't figure out is why Jack and Barry are fighting about me playing Layanette. I'm auditioning for the role of Char.

A fuss kicks up in the big studio I was just pulled from. I don't have to eavesdrop. People in Michigan can likely hear Molly when she screams, "Why?" There's a pause before she bellows, "Do you know who I am? A SCREEN TEST?" Another pause, and then, "I *dated* him! I think we're good."

I wince. I had no idea Zane and Molly Horwitz dated. My heart sinks. I've been naïve enough to think there was a chance between me and Zane. Meanwhile, he's dating women like Molly. Humiliation bubbles in me, but I try to ignore it and go over the lines so I don't make a fool of myself when it's my turn.

CHAPTER 15

The audition yesterday seems like it was a million years ago as I stare at the closed main curtain. I'm a bundle of nerves while we wait for the start of our opening performance of a new year at Hollywood High. I'm nervously pacing back and forth on the stage. The chatter of fifteen hundred students wafts through the fabric barrier. First day of school jitters, the Demitri drama, the Tiffany disaster, the whole movie-audition-Molly-Horwitz thing, knowing I'm not ready to perform Kendra's parts—it all has me spun out.

The awkwardness between Demitri and me after what happened with Ms. Alice doesn't help as he crosses the stage to me. "How are you holding up, Meley?" he asks hesitantly.

"I'm a nervous wreck."

"You've got this."

It's a little surprising when he pulls me in and hugs me, and it's even more surprising when my new memory-reading ability blazes to life unchecked. A memory leaps into my head from Demitri, and I find myself unable to stop watching. It's of him watching me try to figure out the duet on the first day it was decided that I would replace Kendra. In the memory, he thinks, *The last thing I want to do is work twice as hard while Melanie figures this out. She can't pull this off. We need Kendra back, or this show's Titanic-doomed.* A sense of blazing irritation about me rips through him. He rubs his face, trying to curb it.

The memory ends, and I step away from Demitri. My cheeks blaze a humiliating crimson as I realize that I'm truly not good enough for him, even as a dancer.

He looks at me quizzically.

I walk away before Demitri can ask anything. I didn't intend to hear or see any of that. I need to get this ability under control.

I head down the hall to the dressing room, where Tanner's finishing Jayla's makeup.

"You good, Mel?" he asks.

With a terse nod, I survey myself in the fancy mirror. Shiny black cropped halter bra top. Black Lycra pants covered in gemstones. My chestnut-brown hair's slicked back in a harsh ponytail. The makeup for this show makes us look evil. Black eyeshadow, heavy eyeliner, and dark-red lips.

I look intimidating, but I feel so tired. Dancing at the school has been one of the few things that's held me together. *But if Demitri's done dancing with me, then that's the last straw.*

My thoughts are interrupted as Susan's voice drifts through the dressing room monitor system. "Places, please. Places for the top of the show."

One last glance at the mirror before I close my eyes and take a breath.

Tanner squeezes my hand. "You've got this, girl. I'll be right there in the wings cheering you on."

I open my eyes and smile at him before turning and heading with the cast of identically costumed dancers through the hallway. I get to the second wing on stage left and wait nervously.

Arch's voice booms through the speakers. "Hellooo, Hollywood High, and welcome to your 1993–1994 school year! I'm Arch Terani, your student council president. A big welcome to all our new students. You're a member of the best high school in the world!"

The audience screams and applauds.

I drift off on a wave of insecurity as I nervously replay Demitri's memory. Panic and self-doubt climb to a rolling boil in my gut.

Unexpectedly, Trey sends through our connection, *"Demitri would be mortified if he knew you'd seen that. He's bragged that you worked yourself sick getting this down."*

Without responding to Trey, I slam my shields back into place.

Arch quiets the enthusiastic audience before continuing. "To kick off this epic school year, I now present to you our first performance in our brand-new state-of-the-art theater! Now presenting Mr. Isley's award-winning Allstar dance team, in their original production, '*Vibes!*'"

The curtain opens, and we stand for an extended moment in the dark. My heart feels like it's going to pound out of my chest. The lights start glowing onstage, and suddenly, Janet Jackson's "If" blasts through the high-end speakers. The sound is incredible enough to make me grin and forget all of my doubts.

I've got this.

— —

Changed into regular school clothes, I make my way down the hall and out the alcove into the audience area. My friends are waiting for all the dancers from our group. Kelsey tries imploringly to make eye contact with me, but I avoid her gaze. Trey puts a reassuring hand on her arm. I'm positive he plans to yap about how bad his sister feels about the Tiffany mess at some point today.

Mr. Isley rushes down the audience aisle with Ms. Ferry and Ms. G, and he makes a beeline for me. "I TOLD YOU!" he gushes. "I knew you could do it. You were fantastic."

I smile, preening a bit from the praise. "Thank you for giving me a shot, Mr. Isley."

Ms. Alice and Zane walk up, beaming. My heart skips a beat, because I didn't know they were here.

"You were just spectacular," Ms. Alice says, raising an eyebrow Demitri's way. "That duet was a different ball game."

Demitri smiles a little. "I've decided not to hold back. I need to do the work justice."

From beside him, Victoria gives Demitri a nasty look that he ignores.

"Well, I can't overlook your talent," Ms. Alice says. "So I'd like to change my mind again and offer you a spot with the agency. And I'd like to partner you with Melanie."

"Excuse you!" Zane explodes.

My eyes snap wide. "Ms. Alice, may I speak with you?"

"Just say what you need to," she encourages.

"Demitri doesn't want to be partnered with me," I calmly inform, seething a little about what I'd learned from Demitri's memory. "When preparing for this show, he got stuck with me." I shake my head. "He didn't feel that I learn fast enough, was good enough, and he thought the piece was doomed because of me."

Demitri looks stunned. "Why would you say that?" he asks in disbelief. He looks to Ms. Alice. "I would love to be partnered with Melanie."

With a touch on his arm, I send his own memory back to him. He deflates.

"Please," Zane implores. "The whole reason I was coming back to the dance division was because of Melanie."

Ms. Alice looks to Zane and smiles. "You've got an entire movie with her, right?"

Zane grins. "I guess I do."

"What?" I ask with huge eyes.

Ms. Alice beams as she announces, "Melanie, your contract has been delivered. I'll need to meet with you and your parents, but you got the part of Layanette."

"I got the *lead*?" I breathe out in disbelief.

Ms. Alice nods. My friends all cheer. I'm shaken and hugged from every side.

Over the cacophony, Ms. Alice informs, "The director told me that he had no choice but to overlook your age. You were spectacular in your screen test and dance audition. There was apparently no comparison."

My mom and Rich choose this moment to come join the congratulatory crew.

"We'll need to have a discussion," Ms. Alice says to my parents, leveling them with a serious gaze. "The movie is full of nudity and sex scenes. She'll need your signed permission to perform."

Jubilance quickly turns to silent shock from most of my friends.

"What?" Rich says.

"There are regulations," Ms. Alice assures. "They can't show Melanie's bare chest. Everything is simulated. It'll look steamy, but in the end, it's just work."

Rich steers an almost accusatory glare Zane's way. "Did you know about this?"

Zane wobbles his head. "Yes, regarding the regulations. I hadn't seen a full script until this morning. I have yet to read the whole thing, but we were briefed in a meeting before we came here."

My mom blinks rapidly. "I thought Melanie was auditioning for the role of a dancer in the movie?"

"She was," Ms. Alice says. "But she blew them away and scored the lead."

"How old is the lead character supposed to be?" Rich asks.

"Twenty-one," Ms. Alice says. "The producer and director are aware of Melanie's age and are working on camera angles. They can't go against regulations for minors. They know that and still gave her a shot." Ms. Alice gives Rich a pointed look. "This is a huge deal. They believe so much in Melanie that they greatly complicated their lives to give her the part."

I'm mortified that this discussion is happening publicly, but I don't get a chance to say anything.

Victoria turns scathing eyes on Demitri. "You ARE NOT partnering with *Melanie* at the agency. She's about to be a giant slut in a movie. Have some self-respect."

Trey glares at my stepfather. "That won't be an issue because Melanie isn't doing a movie like that. Right?"

My head drops as my cheeks burn fuchsia.

Ms. Alice looks around, seeming surprised. "I . . . I was so excited for you. I thought everyone would be excited. Your first feature film is a huge deal."

"We are excited for her," Bear attempts to reassure, but it comes across as doubtful.

Trey levels Zane with a furious glare. "Stay away from Melanie."

Zane grimaces while Ms. Alice whips her gaze from Trey to Zane. She rushes to say to Trey, "It's a movie. None of it is real."

"Are you guaranteeing she won't have to touch, kiss, or simulate anything with him?" Trey demands as he fires an angry finger Zane's way.

"Trey, please stop," I plead quietly. "We'll talk privately."

"I'm not facing everyone at this school after my girl acts like a giant hoe on the big screen." Trey glares at me. "We already deal with enough in this fucking place!"

"We aren't even together," I panic mind-to-mind down the connection.

Trey's eyes snap wide at my take on our status.

"I apologize for not informing you privately, Melanie," Ms. Alice implores. She looks to Trey. "Melanie is an actress, and this is part of it." She gestures to Demitri. "It's no different than what she just did onstage with Demitri. They were playing roles in a show."

Trey glares at Demitri. "Melanie's done dancing with you."

Realization that Trey is doing the exact same thing that Victoria did in the audition yesterday has me in a panic. The fact that we aren't together makes it even worse.

Victoria crosses her arms over her chest. "It's Melanie or me," she barks at Demitri.

I close my eyes, trying to pull it together. "Enough. The next person who attempts to ruin my special moment is getting blasted through a wall."

Arch chooses now to storm down the center audience aisle from the double doors at the back of the auditorium. He stops, winded, and announces, "We have a serious problem." He slides a horrified expression my way before distributing flyers around the group. "The cheerleaders left the assembly before everyone else was excused. They looked like they were up to something, so I followed to do recon. They handed these out to all the students as they exited the theater. Tiffany's behind it."

I look down at the paper, and it's a xeroxed copy of the article that ran about my medical condition this summer. Trey looks like he just got punched in the gut.

"I swear to you that I didn't know Tiffany was going to do this," Trey gasps.

"YOU had to have known," I say, glaring at Kelsey.

Mortified, Kelsey shakes her head. "I would have told Trey."

None of this was supposed to get out, but everyone at school now knows. I have a choice to make: cry or get furious. "Get your sorry ass out there and stand with the cheerleaders," I bark at Kelsey. I twist my loose hair into a bun, then hand my backpack and dance bag to my mother.

"What's your plan, Melanie?" Mom asks.

"Time to put Tiffany in her place." I look to Hiram. "You know that speaker that hasn't been hung yet, the one by the four-story switchback door?"

He nods, catching my drift. "What song, Melanie?"

"'Bell,'" I request.

Hiram smiles, slow and wicked. "I'm on it."

Everyone watches him as he runs up the aisle to the speaker, props open the door with it, and aims it outside before hauling ass to the booth.

"All right, girls," Deb says as she opens her backpack and pulls out a little zippered black pouch. "It's time to kick ass."

She dumps the pouch's contents into the enormous hands of her boyfriend, Drake, before selecting a set of brass knuckles and sliding them onto her right hand. She twists her hair into a bun while Presley, followed by Finley and Jayla, each choose spiked rings that they slide onto their fingers. To my surprise, Susan grabs a spiked ring, then piles her long hair into an impressive cinnamon-roll-sized bun.

Kelsey starts to join, but Deb glares at her. "Get away from my stuff. You're one of the asses I plan to beat outside."

Trey pulls his sister behind him, and Tanner steps up to Trey, radiating menace.

"I assure you," Tanner says threateningly, "that if you protect Kelsey, you and I are going to have at it."

Trey's eyes widen at his best friend. From my empathic gift, I can sense his surprise. He and Tanner are *always* on the same side.

"Please," Trey says, "I'm asking you to back off with Kels. She's not on Team Tiffany."

"She is now," Presley says, glaring at Kelsey.

Arch steps in front of his girlfriend. "Leave Kelsey alone."

In turn, Marcus steps in front of his girlfriend, Presley. "Don't threaten my girl."

I chuckle sardonically. "I'll be the one to beat Kelsey's ass, right after I finish with Tiffany." I glare at Trey. "Then you and I can have this out."

Kelsey tears up. "Please! I'm so sorry I hid things from you, Melanie. I want nothing to do with Tiffany."

"Get ready, Kelsey!" I crow. "I throw a mean right hook."

"They aren't seriously about to have a tacky brawl in the middle of this school, right?" Ms. Alice asks Mr. Isley.

"No, no, no," Ms. G squawks. "No, they aren't. I'm handling this. Just leave them alone, and I'll expel Tiffany and the cheerleaders."

Presley opens and closes her fist, testing the ring's placement. "You're going to have to expel us too. No one humiliates Melanie."

Metallica's "For Whom the Bell Tolls" bongs ominously through the speakers at earsplitting volume.

"Tiffany is mine," I say with a grin. "Let's crack skulls."

"FINALLY, those cheerleaders are going to get it!" Deb crows.

I strut up the aisle with Zane, Mr. Isley, Ms. Ferry, Ms. G, and

Ms. Alice begging me to stop. Surprisingly, my parents don't say a word. I step out the door and to the railing, surveying the mass gathering of students below. Loud laughter rises as many point in my direction. Naturally, the students are doing precisely what I expected. This population isn't mature enough to be compassionate and realize what I went through.

"You have to stop them from fighting," Zane begs of Trey.

"Hell no." Trey grins maniacally. "The football players are going to defend the cheerleaders. Melanie needs all the help she can get." He unhooks the chain he keeps clipped on his belt loops and wraps it around his knuckles. "Pop the popcorn and watch the bloodbath, Beastie Boy."

Arch steps up beside him, having done the same with his own chain.

I look at Trey, unsure about whose side he's really on since he just screamed at me about the movie. He crooks a finger my way while stepping against the railing, in full view of the students. "I'm going to back you," he says to me. "But I'm asking you to leave Kelsey out of this."

Tearfully, Kelsey stands beside her brother.

"It's her or me," I say. "If she stays in this group, I'm out."

"Me too," says half of the group.

Arch rolls his eyes. "Can we deal with the real problem?" he asks, while flourishing an arm toward the taunting crowd below.

I glare at Kelsey. "You're dead to me."

Trey shakes his head. "We're not arguing about my sister right now." Without warning, he steps in and kisses me passionately. My head spins with confusion.

The crowd silences as Trey proves his loyalty.

When he's finished, he surveys them, radiating rage. "You better be ready!" he calls.

Our whole group crushes against the railing, smirking in challenge.

Tanner cracks his chained knuckles, and yells to the crowd below, "Have you forgotten who the FUCK we are? We're the ones who masterminded your escape from this shitbox."

When the next song comes on, I crack up. This must be from one of Hiram's mixed CDs. Eazy-E's "Cruisin' in My 64" blares to life. We watch as everyone who's been treated like crap at this school starts to get ready. Nerds, burners, the school's social ghosts—they all start dumping backpacks. Even though most of them have no idea how to fight, many of the girls take our lead and start twisting up their hair. The camaraderie is appreciated.

"Looks like not everyone forgot how Melanie has backed them, over and over," Arch says.

Tad and his surfer dude click dump their backpacks in a pile. He grins up at me, flashing a double set of devil horns.

My mother raises a disgusted eyebrow at Rich. "Every security guard and teacher who tries to stop Melanie is gonna get it."

Rich nods with a tight jaw. "We can afford bail. I'm with you."

Mr. Cantrell, Demitri's dad, steps up next to Rich. "I can also afford bail." He looks to Demitri. "Level anyone who comes near Melanie."

Demitri nods.

Victoria hits Mr. Cantrell with a death glare. He replies with a look that clearly communicates his extreme disdain for her.

She rolls her eyes. "Well, *I'm* not getting in a fight with the whole school just because Melanie's a hooker who craps her pants."

I turn on Victoria, draw back a fist, lightning fast, and hit her with a mean right hook that launches her into Demitri. He grabs Victoria before she falls.

"One down," I snarl. "Thousands more to go."

"Holy crap," Mr. Isley says.

Zane's slack-jawed. "You can't be serious," he admonishes my parents.

Rich glares at him. "You can stay out of this, hiding behind your agent and your uppity reputation, but we're backing our kid." He points to me. "I'll be damned if this school full of assholes tortures her after everything she went through."

Trey cups my cheek. "No mercy. Level Tiffany."

"You sure you aren't on her team?" I ask.

"I'm with you. Fuck Tiffany."

"You already covered that twenty-two times," I say with a wince.

Trey's head drops back. "Never again, Melanie."

With the girls from my group following behind, I strut down the stairs. Quickly, I spot Tiffany backing away into the crowd. "Where you going, Twenty-Two?" I bellow.

Fury blasts from her as she screams, "Don't call me Twenty-Two!"

I smirk.

Tiffany rushes me, and I hit her with a wicked upper cut. She launches in the air before thudding to the pavement. I survey her prone body before panning the crowd. "One shot!" I gesture to Tiffany. "Who's next?"

"You might shit your pants if I attack you," quips Brad, a jerk football player who leads the other jerks.

Laughter peels from the crowd. I give Brad the look he deserves and gesture him forward. He steps up to me and cocks back a fist. Coming in from the left, Trey sucker-punches Brad, dropping him to his knees. This seems to be the signal everyone was subconsciously waiting for, because the football players and cheerleaders all surge forward. Our group fans out, and the brawl is on.

The baseball players pour through the crowd, backing Trey. The basketball players join the fray, backing Drake. Football players and cheerleaders start hitting the pavement as we swing, kick, and rush everyone who has it coming.

Security finds itself in a standoff with Mr. Cantrell, my parents, and surprisingly, Mr. Isley. They haven't rushed into the brawl out of fear, because the adults in my life are just as scary as the teens are.

I turn, sighting on Kelsey. She backs up rapidly. I smirk, stalking her way.

Principal Walker storms into the rumble, bellowing, "STOP!"

Everyone freezes.

"Who started this?" Principal Walker demands.

"Melanie," Brad accuses.

"You're expelled, Melanie," Principal Walker hollers loud enough to be heard at the back of the crowd.

Mr. Isley struts forward and jabs one of the flyers at Principal Walker. "Tiffany Savoy distributed these to the entire school as the assembly let out. *She* started it."

Principal Walker reads the article before turning on Tiffany, who's slowly getting to her feet. "What's the meaning of this?" He rustles the paper in her direction.

Tiffany turns red but doesn't answer.

Screw it. I decide to throw caution to the wind. "Tiffany didn't want me to share the dirt about her having an affair with my boyfriend Trey."

Many in the crowd slide scandalized glares Trey's way. He winces as I keep barreling my honesty train down the tracks.

"So, she decided that her best course of action was to destroy me before I aired her dirty laundry. Unfortunately for old Twenty-Two here—" I gesture Tiffany's way—"I've taken all I can stand. I rung her bell, like she deserved."

Tanner steps forward. "Now, *I'd* like to ring her bell. Not only is Tiffany a homewrecker with Trey, she's also been with . . ." He rattles off a list that's truly impressive.

Angry girls start squabbling with their boyfriends all over the quad.

After a harrowing stretch of names, Tanner takes a deep breath, looking satisfied. He loves gossip. "Last but not least, Tiffany has been hunching Mr. Hutchins in the chemistry lab storage room connected to his classroom!"

Mouths drop open all over the quad.

Tanner smiles at Mr. Hutchins. "Sorry, my dude, but Tiffany must be stopped, and you're a douche-canoe."

Everyone stares at Tiffany while Principal Walker appears at a loss. Trey looks at her like she's lost her mind. I suspect he thought he was special when he was humping her. Turns out he was just one small checkbox on an impressive conquest list.

I look to Zane and Ms. Alice, who are standing at the base of the stairs, appearing gobsmacked by what they're witnessing.

A moment of stone-cold, intuitive clarity breathes through my chest, and suddenly I'm sure of my path. I turn to my mom and Rich. My voice confident, I say into the silence, "I'd like to enroll at Canoga Park High School. If we head that way now, I can still make it to half my classes for the day."

Everyone stares at me, so shocked they can't blink, and then all hell breaks loose. Trey moves past Kelsey, making his way to me, trying everything he can think of to change my mind. My friends all start yelling over each other, trying to talk me out of it. Mr. Isley and Ms. Ferry turn on Principal Walker, begging him to do something.

Ms. G puts two fingers between her lips and whistles at ear-splitting volume over the ruckus. She loudly says, "Melanie isn't expelled!"

I smile at Ms. G. "I appreciate your support more than you know, but I'm firmly decided."

"If you leave, you lose your spot here," Ms. G implores.

"If I stay, I lose my soul here."

"What does this mean for us?" Trey asks in a rush.

I level him with exhausted eyes. "I have no clue. Maybe when you can explain why Tiffany warranted a whopping twenty-two, you'll have a shot again." I gesture to Kelsey. "As usual, your loyalties are a mess." I cock a hip. "And I'll do any movie I damn well please."

Trey rubs his face hard with his right hand before saying to Ms. Alice, "I apologize for my outburst earlier about the movie." He puts a hand on my cheek. "One indiscretion down, now for the next." Trey glares at Tiffany. "Don't EVER speak to me again." He looks in my eyes again. "You, Kelsey, and I need to talk." He turns to Ms. G. "Will you please guide that discussion?"

"Absolutely," Ms. G assures.

Kelsey exhales hard, clearly thinking things will be on the mend.

"My lawyer had a cease-and-desist notice delivered to your home two days ago," Zane fires at Tiffany. "Per that court order you violated, you can expect to be arrested." He pulls out his phone, I suspect to call his attorney.

Tiffany turns pale. "I didn't physically attack Melanie! She attacked *me*."

"It was a restraining order! You didn't restrain. Distributing flyers to humiliate Melanie is a direct violation of that restraining order," Zane barks back.

"I'll meet you at Canoga Park High," I tell my parents calmly.

As everyone erupts into another fit, I make my way through the crowd, into the alley, and head toward the student parking lot.

As we cross the front lawn, Canoga Park High School sprawls in front of us.

"You sure about this?" Rich asks as he surveys the expansive campus.

"I'm sick of the drama at Hollywood High."

Mom sighs. "All I've wanted is to get you away from the danger at that place, but now that I'm getting my wish, I want to drag you back there immediately."

"The vibe at this school is so bland," Rich says hesitantly.

"You're making a mistake," Mom says, turning to me in a rush. "I know I don't have your intuition, but this just doesn't seem right."

"Let's give it a shot, okay, Mom?"

I lead the way down the front breezeway and through the door with a big sign reading, *Main Office*. We cross the threshold and are met by a slumpy receptionist. Her clothing, quaffed hair, and horn-rimmed glasses are so drab.

"Good morning. How may I help you?"

"We'd like to discuss enrolling our daughter, Melanie Slate, in classes," Mom says nervously. "She's a tenth grader."

The receptionist flops a hand, without looking up from her paperwork she's perusing. "Transcripts from your previous school, please."

Anxiously, I glance at my parents, but my mom is prepared. She takes my transcripts out of her purse and hands them over with a reluctant smile. She murmurs to me, "Ms. G gathered them before Rich and I rushed over here."

The receptionist looks them over and frowns. "There are no PE credits on here."

"Dance classes counted as PE credits at Hollywood High," I explain.

"They don't count here. This makes you six credits behind. You'll have to take two PE classes a semester this year to make up for it."

My heart sinks. I hate PE with a passion. I glance at Mom and Rich, and they both look unsure.

The receptionist calls out to a counselor, who steps to us and looks over my transcripts, her scowl lines working overtime. She wears various shades of beige, ill-fitting clothing. I wince a little as I survey the office. It's painted in puke green that I guarantee was purchased in bulk back when dinosaurs roamed the earth. Everyone who works in this tomb kind of shuffles and sighs about. I'm hoping it's not a bad omen.

"Welcome, Melanie," the counselor says, without offering her name. "You're a little late to the game, but I'll get you plugged into tenth grade classes. The pickings are slim for electives. We have room in shop class, and your two PE classes will fill the other two spots."

"Shop class?" I say skeptically.

The counselor just sort of huffs a response.

"Do you have theater or dance classes?"

"We do," she grunts, "but they're reserved for seniors."

Before I can even decide whether this is what I'm definitely going to do, she heads to the copier. She returns, handing me my not-so-exciting schedule. She gestures to a high-school-age boy sitting next to her at the desk. He seems to have more life in him than the old hags that molt in this artifact of misery past. He smiles and his eyes sparkle. His blue-and-yellow letterman jacket hints at the likelihood that he's popular. I sneak a peek at the arm patch, discovering that he plays water polo.

Weird. I didn't even know water polo was a high school thing.

Trevor looks like the stock hot-guy teen from every cartoon I've ever watched featuring high school kids: blue eyes, brunette with the haircut every nice guy has lately, well-defined jaw, a real boy-next-door type.

"Melanie, this is Trevor, one of our office TAs. He'll take you on a tour of campus. Lunch starts in thirty minutes. That should be plenty of time to give you a lay of the land."

My head is spinning as I thank her.

Trevor lifts the counter passthrough section and smiles brightly as he crosses to us. "Melanie is in good hands," he says to my parents. He turns to me and sweeps his arm toward the door. "We're off and running. Welcome to your new home sweet home."

I glance at my parents over my shoulder, but Trevor sweeps me out of the room before I can say anything.

— —

Trevor's pleasant in an oddly innocent way. He has a personality, but it's more like a shell. He's supposed to act like a nice hot guy who runs his hand through his hair, and he does. He stands like "that" guy stands. Everything about him looks and sounds right, but there's nothing soul deep about it. It's a bit baffling. As we get to the end of the tour, we turn into the empty cafeteria. We pass an announcement corkboard, where I stop to survey the club selections. When I find a flyer for a dance club, I break into a grin.

"You're a dancer?" Trevor asks, sounding intrigued.

"Would you show me where tryouts will be, really quick?"

He grins. "They're here in the cafeteria after school."

I survey the concrete floor—a disaster for a dancer's joints during leaps. *Oh boy . . .*

My concern is swept away by the ringing of the bell.

Trevor takes my elbow and guides me to the lunch line. "Let's get in line first," he says. "I want to snag my usual table and introduce you to my friends."

"That's really thoughtful of you, Trevor. Thank you."

We work down the lunch line. The choices are the typical sludgy cafeteria mess one would expect. With internal disdain, I survey the grayish Salisbury steak, then tell the jovial cafeteria lady, "I think I'd like a yogurt and a banana."

She chuckles, her ample bosom vibrating. "Full tray, young lady. You're tiny, and I plan to feed you. Don't let the steaming pans fool you. I'm a good cook."

Charmed by the fact that she has an actual personality, I nod. "Deal."

The cafeteria lady fills my tray and grins at me as she slides it over the metal counter. "I'm Miss Tyra."

I return the smile and introduce myself.

Miss Tyra cheerfully waves us through, and Trevor pulls out his wallet when we get to the cashier.

"I'd like to treat Melanie to lunch." He takes a twenty out and accepts his change from the lackluster cashier.

I pick up my tray and turn to Trevor. "Thank you!"

Trevor guides me to a lunch table. "You're more than welcome."

As people join us at the table, it's more of the same. They say the things, give the looks, and have a popular air, but something is wrong. Dread starts to bubble in my gut. Against my better judgment, I open my connection with Trey.

"Something's wrong here. I think this whole school is possessed . . . or something," I send.

Trey watches through my eyes and listens through my ears, while the cheerleaders and water polo guys laugh, fist pound, and chatter about inane nonsense.

"Do you feel that?" I send. *"It's like their bodies are animated but empty."*

A wave of sadness wafts through the connection from Trey. *"That's the feeling of normal teens, Melanie. They haven't figured themselves out. They act like they think teens act. They hide real emotions. It's all a façade, but it's standard-issue normal stuff. Hollywood High is weird. We all act like explosive volcanoes. You're experiencing normalcy, but it's not evil."*

I slam my wall tight, blocking out Trey.

Holy crap, I think as I survey mundane reality, that's now my reality.

— —

The last bell of the day rings, and I dust the wood shavings from my flannel. *What a nightmare!* Shop class was a messy, loud, anxiety-inducing slog.

Let's see if I can salvage the day with dance club.

I gather my backpack and hightail it out of the classroom into the buzzing hall. It seems there's more excitement at the end of the school day than during it. Trevor is leaning against the lockers across the way, his foot up. He's looking at his pager. I stop short, my heart suddenly aching as Trevor's casual stance reminds me of the hundreds of times Trey has waited for me the exact same way.

I close my eyes and make a rash decision to drop the blockage between Trey and me again. I feel his surprise about my sudden presence.

On a wave of almost frantic energy, Trey sends, *"I can explain everything about the twenty-two situation. Give me a chance to discuss this with you."*

"Hello to you too. Right out the gate with a Tiffany mention, huh?"

Alarm zings from him before he sends, *"I apologize. Hi, Melanie."*

I sigh. *"I don't want a Tiffany reminder before you even greet me. I missed you and had a moment of weakness. Forget it."*

I wall our connection back off.

Trevor clips his pager on his jeans pocket and crosses to me, his brow furrowed. "Are you okay?"

"Just a little overwhelmed with all the newness," I say evasively.

Trevor nods. "If it's okay with you, I thought I'd stay after and watch you audition for the dance team. My mom's the coach."

I grin at his thoughtfulness. *He really is nice.* I feel bad for viewing him as an automaton earlier. I need to try a little harder here.

We make our way through the halls in comfortable silence and arrive at the cafeteria. Through the doors, I quickly discover that my fellow auditionees are a motley crew. I strip off my flannel, already ready in a black tank top and black leggings. Trevor takes my flannel, and I pull my jazz shoes out of my backpack. He crosses the room and speaks to a woman who's standing by a boombox. She's wearing a color-block pink, teal, and purple track suit that was likely all the rage in 1983. Her blond hair is pulled back in a tight, high ponytail. Her white high-top Reeboks and popped collar make me wince internally. Back in the day, she was likely the super popular Tiffany of her school.

The woman glances my way, and her eyebrows rise as she looks me up and down. She nods at Trevor, who crosses the room again and takes a seat by our stuff.

With a clap of her hands, the woman catches out attention, and the room silences. "All right, for those who don't know, I'm Coach Sheila. I need everyone to run their prepared solos one at a time. Please have your music ready."

I inhale, thinking quick and improvising. I settle on a routine, then rush to my backpack to pull my homemade mix CD from my Discman.

Coach Sheila announces that Delilah, last year's team captain, will be up first. When Delilah's song selection starts pulsing through the speakers, my eyes widen a touch. What she lacks in training, she certainly makes up for with enthusiasm. Her piece draws to a close, and I clap along with the other auditionees, who seem devotionally impressed.

That was a wreck. SHE was team captain?

The next girl takes her place in the center of the room, and a similar fiasco unfolds. This continues, one girl after another, until the coach calls me up last. I rub my face, realizing that this dance team has no actual trained dancers.

Quickly, I rally, gather myself with a smile, and hand my CD to Coach Sheila. "Track four, please."

The coach nods, and I take my spot in the center of the cafeteria. My favorite song, the Jeff Healey version of "Blue Jean Blues," wafts and thrums through the speakers. The song brings down my wall between Trey and me as I struggle to split my focus between my connection blockage and my nerves. He hovers in the back of my psyche, and I make the split-second decision to leave the wall down until I have time to focus on putting it back up.

I improvise a solo, reaching and turning, leaping and splitting. I use the entire space, my dance training clicking with ease.

As the song thrums to a close, I do my best to ignore my aching heart. Trey sends a memory through our connection from when he won my affections while this song played.

"That was *unbelievable*," Coach Sheila says. She looks over my audition form and asks, "You have an agent?"

"Yes, ma'am. I'm free to perform without hinderance if it's not paid. Any paid dance contracts must go through my agency."

The coach looks like she just got hit with a semitruck. "There's nothing paid through the dance team. We just do this for fun."

I smile enthusiastically. "Good. I like to dance for fun."

All the auditionees stare at me with their mouths open, some shocked and others discouraged.

Coach Sheila announces that the team list will be posted tomorrow, then dismisses us.

I make my way through the crowd to Trevor.

"We've never had an actual *dancer* dancer on the team before," Trevor gushes. "You were INSANE."

"The others don't seem to share your sentiment," I say with a sad smile.

"You just scared them to death. I've never seen someone do that in person. Why aren't you at a fancy performing arts school?"

"I was, but I got sick of the drama."

"No offense, but you should really think about going back. Based on what I just saw, you've got a future ahead of you."

We're interrupted by the coach, who steps up next to Trevor and hugs him. She smiles at me. "Well, that was a first." She sighs. "I should probably tell you that I'm not an actual trained dancer. I don't even know where to start with coaching you. I feel like I should hand the team to you and let you coach it."

"Not at all!" I implore. "I bet you do a great job. The girls all seem really nice."

Coach Sheila smiles at me. "Trevor, why don't you walk Melanie to her car? I'll see you at home."

"That's okay," I say hastily. "I've got some thinking to do. Thank you, though."

We say our goodbyes, and I head out the door.

Now that I'm alone, Trey sighs in my head. *"Can we discuss this?"*

I send back my exhaustion with all the drama. I know he can feel how done I am.

He sends, *"I'd like to remind you that when this all came up, we had JUST decided to go on a date again. I'm begging you not to shut me out. I really was happy that you wanted to give me another chance. I wanted our City Walk night to be special."*

"Stop, Trey. I'm going to walk away because I deserve better. I love you, and always will, but I have to love me more."

On that note, I cut off our connection. *I choose me, and I deserve it.*

CHAPTER 17

The next morning, Trevor's waiting for me as I head for the front gates of my new school. He smiles, the early morning sun glinting off his brown hair. I grin back, happy to see a familiar face. We turn together and make our way into the building.

"I thought I'd walk you to class."

"Thank you, Trevor. You've made this new-school transition surprisingly easy."

When he nervously puts his arm around my shoulder, I try not to chuckle. I'm used to guys being more comfortable around girls. My encouraging smile causes his arm to relax, and we walk together in comfortable silence.

At the other end of the hallway, Trevor stops us. "Your English class is here." He gestures to the door.

"Thank you. I really appreciate you."

He glances away, looking uncomfortable again. "I want to be the one to tell you that you didn't make the dance team," he says quietly.

Surprise reverberating through me, I lose control of my carefully held shields, and they slip down. I allow Trey to see and hear through me, somehow feeling better by the familiar presence as I digest the bad news. "Can I ask why?"

Trevor glances down. "Mom thought you were too good. She needs the dance team to look cohesive, and you would make it obvious how mediocre the rest of the dancers are." He meets my gaze and adds, "I spent an hour arguing with her after dinner last night, but she felt strongly about it."

I scoff. "I didn't make the team because I'm too good?"

In the back of my mind, Trey snorts.

"It's insane," Trevor agrees. "I told her to make you a soloist. She considered it, but said it'll just create bad blood with the rest of the team."

Trey radiates heartbreak on my behalf.

Trevor interrupts my internal studying of Trey's sentiment. "This might create some social static for you. Everyone knows that the dance team auditions aren't real. In its nearly twenty-year history, everyone's made the team."

My cheeks burn with the knowledge that I'm the first loser to not be granted a spot.

He seems to notice the blush. "I'm sorry, Melanie. I think this is backward."

"Maybe I should slip away and ditch a few class periods to think about this."

He looks at me like I'm nuts. "You can't ditch class because you're upset. Who does that?"

Trey snorts in my mind.

This place is gonna be weird.

Trevor says goodbye and heads down the hall to his class.

Trey sends, *"You don't fit in there, Melanie. You need to come home."*

I give in and send back, *"How are things at Hollywood High?"*

Through Trey's eyes, I see that he's sitting at Smokers' Corner at Hollywood High with Bear and Tanner. *"Tense. The school is clearly divided, but the usual smack talkers have been beaten into cowering. The power dynamic is shifting."*

"What's happening with the restraining order?" I ask, feeling out of the loop.

"Tiffany has a court date. She's taking it seriously. Apparently, her parents are at a loss. They've never dealt with anything like this, and Zane's lawyer is a shark. He's pushing for her to be locked up because of the combination of her recorded messages and the flyer distribution."

"Wow. That's just . . ."

"If it helps, she now understands the gravity. She's up against aggravated stalking charges, and she's a panicked disaster. She begged me to help get the charges dropped. Full disclosure, I called Zane. He laughed hysterically at me. I don't really care if she's locked up, honestly. I just wanted her to shut up."

"Zane isn't going to drop this," I send back, amused.

"She gets it, Melanie," Trey assures.

I watch through Trey's eyes as Demitri rounds the edge of the hedges and sits down. I hear through Trey as Demitri asks, "Did you get a chance to apologize to Meley for me? She's ignoring my calls."

Trey smiles. "I'm talking mind-to-mind with her now. She's a little spun out, but she can see and hear you through me if you want to just tell her."

"There's no time for a Demitri chat right now. Tell Bear and Tanner that I say hello."

Trey passes along the message, and I watch Tanner and Bear smile. Demitri winces, likely because I left him out of the hellos.

The bell rings, and I'm pulled back to reality. I send to Trey, *"Thank you for your help with all this. We've got more to discuss, just you and me."*

A wave of hope breezes through our connection. *"Ditch class so we can get back to a good place."*

Just as I send a bubble that I'll give talking a shot, Tiffany rounds the hedges and enters Trey's field of vision.

"Trey, can I talk to you?" she asks.

"Damn it," Trey sends. *"Of all the shitty timing."*

I radiate annoyance. *"You almost had me, but I'm not going to be interrupted by her. If she's still in your life, I'm out. Looks like you're ditching with her."*

"Just give me a sec . . ."

I shut down our connection. A thousand conflicting emotions course through me as I head into my first-period class. All I want is to have Pierre back. This is ridiculous.

CHAPTER 18

I make my way through the lunch line, and Trevor steps up next to me by the cashier as I finish paying for my lunch. He smiles, his eyes sparkling. "Can I talk you into sitting with my group again?"

"I would love that," I say, returning the smile. "Thank you."

He leads me to his table. I don't know why he keeps asking me, considering that I've sat with his group every day for two weeks. Meanwhile, I haven't talked to Trey since our empathic discussion that was interrupted by Tiffany.

When I set my tray at an empty spot, the girls all grin my way. One of the guys shifts over, making room for Trevor to sit next to me.

"Aw," Bethany, the lead cheerleader, says coyly. "Trevor gets to sit next to Melanie."

Trevor blushes a touch. "Do you have plans tonight?" he asks me.

I'm startled by the question, but realistically, this sweet guy has practically done backflips trying to flirt the past two weeks. "I don't. What did you have in mind?"

His eyebrows rise, his face a mask of shock. He rattles his head, surprised, and manages to croak out, "Are you serious?"

"Was that not you asking me out?"

Trevor stares at me, the silence stretching as I wait for a reply.

After a long moment, his buddy Jerome thumps him twice on the back and pointedly says, "Trevor, would you like to go on a date with Melanie?"

Finally, Trevor remembers how to speak. "I would love to. Where would you like to go?"

I'm baffled. I don't know who just asked out who, but whatever. I shrug. "How about you choose?"

Let's see what makes Trevor tick. I don't know what innocent water polo players do for fun, but I'm guessing my usual shenanigans aren't on his radar.

Everyone leans in, radiating anticipation as he considers the question for a moment. Finally, he suggests, "How about we go to your old stomping grounds, and you can show me around? I've never been to Hollywood Boulevard."

Shit. Not good. Rally, Melanie.

My smile only shows a touch of my hesitation about this idea. "Sounds like . . . a plan . . . of sorts. How about you pick me up at six?"

He grins at me. "Thank you, Melanie," he says politely. He surveys his friends with innocent glee. Then, unexpectedly, he blurts, "You guys should all come too."

I slide a baffled gaze Trevor's way.

He grins back at me, oblivious to my apparent discomfort. "It'll be fun."

"All right," I say reluctantly. "One big happy group date, coming right up."

Everyone sets to yammering, excited by the prospect of "edgy new Melanie" taking them on a Hollywood adventure.

I close my eyes, and my dark-water side slides up through my mind. She's radiating revulsion at Trevor's innocent enthusiasm and group-date hijinks.

Awareness dawns that the cafeteria has gone completely silent. I open my eyes, glancing Trevor's way, and my dark-water side gags in my mind. I ignore her and look around. Everyone's staring at me. A hand lands on the table next to me. I whip around, meeting Demitri's gray-blue eyes.

My mouth drops open. "Why are you here? This is my *new* nightmare. You're a part of my *old* nightmare."

Demitri looks around pensively. "Apparently new people aren't the usual around here."

Everyone stares at him slack-jawed. Demitri is one of the most gorgeous humans I've ever seen, with his perfectly muscled physique and stunning face. He looks like an underwear model, and while that's common at my old school, this pack of Normals I'm saddled with at Canoga Park High are clearly floored by him.

"The problem isn't that you're new," I tell him. "It's that you're drop-dead gorgeous. What do you want?"

Demitri rolls his eyes and holds out his hand. "We're leaving. We need to talk."

"If I wanted to talk, I would have answered the phone."

"*I* want to talk, so I hauled my ass down here. Come on."

I take his hand and stand, getting my legs out from between the bench and the table. I turn to my friends and inform, "Gotta jet. Apparently, I have a discussion looming."

With dreamy eyes, Bethany says, "I've never been more jealous in my life. I want every detail when I see you tonight."

"I fear you'll be disappointed. He's not interested in me."

Bethany points at me and says to Demitri, "You do realize she's single, right?"

Demitri looks amused. "I'm aware, but thanks for the heads-up."

Jerome whistles low as Demitri puts his arm around my waist. "Does everyone at Hollywood High look like a model?"

"Actually, pretty much," Demitri says with a shrug. "At least in our group."

"I'll see you later," I say, aiming for a little coy flirtation with Trevor.

He blushes crimson and stammers out, "Yeah. Okay." He's radiating insecurity as Demitri escorts me out the door.

We head down the hall and out the front gate. No one attempts to stop us as Demitri guides me to his Jeep. I get settled in his passenger seat, and he rounds the back, getting in and pulling out of his parking spot.

When he looks at me, his gorgeous eyes are sad. "You haven't returned anyone's calls. Trey's a wreck. He says you've had him blocked since the morning Tiffany interrupted your talk."

"I'm done with the Hollywood crowd."

"We're your friends," Demitri reminds.

I offer an evil side-eye. "Really? Are you?"

Demitri exhales with exasperation. "We all *brawled* with you."

"Your girlfriend is a monumental problem."

"I'm aware," is the only response I get in return.

We listen to his Boyz II Men CD all through the first half of a seemingly long drive. I curl up and roll down my window, letting the breeze drift through my hair. To my dismay, it's nice to be back in Demitri's Jeep.

He pops his glove box in front of me and pulls out a handful of candies. He holds one out to me. "Want a lala?"

I can't help a giggle. "A what?"

Demitri waggles the wrapped peppermint candy around. "A lala."

"I don't care for peppermint, but thank you."

"The sacrilege!" His tone is one of mock horror. "Peppermints are gifts from the gods." He gives me puppy dog eyes. "You don't want my lala?"

"That sounds so wrong!"

Demitri chuckles. "Lala's are meant to be shared. I won't enjoy mine unless you get yours."

"That also sounded so wrong." With a laugh, I take the peppermint. "I'll suffer through your lala, but I won't enjoy it."

"I'm a little offended."

My amusement is quickly interrupted when I pop the peppermint in my mouth.

Demitri studies my reaction and seems shocked. "You really don't like it, do you?"

I wince dramatically. "It's like eating mace-covered cotton candy."

He holds out his hand. "Spit out my lala, Meley."

I shake my head and garble out, "I'll just swallow it," while I try not to let the candy touch my tongue.

"You don't have to swallow it. You can spit it out."

"This conversation's taking a sharp skid I didn't expect." The awful candy rolls over on my tongue. I make a "haaah" sound, and Demitri cracks up.

"That sound sounded wrong."

I rattle my head. "I can do it." A particularly spicy moment hits my tongue, and I gag while I spit out the candy into Demitri's hand. "Nope. Can't do it. I tried. Your lala isn't swallowable."

Demitri chuckles and tosses the candy out the window. "I'm flummoxed, bereaved, and astounded that you didn't enjoy my lala." He opens a pack of baby wipes and cleans up his hand while he drives with his knee.

I glance in amusement at the baby wipe package. "Why do you always have those in here?"

"Don't deflect. My former best friend apparently has the taste buds of a peasant and can't appreciate the fine complexities of a lala," he chastises. He wobbles his head. "Also, I don't like sticky."

"There goes your romantic life!" I crow.

Demitri smirks. "I don't keep baby wipes in here for romantic cleanup."

I hack. "It lingers. Lord help me, that's vile."

When he offers me a drink from the water bottle in his cup-holder, I give it a more judgmental look than I had for the candy. "I'd rather just suffer, but thank you."

"You've always drunk from my water bottles."

I side-eye him. "I'm sure Victoria is *teeming* with exotic crawlers. No reason to expose myself to any further risk. I should get tested as it is."

Demitri's face falls. "You've kissed me a few times, Melanie. I think you're fine."

I wave my hand his way dismissively. "Enjoy your lala. Boyz II Men have something important to say." Like it always does in my life, the music times itself perfectly, and "End of the Road" croons through the speakers.

— —

The Jeep stops, and I open my eyes. I'd been drifting through thoughts. When I see where he's driven us, my mouth drops open and I turn to Demitri with happy eyes.

"You brought me to the Getty Museum?"

There's hope in his eyes. "I thought an art museum would make you happy."

"I *love* this place."

Demitri hops out of the Jeep. He comes around to my side, opens my door, and asks, "Are you still mad at me?"

"Your question doesn't do the sheer magnitude of this mess justice."

He steers me toward the museum entrance and pays for two tickets. We walk through several of the halls, taking our time looking at paintings. I stop at the ones that interest me and really study them. I know a lot of the history of several of the painters, and I tell Demitri fun facts here and there.

After some time, we head out to the courtyard and sit on a bench. The elegant courtyard is beautiful with its reflection pool and pillars.

"I remember coming here on a field trip when I was little," I say. "I sat here and thought it was the prettiest place I'd ever been."

He ignores the line of conversation. "Your friends miss you. Trey misses you. Mr. Isley is DESPERATE for you to come back." He glances down at his hands in his lap. "I'm partnered with Justine as of three days ago."

I belt surprised laughter. Justine is a sweet girl, and she tries, but her abilities are not even close to Demitri's.

Once I calm down, I pat him on the shoulder. "I'm not looking so bad anymore, am I?"

"Not only is Justine a disaster, but she paws at me like a panther in heat."

I giggle. "You *love* getting pawed at."

"Not by her." He taps my hip. "Sit in front of me."

As soon as I'm in front of him on the pavement, he takes my hair tie off my wrist and bundles my hair up in a messy bun. He starts rubbing my shoulders. My muscles have been tense for weeks. I drop my head as he sends a calm wave through his hands. Being around another energy worker again is a welcome relief.

"Why did you come on this little recon mission?"

"Everyone sent me, Meley. And for the record, they were sending best-friend Demitri. They don't know about our date issue."

"Get to it, then. We're burning daylight."

He takes his time before saying, "I'll start with the easiest piece. There's no more laughter in the dance studio. Everyone is bored and in a bad mood. You and I brought the fun shenanigans, but that requires both of us to be there."

I look up at him over my shoulder. "Most of the dancers there hate me."

"Yeah, well, that may have changed. The flyer debacle put them on the defensive. You're one of the dancers, and they've taken to defending you with gusto. It's now the dancers versus the cheerleaders." Demitri grins. "The only ones better than the cheerleaders at ferreting out and spreading gossip are the dancers who used to hate you so much."

"They're on my side?"

"Dell is leading that charge, if you can believe it."

"She despises me!"

Demitri shrugs. "You remember when Tanner barked out Tiffany's little *indiscretion* list? Dell's boyfriend was on it."

"Oooh."

"Dell's firmly on Team Mel. The cheerleaders have quite the list of indiscretions, and EVERYONE knows all of it now. Cheerleaders apparently had a secret boyfriend-steeling competition going, so they've been getting their asses beaten right and left."

I crack up. "I can't believe Trey was dumb enough to fall for that."

"Tiffany didn't know about you when she hit on Trey. I talked to her, and she thought he was still with Victoria, who she hates. I told Vic, and she beat Tiffany's ass on the grounds that Tiffany tried to steal her boyfriend, even though he wasn't her boyfriend anymore."

I look up at him again. "Considering that *you're* her boyfriend, how do you feel about that?"

He shrugs. "She screamed, 'This is from Melanie,' before hitting Tiffany with a right hook that left her cross-eyed for a second. Vic actually went to bat for you."

"Weird."

He drapes his arms over my shoulders and says quietly, "Second easy issue: You need to reconnect with your friends, even if you leave Trey in the dust."

Unsure about the intimate vibe I'm picking up from Demitri, I stand and head out to the grassy edge of the courtyard. I stretch out under a tree, and Demitri lies down next to me.

After some time, he says, "I need you to know that I'm truly sorry about the date night."

I sigh. "I already have two lying, scheming, manipulative players in my life. You're just another Trey or Adam, and I'm over it."

Demitri groans and sits up. "I've been called a lot of things, but damn, that hurt."

My head tilts right and left. "Actually, that's not fair. You're an Adam, because Trey's got enough class to at least shower and change clothes between hookups."

He grimaces. "I was freaking floored by how perfect our Disneyland date was. I was so excited to see you again. I went to Victoria's house with all the right intentions. Old habits boiled up. I truly don't know what I was thinking."

"*I* know what you were thinking." My anger abates, and I take pity on him. He needs to understand something I know all too well. "Soulmate connections work that way. You make tangible, well-intentioned plans, and then it all goes south the moment you're with your soulmate. Look at what it took for Adam and me to finally call it quits."

Demitri rubs his face. "Can I show you what happened when I left?"

I side-eye him. "I don't know. Where have your hands been?"

He scoffs. "Nowhere near any girls."

"Fine." I hold out my hand, and he takes it. I accept the memory he offers.

In the memory, he puts his hands up and says, "Huge mistake, Vic. We're done. I'm sorry. That was totally out of line."

Victoria blathers on, but it does no good. Demitri heads through her massive rich-girl mansion and out the door. He climbs in his Jeep and manages to get away from Victoria's house while she's still clamoring and carrying on.

He drives to his house while his mind is whirling through guilt and conflict. He rushes to his bathroom and jumps in the shower. *If Melanie searches my memories*, he thinks, *I'm so screwed*. He ponders the chances and settles on me being unlikely to do it because I wouldn't violate him that way.

I pause the memory and exclaim, "Looky there! You *did* shower!"

"Yes, Melanie, I showered," he says, giving me a look. "That's why I was late."

"I appreciate that *so much*!" I say with my trademark sarcasm. "I had you all wrong."

"Will you please finish watching the memory?" Demitri asks.

"Nope. You ended up on a date with her that same night. Whatever."

Demitri shifts pensive. "I mean it when I say I loved everything about that Disneyland day."

"That I'll discuss. The Disneyland day was the first truly happy time I've had since I was with Pierre. My life suddenly felt right again. Thank you for that day. I needed it."

"I need *you*, Melanie," he confides. "You're my best friend."

"Well, I'm sorry, but you make me feel like I'm not good enough, Demitri. There's no more room in my life for that. I'm grateful that this happened before we got too tangled up. Considering the direction my intentions were headed, your dickhead timing was kind of a gift."

He seems to shrink. "Don't tell me that."

"I guess you were getting laid either way," I prod tactlessly. "You just happened to choose Victoria over me."

He groans and flops onto his back on the grass.

I pat his arm. "There, there," I say mischievously. "You cleared the way for me to go on a truly MAGICAL date with Zane." My bright smile carries sarcasm. "Dinner at Musso & Frank, a movie where I was noticed by the director of a movie I'm now in, AND an amazing formal dance after. Thank you, Demitri."

He looks mortified. "I'm so incredibly sorry."

I laugh. "Yeah, yeah. You got caught. Poor guy has my dead husband in his head and can't get away with being gross. For the record, no girl likes to find out her date just left another girl's bed." I hit him with a pointed look. "Particularly Victoria's."

Demitri nods. "I'm aware and I respect that. I'm also aware that I made promises to change my ways specifically because I wanted to be worthy of Riptide's approval."

"How's that approval going?"

Demitri huffs. "About like you'd think. He's thoroughly disgusted with me."

"I have no clue why I thought I should get so comfortable with you." I roll my eyes. "That's not true. Our whole former spirit-guide eternal bond is why."

He grabs my hand. "Can we please try to work this out between us? I swear to you that I want our eternal bond back."

I roll my eyes. "You remember that goober in the lunchroom who was all freaked out about you?"

"Letterman jacket. Sweet and innocent like a cartoon high school popular guy?"

"Those were my thoughts exactly when I met him!" I huff. "I have a date with him tonight."

Demitri hits me with a baffled stare. "You DO NOT! Melanie, that's insane. He's so nice and normal. *Why*?"

"I don't know. Why not? I might as well try out a Normal. He's nice. He's smart. He's cute. On the other hand, he's boring, his mom is an uppity bitch, and he's boring. Oh, wait. Did I mention he's boring?"

Demitri scoffs. "With your dark-water side, you're going to screw . . . What's his name?"

"Trevor."

He gives me a deadpan look. "You're going to screw Trevor?"

I scrunch my face. "Eww. I'm just going on a date with him because I'm bored. I'm not screwing him." I give him a nasty look. "You chose a Normal over me. Maybe Normals are the best thing ever. I've never tested one out."

"What about Zane?"

"He's never even kissed me," I inform.

Demitri groans. "Oh, the disappointment waiting for you."

I start massaging my temples. Somehow, I'm not surprised that Demitri shoved me aside for Victoria. All candor aside, I'm truly feeling rejected. My self-esteem takes a nosedive.

"Meley, what are you thinking?"

My expression guarded, I look at him flatly. "I actually think Trevor might be in my league."

Demitri rattles his head. "Are you insane?"

"Adam was so desperate to move on that he proposed to Valerie, who he fought with *constantly*, might I add. Full-blown, mind-blowing soulmate connection with Adam. Yet, he bailed. Then there's Trey. Full-blown soulmate connection, yet he was more interested in Tiffany." *I can't keep my soulmates around, yet I think I have a shot with Demitri? What is* wrong *with me?*

"True on both counts," Demitri says, "but they ran because the connections were too perfect. They didn't bail because Tiffany and Valerie were so mind-bending."

"You gave up a spirit-guide eternity with me."

He rushes to say, "I didn't know that at the time."

"You knew it when you were an hour late to get me because you were with Victoria."

"For the record, I intended to call you while I raced to your house. I forgot my phone on my dresser."

I look down at my lap. "We need to come to terms with the fact that I'm never going to be good enough for you."

"That's not true, Melanie. I'm devastated about this. I'm mortified by my actions. All I've wanted is a chance to beg you to forgive me."

The sudden urge to go back to my car hits me. I need to go to the mall to get an outfit for tonight's date because none of my edgy stuff will work. I need to try with Trevor. Spending time with a nice, cute guy who's actually interested might be a breath of fresh air. "I'd like to head out," I say quietly. My expression bunches as self-doubt builds. "Thank you for coming to get me. It means a lot. I promise I'll call our friends. Your mission is accomplished."

I stand, and Demitri hesitantly stands with me.

"How do we get past this?"

"We don't, Demitri. I just want to hide in my new life. I don't fit in at Canoga Park High, but I'm good enough there."

His eyes widen. "You're the fire in our group. You're the humor in my life."

I settle firmly into melancholy. "True and true. I'm also Trey's consolation prize when there's no one hotter around. The same can now be said about you. I'm sick of being the funny, quirky one that everyone keeps around as the group's mascot. With Trevor, at least I've got a shot at actually mattering."

His mouth drops open. "No one has meant for you to feel that way, Meley. Least of all me."

I flop my head back. "Do you have any idea how ridiculous I felt, all dressed up, finding out that you chose someone else over me?"

"Melanie . . ." He doesn't seem to know what to say.

"I'm just not one of those girls, D."

"What girls?"

"The kind that are real to you."

Demitri shakes his head slowly. "That's absolutely not true."

"You call me your Fraggle." I give him a weighted look.

"Ummm . . . Yeah. You're Red from *Fraggle Rock*. It's the best show EVER."

Irritation surges through me. "I'm not a Fraggle. Your demeaning bullshit is insulting."

He looks like he's just been gut-punched.

I close my eyes and open my connection with Trey, who blasts shock my way at having me in his mind again after two long weeks. I see through his eyes that he's with our friends at Snow White Café.

"Melanie, talk to me," he sends in a rush.

"I never want to be your obligation, your mistake, or your consolation prize again." I take a deep breath. "I want to matter, Trey.

I'm not a quirky fucking Fraggle. No one calls Victoria, Valerie, or Tiffany a Fraggle. I can't be the group's mascot anymore. It's humiliating."

I wall off my connection hard and fast. My cell phone immediately starts ringing, and I turn the ringer off. I cross the lawn and head to Demitri's Jeep. He rushes to catch up and tries to touch my cheek. I pull away, and he settles for penetrating eye contact.

"Melanie, I'm telling you now that you're wrong." He looks pained. "I want to describe something."

I give my blasé agreement with a nod.

Demitri contemplates for a moment. "Part of this is gross, but important. Here goes. Victoria is . . . well, she looks good, but . . . it's not all good." Dramatically, he scrunches his face, and I unintentionally make a Fraggle face in return. He laughs the slightest bit at my cartoon confusion. Then, his whole expression contorts, somehow getting worse than before.

"Oh God, it's like witnessing a train wreck," I say. "I'm committed to morbid curiosity because that expression of yours is extraordinary."

He squeezes his eyes closed and wrenches his head to the side. My eyes widen with feigned horror.

Finally, he shakes his head. "I can't say it. It gives me bubble guts."

"Now, I definitely have to know . . . but I really don't want to know. You know?"

A "ga, ga, ga, ga," sound escapes him, and my irritation over our squabble dies away on a burst of giggling.

"Tell me!" I squeal.

"Let me come at this from another angle, because buhhhhhhh." He shudders from head to toe, and I crack up.

"You know how you smell like vanilla?"

I scrunch up my Fraggly face again. "Uh-huh . . ." Late last school year, I learned that I have a vanilla pheromone. At first, it didn't occur to me, but now I'm finally able to smell it. It makes guys a little bonkers, and I'm not a fan.

"My tank top smells like vanilla-you every time you sweat all over me in the studio."

Silently, I stare at him. He clears his throat.

Eyebrows raised, I say, "No clue where you're headed with this. Just say it, D. You don't want to wander away mid-conversation about how I smell weird. I'm still not comfortable with the whole vanilla pheromone issue."

Demitri laughs and rubs his hands lightly down my arms. "No, no. It's not a bad thing. Quite the opposite." He smirks at me. "I just don't want you to get mad for what Adam suggested."

"I'm fully aware that he's a dirty bastard. I guarantee he's done worse than whatever this is about. Out with it."

"He suggested that if I ever rev you up, I inhale here," he runs a finger lightly behind my ear, and my eyebrows fly up again. He chuckles deviously. "So, I had my arms wrapped around you during the fireworks show at Disneyland, and apparently me squeezing your ribs sparks your dark-water side."

An awkward expression contorts my face.

He rolls his eyes. "I did what he suggested, and damn if that vanilla pheromone doesn't get stronger when you're turned on. He warned me that it would nearly buckle my knees, and he was right. I got lightheaded and couldn't even function for a hot second."

The look I give him says he's insane.

"Totally true," he says, hands raised. "It makes my head spin. Like I said, my tank top smells like you after you've sweated all over me in rehearsals. I'll wear the damn thing until I go to bed, and then I'll sleep with it bunched up under my head."

Mouth agape, my eyes widen to the size of dinner plates.

Demitri waves his hands around as if to clear the air. "I told you all of that to reassure you that I do, quite seriously, view you as an actual possibility. The smell of you makes my brain crater." His eyes roll into the back of his head. "You have no freaking idea."

A little giggle escapes me as I'm caught between flattery and horror. I already knew my pheromone is intoxicating to my guys, but I don't like being compared to Victoria. "Okay, now get to the Victoria part of this smell-tacular."

A liberal "Buhhhhhh" escapes him as he shudders again. "She's—" He urps.

"You picked buhhhhhhh over vanilla?"

He scrunches his face in a way that shows his vulnerability. "Honestly, I think I was convinced I wasn't good enough."

"For ME?"

He shrugs a little. "You're not what you think I think you are."

Apart from me, he's the only person I know who talks in riddles like this, and it makes me smile, despite my insecurities. "I'd rather not be turned down for a buhhhhhh."

"And I'd rather not turn you down for one." His eyes narrow mischievously. "Especially considering how Adam let it slip that the whole vanilla pheromone situation goes into overdrive when you blow."

Jaw dropping, I exclaim, "Did he? Oh, how charming! I'm gonna kill that blabbermouth."

Demitri chuckles before begging, "No, seriously. You can't say anything. He's been really cool with me. I don't want to lose his trust, and I really do enjoy being his friend."

"His vanilla-gossip friend?" My eyebrows rise.

He grimaces. "I really am sorry, Melanie. I've been devastated over this. I'm a lot more captivated by you than I let on."

I give him a blazingly serious look. "If you ever shudder and describe me as buhhhhhhh, I swear I'll die of shame."

"She's buhhhhhhhh because she doesn't shower," he says with a laugh.

A shudder runs through me.

"Yeah. Epic failure. Please forgive me, at least as my friend."

Wincing, I ask, "Is your soulmate connection with her really that earth-shattering, D?"

"No. I flat don't get the thrill of a soulmate connection. All it does is make me feel trapped."

I scoff. "You have no idea how much I can relate. I want to be done with Trey, but we're always connected." I take a nervous breath. "While this has been riveting, I need to purchase an outfit for this date." I give Demitri a look. "I'd hate for Mr. Innocent to discover the shocking world of cleavage." I grimace. "I'm already about to expose him to Friday night fun on Hollywood Boulevard. Hookers, punk rockers, and tourists await."

"You're taking Trevor to the *boulevard*?"

"Lucky me. It wasn't my choice, if it helps."

"Why does he want to go there?" Demitri asks skeptically.

I make a sarcastically enthusiastic face. "To compare handprints at Mann's Chinese Theater and dodge slimy randoms, I guess."

"So, you're a tour guide now?" Demitri scoffs. "How romantic."

I quirk my mouth as I get into the passenger seat. "It gets worse. He invited all his friends to join us."

Demitri's whole face scrunches. "How the hell does he plan to get lucky while you have an entourage?"

"Trevor wasn't getting lucky tonight." I raise an eyebrow. "I bet he'll show up on time, though."

Demitri's head drops back, and he gives a frustrated exhale. I smirk to myself, satisfied that I got in one more little jab.

"Just tell me that you understand how sorry I am," he murmurs as he gets into the Jeep.

"I don't hold it against you. You're a shallow guy. I can't expect you to turn down a hoe or have respect for our date. That would be ridiculous."

"I'm not some random asshole, Melanie," Demitri breathes on a wave of dejection.

"So, you not showing up for our date because you were screwing Victoria makes you a *good* guy?"

His eyes close. "No, but I'm not . . ." It takes him a moment of pondering before his head drops. "My actions were very 'that guy' but I'm not that guy." He looks at me mournfully. "The fact that I was 'that guy' with you is humiliating."

"Every guy is 'that guy' with me. This happens to me all the time. Adam stood me up. Trey cheated on me. You ditched me for Victoria." I meet Demitri's dejected gaze. "I thought maybe I have horrible taste in men. You're different, yet you did it too. I think I'm the problem."

"You aren't the problem, Melanie," Demitri murmurs. He pulls out of our parking spot while he radiates shame.

CHAPTER 19

I turn the corner from the hall into the living room, and Mom and Rich look me up and down, surprised.

Mom does little to hide her bewilderment. "What are you wearing?"

I glance down at my new outfit: knee-high black stockings, pleated purple-and-black plaid skirt, and an open purple blouse with a black cami tank top.

"Let's just say I fit in wearing this." I sigh.

Rich raises his eyebrows, his face awash with shock.

"The water polo team and cheerleaders are the group that took me in at Canoga Park High," I explain. "If it helps, they're the least troublemaking group you'll ever meet. They're nothing like the Hollywood High kids."

The ringing of the doorbell interrupts my parents' response. Rich crosses to the door, and in walks Trevor, followed by nine of my new friends. Trevor and the guys are all in jeans and their water polo letterman jackets. The girls have on cute skirts that are far more conservative than my previous crew tends to wear. They all look preppy and innocent.

Rich's mouth drops open, and he bluntly says to me, "I thought you were going on a date?"

Radiating amusement, I gesture to my date. "Trevor asked everyone to come on our date with us."

Mom's eyebrows furrow. "How nice," she says hesitantly.

Clearly amused, Rich steps forward and enthusiastically pumps Trevor's hand. "It's so nice to meet you, Trevor, and if I don't see you again, I'd like to wish you well with your water polo endeavors."

Trevor looks confused as he politely shakes Rich's hand. "It's so nice to meet you officially, sir. I should've properly introduced myself in the office before I took Melanie on the campus tour." He turns to my mom. "Ma'am, you're radiant. It's a pleasure."

Mom is clearly tickled by Trevor's formality—so much so that she has to excuse herself. She heads to the backyard, and through the sliding door, I can see her shoulders shaking.

Left on his own, Rich closes his eyes, trying to hold it together. "Melanie, home by one, please," he says once he's gathered.

Trevor looks shocked. "I have to be home by ten, so I'll have her here no later than nine-thirty."

Mom chooses that moment to scoot through the sliding glass door. Hearing Trevor's curfew announcement, she guffaws. She rushes back through the door and closes it briskly behind her.

"Nine-thirty, huh?" Rich asks, having a hard time holding it together himself. "Boy howdy! Sounds like a wicked good time. You crazy kids have fun."

I fight not to laugh. My new friends leave through the front door, and Trevor and I scoot out last. We get halfway down the walkway before I hear my parents roaring with laughter.

Trevor turns to me, totally oblivious that he's the source of their mirth. "They sure are jovial. I really like them, Melanie."

My new friends enthusiastically compare their hand and footprints to the cement stamps at the Mann's Chinese Theater. I try not to roll my eyes as they carry on like tourists.

These kids are so basic. I had no idea this was what most teenagers were like.

As if to answer my thought, Trevor says, "This has been so much fun! Heck of an idea, Melanie."

A bit baffled, I remind him, "Hollywood Boulevard was your plan, remember?"

The group all bunches up next to us as Bethany bubbles out, "What's next? This is awesome!"

"Isn't it though? Ummm . . ."

I'm interrupted by an enthusiastic voice behind me. "Look what the cat dragged in! If it isn't Melanie!"

Closing my eyes, I inhale, both amused and terrified about the inevitable exchange. I turn around and see Arch grinning at me in his trademark trench coat with the anarchy symbol on the back. Fanned out behind him are all my Hollywood High friends, most of them wearing their Hellcats leather vests.

"Shit," I say under my breath.

Arch grins from ear to ear. "Shit, indeed." He gestures to the Hollywood group. "We went by your house to surprise you, but your parents GLEEFULLY informed us that you're hosting your new friends on our stomping grounds." He gives me an overexaggerated wink. "We raced right over to say hi."

Mom and Rich strike again.

Apparently, Demitri didn't inform the group of my date plans. Points for him. I look the group over, noticing that Kelsey and Victoria are absent. I relax a little.

Trevor surprises me by crossing the distance and putting out a hand to Arch. "I'm Trevor, Melanie's boyfriend," he says cheerfully.

Arch smirks as he enthusiastically pumps Trevor's hand.

As they survey Trevor's letterman jacket-clad preppiness, my Hollywood friends' mouths drop open.

Bluntly, I ask, "I'm sorry, Trevor . . . You're my *what*?"

Awareness seems to dawn on him that he might have jumped the gun with that title.

Adam saunters forward before Trevor gets a chance to say anything. Arch thumps Adam on the back, grinning.

Adam sends his amused, ocean-blue eyes my way before looking down at Trevor, who's six inches shorter than him. "Melanie's boyfriend! Would ya looky here, guys!" Adam glances around at my Hollywood friends, who all nod gleefully. He turns back to Trevor and sneers. "I'm Melanie's ex-boyfriend, Adam. Nice to meet you."

"Hi," Trevor says uncomfortably.

Adam takes a drag from his cigarette and *accidentally* blows it Trevor's way. I wince as Trevor spastically waves his hand around, trying to avoid the smoke.

"Trey, come here and meet Melanie's boyfriend, Trevor." Adam gestures to Trey. Then, he leans to Trevor and says in a gossipy tone, "This is Melanie's other ex. I'd hate to be the only one standing here intimidated by the new competition."

My Hollywood friends all snicker while I cower a little.

Trey steps forward, radiating amusement. He snorts and raises an eyebrow at me before surveying Trevor. "I'd love to be a fly on the wall when her dark-water side slithers to the surface in *his* back seat," he says to Adam.

"Please no," I mutter under my breath.

Adam throws his head back and belts laughter while my friends all chortle. Instantly, I turn red. My hard glare at Trey draws out his mischievous grin.

"Okaaay," I say loudly, plastering a fake smile on my face. "My new friends, these are my old friends. Old friends, meet my new friends." Vaguely, I gesture to each group in turn. "If you'll excuse us," I say to the Hollywood crowd.

My attempt to get away is rendered fruitless by Trevor.

"Melanie dated you guys?" he asks hesitantly of my exes.

"Yeah, Melanie and I broke up because she's a rattlesnake." Adam grins at me as I blush.

"We miss you, Firebird," Tanner says.

My new friends all look curious, and Bethany asks, "Firebird?"

"It's the nickname she got from the leader of the Hellhounds," Tanner says exuberantly.

"Please don't," I plead.

Bethany looks confused. "The Hellhounds? What's that?"

Big Joe, Stubbs, and Stealth choose that moment to come through the crowd and join my friends.

"We're *so excited* that Arch called us," Stubbs says with a grin. "We were right around the corner."

They cross the short distance and hug me. My new friends look baffled by my friendship with these middle-aged, rough-and-tumble bikers.

Big Joe answers Bethany's question. "We're the Hellhounds, a biker gang that runs the Hollywood underground."

Trevor's eyes bug out. "You're in a *biker gang*?" he practically yells at me.

Marcus answers for me. "Actually, she's in an associate gang called the Hellcats."

This is all unraveling so fast that I don't know what to do.

Trevor chuckles good-naturedly. "Come on, Melanie. These guys are pulling our legs."

"Show them, Firebird," Trey says, jutting his chin toward me.

Eyes closed, I shake my head and sigh. Maybe if I confidently get on board with all this, my new friends will handle it well. They seem to like me.

I slide down my blouse and pull the left strap aside on my tank top, showing my new friends my firebird tattoo.

Trevor steps up behind me and licks his thumb before rubbing the tattoo.

His spit on my shoulder makes me shudder and nearly gag. "Buuuh!"

Demitri cracks up.

"You have a *tattoo*?" Trevor croaks with disgust.

I nod.

"She got it to cover a gunshot wound to the shoulder," Trey announces.

My new friends gape at me.

"It's so trashy, though," Trevor says.

Radiating irritation at being called trashy, I glance at my Hollywood friends.

Arch pushes up his sleeves, displaying his ink. "You might want to can it with the tattoo talk around this crew."

Trevor blanches at my intimidating friend. "Well, I mean . . . Your tattoos are fine, but Melanie's seems . . ."

Big Joe crosses his arms over his chest. "Seems what? I'm the one who inked her. You should see the other one."

Trevor looks like he's going to keel over. "You have TWO tattoos?"

I raise an eyebrow. "The other one's none of your business." I have Pierre's seashell sketch tattooed on my hip. He drew it with the intention of getting matching tattoos with his future wife. It was the night of his memorial when I received this ink.

Trevor rapidly changes the subject. "How did you get into a biker gang?"

Before I can answer, Trey says, "She murdered a serial killer who was stalking her, earning Big Joe's respect."

"SHIT!" Jerome exclaims. "Are you serious?"

The Canoga Park group looks a little surprised by Jerome's profane outburst. They quickly shake off their revulsion at the cussing and switch to staring at me like I'm some kind of alien being. Trey's account of the matter is a little out of order, but I let it go because I'm so stunned to find myself in such a sharp downward social spiral.

Arch laughs. "If cussing shocks you, Melanie's gonna be a real treat."

"Okay, so," Trevor stammers, "I'm still hung up on this motorcycle gang thing."

"It's a group, not a gang," I explain. "They're all exaggerating a bit about that." I swing my arm wide. "Meet the Hellcats."

Flamboyantly, Tanner says, "Roll call!"

My friends all smirk.

Arch raises his hand, casually saying, "Anarchy."

Everyone calls out their Hellcat handles with gusto, one after the other.

Trey steps forward last and snarls, "I'm Shivers." He turns to me. "Seeing as how your naughty boy toy has to be home by ten, your parents gave you permission to come to a party at Mama Mabel's with us."

I raise my eyebrows, but before I can answer, Trevor looks curiously at my Hollywood group and asks, "Is that a nightclub? Sounds like fun. We might be able to get our curfews extended so we can join you."

Trey smirks. "It's a brothel."

I want to die.

Trevor looks confused. "A brothel? What's that?"

"House of ill repute," Arch says.

Trevor still looks baffled.

Bear offers, "Ladies of the night?"

Of all people, Mama Mabel sways into the center of the group, stops, cocks a hip, and purrs, "Whorehouse, sugar!"

I turn fuchsia and pray that the ground swallows me whole.

"You go to whorehouses?" Trevor squeaks at me.

"Only Mama Mabel's," I say sheepishly.

"And you are?" Jerome asks of our new company.

Mama Mabel flourishes her hands, her eclectic outfit fully on display. "Mama Mabel, at your service."

"Melanie?" Bethany says hesitantly. "How do you know Mama Mabel?"

Mama Mabel grins, announcing with glee before I can reply, "Melanie and I met when she was in jail for assault."

My new friends all turn to me in unison, shock written on their faces.

"Every one of you knows there are much more reasonable explanations for all of this," I say, side-eying my Hollywood Hellcats.

Tanner stomps over in a huff and pulls me to the center of the two groups, giving himself some elbow room. "I can't take it anymore. What the hell are you wearing?"

I'm too flummoxed to protest as he takes my blouse off, drapes it over his shoulder, ties up my camisole tank top, and makes it into a crop top. Then, he yanks my plaid pleated skirt down, instantly turning it into an edgy hip-hugger number. He kneels beside me and gestures to Trey. "Pocketknife."

Trey doesn't hesitate to pull his pocketknife and hand it to Tanner, who carefully cuts big gashes into my black knee-highs on both legs. Looking satisfied, he stands and wraps my purple blouse around my waist, knotting it. With a finishing flourish, he opens his side satchel and pulls out my Hellhounds black leather vest. "Rich got it out of your closet for me," he explains as he hands it to me.

I hold it limply in my hand.

Tanner takes a step back and grins with satisfaction.

Presley exhales. "Thank you, Tanner! That fashion crisis was narrowly averted." She gestures toward the leather vest in my sweaty hand. "Put it on, put it on!"

I slip the vest on and try not to huff.

"Well, I thought Melanie looked cute," Trevor says in a lame attempt to defend me.

Presley snorts. "Melanie LOVES to be called cute. That's gonna win you romance points, FOR SURE."

The Hellcats all crack up.

My expression slides to dejection so hard that a few of my Hollywood friends suddenly look concerned. "I *liked* feeling cute," I admit.

"Uh-oh," Finley says softly. She looks up at Tanner, and his eyes pinch around the edges as he studies me.

"Melanie, did you like your outfit before I fixed you?" Tanner asks.

I nod bashfully.

Adam hands me his cigarette. "Be who you are, Melanie," he scolds. "This whole good-girl act is bullshit."

My head hangs for a second before I groan and look to my new friends. "Meet Melanie," I say dejectedly before taking a drag.

Trevor looks mortified.

"She's a bad, bad girl," Trey says to Trevor.

"Trey, this needs to stop," Demitri says.

After a glance at Demitri, who clearly doesn't approve of the cigarette, I look to Trey. He stares into my eyes, knocking on the blockage in our soulmate connection as he slowly walks my way. Reluctantly, I drop the blockage. He sends a quaking wave of seduction before I can beg him to make this vapid display in front of my new friends stop. Trey's seduction roars my dark-water side to life. I moan as my head drops back. Completely overcome by my dark side, I slowly lift my head to stare into Trey's eyes. What he sees causes him to smirk, slow and seductive.

"I'm in a mood," I purr. Waves of my vanilla pheromone pour from me.

"It's likely one I can fix, if you'll let me."

"Possible," I gravel back.

Mama Mabel snorts. "*Probable*," she says to Trey. "If you'll get her to come to my place with us, that is."

My Hollywood friends all break into evil laughter—except for Demitri.

Trevor looks uncomfortable. He quickly switches gears, checking his watch. "I better get you home, Melanie. It's eight forty-five and we have a long drive. I'd hate to have to speed."

"God forbid a person had to speed." Adam scoffs.

My new friends stare at me with fear in their eyes. My dark-water side has clearly triggered their flight instincts. The reality is that Normals generally subconsciously view me as a predator to their prey. I'm panicking in the back of my mind, but my dark-water side has such a solid grip on me that I don't care at the moment.

Trey steps behind me and drapes his arms over my shoulders. "Don't worry about getting Melanie home."

"I promised Rich and Carol that I'd get her home safely," Trevor argues politely.

"Well, after you made that promise, *I* promised Rich and Carol that Melanie would stay at Mama Mabel's tonight. Her overnight bag's in my car as we speak."

My stomach clenches. I didn't expect this news, and it burns through a little of my dark-water side.

"I am NOT allowing Melanie to stay at a house of nighttime, or whatever you people called it!" Trevor exclaims.

"Whorehouse, dear," Mama Mabel reminds cheerfully.

Some of the Hellcats and Hellhounds snicker.

Playfully, Trey bites my neck. It makes me gasp, and my dark-water side rages again. My head spins. The proper part of me drowns in the dark water in my mind. Unchecked, I press my back and tush hard against Trey. The sudden assault of hormones causes my vision to lose focus. It leaves me reeling, helpless against the call of my primal instincts.

"Let loose, Melanie," Trey whispers in my ear. "I can feel you fighting this."

"We need to talk," I murmur back.

Trey growls, the vibration in his chest running along my back. My lips part, and I sharply inhale as my body collapses against him. He chuckles deep and holds me up by the waist with one arm while I relearn how to breathe. In the back of my mind, I'm panicking, but Trey seems oblivious.

"Those two are going to get arrested for indecent exposure if we don't get them out of here," Tanner quips.

"She'll be in good hands," Trey says to Trevor. "She's staying with me in the guest room."

At the prospect, my eyes widen. Trey and I aren't even close to being in a good enough place to reconnect like that. A blush blooms on my cheeks. The last thing I want is word of all this getting around my new school. My Hollywood life will sound INSANE to all the Normals. As I slide a desperate gaze Demitri's way, my dark-water side finally subsides. I'm left humiliated.

Demitri surveys me with growing concern. "Wrap this up," he orders quietly. He gives Trey a look and gestures him over.

Trey steps to him, and the rest of the Hollywood crew crowd around the two of them, leaving me to stand mortified before my new friends.

Through my soulmate connection with Trey, I hear Demitri ask, "Do you really think this little meet and greet was best for Melanie's reputation at her new school?"

Trey shrugs. "We want her back at our school. Hearing her new *friends* talk shit will drive her home."

"She's a Magnet student," Demitri explains stoically. "Her spot has already been filled. She can't enroll at Hollywood as a Regular. She lives out of district, remember?"

Panic bursts through Trey. "Shit. I didn't think about that."

"Given her outfit tonight, and her choice of new friends, it appears she was trying for a fresh start as the kind of girl she wants to be." Demitri juts a thumb Finley's way. "That type of girl. Now, it's been outed that Melanie was in jail, is in a biker gang, has tattoos, and sleeps at whorehouses with you." Demitri gives mortified Trey a hard look. "You just dragged her past—a past that makes her very unhappy—into her present. She deserved a fresh start, Trey."

Trey turns to me, but he clearly doesn't know what to say.

"I'm sorry, Melanie," Arch says. "We weren't thinking."

My ears feel like they're on fire, I'm blushing so hard.

"Melanie," Mama Mabel says, radiating mortification. "I'm so sorry. I thought you were on board with this whole display. When Marcus called me, the Hellcats acted like it was all a big joke."

"That's because I *am* a big joke to them." I gesture to the Hollywood crowd.

"That's not true, Melanie," Presley rushes to say.

"I was just trying to go on a date and hang with friends," I whimper.

"Hey," Trevor says softly as he takes me gently by the arms. "You're okay." He looks to his friends. "Right, guys?"

"Absolutely," Jerome says, rallying.

Bethany squeezes my shoulder. "I was having so much fun before we were interrupted."

Trevor smiles softly at me. "I was nervous to go on a date with you. That's why I asked my friends to come with." He quirks his mouth. "Thank you for taking us on an adventure. We're going to head out."

"I'm sorry," I say, ashamed.

He shakes his head and smiles. "Don't be. Can I pick up coffee for us and meet you in front of the school on Monday? I'll walk you to class."

"Yes, please. That's really thoughtful of you."

"All right. You've got yourself a deal." He hugs me.

"I can't wait to hear your stories sometime!" Bethany bubbles.

Bashfully, I smile her way. "I promise to regale you with the tales."

The other girls Bethany is friends with exchange unsure looks that cause me to wince internally.

Jerome gives a flirtatious grin. "Would it offend you if I said I think your whole bad-girl side is hot?"

"Not at all," I say, amused despite my humiliation. I turn to Trevor and add sincerely, "Thank you for a lovely evening. Please drive home safe."

Hoping they still like me, I watch them walk away.

"Melanie," Trey says.

Slowly, I turn and survey a very dejected huddle of my Hollywood friends.

"We're so sorry," Presley says. "You know how we all joke around. We forget how our insanity sounds to outsiders."

"It wasn't *your* insanity that was revealed," I say quietly. "It was *my* insanity." My head drops.

"I'm sorry, Melanie," Trey says.

"Let's just go." I pivot and start walking.

"I'm parked the other way," Trey calls out.

Looking over my shoulder, I say, "I'd rather walk."

Presley jogs to catch up with me. "I'll walk with you."

CHAPTER 20

Mama Mabel guides us into the guest room. I've stayed here before, so in some ways, it feels a little like home. Two empty duffel bags are on the floor by the door, one of them Trey's and the other mine. My heart pounds.

"I took the liberty of having my housekeeper unpack for both of you," Mabel informs. "Your stuff is in the dresser. I spoke with both of your parents, and you're staying here tonight *and* tomorrow night. I'm going to help you get through this, and the weekend is the perfect time." When Trey takes a shuddering breath, Mabel points a finger his way. "Is there *anything* else you're hiding?"

Trey shakes his head.

Mabel nods. "If you EVER cheat on her again, you have my promise that I'll whoop you Mama Mabel style."

Trey grins mischievously. "That's oddly intriguing."

Mabel belts laughter. "*You* are trouble!" she croons. She turns my way and implores, "He can't change what he's done, but I truly believe he's learned from it. He and I have talked at length."

I snort. "Your side and my side are rarely the same side," I say to Trey, "but this is your shot at fixing us, and Mabel seems to think you're the only one who deserves a discussion." I gesture to the duffel bags. "And you both seem to think that us shacking up for a weekend is inevitable, because Trey's charm will outweigh his indiscretions."

His eyes widen as he looks to Mabel. "Um, seems we were shortsighted. We should have included her in this decision."

"You were incredibly honest with me, Trey. Give honesty a shot with Firebird." Mabel turns a bright smile on me. "You have an hour before I expect you to come out to the party."

We nod, and Mama Mabel leaves.

Trey cracks his neck nervously. It's one of his tells. This conversation is going to be hard for him. "Drop the wall blocking our connection."

At once, I crash the wall down.

Trey exhales loudly, radiating relief. "Please don't put it up again."

"We'll see."

"I love the hell out of you, girl," Trey says with conviction. "Every minute of every day. Without fail or compromise. It scares the shit out of me."

My heart flutters, and I melt a little.

"I want to discuss Tiffany."

Hope dissolves in a huff. *That was quick.* "Seriously?" *All I want to do is discuss us.*

"Just hear me out," Trey implores. "As hard as it is for me to admit, having a relationship with someone I had no deeper soulmate connection with was hugely appealing—at the time—mostly because it was simple."

As he takes a breath, I scoot to the wall and lean against it, needing to be against something solid.

After a moment, he continues. "I took her to Big Bear, and I'm going to level with you that I had a blast. It was the most uncomplicated weekend I've had since the day I met you. I was intensely relieved because the trip balanced out the pressure I felt while you were in the hospital the first time."

I hate the direction this conversation is going. *"I'm headed out now,"* I send to him.

"No, wait. I'll get to the point. Please take the memory compilation I've got ready."

At a cursory glance, the thought bubble I take contains every detail of his Big Bear trip all lumped into one. "Mama Mabel insists that I need to spill all of it at once so we can clear the air," he says out loud.

"Mama Mabel doesn't get to decide that. I'm warning you that if ANYTHING so much as kissing is in this memory, I'll never speak to you again."

"Then wait, Melanie. Don't dig through it."

Out of spite, I start to study the bubble. He offered every detail, but it would take me days to get through all of it. My heart hurts as I watch how madly in love with Tiffany he is in the memories. The sex was spirited and constant. The hand-holding was dreamy. All of it was truly perfect.

Tears roll down my cheeks. *I just can't anymore.* "You are so out of line with this that there aren't words, Trey."

Trey panics as I open the door. Mabel, Demitri, and Presley are waiting in the hall.

Mabel stops me as I storm out. She gently directs me back into the room. "What happened?"

"He took your advice and gave me a complete set of memories of him screwing Tiffany," I spit out accusingly. "Apparently, they were madly in love."

Mama Mabel squawks at Trey, "You WHAT?"

"You told me to tell her everything!"

Presley steps through the still-open door and hugs me. "What is *wrong* with you, Trey? Melanie, I swear I've never met stupider guys than yours."

"Come on, Trey. That's ridiculous." Demitri looks down at me. "Are you okay?"

I stare at the floor and don't respond.

Mama Mabel looks from Trey to me. "You're an idiot, Trey. That is NOT what I meant. I was telling you to be honest about how you feel about Melanie, not show her your orgasms with your fling."

She steps to me and puts her hand on my forehead. Suddenly, the memories he offered are gone from my mind. I'm aware that it happened, but the graphic details are wiped.

I exhale. "Thank you."

Mama Mabel glares at Trey. "Pull your head out of your ass. I wiped the details from Melanie's mind. You get ONE do-over. It was cruel for you to show that to her, and you have a lot to learn."

Down our connection, Trey sends agony at how complicated this is for him. "I'm sorry, Melanie. I'm trying, and I obviously misunderstood Mabel."

"I was shortsighted in assuming that I didn't need to get your side of things," Mabel says to me as she puts a hand on my arm. She looks to Trey. "I'm starting to see that you make serious mistakes. You're lucky Melanie is even standing in this room with you."

"At some point," I say, swallowing hard, "I'd like to matter enough to have some consideration."

"I respect that," Mabel assures. "I'm going to ask a hard thing of you. If Trey can't handle fixing this with the discussion we had, please give him another chance. I'm getting to know you kids, and I may have been naïve about how to help."

Trey looks desperate for a chance with me.

"I'm going to try." Then, bashfully, I add, "This matters to me."

My friends follow Mama Mabel into the hall. She pulls the door closed, and I'm left with little to say.

"I'm telling you now that I was completely out of my mind when Tiffany happened," Trey says. "That's what I was aiming for you to see."

"Gleeful happiness is you being out of your mind?"

Trey snorts. "Yeah. You've met me, right?"

"I want to be part of your gleeful happiness," I whisper back. "Not part of your unhappiness."

Trey closes his eyes and seems to wilt at my take on things. "It's not like that, Melanie. It's just that I'm not a carefree, happy goofball." He evokes intense longing for me to understand him. "Do you have any idea how much pressure there is when you have to watch your soulmate dying in a hospital bed?"

I don't respond. The silence extends long.

Finally, I say, "I don't understand that pressure from your side, but Zane and I have discussed his experience after he took care of me. He handled it well, but . . ."

"I wish I had handled things better. I'm glad Zane was there for you this last round." Trey inhales. "Bottom line, it didn't take long before the relief of 'gleeful normalcy' slipped into mind-numbing boredom. I realized it the moment you came out of the coma. I looked into your eyes and knew in that instant that I had completely fooled myself into thinking Tiffany meant anything to me. The guilt I've felt since then has been suffocating."

"I can't trust you."

"Yes, you can," he implores. "I'm fully aware that you've been through extra layers of hell because I didn't love you the way I should have. Pierre and Zane would have never happened if I'd had the balls to be your man. Being your man is a damn hard thing.

But I'm going to ask something difficult of you too."

"Ask."

"The Melanie I watched on TV while you were in Hawaii with Pierre was a calm, happily confident woman. I need to understand that version of you, because you're never happy like that with me. Will you send me a memory of what it was like with Pierre so that I understand what makes you happy?"

I send him the memory of Pierre and me the first time we got in the hot tub. Pierre kisses me in the memory, and then holds me with his head on my shoulder. There's no pressure or insecurity, only calm vibes and trust. His hands shift to my hips, and I float back in the warm water. Pierre waits patiently while I float, content. Trey hears a bit of the conversation, but my emotional vibes and thoughts about Pierre are far more telling than the words.

When the memory ends, Trey exhales. "He made you feel attractive, safe, and like you had time to just *be*."

"Indeed he did. I've never felt that comfortable. He never said anything misleading. He thought I was beautiful for who I was. There was nothing for me to second-guess or fear. I was safe. That's what I need, Trey. But you make me feel insecure. I don't feel good enough with you. It's always more like I'm being compared to other girls in your head. I don't trust you."

"I know," he replies. "And everything you feel about this is valid. I have a lot of work to do on how I handle things with you. Please understand, though, that I truly have no interest in Tiffany." In a rush, Trey pleads, "Trust me enough to take one more memory."

I decide to trust him, close my eyes, and watch as the memory unfolds. It depicts him warning Tiffany, "Stay away from Melanie and me. I'm done with this. No more discussions. As much as this will hurt you to hear, I'm telling you that you're the biggest mistake I've ever made. I'm not in love with you. All I feel about you is horrific regret. If I could take it back, I wouldn't even give you the time of day. I want my Melanie back. Period."

I watch in the memory as he leaves a sobbing Tiffany at Smokers' Corner. It occurs to me that this was the same day she interrupted us while we were communicating through our soulmate connection.

As the memory ends, Trey's hands slide along my back, and he pulls me into a hug.

"Did you mean what you said to her?" I ask.

"Every word," he sends. *"She means nothing to me. I'm not in love with her. I was a confused mess."*

Seeing as how it's close to impossible to lie mind-to-mind, I know he's telling the truth.

I lay my cheek on his chest, and he rubs the back of my head. "You called me your Melanie." For me, the tone is oddly girly.

"I view you that way. I don't voice it like I should." He pauses before softly asking, "Is that the kind of thing that makes you happy?"

"Yes. I like feeling like I'm wanted and have a spot."

"I can do that, love," he says. "I've had that all wrong. You need something a lot closer to what I gave Tiffany."

In frustration, I thump my forehead against his chest. After a moment's contemplation, I turn and open the door. Demitri and Presley are still in the hall.

"Every damn time we head the right direction, he circles back around to yapping about Tiffany." I point at Presley. "Tag, you're it."

"That's *not* what I was trying to do!" Trey rushes to say. "I was trying to explain—"

"Shut up, Trey," Presley cuts in. She and I switch spots, and she slams the door behind her.

"Come on, Meley." Demitri takes my hand and pulls me down the hall.

We meet Mabel, who looks at Demitri expectantly.

"Presley's dealing with the moron," he explains. "Melanie stormed out."

Mabel takes out her keys and unlocks the room next to us. Demitri pushes open the door to what turns out to be another guest room. I step in, and he closes the door behind us.

"What did he say?" he asks.

"I don't want to discuss Trey," I blurt out. "We need to deal with us, Demitri."

"You need to see what Presley discussed with me in the hall then." Demitri holds out his hand, and I take it, along with the memory he offers.

I close my eyes and watch as Presley quietly says to Demitri, "Melanie's been in love with you for forever. What's wrong with you, D?"

"I take it she filled you in on my date nightmare?"

"She did."

Defeated, Demitri shakes his head. "That night at Disneyland, I had it all." He smiles a little. "I'm going to let you in on something I never tell anyone."

"I won't even tell Marcus," Presley promises.

"I'm a healer. I healed Melanie's condition." He chokes up a little. "What I found . . . Melanie would have ended up a vegetable within a few years. She sustained severe brain damage. I was in her mind as I healed her brain." His expression crumples with vulnerability. "She's so sweet, Presley. I've always loved her, but after being in her mind, I had to try a date. It was so perfect. I never in a million years thought I could have something like *that* with someone."

"What was perfect about it?" Presley asks.

"She never once looked at me the way girls do." Demitri smiles to himself. "I wasn't some kind of trophy. I was a real person." In the memory, he feels giddy. "She talked to me like we've always talked, but she was also snuggly in a new way. It was like having a girlfriend who's also my best friend."

Presley's eyebrows rise. "That's how it's supposed to be. You've always been the perfect couple, but you never seemed to grasp that. Melanie's never seen you as a pretty shell, D."

"She really hasn't, has she?"

Presley shakes her head. "Melanie deserves someone other than Trey, and you know it. I'm not even going to get into you and Victoria because that situation is a joke. Victoria's a total waste of your time."

"Correct on all counts."

Presley puts a hand on Demitri's shoulder. "Get your head out of your ass, D. You run from Melanie because you know that if you give in, she'll be capable of truly destroying your heart. It's why you stay with Victoria. If *she* leaves you, you won't give a shit."

"Harsh, and true."

"Melanie's earned happiness," Presley implores. "Whoever makes her happy will be who she latches onto. If you want her, you damn well better figure this out. Even if she tells Trey it's over for good, that Zane guy's still looming. Not even *you* can compete with him, I'm sorry to say."

"Zane is my biggest fear," Demitri admits. "If I lose her . . ."

"You may have already lost her."

Internally, Demitri seizes around Presley's blunt words.

We come out of the memory, and now the Demitri standing in front of me is wearing an odd combination of pale and mottled blush.

"Revealing all that had to have been very difficult for you," I say quietly.

"It was, but I can't keep hiding behind my pride."

"I've never viewed you like other girls do," I inform. "Being honest, I don't even notice your looks."

Demitri looks confused. "Then why are you interested in me?"

"Because of what's *behind* your eyes," I explain, to his surprise. "You have a world in your eyes. I love that. It's all I see. Trey's eyes scare me. Adam's are blank most of the time because he hides. You, Zane, and Pierre have the eyes, though."

Demitri scoffs. "Your list of men is pretty impressive physically."

"Hence the eyes," I insist. "If I was a body chaser, I'd be a happy piggy wallowing in all the hot mud, instead of attempting these deep connections."

The door opens, interrupting our conversation that was actually going somewhere. It's always like that, and I hate it.

Adam steps in and closes the door behind him. With a clenched jaw, he turns on Demitri. "Presley just told me you stood Melanie up for Victoria," he accuses. "Stay away from Melanie!"

"Stay out of it, Adam," Demitri snarls back. "You did the same damn thing with Valerie."

Adam hisses back menacingly, "That girl has been mine for over two hundred lifetimes. I'll never stop protecting her."

"Why?"

"Because that's what I fucking do. Welcome to the big leagues, Peter Pan. There's more to life with Melanie than making her giggle. Go be pretty. Drape yourself all over worthless girls and leave Melanie to the two people who actually understand her."

"You, I'll buy," Demitri snarls back. "But Trey doesn't understand shit about her!"

"You and Trey are both a fucking joke."

Both guys ramp up, and the room suddenly quakes with testosterone. Emotionally exhausted, I toss my hands while Demitri and Adam scream at each other. The door flies open, and Trey strides through with Presley.

"Enough!" Trey bellows.

"You people are all insane," I say, exasperated. "Now that I've spent two weeks in a new school, I'm seeing it. I thought I was going to come to Mabel's, talk with Trey, and have fun. Instead, it's been nothing but hearing about Tiffany and then listening to you people scream at each other about what *I* supposedly want and need."

Adam and Demitri's expressions soften, but I don't give them a chance to respond. "Do any of you realize how lost I am?" My face falls. "This was a massive mistake."

"Melanie, we need to talk."

I look at Adam like he's insane. "You haven't been around for *how* long?"

He sighs. "I couldn't help that. My life is in freefall, and I don't want to drag you into it." He gestures to me. "You clearly need someone to talk to, though."

"Peas in a pod, you and me," I crow.

"I need you to understand that I ran to Tiffany because it's been hell," Trey implores. "In one year, we've been through two rape attempts by Joel. The balcony nightmare. Almost dying as Adam's psyche collapsed. The kidnapping attempt. Coach Stamp trying to kill you. Getting shot. Jet trying to kill you at Riptide's. Jet attacking you while you surfed. Bomb scare." He holds up his ten fingers. "I'm already out of room to keep counting. And there's still you drowning. Plunging off a cliff with Jet."

Adam adds more fingers to the list. "Also, the seizures during your first round in the hospital. She *did* die that time. Then there was the woman trying to kill you in rehab. That makes fourteen close calls."

"That gives you the right to impregnate the school sleaze?" I ask Trey.

Out of the loop, Adam points to Demitri. "Wait, I thought *he's* attempting to impregnate the school sleaze!"

Presley scrunches her face. "Since when is Melanie the school sleaze?"

"What?" Trey barks, while I give Presley a look.

Adam waves his hands about. "I thought Melanie switched schools and started screwing Terrance?"

"Who's Terrance?" Trey yelps my way.

"I have no idea!"

We all look to Adam.

He waves his hand about. "Mr. Innocent who doesn't know what a whorehouse is."

I roll my eyes. "His name is Trevor, and I'm not sleeping with him." I scrunch my face at Adam. "Not every teenage boy frequents Hollywood's finest whorehouse."

Mama Mabel chooses this moment to sweep in. "Why, thank you. We aim to please."

Adam points at me and asks Mabel, "Since when is Demitri attempting to impregnate Melanie?"

"Oh my!" Mabel gives me a confused look. "I'm unsure what's in order. Birth control pills? Congratulations? Wedding planning?"

I scrunch my face at Demitri. "*What* is happening?"

Demitri shrugs. "Unsure."

Trey huffs. "I meant that he's trying to woo you."

"How does that justify you calling me the school whore?" I yelp at Trey.

"The school sleaze," Adam corrects. He looks to Demitri. "I

thought you were hunching *Victoria*."

"I quit hunching Victoria. She's buhhhhhhh." Demitri shudders all over.

"*Victoria* is the school sleaze," Trey explains, "not Melanie."

"I don't even go to Hollywood High anymore!" I cry out. "And I'm not the Canoga Park High sleaze either."

Adam rolls his eyes before leveling Trey with a scornful look. "I thought *you* planned to hump Melanie?"

Trey winces. "I talked about Tiffany too much and things went south."

"Who's pregnant?" Adam asks, beyond confused.

"Trey knocked up Tiffany, but she's not pregnant," Demitri clarifies.

"Pregnant is pregnant," Adam warns Trey. "I'd know."

"Miscarriage," Trey says sheepishly.

Adam squints. "Dodged that bullet. Tiffany would be a horrible mother." He grins at Trey. "Back to the point. You thought talking about your mistress would get your ex in the sack?"

"I wasn't trying to get Melanie in the sack," Trey says defensively. "I was trying to get her to love me again so we could spend the weekend snuggling!"

I grimace. "About that." I turn to Mabel. "I don't want to shack up with Trey, in a brothel, while he talks about the delights of his affair."

Mama Mabel looks stunned. "You don't want to stay in the guest room with Trey?"

"Why would I want to stay in your guest room with my ex-boyfriend?"

Mabel looks to Trey. "You said she wanted to fix things!"

"She does, but we had no business moving her in with me for the weekend," Trey informs. "We didn't think this through."

As if this crazy isn't enough, in walks Zane. He's sipping the biggest Slurpee I've ever seen. "Hello, all," he says jovially.

"What are YOU doing here?" Trey bellows.

Zane grins. "Melanie, will you please check your phone?"

I pull the phone from my skirt pocket, and it's thirty-three minutes into a phone call to Zane's number.

He waggles his phone in his hand. "You accidently dialed me—hence, why I'm here instead of at my apartment fifteen minutes away."

"How much of this mess did you hear?" Trey asks.

Zane raises an eyebrow. "You're your own worst enemy. 'You need what I gave Tiffany?'"

Everyone gives Trey a look.

He blushes. "I admit that I didn't exactly suave my way through this."

"No, you certainly didn't," Zane says. "Watch and learn, young Jedi." He hands me his Slurpee, and I take a sip. I wiggle my shoulders as he smiles softly at me. "That one can be yours. I have another one in the car."

"You drink two trash-can-sized Slurpee's at once?" Demitri asks.

"No," Zane replies. "I listened to Trey's debacle, followed by Demitri's debacle, although there was a weird amount of silence during that one."

"Memory watching," I explain.

"Ahh, that makes sense," Zane says. "Then I listened to *all* of your nonsense." He grins gleefully at the guys. "I stopped for Slurpees. Half cherry, half Coke, layered, just like she likes it."

I wiggle about happily.

Zane chuckles. "Honey, when's the last time you ate?"

"Demitri got me before I could have lunch," I say after thinking about it a moment. "Trey and company interrupted my date before we got cheeseburgers. I didn't eat breakfast." I pull another sip. "Dinner last night was when I last ate."

"We've talked about this," Zane says, giving me a paternal look. "You get emotional, snarky, and irrational when you don't eat."

"I know. I'm hungry."

He chuckles. "You're the cutest thing ever with that giant cup. What kind of hamburgers were you supposed to get?"

"In-N-Out."

"Best news ever. They're my favorite." He claps his hands together. "Okay, Mighty Mouse. Food time." He smiles. "Are your parents gone for the night again?"

My eyes big, I nod. "I get scared alone."

"I know you do," Zane says with a compassionate lilt. "Do you want to stay in Mabel's guest room with Trey?" He purses his lips playfully while he shakes his head.

I giggle, in a far better mood now that Zane is here. "No. I don't like all this stress."

"Good choice, gorgeous." He holds a bag my way.

From the bag, I pull out a fluffy, gigantic, pink abomination with big colorful gummy bears printed on it. It has a hood and is the squishiest pile of nonsense I've ever seen. With a squeal, I hand Presley my Slurpee so I can put this thing on. The giant hoodie hangs to my thighs. Zane chuckles as I put up the fuzzy hood.

"Thank you!" I chirp.

"You're welcome. You see, I went into Spencer's Gifts yesterday." He gives me another playful pursing of his lips. "The front of the store, not the back where it's all naughty and weird." I giggle again, and he smiles. "I saw that and knew my favorite gummy bear girl needed it. So, if I promise that it's a gummy bear hoodie night—" he gives Trey a look—"and not a 'tricking you into sex when we really need to talk night,' will you let me stay with you and keep you safe?"

Gratefully, I nod, and he produces a bag of gummy bears from his hoodie pocket, handing them to me.

"For me?"

"Yes, dear. You love gummy bears."

"She does?" Trey murmurs to Adam.

Adam shrugs. "News to me."

Demitri surveys Zane with narrowed eyes. "Where did you learn this?"

"I lived in a hospital room with her for a long time." Zane clears his throat before giving all the guys a look. "One of you said, 'There's more to life with Melanie than making her giggle.' I disagree. When she was in the hospital, that sound was my life's goal. After listening to her—terrified because she wasn't getting better—I found every single way to make her happy."

I pop a red gummy bear in my mouth.

"These squishy little bastards were my heroes then." Zane selects a green bear from the bag. "They made my girl quit crying. She was so scared." He holds an arm my way, and I curl up, closing my eyes with my cheek on his chest. He squeezes me tight with one arm.

I look up at him with big eyes. "I'm supposed to leave you alone."

Zane grins. "I know, but your life is such a mess that you can't." He tips his head back and comically yowls, "Thank GOD!"

Presley shakes her head. "Boys, you've missed the boat." She smiles at Zane. "Thank you for understanding Melanie. We were all treating tonight like it was complicated." She gestures his way as she says to my defunct trio of attachments, "It's not complicated."

"You're trying to tell me that her dark-water side isn't of interest to you?" Trey snarks.

Zane shakes his head. "It's not. I ignore it intentionally. I don't ever want her to question my intentions. One day, that side of her will get the best of me, but I'll be damned if that happens before she's sure of where I stand with the actual Melanie." He looks down at me. "She isn't all that dark-water distraction anyway. She's *this* girl, and that's who I'm here for."

"Looks like you found a hero," Adam accuses.

"Nope!" Zane bellows. "Melanie isn't a princess who needs saving. She's a warrior who needs to rest. I'm the safe space where she can do that."

Relief at actually being understood ripples through me. I exhale so hard and fast, it makes me dizzy.

Zane smiles down at me from his mammoth height. "I know you, girl."

On that note, he steers me from the room, leaving the guys gaping and Presley and Mama Mabel grinning.

CHAPTER 21

I finish changing and survey myself in the mirror. Luckily, I can still pull off my black bikini even though I'm full to busting with hamburger happiness. I toss on my new gummy bear puff-puff and head outside. It's well past midnight, but I have nowhere to be tomorrow, so why not enjoy a night swim?

After walking to the far side of the pool, I take off my puff-puff and toss it from the top of the waterfall to land on a lounger. I stare down at the dark, deep water. Night swims have become a ritual for me. This dark pool is a perfect actualization of the dark water in my mind, except I'm not in danger when I'm in this water. I've started using the pool to help me grasp the calm part of my dark-water side.

I stretch long before leaping up, jackknifing, and diving in with what I'm positive was little splash. I torpedo to the bottom, waiting for my hands to touch the deep drain. I roll over, lying at the bottom while I grip the drain with my fingertips. As is my custom, I hold my breath as long as I can and experience the stillness of the deep, cool water.

Just as I decide it's time to come up for air, I'm grabbed and yanked up so fast that I can't figure out what's happening. My head breaks the surface, and I find my back against Zane's chest. His arm is wrapped around my chest, his hand inappropriately squeezing the daylights out of my left teehee. He gets me to the edge and grips the railing to the ladder out of the pool with his free hand.

I'm amused by his frantic vibe. A glance over my shoulder reveals his stunned gaze as he realizes I'm okay. I go limp against him as I laugh harder.

"If you wanted to grab a boob, you didn't have to superhero up an excuse."

"Crap," Zane says, releasing me. He holds his hand up like this somehow negates his indiscretion. "I'm so sorry. I thought you were dead."

I giggle. "I lie at the bottom and hold my breath when I first dive in every time."

"Why?"

I explain about finding balance for my dark-water side, searching for calm in the chaos.

"That's an excellent idea," he compliments.

"It's worked wonders. I feel a lot calmer now that I've started doing this."

Zane's head gently drops to my shoulder. He holds me tight. At some point, my legs landed around his waist, but it's not weird, so I let it be.

"You okay?" I ask quietly.

He nods without taking his forehead from my shoulder. "When you dove in I thought, *Damn, did Pierre have good taste in swimsuits and wives.* You didn't surface, and fear that you'd broken your neck again followed." He seems to realize suddenly that there's zero space between us and lets me go. He pushes away from the pool edge as he stares at me.

I giggle a little. "Thank you for rescuing me from impending death." I raise an eyebrow as my blunt tendencies bubble up. "Your self-control is astounding."

"You're not the only one learning balance and control," he says flirtatiously. "In the past, I took a little too much advantage of my celebrity status in some areas of my life. I'm working on that."

"That involves the here and now how?"

"Zane *Drell*," he says with sarcasm, "isn't taking advantage of Melanie Slate."

"You aren't Zane *Drell* to me," I inform, imitating his tone. "You're Zaney." I shrug a little. "You heard my conversation with the Three Stooges earlier. Looks like it's time for you to get the speech." I start swimming his way. "I don't give a damn that you're six four, muscled, the best dancer on the planet, or a hotshot movie star. I also don't give a damn that you can afford FABULOUS couture." I gesture to the lounger, where my pink puff-puff hoodie came to rest, and Zane cracks up.

"That puffy abomination you seem to love ran me fifteen dollars."

"Very impressive," I say as I swim closer to him. "I *do* give a damn that you're hilarious, attentive, and altogether adorable." I boop his nose with my forefinger. "So don't get all pretzeled because you have to curb your swollen ego."

Zane's eyes narrow contemplatively. "You're the *weirdest* girl."

"I'm weird because I'm not shallowly panting about your massive bank account?"

He stares at me like a confused basset hound.

"I'm much more captivated by your sense of humor."

My empathic gift picks up on the shock rolling off him. I take advantage of his flummoxed state and kiss him while his guard is down. My head spins as he gasps and quakes. Before things can get overly heated, I pull back and grin. His mouth drops open, and he suddenly looks like a young guy who's completely out of his element.

"There," I say. "We've gotten that pesky kiss out of the way, and you survived it. Now it won't be weird when we film naughty scenes in a movie." I swim to the shallow end, step out of the pool, and grab a towel. "Come on. I want to watch the Chipmunks Christmas special on VHS."

Zane is staring up at me from the pool like I'm some kind of a bizarre creature.

I giggle again and toss my towel onto a lounge chair. I grab my puffy hoodie and pull it on. "Covered to my knees, I am."

My horrible imitation of Yoda breaks the spell Zane appears to be under. He laughs sheepishly, and I wink before heading inside.

I wake to a ringing phone. My head is resting on Zane's T-shirt-clad chest. He leans, putting a hand on my back to make sure I don't fall off the couch as he grabs his cell phone. He answers with a groggy, "Hello?"

The VCR clock says it's seven in the morning. Apparently, we fell asleep watching the Christmas special. I groan a little.

"Talk to me," Zane says into the phone, his energy shifting excitedly.

I sit up and scoot to the other end of the couch. Zane sits up and rubs tired eyes.

He listens for a long stretch before smiling. "That quick? I'd love that. Call her and see what she says." He listens again before assuring, "I bet she's awake." He says goodbye and hangs up. Then, he rolls his head around and looks at me playfully. "Good morning."

"Good morning," I reply, wiggling down and putting my head on the cushy couch arm. My eyes drift closed just as my cell phone rings from the coffee table. I wince. "Need coffee."

As I answer the phone, Zane gets up and heads out of the den.

"Melanie," Ms. Alice bubbles out, "did I wake you?"

"No, ma'am," I rush to say as I sit up straight. "I'm so incredibly sorry about the last time I saw you. I promise I don't normally start brawls."

Ms. Alice laughs a little. "I must admit I was worried. You fight like an Alcatraz convict."

"I was irked."

"With good reason. I can't believe that girl put that article out there."

"How can I help you?"

"How do you feel about filming for *Glamour* starting in a week?"

"You're kidding," I gasp out.

Zane strides back into the den and grins at me as he hands me a mug of coffee.

"Have you talked to Zane?" I ask, keeping up the ruse that we aren't in my house together.

"Yes, and he's ready to head to set." I can hear Ms. Alice smiling.

"Yes, please. Get me out of as much school as you can." I look at Zane in disbelief.

"All right, that's settled. So you're aware, because you're underage, the money from your contract will need to be deposited into a trust. You won't be able to touch the money until you're eighteen."

"That's no problem," I say. "Because of Pierre's insurance settlement, I already have a trust in my name."

"Then I need you at my office at noon today to sign the contract," Ms. Alice requests.

"Thank you so much! My parents should be home in time. We'll be there. Have a great day."

Ms. Alice chuckles. "Wouldn't you like to know what you're being paid?"

"Oh, umm, sure," I reply bashfully.

"Five hundred thousand," she informs.

"Excuse the fuck out of you!" I bark before wincing dramatically.

Through a silent, sudden belt of laughter, Zane sprays coffee all over the den. He starts cleaning up as I say into the phone, "I'm so sorry. You caught me off guard. May I try again?"

"Sure," Ms. Alice says jovially.

I make a prim face, causing another round of quiet chuckles from Zane. "Pardon? How much?" I ask like a debutant at a cotillion.

"Five hundred thousand. It's less than it should be, but you're unknown in the industry. You're also female, and sexism runs rampant in this business. I got the amount negotiated up from the two hundred thousand they initially offered. You're the lead in this movie, and I won't let them screw you."

"I suppose I can make that work," I reply with a grin. "Thank you!"

"You got it, kiddo," Ms. Alice muses.

I hang up and toss my phone as I fly off the couch. I leap Zane's way, and he catches me. "We're going to be in a movieee," I squeal.

Zane smiles while he hugs me tight. "I'm so excited. For the record, you got that part on your own."

"I really did it?" I ask.

"You really did it."

"I need to call my parents," I gasp in disbelief.

He sets me on my feet. "I'll get us bagels while you handle that."

A few seconds after he leaves the room, I hear the front door open and close. I dial my stepfather's cell phone as I start cleaning up our snack mess from last night.

The audience goes wild as the announcement is made, "Give a *Tradewinds* welcome to Zane Drell." I watch on the monitor as Zane strides onto the show stage. He shakes hands with the talk show host, Charlie Trade.

I'm amazed by how calm Zane is. I'm a nervous wreck as I slide unsure eyes to Ms. Alice.

She smiles my way encouragingly. "You'll be fine."

This all moved so fast. We signed the contract at noon, and already we're filming a talk show at two-thirty. This is the craziest Saturday of my life.

Zane and Charlie chat for a bit before Charlie asks, "Would you like a sneak peek of the ooh la la we can expect?"

The audience cheers.

The host flourishes a hand. "Please welcome Melanie Slate, costar of the upcoming movie, *Glamour*."

Nervously, I walk onto the set and smile as Zane stands.

Charlie coos to Zane, "She's so cute!"

Zane chuckles as Charlie crosses to greet me.

"Welcome, Melanie."

"Thank you," I reply before smiling at the audience and waving shyly.

There's a friendly feel, and I relax into the excitement of it all. Charlie guides me to the couch. Zane side-hugs me and only sits after I do. In my black evening gown, I cross my heel-clad ankles primly.

Charlie Trade cracks a friendly chuckle as he surveys us. "You two are SO cute," he informs. "But she looks twelve next to you, Zane."

Zane rolls his eyes a little. "Trust me, when she dances, she doesn't come across as twelve."

The audience gives an "ooo."

Charlie looks to me. "How does it feel to get your big break?"

"This is wild." I giggle a little. "Thank you for having me." I look up at Zane. "This is going to be an amazing adventure."

After winking at me, Zane looks to Charlie. "Would you like to see a duet from the movie?"

The audience goes wild. Zane grins as he stands and holds a hand my way. He guides me to the performance stage to the left of the desk. Our sultry duet to Santana's "Your Touch" starts, and we do it justice. We get through a minute of the piece before the music fades and Zane dips me low. The audience whoops and hollers as he pulls me to my feet.

Charlie Trade rushes our way, beaming. "That was remarkable!" He gives Zane a scandalized look. "You two are smoking hot together. I have never been more wrong to call someone twelve."

Grinning uncomfortably, Zane leads us back to the couch. Given my age and how we've already been linked publicly at least once before, I know that Zane wants to tamp down mention of any attraction between us. I have no clue how to curb the direction this discussion is headed.

"Melanie and I have worked together before, and we've been friends for a while," Zane says. "She dated my best friend, who passed away."

"That," Charlie points to the dance stage we just vacated, "was NOT a best friend's girl vibe."

Zane holds up a hand to the audience. "Do you want to meet the real Meley and Zaney?"

The audience cheers. Charlie assumes that delightedly befuddled expression talk show hosts are known for whenever they don't know what's coming but trust the guest anyway.

Behind the couch, Zane pulls out the duffel bag he apparently stashed there before filming started. When he takes out a pair of squishy gummy bear slippers, I start to laugh.

"Yesss! I love Zaney time." I take off my heels and put on my silly new slippers.

Next, Zane hands me my pink puff-puff gummy bear hoodie. I pull it on over my evening gown, and the audience is in stitches.

I smile up at Zane as he pulls on a Skeletor hoodie, zips it shut, and puts up the hood. Next, two chocolate milk cartons materialize out of the bag, followed by a sack of donuts. I take the milk carton he opens for me, followed by a glazed donut. I snuggle in with my usual slumpy comfort level against Zane's side and chomp on my donut.

Zane puts his hands out to the sides, flourishing his donut and chocolate milk. "Meley and Zaney."

The audience cheers.

Charlie laughs gleefully. "You know, Zane, when you come on this show, we never know what you're going to do, but it's always a good time."

With a smirk, Zane casually slings an arm around my stomach as I happily snack on my donut. The audience coos out a collective, "Ooooohhhh." Apparently, our silly chill side is cuter than our sultry dancing side.

"Melanie, I'm so sorry that you lost Riptide Strader," Charlie says sincerely, as a few pictures of Riptide surfing flash across the monitor looking up at us from the foot of the stage. Next is a picture of Zane and Riptide, followed by Riptide and me with the sunset in the background.

I give a sad, awkward little smile and find that I don't have the words to reply.

Zane grasps my hand. "We lost so much when he died," he admits. "Melanie was the love of his life, and he was my best friend and self-proclaimed little brother." He hugs me a little. "The fun lives on though. Melanie is my best friend, and we hold Riptide in our hearts."

I look up at Zane with soft eyes, bumping him affectionately with my shoulder as I sit up straight.

Charlie raises an eyebrow. "Now that we know about this best-friend status, I look forward to seeing if you two can pull off the romantic heat."

Zane and I laugh. I stuff what's left of my donut in Zane's gaping mouth, and he crumbles with laughter.

I grin at Charlie.

"We've got this," Zane says after swallowing down the donut. "We're going to blow you away."

He stands and guides me to my feet. He hits his hot-guy pose, and I cock a hip. We each make our model faces, even as we're dressed as Skeletor and a gummy bear. The audience screams their approval. Charlie Trade beams and comes around his desk to shake our hands and say goodbye.

The show segment cuts, and Charlie hugs me again while Zane tosses my heels into the duffel bag and gathers our trash.

"You did great, Melanie," Charlie says. "I'll have you back on the show in a New York minute."

I thank him. Zane says goodbye, and we rush backstage, making room for the next guest. Rich, my mom, and Ms. Alice hug us both in turn, all smiles.

"That was brilliant," Ms. Alice murmurs.

Zane shrugs. "I had a choice to make. We could suffer through the 'what are they?' scrutiny, or I could curb the rumors with our quirky vibe. Gummy Bear and Skeletor should create the kind of interest that will be much easier to manage."

Ms. Alice wholeheartedly agrees.

"Ready to go?" Rich asks.

I take off the hoodie and slippers. Zane hands back my heels. Mom takes my slippers and puff-puff.

"We need to be at the airport Wednesday at noon," Zane reminds. "You're flying with me. Don't be late."

"I wonder what the principal is going to say." I ponder. "Missing school because of a movie isn't the norm at Canoga Park High."

"That'll teach Hollywood High for the Performing Arts to drive you away," Zane says with a wink.

"Your segment airs tomorrow night at nine," Ms. Alice informs.

"On a Sunday?" I ask.

Ms. Alice nods. "It's the only night they air. The show is right before the news, when there's nothing else on, and the *Tradewinds* viewership is through the roof because of it."

Zane softly smiles at me. "I'll see you in a few days, movie star."

"Your script will be in my office Monday morning," Ms. Alice says. "Come by and get it."

I bounce and grin. "I'm so excited!" I hug Zane tight while I beam.

CHAPTER **22**

Halfway across the parking lot outside Canoga Park High, I realize that people are staring at me.

One of the cheerleaders who went out with us to Hollywood Boulevard sneers. "What's up, movie star?" she says with derision.

Fantastic. She must've seen Tradewinds. *A new reason for scrutiny.*

With a sigh, I slog to the front gates. I find Trevor and Jerome waiting for me. As I step up to them, two of the other guys who joined us at Hollywood Boulevard, Dan and Barry, join us. Trevor hands me a coffee.

"It appears that I'm the source of copious amounts of attention."

"The guys have your back." Trevor gestures around the circle. "But the girls who went on our adventure turned on you. After your movie news spread, they told all your dirt to everyone."

Shit! Not only am I hated for the movie, but my dirt has also been spread.

Bethany steps up to our circle and furrows her brow at Trevor. "Don't lump me in with the other girls." She turns to me, her bouncy ponytail swishing, and bubbles over, "I'm SO excited for you. I'm on Team Melanie *all* the way." She narrows her eyes. "I'm working on the girls who talked crap about you."

"Why, *Bethany*," I say in a jovial tone, "you just said 'crap'!"

Bethany grins conspiratorially. "You're a breath of fresh air, and you might be rubbing off on me."

"You don't seem upset about what I just told you," Trevor says.

I shrug. "Eh. I don't really care. I leave Wednesday for a movie set. I just have to get through the next two days."

Deep in contemplation, Bethany stares at me. "I've never met anyone like you."

"Thank you for being nice to me," I say with a smile. "Friday night was mortifying."

The bell rings, cutting off any further discussion. We wave goodbye and go our separate ways.

In my first-period classroom, I greet my teacher, Mr. Harring, as I pass his desk. Just as I take a seat and start pulling my stuff from my backpack, I hear behind me, "You think that's bad? My aunt's best friend's daughter's cousin goes to Hollywood High! SHE told me that Melanie is a *witch*!"

"You can't be serious."

"Dead serious. AND she burned down the auditorium!"

Dejection fills me. My eyes close.

"Not only *that*, but look what her best friend, Tiffany, handed out on the first day of school."

Oh NO. This girl is talking about Tiffany's best friend Sheila.

I'm overcome with dread as I hear a paper rustle.

A stretch of silence passes before I hear, "Oh. MY. GOD," hissed behind me. "I wonder if she wears diapers."

Evil giggles bubble up, and I think I might die in this seat.

Not this. I can't believe Tiffany's managing to ruin me here too.

My rumination is broken when the office receptionist, Ms. Flowers, enters the room with clipped steps. She has a murmured discussion with the teacher before demanding, "Melanie Slate.

Come to the office. Bring your stuff."

Thank God. Get me out of here.

I quickly pack my bag and follow a rather pissy Ms. Flowers down the winding halls to the main office. We enter, and I'm escorted to Principal McGregor's office in the back.

Principal McGregor looks tired. A girl I vaguely remember from my fourth-period class is sitting across from him. She's a swishy ponytail clone like all the other cheerleaders in this place. I survey her blue-and-yellow uniform and *enormous* bow with internal disdain.

Principal McGregor steeples his hands, his elbows resting on his desk. "Melanie, I need you to put your belongings on the floor next to me."

I round the corner of the desk and deposit my backpack. I sit in the spot the principal indicates and then hit him with nearly dead eyes.

"Theresa, what does the necklace look like?"

Theresa side-eyes me, seeming terrified. "It's a silver locket on a chain," she whispers. Meekly, she gestures in my direction with her finger. "She put it in the front pouch of her backpack on Friday."

I snort. "I put MY locket in my backpack, but it's not floating around in the pouch Little Miss Accusation over here suggested," I say defensively. "My locket's in the zipper coin section of my wallet."

Principal McGregor hefts my backpack on the table. "I'm doing a full belongings search."

"Does it make ANY difference that I'm telling you I didn't take anything from her? I've never stolen something in my life."

Principal McGregor levels me with a condescending look as he unzips the largest section of the backpack.

"Guess not," I mutter under my breath.

"Hoodie. Correct?"

I give him a baffled look. "Yes, sir, that is indeed a hoodie."

He pulls out my notebook. "Notebook. Correct?"

"I'm sensing a pattern. Science notebook. Check." *This guy's gonna go through this bizarre ritual with every item.*

Principal McGregor takes out the rest of my notebooks in one clump. "Let's speed this up. Notebooks."

Sarcastically, I grin. "Very good. Those *are* notebooks."

My phone comes out next. "Phone."

"Phone," I repeat.

"Hairbrush."

"Hairbrush."

He turns red and pulls out the pack of condoms.

I grin from ear to ear at him. "Come on!" I tease. "Say it! You can do it."

"Condoms," he says quietly.

"Correct!" I bellow. "Condoms."

"Why do you have condoms in your backpack at school?" the principal asks incredulously.

"Well, sir, you never know when a good time'll pop up in third period," I quip.

"We have rules about sexual activity at school," Principal McGregor says gruffly.

With an aghast expression, I sarcastically blurt, "There goes my popularity plan! I guess I'll have to lean on my charming personality to make friends."

Theresa laughs a little and gives me a slightly warmer and more accepting look. Apparently, my abrasive humor has burned through her suspicion that I'm a kleptomaniac.

My face scrunches up. "*Why* do you care what I have in my backpack?" I ask irritably. "Nothing you've pulled out has anything to do with Theresa's lost locket."

He finally gets sick of the process and turns my backpack over, shaking out the remaining contents. Principal McGregor picks up my wallet and unzips the little pouch.

"Quite the production you just went through to get to this step that you could've started with," I say.

He pulls my locket out and holds it up. "Is this the locket you're missing?"

Theresa turns red and almost imperceptivity shakes her head. "I apologize, Melanie," she says. "I just assumed."

I raise an eyebrow her way. "You assumed *what*?"

She blushes. "Everyone's saying you're a witch, so when my locket went missing, I thought you took it."

"I've been called a lot of things, but Klepto-Witch is a new one."

Principal McGregor cracks a smile, fighting to control his amusement.

Screw it. I'm going for big air. I stand and haphazardly stuff my items in my backpack, clearing space on the principal's otherwise tidy desk. I drop the backpack on my assigned seat and gesture for the principal to move. "I need space. I'm going to do something *witchy*."

He jumps up so quickly, his rolling chair bounces into the wall. He scurries around the desk and stares at me. I hop up on the desk and face my captive audience. I sit cross-legged, putting the back of my hands on my knees in an overexaggerated mediation pose. A dramatic breath, and I, "Oooooooooooohhhhhmmmmmmmmmm." In a deep, dragging voice, I say, "Spiriiits of lost thiiiings, guide me. Ssshow me where Theresa's locket iiiis."

Though she can't sense it, I riffle through Theresa's memories until I get to the moment she went through her backpack that day. In the memory, I see Theresa's hand grab a compact. She puts on a heavy coat of horrific cotton-candy-pink lipstick. She tosses the lipstick back in the little pouch of her backpack. Out of the corner of her memory, I watch the locket get snapped into the compact as she closes it before pulling her empty hand back and grabbing her pencil to work on her assignment.

I pop open my eyes and condescendingly inform Principal McGregor, "Front pocket of Theresa's backpack, inside her purple glitter compact."

Theresa hesitantly pulls out the compact. A delicate silver chain dangles a bit from the side. She opens the compact and pulls out a tiny heart-shaped locket.

"Voila!" I say sarcastically. "Mystery solved."

Principal McGregor's mouth flops open. "How did you *do* that?" he squawks.

I hop off his desk. "Witch, remember?" I chirp.

"Thank you, Melanie," Theresa says bashfully. "I'm so sorry."

I hit her with a dirty look. "Now for the klepto part." I snag a rubber band from a supply organizer on the corner of the principal's desk. "I'm stealing this. Can't find my hair tie."

"I'm sorry, Melanie," the principal says sincerely.

"I've tried really hard to fit in at this school," I tell him with tired eyes. "I don't need these assumptions. I don't steal from others."

The principal turns a weighted look toward Theresa. "I took you at your word that there was a problem. Please be more thorough before you accuse another student of something like this."

"Yes, sir," Theresa says, head hanging.

I throw my hair back in a ponytail and toss my backpack on my shoulder before breezing out.

CHAPTER 23

I smile to myself as I ignore the show on the TV. I'm so excited about the movie. Mom helped me pack after dinner, and I can't wait. I just have to get through tomorrow, and then we leave.

There's a knock at the front door.

Rich gives me a look. "It's a little late."

"I didn't invite anyone over," I assure.

I follow Rich to the door. He opens it, revealing Trey.

He looks cautiously upset. "Hey, I'm sorry for the invasion."

"Is everything okay?" Rich asks.

It's ten on a school night, and we're not speaking, so Trey must have a reason for coming over.

Trey nods, but it's caged. "I was hoping to talk to Melanie for a few minutes. I promise I won't stay long."

Rich gestures him in before hugging me. "I'm headed to bed. Make sure to lock up after Trey leaves." He says goodnight to Trey and leaves down the hall. I hear my parents' bedroom door close.

Alone, I look at Trey with caged eyes. "Why are you here?"

"I know you're mad at me, but this is important," he says quietly. "I need to show you something."

I follow him to the den. He swings his backpack off his shoulder and unzips it.

With a VHS tape in hand, he says, "You might want to sit down."

"What's happening, Trey?" I ask as dread froths in my gut.

He slides the tape into the machine before sitting next to me. Trey looks in my eyes intensely. "I want you to know that I love you, and I'm here because I care. I'm not trying to cause problems for you. I'd rather you heard this from me than get blindsided."

"Cryptic, and possibly conniving," I reply quietly.

"I'm not trying to con you. The last thing I want to do is deal with this. I'd much rather find a charming way to weasel back into your good graces."

I roll my eyes.

Trey hits play, and a gossip show clip comes on. My brow furrows. Everyone knows that *Splash TV* is a pain in the ass. Celebrities despise the hosts, but they offer thorough gossip reports. Their exuberant reporter, Franky Fabulous, barks out, "Coming to you live, let's check in with A-lister Zane Drell."

"Oh no," I breathe. "Zane hates paparazzi."

The camera jostles a bit as it follows Franky Fabulous's swishing hips down a pathway. The view between two iron fenceposts comes into focus before the camera operator stuffs the video camera through the posts and zooms in. There's Zane leaning close to Molly Horwitz at a patio dinner table.

"This aired live an hour ago," Trey informs.

"Looks like Eden is the newest celebrity hot spot," Franky says excitedly, just as Zane passionately kisses Molly. *Passionate* isn't even the word. Those two burn red-hot, and the public display is cringe inducing.

"He hates her," I murmur. My heart hurts.

We watch a few more moments before the clip ends.

Trey hits stop before taking the tape from the machine and returning it to his backpack. "I'm sorry, Melanie." He kneels by my side.

"I'm not dating Zane," I inform softly.

"You're really not?"

I shake my head. "I'm too young for him. We're just friends." My clenched stomach and the pain in my chest defy my pronouncement. It's true that I've fallen for Zane. But it's also true that he's free to do as he pleases.

Fighting not to tear up, I close my eyes. Losing the battle to remain stoic, hot tears fall down my cheeks. I can't stop them. The last thing I want to do is cry about this in front of Trey. He sits next me without saying anything.

I cry for a while before finally whispering, "I'm sorry. I know this is ridiculous."

"No, it's not," Trey says compassionately. "I knew you'd be hurt, and I didn't want you to find out in public in case you fell apart."

"Thank you," I manage to get out.

Gathered, I look in his eyes.

"I love you, Melanie," he says calmly.

There's something about his face in the lamplit intimacy of my quiet house.

"I'm so sorry we've had issues," he says. "I'm sorry I've been a jerk. I'm sorry for everything that happened at Mabel's, and my indiscretions that led up to it. I'm sorry that you're sixteen and in love with an older guy. I'm sorry for all of this, but I'm here for it."

"I can't believe you're here for it," I reply. "You usually run from deeply personal."

He smiles. "I can't be an idiot forever, right?"

I laugh a little. "It means a lot that you showed me."

"What do you want to do about what you just saw?"

I shrug. "There's nothing to be done. He's not mine, and he's free to slop about any way he sees fit." I grimace at the blank TV screen. "Gross, though."

"It was . . . sloppy," Trey says with disgust.

When I shudder, he chuckles at my expression.

Trey appears a little unsure as he starts to stand. Against my better judgment, I say, "Trey, the way you handled that apology was exactly right."

"Yeah?" he asks hopefully.

I nod.

"I talked to Sheila today," he says. "Presley filled me in on the girls talking about you in first period. She was mortified by what the girls at your school did." He winces. "Sheila didn't understand at the time that the flyers were distributed what was wrong with you. She has a brother with a degenerative disease. She said her mom sat her down after the cheerleaders squealed and carried on about the flyers they distributed the first day at Hollywood. Her mom explained that it's like what her brother Scott goes through every day. Scott's in a wheelchair, I guess. Sheila felt terrible."

"I suppose it's nice of her to realize it, even though it's too late."

Trey quirks his mouth. "Hollywood High isn't against you anymore. Tanner spread that Sheila ruined you at your new school, and she's joined Tiffany among the most unpopular. She's being eaten alive."

"Can't help her with that," I say with a shrug. "Karma's a mean one."

Trey heads to the door with his hands stuffed in the pockets of his letterman jacket. He exits to the porch before turning around and looking at me wistfully, like he wishes there was something else he could say or do. "Goodnight, Melanie."

"Goodnight, Trey."

I close the door and slide down the wall, my tush thumping the floor. Tears pour.

I have no idea what I was thinking. Of course, Zane Drell isn't interested. He's got women like Molly after him, and I'm just a kid.

CHAPTER 24

Today can't end soon enough. Heartbroken over Zane, I tossed and turned all night. Yeah, I already know it's idiotic of me to think Zane and I would ever be together. Sometimes the sixteen-year-old girl in me shines through, and it chaps my ass.

I'm waiting in the cafeteria line, a touch peeved that it's taking forever. Today might be my last day before heading out for filming, but that doesn't mean it hasn't been painful. I've been on the receiving end of dirty looks, hostility, and snotty one-liners. Apparently, the reality of my edgy past, in combination with my supposed success, coupled with my pants-crapping summer, hasn't been well received. Sheila's cousin's friend, along with her posse of ass-bags, have spread my dirt far and wide. Trevor's friends are pleasant with me when we pass in the halls, but I can't sit with them anymore due to their concern about reputation by association. There's no loyalty in this lackluster swamp. The only thing worse than Hollywood High is this normal high school full of numb-brained slugs.

I pay for my lunch and make my way to an empty table.

Just as I get to my little corner spot, a catty voice behind me says, "What's up, Tattoo?"

I roll my eyes. *Damn it. Here we go.*

A slow turn reveals the school bully, Cassidy, who I've managed to evade thus far. Looks like my luck's run out. I've been dreading this. Cassidy is the quintessential tough girl. Hefty in both reputation and girth, she rules this place with fear and cheap one-liners. I survey her cargo shorts and *Who farted?* shirt with disdain.

"Hello, Cassidy. How can I help you?"

Cassidy stamps her foot and cocks her lumpy hip. "New giiirl," she sort of growls.

I cock my head quizzically, unsure if she's hitting on me or just catching a whiff of fresh victim. Either way, she isn't getting anywhere with me.

Out of nowhere, she slaps my lunch tray out of my hand. The entire room hushes, every pair of eyes on us.

Cassidy radiates hostility in waves, clearly waiting to see what I do.

I amp up, radiating back how much she really doesn't want to do this. My dark-water side rises, and I welcome it.

Surprise crosses her face, but to her credit, she doesn't step back.

Just when the tension's so thick I could cut it with a knife, she lunges. I step gracefully aside, and she falls off-balance, stumbling into the table behind me.

I sigh and make eye contact with the duty teacher across the way. "Didn't touch her."

The teacher stands frozen in place. Apparently, fights are rare around here. Cassidy bullies people all the time, but they generally submit to her and things don't escalate to this point.

Cassidy rights herself and turns like a lumbering bull. She swings wildly as she plows toward me. I hop over a table nimbly and watch as Cassidy fails to stop and slams her knee into the bench attached to the table.

I give the duty teacher another pointed look. "Again, I didn't touch her."

Cassidy finishes hopping about in pain and turns on me with a roar.

"Incoming," Trevor caws.

My lips twitch with the effort not to laugh.

Cassidy hefts herself onto the table, and it groans and creaks as she slogs over.

"Damn, that's asking a lot of a defenseless table," Jerome mutters, earning smattered laughter from the otherwise silent room.

I step onto the attached bench and ping-pong skip over the table to the other side.

"The table didn't protest *that* time," Trevor mutters.

Cassidy pants and gasps, sweating profusely while she glares at me from the other side of the table.

I turn to the duty teacher and spread my hands wide. "Guess what I didn't do? Touch Cassidy!"

Jerome, Trevor, and Bethany all howl with laughter from their vantage at the table next to the showdown. Given how popular they are, their laughter apparently offers permission to the rest of the slack-mouth students, who all double over cackling.

I take a deep breath, intentionally maintaining a straight face so I can't be accused of making fun of Cassidy. Cassidy bellows and leaps at surprising speed over the table. Left with no other choice, I drop to the ground and roll under two tables, springing up and grinning at an exhausted Cassidy.

I turn to the duty teacher, but before I can say it, she says, "I know, I know. You didn't touch Cassidy. Come on, you two. We're headed to the office."

"Wait, *I'm* in trouble?"

The duty teacher nods. "Rules state that everyone in a fight get suspended for a week, regardless of who started it."

"Of course they do. How logical."

Whatever, I think triumphantly. *I leave for New York tomorrow anyway.*

— —

Somehow, it turns out that my parents listed Trey as my third emergency contact in the event they were unavailable to pick me up. And yep, they were unavailable. So now, even though Trey and I aren't exactly on the best terms, the universe seems to be pushing us together once again. I slide into his passenger seat and inhale. Even though there are about a dozen people I'd rather be riding with at the moment, I find relief washing over me. His car always smells like home.

"Thank you *so* much for picking me up," I say spastically as Trey gets into the driver's seat. "Rich is in a big production meeting all day, and Mom has jury duty. Guess you were next on the emergency contact list."

"Where's your car?" Trey asks.

"In the shop for maintenance. I was supposed to take the bus, but I apparently can't be trusted to grace campus for the remainder of the day." I wobble my head sarcastically.

He pans an amused gaze my way. "What did you DO?"

"I *didn't* get in a fight with 'Who farted.'"

"What?"

I nod, sharing in Trey's confusion. "She was the girl who was glaring at me from the other office chair. You have to see this." I hold a hand his way, and he takes it. I pass the memory of the cafeteria showdown.

Trey closes his eyes and melts into the center console, howling laughter. Done with the memory, his eyes open. "Canoga Park High is insane," he says.

"You have no idea."

Trey shrugs. "Well, at least we're talking again."

"I guess," I commiserate, accepting the bizarre bonding moment. "Since we're talking again, I should tell you that my intuition's nagging at me. Something big is coming."

Trey shifts next to me and narrows his eyes. I send him a thought bubble of the intuitive information I've been picking up. He looks to the side, his eyes un-focusing as he studies it. After a time, he shakes his head to clear it. "It involves school, a large crowd, and a lot of heavy weight. That's all I can figure out."

"That's a good description. Not sure what else it means." I shrug. "I'm sorry about today. I swear I'm doing *nothing* that should get me in trouble."

"I know," he says quietly. "Will you let me take you to lunch since I don't feel like going back to school today?"

Deciding that we've earned lunch, I side-eye him hopefully. "Jinky's Café?"

He grins. "Jinky's it is."

— —

Just as we finish lunch, my cell phone rings.

I answer, and Ms. Alice asks, "Can you leave school? I need to meet with you."

"I'm already off for the day. Should I head to your office?"

"Yes, please," she says before hanging up without saying goodbye.

I look quizzically at Trey. "You up for taking me to the Alice Agency?"

"Of course." Trey's brow furrows. "What's up?"

I shrug. "Maybe there's more paperwork for the movie." I bounce in my seat. "I'm so freaking excited."

He puts cash in the payment folder. We head to his car, and I give him the address. The drive proves to be quick, as the office is right down the street. Trey wheels into a spot in the underground garage. We take a trip up the glass elevator to the sixth floor.

The doors open, and Ms. Alice's assistant, Bianca, is waiting for us. "Come with me, Melanie," she rushes to say. "Please wait here," she says to Trey.

Nervously, he takes a seat in the luxuriously modern waiting room. I glance over my shoulder at him. A bad feeling about this meeting creeps up. Bianca is clearly all a tizzy.

I open my connection with Trey so he can listen in as I follow Bianca down the hall at something close to a jog. She opens an office door, revealing Ms. Alice screaming at Zane. My eyes snap wide as she bellows, "What the HELL were you thinking?"

Bianca quickly closes the door. Considering that we couldn't hear the screaming as we approached, my guess is that Ms. Alice is trying to keep this raging fight under wraps in what seems to be a soundproof office.

"Melanie," Ms. Alice barks, "we have a problem."

"What did I do?" I ask sheepishly.

"YOU didn't do anything but try your best," Ms. Alice bellows. She points at Zane. "He, on the other hand, is at the very top of my *incredibly* impressive shit list right now."

With big eyes, I look to Zane. My heartbreak bubbles at the sight of him, and it's so strong, I have to fuzz out Trey.

"Don't, Melanie," he sends. *"I need to know what's happening in case I have to get you out of there. I already know you're upset about Zane."*

"Fix it, and I swear to you, there will never be an issue again," Zane is pleading.

"FIX it? How would you like me to fix this, Zane?" Ms. Alice shouts this so loudly that I involuntarily take a few steps back. She leans aggressively toward Zane from the other side of her desk. "If I had a TIME MACHINE, I could!" She throws her hands in the air. "*Eden*, Zane? Really? That place wasn't even on the *map* before last night!" Her eyes narrow. "HOW do you think that weasel got wind you would be there?"

Even though I'm clearly not the problem, my face burns fuchsia along with Zane's.

Ms. Alice takes a massive breath that explodes on the exhale before calmly turning to me. "I need to be the one to fill you in on what happened at a tacky little porn hut last night."

"I already know," I inform bashfully. "I saw the footage."

Zane's face goes slack. Just after he hits the white-as-a-sheet phase of shock, bright-red humiliation starts creeping up his neck.

"*While I don't want you with Zane, you just got proof that he loves you too,*" Trey sends.

"*Not helpful,*" I send back.

"How is Eden a tacky porn hut?" I ask Ms. Alice.

She rolls her eyes. "Before Zane decided to turn it into a Motel 6, it was where all the porn stars ate. No one credible would ever be caught dead there. Now, it's overrun with hopeful starlets." She glares at Zane. "Starlets who want to be the next hussy he humps in the flower bed."

"I didn't hump Molly in the flower bed," Zane insists.

"No, you just groped her, slathered your tongue in her ear on *national* television, and then FELL as you exited the building! Thank GOD you tumbling ass over teakettle down the stairs wasn't caught on film, but it's sure making its way through the gossip circuit."

I whimper a little. "Ew."

"Yeah, Melanie. Ew." Ms. Alice sighs before asking me to sit.

Dread bubbling in my gut, I take the offered chair.

"I have some news, and as your agent, I have to be the one to deliver it," Ms. Alice gently says as she takes a seat behind her desk.

"This isn't about paperwork, is it?" I ask, barely over a whisper.

She shakes her head. "No, sweetheart, it isn't. When everyone heads to New York tomorrow, you won't be going."

"But my parents signed the consent forms. I'm allowed to travel."

Ms. Alice's expression sags with regret. "That's not the issue." She glares at Zane. I look his way, and he has his hands over his face, standing frozen behind the chair next to me.

"Melanie," Ms. Alice says gently, "I know Molly. She's a manipulative schemer. She suggested Eden because there's clear views for the paparazzi. I guarantee she called Franky Fabulous after Zane agreed to have dinner with her. She set up that exclusive for *Splash TV*."

"Why?" I ask, not understanding.

Somehow, Ms. Alice's expression becomes more pained. "Heaven help me," she breathes. "You're so new to this." She sighs. "Melanie, this industry isn't what it seems. Molly asked out Zane, got him drunk, and intentionally made sure they were filmed. *Glamour* has an erotic edge to it. The producers were already concerned about your age, but they were on board until they saw the footage of Zane all over Molly. I guarantee Molly personally delivered a tape at the crack of dawn." Ms. Alice takes my hand. "Long story short, you've been replaced in the movie."

As I gasp out loud, Trey gasps in my head.

"I signed a contract," I whimper in disbelief.

"The contract has a retraction clause," Ms. Alice explains. "They have the legal right to rescind. It makes zero difference that Molly manipulated the situation. In this business, all that matters is the look they're after. I've tried all morning to stop this, and there's nothing I can do." She glares at Zane.

Shock ricochets through my rattling brain. My mind and body are suddenly numb as I process the news. I send to Trey, *"I so badly wanted to do this movie."*

"I know, love. Wrap this up and we'll talk."

I collect enough of myself to manage, "Everyone at school hates me because of the movie. When it comes out that I got canned, maybe I'll have friends again."

Ms. Alice squeezes her eyes closed, and her head drops. It takes her a moment to get back to a professional expression. "It's not going to help, Melanie. The people at school are going to turn on you worse now. Before, I guarantee you faced jealousy. Now, you'll face scrutiny. I've been through this with teen talent before."

"Wonderful." I exhale hard, pulling a little resilience from my core. "That's not new. I've been made fun of before. I can take it."

Zane collapses in the chair next to me with his left hand over his face. When he finally drops his hand, his cheeks are wet. "I'm begging you to get your legal team on this," he pleads of Ms. Alice. He points my way. "I guarantee the producers are making a mistake."

Ms. Alice arrogantly leans back in her chair with her hands laced in her lap. "You think I didn't meet with legal? There's nothing they can do. *You* are the problem, not the ironclad contract. You know better than anyone that in this industry, you lie low, keep your brain intact, and your dick in your PANTS."

Tears continue to fall as Zane wrestles with himself. "It's one thing for me to ruin my own career and reputation, but . . ." He looks my way and can't seem to speak through his tight throat.

"But," Ms. Alice finishes for him, "it's another to ruin Melanie's big break." Zane nods wordlessly, and Ms. Alice's tone softens. "I'm going to say it, so we all understand. Zane, you've not only ruined Melanie's big break—a break that, as we both know, is as rare as being struck by lightning—but you also destroyed this opportunity for *Pierre's girl*. THAT is what makes me the maddest. Pierre would have done anything to help her."

Zane leans forward, his face in his hands.

I decide that my purpose at this meeting has been fulfilled. "Thank you for meeting with me, Ms. Alice," I say, coming to my feet.

She steps around her desk and hugs me hard. "I'm so sorry, Melanie. You have my word that I'm going to submit you for every audition that comes across my desk. One way or another, we're going to get you there." She smiles conspiratorially. "The Zane route was too easy. Let's claw our way to the top like everyone else does." She squeezes my arms. "It'll mean more."

"Yes, ma'am," I say dejectedly.

"Hey," Ms. Alice adds, "you're gorgeous, talented, and adorable." She smiles. "You're also so incredibly professional. I've never had anyone take news as stoically as this. You're going to make it."

"Thank you," I reply bashfully.

Ms. Alice heads for the door and opens it for me. Trey takes two steps in as the door opens. I cross to him, and he drapes his arm around my waist, careful not to hug me for fear that I'll cry.

"Trey," Ms. Alice says, "it's good to see you again."

He nods formally. "Ma'am." His gaze slides to Zane, and he says nothing, maintaining a tightly professional expression. Trey chuckles a little, breaking the tension, as he steers his gaze my way. "Wanna go to Eden? I hear that's where all the hopeful starlets hang out."

I spurt surprised laughter. "Only if you defile me in the flower bed."

Zane looks like he wants to die.

Trey chuckles, squeezing my waist as he steers me through the door.

Ms. Alice laughs from behind us. "I'm proud of you, Melanie."

I look over my shoulder. "Thank you."

Zane is behind Ms. Alice, and he doesn't even look like himself. His expression is so full of regret, remorse, heartbreak, and humiliation that it's painful to witness.

"I hope the movie goes well," I say his way sincerely. "I look forward to seeing it."

As Trey guides me away, we hear Ms. Alice say, "That girl is so sweet! She doesn't deser—" The door must have closed because her words are cut off.

Trey guides me along hallways, through the lobby, and down the elevator, but I see none of it. Now that I'm out of the office meeting, I've given into grief-filled shock. I hold it together until we get into Trey's car, where I fall apart.

Trey gathers me up, leaning me over his armrest. I sob against his chest. All my shields drop, and I pelt him with everything I've been through.

It takes a long stretch before I calm enough that Trey can let me go. When I sit up, his cheeks are soaked with tears. Considering how unemotional he usually is, what I released must have been hard to take.

He grips my cheeks. "Fuck Zane Drell, that movie, Tiffany, Jet, your broken neck, Hollywood High, me being an asshole, every damn cheerleader who's ever existed, and that joke of a school you're stuck at. You're Melanie fucking Slate, and my firebird WILL rise from the ashes. It's what you do, baby."

"Thank you." I huff and puff, scrubbing at my snotty nose.

Trey hands me a fast-food napkin he pulls from his center console. "I believe in you," he says venomously.

"Think I could hold your hand?" I ask pitifully, while I clean up tears with the napkin.

He holds his hand my way. I take it, lacing my fingers with his.

As he pulls out from his parking spot, he says, "Take the memory I've pulled. I made another collection montage for you."

"Another one of you screwing Tiffany?" I huff.

"No. This is the memory collection I *should* have given you at Mabel's."

I pull the memory and close my eyes, watching all the moments since we met when Trey's been enamored by me, and proud of me to the point of busting. I can feel his emotions in each snippet, and it seems that he really does love me. It's truly beautiful. I don't have any idea what to do about it.

CHAPTER 25

Dread sits heavy in me as I pull into the parking lot at school. It's my first day back from my long suspension. I spent a lot of time reading in my room. It seemed better than sobbing about everything I can't fix. My parents were furious about my movie role loss, but they confirmed with Ms. Alice that nothing could be done about it. Zane Drell is quite thoroughly in the doghouse with them. My mom invited Trey to dinner several times, and he's back in their good graces. He's still in the friend zone with me, but we've managed to have fun without all the *together* pressure. I smile a little, recalling how he showed my parents the *Splash TV* clip of Zane slobbering all over Molly. They fumed, right up until Trey gleefully announced that there's another videotape. He popped that one in, and we laughed our asses off at Zane's literal fall from grace right down the stairs of Eden. This hadn't appeared on the first airing of the saga on *Splash* because their cameras hadn't caught it. But when a passerby came forward with the footage, the *Splash* producers happily paid for the rights to it.

Let's see how this goes, I think as I get out of my car.

Heads turn, scrutiny abounds, and everyone stares. Feeling feisty, I raise an eyebrow. My hips sway as I pound down the sidewalk, my motorcycle boots clacking aggressively. I've decided to be me, and have dressed accordingly.

Out of nowhere, I feel a hard tug on the back of the studded belt draped as an accessory statement across my hips. I snarl and whip around, snapping my rear hard to the side and dislodging my belt from the intrusive hand.

I unintentionally send fear down the line to Trey. It tears down the blockage I have up, and he pops into my mind, watching. I hear him say to our friends at Hollywood High, *"Hush!"*

Cassidy steps up toe-to-toe with me.

"Didn't even make it through the front gate."

Trey snarls in my mind.

I glare as Cassidy hisses, "Whatcha gonna do, Has-Been?"

She towers over me, attempting to swallow my personal space. Pissed, I flex my energy shield, allowing it to bubble around me. I accidentally send my plan to Trey and feel his eyes snap wide.

"Don't, Melanie! They won't know how to handle it if you out yourself like that!"

Cassidy narrows her beady eyes at me. "Melanie lost her movie role," she announces loudly enough for everyone within thirty yards to hear. "It was announced on *Splash*."

Laughter peels from the curious spectators.

"Game on."

Trey gasps. *"Shit."*

I push hard, straining nearly to snapping from the effort. The bubble I've created presses against Cassidy and meets with resistance. I draw every ounce of energy I can, pulling it from the crowd when my stress-depleted reserves give out. People sag and gasp as I drain them. I mentally push, forcing the larger girl back. Her feet skid as I march her fifteen feet down the sidewalk. A wave of rage boils in me, and I launch Cassidy in a wide arch through the air. She smacks into a tree trunk. The straining effort nearly buckles me.

I hear the principal exclaim to my right, "What was THAT?"

It seems like the entire school is gaping at me.

"Damn, baby!" Trey fills in my Hollywood friends on what just occurred.

Cassidy stands, her legs shaking with fear. She runs full bore in my direction. When she gets almost to me, I hit her with a well-placed little energy pop. Her knees buckle. She plunges to the pavement and looks up at me in terror. I smirk at her.

People start murmuring around me, and I hear quite a few students call me a witch.

I glare challengingly at Cassidy. Her mouth drops open. She looks around frantically. Finding nothing else that could have caused the attack on her, she looks my way. She gasps as she realizes I did it with an invisible force.

"You're on my radar, Cassidy. I hate it here, and it's time to have some fun. Keep messing with me. I'm begging you!" I send out an energy shove, and Cassidy falls over backward.

She whimpers, terrified, and streams of urine puddle under her. She glances down at her plaid skirt and wet legs. Tears roll as she realizes she just wet herself in front of the whole school. Her face burns crimson.

I raise an eyebrow at her and loudly purr, "You thought you were a big dog around here. Guess what? I'm a monster, and I eat big dogs for lunch."

Cassidy scuttles back rapidly, leaving a wet snail trail in her wake. It takes her two tries before she gets to her feet and turns, loping at a cumbersome jog to the student parking lot. She jumps in her car, slams the door, and a moment later, her car screeches away.

I'm left standing next to the wet concrete spot, unsure what to do. No one in the crowd moves a muscle. The principal is blinking rapidly at me, a frozen tribute to what just occurred.

I watch through Trey's eyes as Mr. Isley steps in front him, and I hear through Trey's ears as Mr. Isley says to me, "Get out of there, NOW! Besides, I need you here for a big grant competition at noon. You're dancing."

I rattle my head and send, *"I'm WHAT?"*

Trey relays the message.

Mr. Isley rushes to say, "Kendra can't dance yet. I need you to take one for your old team. Our program needs to win this competition."

"I know about the grant. My school's busing the theater and dance kids over."

Trey passes on the message.

Mr. Isley asks Trey, "Can you look and tell me what she sees?"

I scan the crowd, and Trey tells Mr. Isley, "She's on the front walkway outside the school. She's surrounded by hundreds of people, and the principal is about ten yards to her right."

Mr. Isley instructs, "Melanie, don't say a word. Walk with purpose to your car. Don't slow down, and don't do anything to cause alarm. Get out of there NOW!"

I start walking.

I hear the principal yell behind me, "Melanie, get back here!"

The crowd's energy suddenly spirals toward violence, and I'm positive I'm about to be attacked by the tense mob.

Trey feels the vibe through me and frantically orders, *"RUN, Melanie!"*

I take off running.

Demitri demands in a panic, "Trey, what's happening to her?"

"Mob. Hang on. She's running."

I make it to my car just ahead of the rushing crowd. I slam the door closed and hit the lock button right as Principal McGregor gets to my car. Flustered, I drop my keys and search for them on the floorboard.

People start pounding on the car.

Trey says aloud for our friends to hear, "She's in the car. Melanie, stop panicking. Find the keys." He sends a wave through our connection, laced with Demitri's calm energy from the hand he puts on Trey's shoulder.

My head clears and my hand makes contact. I snatch the keys up, shove the right one in the ignition, and my car roars to life. Careful not to hit anyone, I pull out of the parking spot and drive away.

"She made it out," Trey informs. "She's headed here."

Through our connection, I hear my friends collectively exhale, relieved.

CHAPTER 26

Arch puts an arm around me, and we set a brisk pace for the theater building. We run up the stairs, and my legs feel like gelatin when we get to the top. When my knees buckle, I hold on to the railing and fight the fear that my brain stem condition has somehow returned. Arch picks me up, hauling me through the door that Mr. Isley holds open.

Mr. Isley shuts the door behind us, and Bear and Darren step to me, each grabbing one of my shaky hands. Demitri stands in front of me and puts his hands on either side of my head. They all close their eyes, and my head drops. I'm quaking with exhaustion. My knees shake.

"Her energy stores are so low," Bear says. "She's running on fumes."

"No physical injuries," Demitri says.

"Are you sure my condition hasn't returned?" I beg. "My legs gave out on the stairs!"

Demitri shakes his head. "It's just energy backlash."

Darren asks Ms. G, "How long until Trey can get here?"

Ms. G checks her watch. "He finishes his test in thirty minutes."

"We don't have thirty minutes," Bear says in a panic. "He has to refill her. They have an energy line. Any of us could do it, but our energy is so different from hers that it'll give her a splitting headache and make her violently ill. She won't be able to dance at the competition."

Darren says to me, "Send a pulse to Trey that we need him here, and fast."

After a moment of effort that makes me see stars, I shake my head. "I can't." My nose starts bleeding, dripping down my chin. Suddenly, it's pouring like a fountain.

"Shit," Darren says. "I shouldn't have suggested that. The effort of trying to reach Trey just drained what was left and pushed her over the edge."

Mr. Isley rushes through the lobby doors. He runs back in with paper towels and says to Ms. G, "Radio for Trey. He must come now. Make something up if you have to." He turns to Arch. "Call Melanie's parents. They need to get over here. She isn't a student here anymore and we need authorization to treat her."

Ms. G snorts. "I'm Mom around here. I'll make decisions for her if I need to. Her parents trust me."

Despite it all, I find myself appreciating how nice it is that Ms. G and Mr. Isley are both energy workers, and we don't have to explain this madness.

When I start to see stars again, Bear and Mr. Isley lower me to the ground. They put me on my back, and the blood pools in my throat. I gurgle around it and turn over, swallowing it. It's revolting. Blood runs from my nose in gushing quantities. I hold the paper towels to my face, but they're completely saturated. Blood oozes all over the carpet and drips in long, sticky lines down my neck.

"We need to call an ambulance," Ms. G says.

Bear shakes his head. "If you send her to the hospital, they won't know how to help her. When she attacked that girl with her energy, she emptied every reserve she had. She must have already been running low. It's hard to reach a meditative state with the kind of pressure she's been under. Once Trey's here, he can fix the energy problem, and in turn, the bleeding should stop."

Ms. G unclips her radio from her belt and pushes the button. "Main office, I need Trey Valdez in the theater building immediately. He's in Mr. Sanchez's chemistry class. They're in the middle of a test, but he needs to drop everything and rush this way."

Darren runs in with a wastebasket, plunking it in front of me. I lean over it. Blood gushes faster from my nose as panic makes my heart race. What's pouring down my throat makes it hard to breathe. I blink rapidly, my breathing bubbly.

"Can you stop the bleeding?" Bear asks Demitri.

"It's not coming from an injury."

"Long shot, but you and Melanie are close. No chance you have a soulmate connection, right?" Darren asks. "She seems to collect soulmates like most people collect bad habits."

"I'm his Fraggle, not his soulmate," I manage to joke raspingly through the blood in my throat.

Ms. G's radio buzzes to life, and the office secretary says, "Mr. Sanchez's classroom phone isn't operational. We sent Tiffany, our TA, to grab him."

I laugh weakly. *Tiffany of all people.*

"The universe certainly has a sense of humor today!" Darren says sarcastically.

Arch comes back from the lobby and announces, "Melanie's parents are on the way. They said they can be here in forty-five minutes. In the meantime, they've given Trey first right on medical decisions, and the rest of us are authorized in his absence."

Someone pounds on the double doors, and Arch rushes to open it.

Just as Trey and Tiffany run through the door, my stomach heaves. I groan out, "Oh NO," and throw up into the wastebasket the gushing tidal wave of blood that had settled in my stomach.

"What the HELL is happening?" Trey screams.

When the heaving stops, I tip my head back, trying to catch my breath. I'm coated in a sticky, crimson slick from my mouth to my waist.

"That was insane." Arch's eyes are huge.

I make eye contact with Tiffany and rasp out, "Nice to see you again, Twenty-Two."

Her eyes bug out of her head. "What's wrong with her?"

"Shut up, Tiffany," I snarl. My heart pounds and blood pours. I stare at Tiffany menacingly, and she seems to shrink in fear. "Your day's coming," I warn.

Bear's attention whips to Trey. "Back to the issue at hand. When Melanie energetically attacked that girl at CPH, she drained every reserve she has. Energy battle can be lethal. You need to boost her. If you need us to help you, we can, but our energy needs to funnel through you, or it'll make her sick."

Trey nods. "Kind of like the right blood type?"

"Exactly," Bear says. "Do you need me to tell you how?"

"No. Energy sharing isn't new to us."

Trey settles on the floor with his legs crossed and yanks me onto his lap. I use the last of my strength to wrap my legs around his waist. He wraps his arms around me, and I sag against him, unable to hold up my head. Blood runs down the shoulder of his white shirt and pools in the crook of his arm, but he ignores it.

He puts his hands on my back, and after a moment, says to the guys, "I can't reach her mind-to-mind. Her energy literally isn't humming at all. We usually connect mentally first."

"Figure it out, Trey," Bear says.

"Here we go, Melanie," Trey says quietly. "I'm dropping into meditation."

After a long moment, I feel a gentle radiation through his hands and into my back. It's like warm sunshine on a cold day. I shiver. My arms goose-bump and my head swims. I feel like I'm falling even though I'm sitting down. A whimper escapes me.

"You're okay," Trey murmurs. "I've got you. Drop into our connection as soon as you can. I'll meet you there."

I relax against him, and suddenly, I'm able to connect mind-to-mind with him as my energy stores rise. He clamps a shield over us, knowing how personal our energy sharing can be. We enter a common space that lives in the soulmate connection we share. I look across the space, and the Trey in my mind smiles at me.

We watch in our shared mind's eye as our energies wrap and braid, swirling and dancing around each other like they always do. His mental presence moves toward me. For the first time, his energy melds into mine like water vapor, and the two energies combine into one energetic being. We gasp as the synergy makes us buzz and hum.

His mental voice breezes through my psyche. *"MEL-anie!"* The sound encompasses everything that makes me who I am.

"Oh my God," I mentally whisper. *"What's happening?"*

"I had no idea our soulmate bond could do that."

After what feels like a lifetime, Bear's voice breaks in from what sounds like far away. "Melanie and Trey, you must come back. Melanie's breathing has evened out. I just checked her energy levels. She's okay."

Finally, I find my way back into reality. Our energy separates as I pull out of our connection, and the physical Trey grips me harder.

"Good, Mel," Bear says.

I moan and blink.

Awareness creeps in. I close my eyes, looking inside our connection. I check on Trey, and his energy is pulsing erratic.

"I'm good," I croak out, "but Trey's not. He won't stop until I'm full, and it's going to hurt him."

Darren and Bear move closer, fighting to pull Trey's hands off my back. He has an iron grip, his head slumped on my shoulder.

I whisper into Trey's ear, "You have to stop or it's going to hurt you."

He doesn't respond, but I understand the problem. Sharing energy like this is the most intimate connection we've ever had. It's tantric and intoxicating. Considering how disconnected we've been lately, he's lost in it.

I whisper in his mind through our connection, *"You need to come back."*

He finds his way back to awareness and eventually lets go of my back willingly.

After a moment of inner assessment, Trey calmly says to Darren and Bear, "You two need to boost me. I'm drained to the point that I'm going to fall over if I try to stand."

Bear and Darren kneel behind Trey, each putting a hand on his shoulders. Trey inhales as their energy pours into him.

As soon as I know Trey's okay, the tantric energy zings and zips through me. I moan, closing my eyes. I feel high. I flop back, bonelessly lying down on the carpet with my legs still wrapped around Trey.

His head drops back, and he sharply inhales. His eyes roll into the back of his head. "God, that's incredible."

He reaches out, pulling up my sticky, blood-soaked shirt. He puts his hand flat on my stomach, and the energy pulses back and forth. My head lolls, my eyes rolling back. He chuckles seductively as he watches my response.

The rest of our friends choose that moment to rush through the double doors. They catch a glimpse of the bizarre scene and freeze mid-run.

"What kind of vampire Kama Sutra shit are you two into?" Presley screeches.

I wince and scoot off Trey's lap. We aren't together, and this is awkward.

Our friends glance toward the trash can full of frothy blood.

"Well, I guess it's official that Melanie's back," Hiram quips. "Shit's weird again."

Everyone laughs hesitantly, shocked by all they're seeing.

Mr. Isley shakes his head. "You all missed a hell of a show. That was the strangest thing I've EVER—"

"I'm going to be sick!" Marcus cuts in.

Tanner holds up the bloody trash can just in time for Marcus to lose his lunch in it.

Everyone grimaces. Some turn pale.

After Marcus finishes his dramatic hurling, everyone turns and stares at Tiffany, who's still crouched on the floor, white as a ghost.

"Welcome, Tiffany!" Tanner exclaims. "So glad you could join us in the cradle of Trey and Melanie's love."

We all crack up.

Trey looks her way. "I'm sure you're beyond confused."

Tiffany meets his gaze. "I was *totally* wrong about us having a bigger connection than you and Melanie!" She asks me, "Are you okay?"

I can't help but laugh. "It's just another Friday. Welcome to our normal."

"Your normal is barfing blood, and having some bizarre tantric energy connection with Trey in the middle of the auditorium during third period?"

Trey shakes his head. "The blood situation is new. The tantric connection is generally something we reserve for a more private setting. But, with me and Mel, it's always something."

"Well, all right," Ms. G barks out sarcastically. "Apparently, Melanie feels better."

Demitri hovers into my view. "Can you stand?"

I nod, and he takes me by the elbows, attempting to avoid the blood that's all over me. He slowly pulls me to my feet.

Bear and Darren help Trey to stand.

"It's never dull," I say to Trey. "Thank you for rushing over here. I was worried for a second there."

He closes his eyes. "I told you not to attack the girl at Canoga High, and you're welcome."

I smirk. "I know, but you have to admit the Cassidy energy attack was cool."

"Being your soulmate is insane," Trey says with a chuckle.

Mr. Isley glances my way. "Do you think you can still do the dance pieces?" he asks hesitantly.

"I'm rock solid to do the show."

Mr. Isley starts barking orders. "Arch, run to my office in the dance building. Behind my desk, there's a box of dance department swag. Grab two shirts and a pair of shorts."

Arch nods and scoots out the door.

Mr. Isley checks his watch. "People are going to arrive soon." He turns to me. "Go to Star Dressing Room Five. Get cleaned up." Then he turns to Susan and says, "Please move Melanie's costume to that dressing room."

Susan jogs off.

"I want Melanie onstage in forty-five minutes, in costume, hair and makeup, to run both pieces." Mr. Isley looks to Ms. G. "Be ready to fill in Melanie's parents when they arrive." He asks me,

"How honest can she be about what just happened?"

"Completely honest," I insist. "Nothing surprises them anymore."

Mr. Isley points at Tanner. "Be ready to glam her when she's not covered in blood anymore."

Tanner nods.

I jog down the audience aisle, running through the alcove to the end of the dressing room hallway. I find my assigned room and rush through. I glance at the costume rack and find that my costume's hanging right where it's supposed to be. I close the door and catch a glimpse of myself in the full-length mirror. The view is stunning. I look like a character from a horror film. My mouth, chin, neck, and chest are completely covered in blood. My shirt's stuck to me, clinging in awkward bunches.

Post-trauma fear makes my mouth run dry. I stare into the reflection of my eyes and realize that my life is cratering. My friendships, the mess at school, my relationships with Trey and Zane, and my metaphysical abilities are all haywire.

I close my eyes and inhale, deciding to enjoy being back at Hollywood High, if only for a few hours.

I pull my shirt off just as the door opens. Trey comes in, surveying me.

"Hi," I say, a little unsure.

He starts to come closer. When I take a step back, he stops, saying, "Walking in on you throwing up blood almost made my heart stop."

"It *was* a little unsettling."

"I need to wash up and change," Trey informs, tossing a dance department shirt on the makeup counter. He puts a shirt and pair of shorts on my bag. "Those are for you."

"Thank you," I reply, leaning against the counter.

Trey pulls his shirt off and washes his arms and neck. He turns to me as he starts drying off with paper towels from the dispenser next to the sink. He snags the shirt and pulls it on before surveying me. "Now that I know you aren't going to die, the blood's kinda hot."

"You're siiiiiick."

He chuckles a little.

"The universe keeps putting you right there when I need you," I say.

"Why do you think that is?" he asks with a gravelly tone.

The mood shifts with weighted seriousness.

"Because I think we're supposed—"

Before I can finish the thought, the door opens, and Tiffany comes in.

Trey looks at Tiffany like she's lost her mind. "WHAT are you doing in here?"

"Can the three of us please talk?" Tiffany implores.

"Last time I checked, there's an active restraining order that you're currently violating," I remind.

She blanches.

Trey turns to me. "Give me a few minutes, and we'll finish our talk. Rinse off."

My head drops. "You have to be kidding."

"I won't be long," Trey promises.

I go into the bathroom and close the door.

So I can hear their talk, Trey opens his side of our connection just as I step into the shower.

"I was talking with Melanie," he says to her. "I'm still trying to fix this disaster. Is there a reason you decided to saunter in here?"

"Yet again, Tiffany wins," I send to him. *"She wandered in, uninvited, and you shut down with me to deal with her. Our talk is over. Please get out of my dressing room."*

I slam my walls up tight, blocking him out.

CHAPTER 27

The second Tanner finishes my makeup and hair, the two of us stalk out of the dressing room. Trey's waiting in the hall, and he immediately steps over to stride beside us.

"What?" I mutter, not wanting anything to do with him right now.

"There's a problem onstage," Trey says sheepishly. "I'm bodyguarding."

We round the corner to the stage and find our group in a stare-down with Coach Shiela and the principal from Canoga Park High School. Since the curtain is down, the CPH dancers are all peeking pensively around the wings at the looming confrontation.

"Can today be over already?" I mutter.

"Tanner, stay on her other side," Trey says quietly. "This might come to blows."

Tanner snarls, "Already plan to."

Our trio pushes through the Hollywood dance crowd and stops next to Mr. Isley and Ms. G.

Principal McGregor demands to know how I shoved Cassidy with an invisible force. Mr. Isley counters threateningly. My dance team friends all amp up, ready for a fight.

Before I can come up with an answer, Darren calmly asks, "Are you referring to the weird earthquake we had?"

Principal McGregor glances curiously at Darren.

Bear smoothly takes up the thread. "It was the strangest thing! Some people didn't feel it at all, but just a few feet away, others were bounced off their feet." He juts a thumb Hiram's way. "This guy flew ten feet across the room and boinged right clean off the wall."

Clearly not in on the plan, Hiram fights not to laugh. He plays along, rubbing his tush. "My rump still smarts."

Trey turns his back, and his shoulders shake with silent laughter. He knocks on our connection blockage, and I drop it.

"The Canoga Park crew are naïve," I send to him, *"not stupid. That's the most asinine thing I've ever heard."*

Trey turns around, having composed himself. *"Just wait for it. They'll buy it because they're desperate for an explanation that's less terrifying than you being a supervillain."*

Sure enough, the principal nods. "I see . . . Huh. That explains it." He turns to me and adds, "I apologize, Melanie. My outburst was out of line. I don't know what I was thinking."

I send to Trey, *"This is the strangest thing I've ever seen, and we're no strangers to strange."*

The Canoga Park dance team coach points her manicured finger my way. "Melanie isn't eligible to dance for your team. She's not enrolled at your school."

"Not true," Ms. G pipes up. "The Los Angeles School District rules state that any student enrolled in the district can participate in after-school activities at any school in said district. I spoke with the district activities supervisor personally to confirm."

The coach looks like she's going to keel over.

The lead dancer from the CPH team, a usually sweet-natured redhead named Tammy, steps forward and narrows her eyes. "We're going to mop the FLOOR with you guys."

Her teammates all look at her like she's nuts.

The Hollywood High dance team fans out, all of us in our impressively bedazzled Lycra outfits. The Canoga Park team, meanwhile, stands in their matching tank tops and bicycle shorts.

Demitri raises his eyebrows. "You should have put Melanie on your team when you had the chance." He bows slightly. "Best of luck to you."

The Canoga Park crew leaves through the stage right alcove.

"Circle up," Mr. Isley says.

We gather around.

"That nonsense took up all the time we had to run our pieces." He looks my way. "Can you get through them without rehearsal?"

"I think so."

"Remember that the opening of 'If' is different because of the smoke wall." Mr. Isley looks to Demitri. "Fill Melanie in on the changes."

"Can you pull the memory of the rehearsal with the changes?" I ask him.

Demitri nods, and I take his hand, accepting the selected memory from him. I watch it on fast-forward and mentally work through what this formation change means for the transitions in the piece.

After a moment, I nod. "Got it."

Mr. Isley says, "Demitri and Melanie, you're doing the duet, but we're changing it from 'This Time' to 'Throb.'"

My eyebrows rise. "'Throb' is almost twice as fast, and the lyrics are filthy. You sure about that?"

"We're doing this our way, and I want you to smoke them," Mr. Isley snarls.

Demitri and I exchange a glance. "Kendra and I ran the piece to 'Throb' when Mr. Isley was trying to decide between the two songs. It's fast, but doable. Do you have the stamina to get through it?"

"She's still riding our energy exchange high," Trey says. "She's got this."

I give Trey a look, sending, *"I can answer for myself."*

"Sorry," he sends back. He steps to the wing, abashed.

Mr. Isley gets a curious, far-off look, contemplating. Finally, he asks, "Can you energetically boost them when 'If' hits the instrumental hum in the middle of the song before the second big build?"

I think about it, remembering when I juiced Presley, Finley, and Valerie at Arch's party during my dark-water issues phase. I smile and nod. "Oh yeah. I can juice them!" I make eye contact with each of the dancers, alive in the knowledge that many of them don't like me.

Tessa smiles warmly. "It's nice to have you back, Melanie." My eyebrows rise, and she adds, "We all feel bad about things. We're sorry."

"Thank you." What she has just said means a great deal to me.

"Who's in?" Mr. Isley asks.

Everyone exchanges glances. Some seem thrilled, others pensive, but all hands go up.

"Isn't this cheating?" Demitri asks.

Mr. Isley shrugs. "There's no test for performance-enhancing Melanie energy."

"Game on," I say. "When we come up on the instrumental breakdown, I'm going to freeze center stage. You all need to do the usual rat-a-tat-tat arm hits. I'm going to have very little time. Don't resist. Be open and receptive to the incoming wave. There's no fixing it if one of you doesn't take the boost. If that happens to you, get offstage because you're gonna get run over by the group."

Everyone nods, and Susan comes to us, announcing, "For now, you all need to head into the auditorium and find seats. There are eight teams competing, and ours goes last."

Trey snags my arm, stopping my trek. *"Melanie, please talk—"*

"No. I get very little time here with my friends. I'm not doing this now. You had time to talk earlier, and you wasted it by talking to Tiffany instead."

His expression falls. I rush to catch up with the dancers as Trey sends, *"I'm sorry, Melanie."*

CHAPTER 28

Hiram gestures for us to follow. We exit the auditorium seats and follow him backstage.

"Canoga Park High are taking the stage," he informs. "You guys are on deck next."

An innocent hip-hop song bounces through the speakers, and the Canoga Park team hops and skips, nods and bobs their way through the piece. They aren't bad, and the piece is cute, but it's lifeless in exactly the way I'd expected from that drudging school.

From the wings across the stage, Trevor catches my eye. He's standing next to his mom, Coach Sheila, who's maniacally spouting confusing orders to her already struggling team. She's hissing so loudly, we can hear her over the music. Trevor rubs his forehead as he surveys me. I'm unclear if it's interest or disapproval. Either way, I really don't care.

Mr. Isley steps up next to Trey, Demitri, and me. "THIS is what they challenged us with?"

I snort.

"It looks like a talent show number," he says quizzically.

"They think this is what a dance team is," I explain. "But in their defense, it's akin to what most of the other teams did also."

"I almost feel sorry for them," Demitri says. "We're bringing an Uzi to a tickle fight."

Mr. Isley chuckles. "Don't hold back. Their coach needs to learn her place."

The Canoga Park team finish their second piece and give us a collectively uppity look before running to the audience to watch our pieces.

Hiram rushes through the alcove, headed to the booth to run the lighting cues he designed for our two pieces. We're the only team that came prepared with a tech-supported show. Arch and Bear rush to place smoke machines in the first and third wings on each side of the stage.

Once they're set, Susan whispers, "Places."

Demitri and I take our places, and the dark stage fills as the smoke machines hiss ominously. The lights slowly build in silence, casting an intense and moody red.

I make eye contact with Demitri across the way, and he nods at me as the first beats of "Throb" moan through the speakers. We jazz walk toward each other, strutting and swaying. Demitri seductively raises one eyebrow, and I smirk as he takes me into a firm tango stance.

The vocals purr, and we start the intricate, weaving-and-snaking footwork section. Demitri shifts his handhold unexpectedly, and I grab his extended finger overhead out of habitual training. He preps and spins me through pirouette finger turns. The speed is unreal, and I spot rapidly as he gets seven turns out of me in four counts before yanking me back into the planned choreography.

My eyes widen as I look at him like he's lost his mind. "Where did that come from?"

He pulls me in, and I slide my leg up his body. "We should have practiced this piece. I forgot some things. Just follow my lead."

I huff, "Shit," as we jazz walk apart.

Mr. Isley hisses from the wing next to me, "No bluebird. Firebird-leap with an up-and-over single-rotation plank toss. Slide down Demitri when he catches you."

These guys HAVE to be kidding.

I run, hit a three-step quick-leap prep, plant my feet, and put everything I've got into a firebird. My back foot touches my head, and Demitri uses my upward momentum to toss me. I plank and hit three spinning revolutions, panicking because I lose track of what direction's up and what's down.

Demitri catches me and slides me down the front of his body. "Holy crap," he hisses. "That was crazy."

Trey pounds on the blockage I have up in our connection. I drop it, and he sends, *"Mr. Isley says the next section is what you know. He's going to warn you of a few other spots through me."*

Demitri whips me right, and I hold my weight like we rehearsed. As I curl and snake down his left side, I tell him, "Mr. Isley's warning me about adjustments through Trey. Don't worry about me. Dance your ass off."

He grins as he développés his left leg well past his usual 180 degrees, his foot expertly pointed. I scorpion over, pointing my foot while I tip my head, giving the audience a sinisterly seductive look. I roll over and land on my back. I point my toe Demitri's way. He pulls up my leg and yanks me to him in a full split against his body. He languishingly meets my eyes. The borrowed seductive energy flares in him, and my dark-water side rises to match his intensity.

Energy thrums through both of us, and Demitri's eyes widen. Trey sends instructions, and I nod slightly at Demitri. He lifts me to his shoulder. I slide through the splits down his back, and he whips around. He takes my hand, guiding me through two cha-cha footwork patterns.

Trey sends, *"Plank. That's the last change."*

I block off Trey. It's distracting having him in my head while I blister through this extravaganza.

I stiffen, and Demitri slides me to the floor. He does a brief solo before baseball sliding my way and crawling over me. I put my hands around his neck, and he looks down at me.

"Victoria and Trey *should* be mad at this point," he whispers.

"Just get through it," I whisper back. "We need to win the prize money."

We both relax, draping against each other, and hold. Demitri is suddenly quaking. My dark-water seduction surges in response to Demitri, and I gasp, my chest rising against him as tantric energy ripples aggressively from me.

He moans in my ear, "Oh my God."

He starts the log roll, and I bury my head in his neck, trying to relearn how to breathe. Everything about what's happening has my head spinning. I'm stunned by how close this energy exchange is to what I had with Pierre, and Demitri and I are still fully clothed.

God only knows what it'll be like in a dark room.

I rattle my head, trying to shake off the thought.

We stop with him on top of me, and my breath catches as we make eye contact. Demitri's eyes are heated in a way I've never seen before.

I might have to give him another shot, after all.

We go through the hand-gripping and sexy arm-grabbing section.

I whisper, "You okay?"

"Nope." Demitri pulls me to standing. He has his arms around my back. We hold, our breathing a little labored from the blazing attraction between us. He holds his arms back in a T and drags me across stage while I hang on around his neck. I arch my back, head dropped toward the audience, lips parted.

The truth is, I've never performed this well, but Demitri and I are suddenly connected. I'm apparently channeling his dance ability, and now that I am, everything about my technique and performance ability has taken a boost.

Demitri swirls me around him. I stop, melting against his back as he gasps.

We get through a split series, and I perfectly time four quick turns and a leap, wrapping my legs around his waist. He catches me and we hold, our faces so close that we're both rattling. He squeezes his eyes shut, and I put my forehead against his to keep from kissing him.

I swoop back and snake up. I body-roll twice against him, and he gets an almost pained look on his face. I close my eyes and take a deep breath to clear my rattling psyche.

He whips me through the "around the world" swing move and slides my feet between his legs, laying me on the stage. I arch my back as he hits a flawless quadruple turn. I tip my face to the audience as the music moans to a close. Demitri leans in like he's supposed to, planked over me on one arm. He lowers himself over me in a one-arm push-up as the lights slowly fade, but instead of looking at the audience, he kisses the side of my neck. I gasp on the final note of the song, and the stage goes black.

I make the mistake of turning my head. Our lips meet in the dark, and it completely stuns both of us. Things escalate as he kisses me, and I moan against his lips. We're both shaking. He slides his hand up my side and lightly bites my shoulder. Fire shoots up my spine. Totally out of control at this point, I wrap my legs around his waist and grab his jaw, pulling him to me and kissing him teasingly. He shudders and presses harder against me. I latch on tighter and moan against his shoulder.

Demitri breathes in my ear, "If you don't unlatch your legs, we're going to end up naked on this stage."

It brings me back to reality. I rattle my head while I unwrap my legs.

There's a moment of deafening silence before the crowd goes insane, cheering and clapping in the dark. I realize only seconds have passed, and I'm relieved that we haven't been lying on the dark stage for the eternity it felt like.

Demitri whispers in my ear, "Damn, baby girl. I need to clear my head." He helps me up.

"No one saw it," I whisper frantically. "Victoria doesn't know."

"What about Trey? We don't need a fistfight on our hands."

"I started fuzzing him out when things got hot. He doesn't know."

"That was insane," he whispers back. "You mad?"

I shake my head against his neck. "No. I'm floored. You mad?"

"No. I'm completely screwed up, though."

We rush offstage to the wings.

From her stage management podium, Susan says, "Sixty seconds to breathe, per competition regulations."

Victoria hands Demitri and me a water bottle each, and we both guzzle before handing them back. Trey hands us towels that we use to mop up our dripping sweat.

Demitri bends with his hands on his knees, trying to catch his breath. He looks to Trey. "Melanie's a beast. I had to fight to keep up. I don't know if I can do the next piece."

"That was the best thing I've ever seen either of you do," Mr. Isley says. "Get through 'If' and you're in the clear. You can do this."

Susan announces, "Thirty seconds."

I toss my towel by the wall. Demitri takes his place in the upstage wing next to me as Victoria and Trey both step away. He murmurs just loud enough for me to hear, "We're going to have to talk later."

"We can discuss it."

"You ready?"

I growl, "Hell yes! We just slaughtered Canoga Park High. Now it's time to bury them."

The stage goes black.

The audience screams and claps so loud, it's deafening.

I'm elated. Not only did the group take on my dark-water energy pulse, but they *flew*. I've never seen the Hollywood High dancers do what they just pulled off.

We gather in the wings.

"I've never felt anything like that before," Javier said. "That was INSANE!"

Mr. Isley rushes to us. He beams from ear to ear and bellows, "THAT'S how you dance! From now on, you do THAT!"

We all laugh.

"I can't believe I dropped you out of that arabesque," Demitri murmurs to me. "I'm sorry."

With a shrug, I decide not to admit that the problem was actually my gooey legs from our dark-stage "Throb" debacle.

The competition judge's voice rings out over the speaker system. "All dancers, please gather onstage."

Trey steps over and squeezes my hand. "I'll be in the audience. I want to watch this with your parents."

I nod and follow my teammates onto the stage. We sit in a spot downstage left, and Canoga Park's team, already looking defeated, slithers to a spot across from us.

The judges come onstage, and the lead judge says into a microphone, "We'd like to thank all our competing teams who came out today to fight for their school's opportunity to receive a HUNDRED-and-FIFTY-THOUSAND-dollar grant!"

My mouth drops open, and I send to Trey, *"A HUNDRED AND FIFTY THOUSAND?"*

"Yup. This is why we needed you. It's enough to fund all the shows for three seasons."

A drum roll thrums through the speakers, and the judge says, "Without further ado! Your grand champion in the first annual Star Shine Grant Competition is HOLLYWOOD HIGH!"

Our Hollywood crowd goes wild. I see my parents screaming and cheering next to Ms. G, and I grin at them. Demitri hops up, holding his hand my way. I take it and stand.

We cross to the judge, and he says into the microphone, "Congratulations, kids. Your pieces were amazing! Do you have anything to say?"

Demitri and I grin at each other before turning to the audience and throwing up devil horns. Our friends go wild, throwing up devil horns from the audience. We turn to the team, and they all have their arms up high, mimicking the gesture.

After Mr. Isley is presented with the school's grant check, we head offstage. Everyone gathers in the hall. We're met first by Coach Sheila, who's pulling Trevor with her.

Principal McGregor is behind her, loudly exclaiming, "You can't be serious, Sheila! They clearly won this competition. No one else even came close."

Sheila rushes up to me, blistering mad, and I catch a glimpse of her memory of her rant with Principal McGregor a few minutes before. I realize with a start that I don't need physical contact to see people's memories anymore.

She jabs her finger against my chest. I look down, staring at her finger. Rage bubbles up as I contemplate knocking her out for touching me.

Trey steps up next to me. *"Stay calm, Melanie. You already won."*

Tension hums through the hall as my Hollywood group waits to see what the coach plans to do.

Coach Sheila snarls, "I've got your number! You're a creepy little witch. You stay away from my son."

Trevor rolls his eyes. "Melanie's my friend, Mother. You're acting like a lunatic."

Sheila grabs Trevor by the collar of his letterman's jacket and practically drags him down the hall.

I raise my eyebrows Principal McGregor's way and smile from ear to ear. "She's such a peach," I quip.

Principal McGregor sighs. "She's just mad at herself because she didn't put you on her team."

"No offense, but I don't want to be on her team."

"I'm sure you'll be transferring back to Hollywood High and that won't be an issue," Principal McGregor says. "This is clearly where you belong."

I shake my head. "There isn't a spot available. I so look forward to seeing you again on Monday at CPH."

His face falls, and he walks away.

"Demitri and Melanie," Mr. Isley calls out, "I'd like a word with you. Everyone else, great job. You're dismissed."

"You, okay?" Trey asks.

"I am," I say. "Please say goodbye to my parents for me. Tell them I'm not sure how long I'll be in this talk, and I'll see them at home."

He hugs me. "Of course." He leaves through the audience portal.

Victoria leans into Demitri and kisses him passionately before following Trey down the hall to the audience area.

Left alone in the hall, Mr. Isley hits Demitri and me with an intense gaze. "Follow me." He heads into my dressing room and closes the door. He turns to us and quietly says, "First, that was spectacular."

We thank him.

He rubs his face. "With the kudos out of the way, I must inform you that I tried to deescalate what was happening with you two out there, and it's the first time in a long while that I couldn't tamp down on something. You're both a force to be reckoned with, and I was outgunned."

I flop back my head. "How many people are aware?"

"No one else. You both did a good job shielding it off. I'm positive not even Trey knows. He was next to me, and awareness never dawned."

Demitri puts his hands on his knees. "You're like a dad to me, Mr. Isley. I need you to keep this between us."

"I'm leaving you two to work this out however you need to." With that, Mr. Isley leaves the room, pulling the door closed behind him.

I lock the door after him. Demitri's staring at me. Neither of us says anything for a long stretch.

Finally, I break the silence. "Where do you stand? Brutal honesty time."

"You're my best friend, Meley. I don't want to lose that."

"We really aren't best friends anymore. We rarely talk."

"That's not fair or accurate."

I cross to the makeup counter and sit on it. He leans on the counter next to me.

"Spill what you're thinking."

"We're both energy workers," Demitri says. "More happened in the fifteen seconds with you than has the entire time I've been with Victoria."

With a sigh, I put my head on his shoulder. He rests his head on mine.

"You're soulmates with a raging bull," he says.

I smile softly and shift my gaze up to him. "True. With that said, I'm not with Trey."

"You aren't back together?" Demitri asks.

"No."

After some thought, he says, "We're both capable of moving forward without an issue."

His response isn't what I expected. *Looks like he's running, yet again. He does this every time there's a decision to make about us.* "Is that what you want to do?" I ask carefully.

"Yes."

I nod and shield off hard, cutting off any chance of him feeling my disappointed vibe.

He thinks for a long moment. Finally, he tips my chin up. "Can you go back to us being best friends?"

My heart squeezes. I really do have it bad for Demitri. I close my eyes and shove the part of me that's in love with Demitri into a locked corner of my mind. "Fraggle reporting for duty," I respond with deadpan emptiness.

Demitri shakes his head. "I'm sorry about earlier. I won't over-step again. I miss being your best friend."

I smile, but it's strained. "Got it."

"You're doing the Fort Knox shielding thing again. What are you thinking?"

"Nothing, D. I'm legit good."

"Okay," Demitri responds, "then we need to have even more rock-solid boundaries. We don't waiver. We don't overstep. Firmly in our own corners. Yes?"

I nod, and he leans down and kisses my cheek.

I wince. "The quirky sidekick vibe freaks me out."

"That wasn't my intention." He sighs.

"You should head out."

"Please don't shut down, Meley," he implores.

"It's Melanie."

He looks surprised. "I always call you Meley."

I push off the counter and scoot past, careful not to accidentally touch him. I grab my clothes, and they're all crusty with dried blood.

"Mr. Isley gave you dance department shorts and a shirt," Demitri reminds.

"I don't go here, and they aren't my vibe." I strip off my costume, ignoring the fact that I'm now in nothing but a thong. I've changed in front of Demitri before, and it's not a thing. I pull on my leather pants and slouch top, tossing my blood-soaked bra in my backpack. I turn to the mirror and touch up my dark-red lipstick before putting on my heeled motorcycle boots. *Time to put all of this to rest and get my life back together.*

"We're not okay, are we?" Demitri asks.

I respond with a caged tone. "No one who touches me is ever okay, Demitri. Get changed and go find Victoria."

As I turn to leave, his hands are suddenly on my shoulders. "I don't want to hurt Victoria with what happened between us."

My smile is strained. "I'm not a gossip, and I'm not new to being a dirty secret. I won't say anything."

"Melanie," he says, looking pained, "I didn't mean to make you feel like you're a dirty secret."

"That's exactly what I *always* become for every guy I love."

There's panic in his eyes.

I grab my stuff and leave, headed through the hall and into the auditorium. Trey's waiting. His eyebrows furrow when he sees me in my battle-stained clothes.

"You're screwed up, aren't you?" he says as he rushes to me.

Demitri comes up behind me. *Ugh.*

I look up at Trey and really study him. "Do you love me?" I finally ask.

"You have no idea how much." Trey's looking at me with guarded optimism, having no clue where this is headed.

"The Tiffany mess?"

Trey inhales sharply before blathering, "I should have never talked to her when we were mid-discussion. I should have never talked to her at all. I can't stress enough how much she's not an issue. Regarding summer, I'm an ass. I had no idea what you were going through. I *should* have known. I've learned from all of that. Having you gone from my life has been sheer hell. As much as I'm sorry that you've needed me here and there lately because your life is chaos, I'm also not sorry because it's all I've got with you. I'll take any excuse to see you."

"What are you capable of?" I ask.

"Monogamy, trust, doing this right, and anything you ask." His eyes are piercing.

Realizing that my options have boiled back down to Demitri being Victoria's, and Zane being with Molly, it becomes clear that Pierre's request that I reconnect with Trey really is the route. Satan only knows that I tried not to. It did no good, and I'm standing here feeling something close to being in love with Trey again.

I smile at him. "Where's my promise ring?"

Trey pulls his wallet from his back pocket and takes the ring out.

"You've been keeping my promise ring in your wallet?"

"This whole time. I couldn't let it go."

My heart flutters. I crinkle my nose at him.

He mouths, "I love you," as he slides the ring on my finger.

I close my eyes and take a moment to ground and center out my whirlwind of conflicting emotions.

"Oh shit," Demitri mutters.

Trey looks at him and says with a hint of wonder, "I don't know what you said to her, but thank you. She went in that dressing room in a totally different place than she came out. I never thought she'd wear that ring again."

Demitri looks pained.

Trey wraps his arms around me. "I love you. I'm sorry. The problems are over." He kisses me. The usual fire and tingles shoot up my spine, and I smile against his lips.

"Can we go do something?" Trey asks.

"I need to head home," I reply. "I'll see you tomorrow night at CityWalk."

Trey winces. "I can't. Mabel is considering me for head of security at her place. I've got a meeting about the system."

"That's okay." I squeeze his hand, relieved to take things slow.

"What about after?" Trey asks. "See if you can come back to Mabel's place."

"I'll be allowed to." I smile a little. "Think you can stay there?"

Trey nods. "I can. I'll be waiting. You should get there when the training ends. We'll spend the night talking."

We hug. He cups my cheek, staring in my eyes, before he kisses me. Everything that I love about Trey slinks up my spine. He ends the kiss and rubs noses with me.

He whispers, "I love you."

"I love you too."

On the way outside, I pass Demitri, who gives me a pointed look. The bright sun reveals the reality of the gore covering my clothes. I earn a few distraught looks from the people I pass on the way to my car, but I choose to ignore them.

I work through the crowd, and finally make it to the movie theater at City Walk. Demitri's apparently the first to arrive.

I huff when I see him, but then quickly rally. "Where's Victoria?" I ask him.

"She had to go to dinner with her grandparents. Arch called and let me know he won't be here either. He's at some training thing with Trey."

My head drops. "You have to be kidding."

"What?"

I hit him with an ironic expression. "Bear and Darren also canceled. They're working on Darren's car, and it's taking longer than they expected."

"So just you and me are going to a movie and dinner?" Demitri asks, clearly unsure.

Apparently, the thought of dinner and a movie with me makes him sick now. "I'll head out, given your pained look."

He takes a deep breath. "Hang on. Are you up for this?"

I think about it for a moment before asking, "Are *you* up for this?"

"We need to talk, so yes."

"Talk about what?" I ask, aiming for blasé. "We decided to land firmly in the friend category. I'm good if you are."

"And then we make the tragic error of going to a movie and dinner."

I laugh hesitantly, feeling like a stranger in my own best friendship.

The theater lights come on, and Demitri guides me up the aisle and out into the lobby.

"Did the dinosaur movie hold up to expectation?" he asks.

"It was SO good!" I say, bouncing happily. "Did you like it?"

"Probably going to have to see it again. I was distracted through most of it. But, yes, I liked it."

"Oh, I'm sorry, D. I know you were looking forward to it."

He shrugs. "I had thinking to do, and it was easier with you present. Are you good if we have dinner at the seafood place down the way?"

Since I'm not a seafood fan, he just picked the one restaurant I don't like at City Walk, but eh, they'll probably have something there that I'll eat. I shrug, and we wander down the busy walkway. We turn into the entrance and are quickly seated.

Trey chooses that moment to pipe into our connection. *"Everything good?"*

"I'm good. How was the meeting?"

"Really interesting. I'm going to study the manual and toy with the system. You almost done?"

"We're eating and then I'll head that way."

"I'll be up when you get home. Have fun."

"Mabel's is home?"

He sends a mysterious chuckle and then fuzzes his side of the connection. I fuzz my side.

I study the menu and find chicken strips and fries in the kids' section. The waitress comes over, Demitri orders, and I follow.

He laughs awkwardly as the waitress leaves. "I take it you don't like seafood."

I shake my head. "The fish and chips at the Beach Bar are the only seafood I'll eat. Apparently, if it's fried, it's no longer icky."

He sighs. "Why didn't you tell me that when I suggested this place?"

I wave my hand. "Quit worrying. I'm fine." I take a weighted breath, my mind roiling with all the things I want to say to him.

He seems to pick up on it. "Spill it, Meley."

There is no hesitation. "I want you to know that I respect your view of me as a Fraggle. Today proved yet again that I'll never be a sensual woman to you." I wince. "I don't get it, and never will, but your feelings are very different from mine."

"What were you expecting when we talked in the dressing room?" He looks me in the eyes, and I blush. He studies me and quietly says, "Melanie . . ."

"I thought you were going to leave Victoria. It's mortifying that what happened onstage today is something you can so easily dismiss."

"What happened was a lot."

"It was a good time. If that wasn't of interest, then you and I are very different animals."

"You have to understand something about me," he says softly. "There's this calm metaphysical ability that lives in me. I depend on it. When I lost control of it in the dark on the stage, I flat couldn't stop any of what I was feeling or doing."

"That's my tantric side. The idea is to give into it, not fight it."

He slowly shakes his head. "I don't give in like that. It makes me incredibly uncomfortable. I'm built for calm and rational."

"Then that's that, because my tantric side gets more intense, not less. You and I have zero shot."

Demitri swallows hard but doesn't respond.

I sigh. "I'm generally good at staying in my lane, and seeing as how my lane with you is more like a bizarre cartoon street in Muppetville, that makes me extra stupid for thinking I had a shot. It won't happen again, and I've landed comfortably back in my quirky sidekick spot."

"And now you and Trey are officially together again because of my dressing room reaction?" he asks guardedly.

"Your dressing room reaction gave me blazing clarity on my confusion about you, which helped steer my direction."

He looks like he's going to be sick. "I . . ." Demitri's eyes close. "Something happened that changed things." He clams up and starts staring off at nothing.

"I can't help you if you won't discuss it," I encourage.

Still nothing.

After a long pause, I hear Pierre in my head, *"Demitri's methodically stubborn. Let's see what happens when we turn the tables."*

I have no clue what that means. Demitri's eyes snap wide, and I realize that Pierre said it to both of us. There's suddenly an energetic swelling all around us. Demitri's expression contorts with panic just before a silent, nuclear-grade explosion detonates in him. He collapses forward, shaking with his forehead on the table. I reach across and touch his arm, but he doesn't respond.

"Playing field leveled," Pierre says in my mind.

After a long moment, Demitri sits back up. He's clammy and pale.

"You okay, D?"

He looks at me with a combination of emotional pain and wonder. His expression morphs to one of panic, and he gasps, "Oh my God." Without another word, he jumps up and rushes out of the restaurant just before our food is delivered.

Blazingly irritated, I pull up to Demitri's house. Thank goodness I had enough cash on me to pay for dinner because Demitri never came back. I've been a lot of things, but the girl abandoned at a seafood restaurant is a new one.

I'm clutching his to-go dinner bag as I ring the doorbell. Mr. Cantrell answers. He looks surprised to see me.

"Where's Demitri?" he asks skeptically.

"I was hoping you'd know."

Mr. Cantrell whisks me into the house, and I hand him Demitri's dinner. He stares down at the bag. "Wasn't he out with all of you?"

"Everyone bailed. It was just us. We made it through the movie, and then he took me to dinner. Just as our food got to the table, he ran out and never came back."

Mr. Cantrell is clearly horrified. "He ditched you, stuck you with the check, and you walked to your car alone?"

I nod.

He grabs his wallet from the coffee table and tries to hand me cash.

"I had some of Pierre's cash on me. I covered the check with no problem."

"There's no way I'm letting you pay for dinner, Melanie. Please take it."

"I'm fine, Mr. Cantrell, but thank you. I just wanted to drop off his dinner and see if he's okay."

"Please fill me in on everything that's happening," Mr. Cantrell says.

I huff. "This isn't my place. Demitri needs to talk to you himself."

He puts his head in his hands. "I'm going to level with you, Melanie. Demitri is saying and doing things that are so out of character for him. I'm at a loss. I had no idea that he had this side, and of all people for him to do this to, you're the last one I'd want to see going through this."

"There are some things you need to know to fully understand this mess," I say with a sigh. "Demitri and I had a very rare connection . . ." As I explain our soulmate bond from our first lifetime, and about how we chose to make a run at an eternal spirit-guide bond, Mr. Cantrell's eyes can't get any bigger. Finally, I inform, "Demitri can't give up Victoria because he dissolved our spirit-guide eternal bond for a soulmate connection with her."

"WHAT?"

"I'm sorry." I grimace a little. "I know you can't stand her." My eyes close as my head drops. "Whatever they have must be worth it."

"Melanie, this can't be!" Mr. Cantrell breathes.

"It is. I wish it wasn't." I fight not to tear up. "You have no idea how much I miss Demitri."

With monumental effort, I pull it together. "I've made mistake after mistake chasing your son. It's humiliating. I flat wouldn't learn. He always shuts down, and now he's literally running. I want you to know that I'm not a crazy stalker."

Mr. Cantrell looks at me with lost eyes. "You aren't the problem, Melanie. He is."

I shake my head. "I repulse him, Mr. Cantrell. Without embarrassing myself by giving too many details, let's just say that no one has ever run from my tantric side. It's alluring, yet he shut down hard in the dressing room. Zero, I mean zilch, in the interest department. It was an ego hit, but it cleared up some stuff. Trey put my promise ring back on my finger right after Demitri proclaimed Victoria the victor."

Mr. Cantrell looks at my hand and sharply inhales. "Are you sure you're ready to be that committed so soon after Pierre died?"

I quirk my mouth. "This is one of my weaknesses, Mr. Cantrell. While I'm aware that being codependent isn't a healthy quality, my life is a dangerous disaster." My expression falls, and I know I look young and vulnerable. "It's scary being alone. I allow myself this one weakness because I'm always forced to be strong in everything else." I pause, unsure, but decide to reveal, "I'm happier with Demitri, but Trey's here for me. He's trying."

"You truly love my son, don't you?"

My eyes begin to water. "I do, but love comes in a lot of forms. I'm just grateful to have him as a friend at this point."

Mr. Cantrell looks pained. "I'm so confused by my son, Melanie."

Rallying, I smile. None of this is Mr. Cantrell's problem. "I should have never spilled Demitri's personal business, but I really did need to talk and there's no one I can discuss this stuff with. I appreciate you."

"I'm dealing with this, Melanie," he says as we both stand. "I promise I'll get through to Demitri."

I shake my head frantically. "Don't do it on my account. He doesn't want me, and that's okay. I'm embarrassed enough already. I'm just not Demitri's girl." I tip my head. "Your dream of me and D is thoroughly squashed. Pulverized. Eradicated."

"Ugh. I don't know what's wrong with him."

"There's someone for everyone, and I think Victoria's just Demitri's person."

Mr. Cantrel leads me to the door, and just as I step outside, Demitri's Jeep pulls into the driveway.

"Your dinner's inside," I tell him as he steps out of his Jeep. "Have a good night, Demitri."

His dad is standing on the front steps, radiating rage, arms crossed over his chest. "You left Melanie sitting at a table, with a dinner check she had to pay?"

I don't wait for the response. I drop into the driver's seat, and drive away.

CHAPTER *30*

I turn into the alley at Mama Mabel's. Her chauffer is waiting by the open garage. He waves me in with a graceful air. I pull into the spot he indicates, and he pushes the button to lower the garage door. Trey opens my car door for me.

"How'd we earn prime garage spots?" I ask the chauffer.

Mama Mabel sweeps into the garage and answers for him. "The Feds are working double-time lately. They've been taking down license plate numbers in my parking lot. The last thing I need is them figuring out that two cars are registered to minors." She grins mischievously. "All my customers are parking in the paid lot down the way, and I'm comping their parking fees." She hustles us through the door into the kitchen. "I called your parents this morning, Melanie. They mentioned that you've had to spend more and more time alone as Rich's career expands."

"It makes me so nervous," I admit. "Ever since Joel attacked me at the house, I'm scared to be alone."

"Well, I told them I'd love for you to stay here anytime you need to."

"That's really thoughtful," I softly reply.

Mabel's eyes sparkle. "Considering that your parents are at Rich's Emmy ceremony tonight, my timing was good, apparently."

"EMMY ceremony?" Trey asks. I nod and he screeches, "Rich got an Emmy, and you didn't tell us?"

I laugh a little. "Rich has quite a few Emmys. At this phase of his career, it's just work. He dislikes the long ceremonies and shmoozing, so we all just kind of downplay it."

"Rich, who we hang out with, has quite a few *Emmys*?" Trey looks like he's going to fall over.

"He's a television producer," I remind. "Cartoons are on TV, hence Emmys."

"Well, all right," Trey mutters, trying to wrap his mind around something that by now just seems normal to me.

"Thank you so much for letting us stay here tonight," I say to Mama Mabel.

Mama Mabel tears up a touch. "I love you kids like you're my own. It means the world to me that you took me on without judgment and criticism about my business."

Trey hugs her. "We love you, and we don't give a flip about hookers."

I giggle. "Just another regular night, right?"

"You two make yourselves at home," Mabel invites, before leaving down a back hall.

Trey holds out his arm. "May I escort you to a big surprise?"

When I giggle suggestively, it makes him laugh.

"That too," he says. "But first, a different surprise awaits."

I take his arm, and he guides me to the door to the guest room. He takes out an enormous key ring and flips to the one that opens the lock. My psyche is raging with guilt over feeling like I do for Trey when I'm still in love with Pierre. The realization of the Demitri mess roars up, adding to the confliction. It's followed by a pang of memory about the Zane disaster. I still haven't heard from him, and don't have any idea what to think.

"What's wrong, Melanie?" Trey asks when he notices my distant look. He leaves the keys dangling in the lock and turns to face me.

"We need to talk about an issue, Trey."

"All right. What is it?"

I take a laboring breath. "Things got heated in the 'Throb' piece, and it was a bit confusing for Demitri and me. We've discussed it."

"Yeah, I was watching. I figured it would spin you out."

"What I'm referring to happened in the dark at the end of the piece."

His eyebrows rise. "What happened?"

"It's going to piss you off," I say with a sigh. "It wasn't intentional, but I turned my head and couldn't see anything. Demitri's face was right there, and my lips landed on his."

"You accidentally kissed him?"

I nod, choosing not to fill in Trey about how I've kissed Demitri before. He omitted plenty about Tiffany, so I'm just taking his lead.

He looks oddly contemplative. "And?"

I roll my eyes. "It was mind-blowing. If it helps, Demitri isn't the least bit interested."

Trey chuckles. "I meant 'And?' as in, 'What about it?' We weren't dating during that show."

My brow creases. "Oh yeah." I tip my head. "You're being really rational."

"I'm not going to screw this up by blowing my stack over a kiss my girlfriend had while she was single." He gives me a soft look. "Considering that I did the unthinkable, and you're giving me a chance, I'm definitely going to be rational."

Gratitude washes through me. "Thank you for that."

He pulls me in, and I rest my forehead on his chest.

"I still feel bad about it. I'm sorry, Trey."

"No apology necessary. I appreciate that you told me."

An evil grin crosses my face as I look up at him. "At least I didn't screw a cheerleader."

He shakes his head. "Nah. You just made out with the hottest guy in school."

"I did," I say with a smirk. "Freaking *fireworks*."

He laughs. "I deserve that." His expression softens. "When I open this door, I want a fresh start. No bad blood. No being pissed about cheerleaders and sexy dancers."

I take a deep breath. "That sounds promising."

Trey's raises his eyebrows, his expression full of anticipation. "Are you ready? This surprise is mind-blowing."

When I nod, he turns the knob, opens the door, and guides me in.

I inhale and turn slowly, studying every inch of the room. Mabel has painted the walls a surprisingly warm shade of dark gray. The homecoming picture Trey and I took together is framed on the dresser next to a pretty jewelry box. I cross to the dresser and run my finger lightly over the lid. I open the jewelry box, and a little ballerina turns gracefully while the song "Music Box Dancer" tinkles and chimes.

"It's perfect," I whisper.

A black-and-silver men's watch box rests next to the jewelry box. *Trey Valdez* is engraved in a bold font on its silver metal plate.

Framed pictures of our friends on all our adventures artfully grace the walls. I laugh as I get to the largest framed picture of me and all my friends shooting double birds at the camera. Spread out behind us is Snow White Café. Above the framed picture is a red-and-black sign that reads in hand painted calligraphy *Love and Light*.

"Mama Mabel gets us," Trey says from behind me.

A black fluffy velvet bedspread adorns the bed. A soft-knit red throw blanket is draped over the corner. I pull back the bedspread a touch to reveal bright-red satin sheets.

"Look in the closet," Trey says.

Through the closet door, a gorgeous array of clothing awaits.

"I checked the sizes, and she nailed it for both of us," Trey informs. "She got all the brands right too. Well, with the exception of a few luxury pieces she thought you might like."

My mouth drops open. "This must have cost a fortune."

"She spared no expense. We have a full wardrobe here. I'm blown away. I had no idea she was doing this."

On the nightstand on my side is a picture of Trey grinning while he dances with me at Adam and Valerie's wedding. "I had no idea she took those pictures."

"I didn't either. They're great though."

We head into the bathroom, and I open the linen closet. Two sets of red and black plush towels are neatly folded on the middle shelf. Every ladies' product and toiletry item I could possibly need is neatly organized on the shelf under the towels.

I shake my head in disbelief. "We have our own place?" In the next breath, a moment of insecurity hits. "Are you sure you're okay with this? It's a lot."

He smiles. "I'd move in here with you in a heartbeat if our parents would let us. When I graduate, I'm hoping your parents will let you live here with me, at least part time. Mama Mabel offered me the head security job, and I accepted. I don't officially start until after I graduate, but the salary is staggering. Sixty grand to start, with full benefits, room, and board. Other than gasoline and fun, my living expenses are covered under the 'room and board' clause. Ten-K yearly raises are promised upon review. My role will be to coordinate, hire, and supervise the security team. She said she's more confident in my abilities than she's been in the bikers she usually hires. She's also offered to pay my full tuition to CSUN. By the time I'm twenty-two, I'll be pulling a hundred grand a year and will have a college degree."

"All this for a teenager not yet out of high school?"

He nods. "She knows I was trained by my dad. His bodyguard security business is no joke in this town. Literally, our future will be set. She's got a job offer in mind for you too, by the way."

My eyebrows shoot into my hairline, and he laughs.

"As her entertainment and events coordinator," he clarifies quickly. "Not as one of her *girls*. Same salary and extra perks I'm getting. It'll be waiting for you when you graduate." He looks down, smirking. "I know working at a brothel wasn't exactly on either of our radars, but her employees are happy, and she's got a solid reputation with the people who matter to us. We really can't beat this deal."

I exhale. "I just thought we were going to roll around on satin sheets for the evening. This has taken a SHOCKING turn."

As if it couldn't get more perfect in here, he reaches for a little CD player tucked on the bookshelf and pushes *play*. Louis Armstrong's "La Vie En Rose" wafts cheerfully through the speaker. Trey takes my hand, turns me twice, and pulls me in to dance with him.

CHAPTER 31

The next morning, Mom and Rich, still glowing from his Emmys win, arrive to inspect our new room at Mama Mabel's.

"Everything about this is perfect!" Mom says to Mabel. "I don't know how you managed to combine Melanie's and Trey's loves like this, but I couldn't have done better myself."

Mama Mabel tips her head in appreciation. "I don't make a habit of moving teenagers in, but these two are a special case. I'm a collector of the eclectic, and they stole my heart. Their oddity is intriguing. They're also here a lot, and I want them to be comfortable."

"We've worked out an agreement," Rich tells me. "You're welcome to stay here one night on the weekends, and one night during the week since you have dinner with your friends at Snow White Café every week. It's okay for Trey to be here with you. We'd also like you to stay here any night your mom and I have a late night out. We learned the hard way that you tend to get into hot water when you're alone. Of course, we're also open to other evenings when things get particularly hectic." He gives me a pointed look. "The only reason we agreed to this is that it really does take a village to keep you safe. Having another safe place for you just might be the key to keeping you alive. We aren't oblivious to your reality lately."

"Does that work for you both?" Mom asks.

"Thank you," Trey says with a grin. "That sounds perfect."

We all head out and take a seat in the parlor.

"Melanie," Mom says, "how do you feel about going back to school at Canoga Park tomorrow?"

I sigh. "Not good. Something's coming, and I'm dreading it."

"Any more clarity on what or when?" Trey asks.

"I'm sick to DEATH of the drama." I stand and start pacing. "I'm talking world class, screw this, hell with everything, flat out DONE. I obviously hate Canoga Park High because it's detestably ordinary. I fully realize that I shouldn't have left Hollywood High, but at the time, I needed to." I flop back on the couch. "Sorry. I needed to get that out."

Everyone sits in silence because there's nothing to say. I just need to ride this out, and we all know it.

After a lengthy moment of contemplation, Rich says, "You're welcome to stay here with Trey tonight. Just make sure to get to school on time tomorrow. Deal?"

"Trey, can you stay?" I ask.

He nods. "At this point, my parents don't even ask where I'll be. They've given up trying to keep up with all the drama. It's been convenient."

With that, Rich and Mom stand and say their goodbyes.

After they leave, Mama Mabel pats me on the arm. "My intuition's buzzing," she warns. "Whatever it is that's coming, you can't control it. Just be vigilant."

CHAPTER 32

The intercom system hums to life, and a lifeless voice says, "We invite all ninth and tenth grade classes to join us in the auditorium for a performance by our dance team and theater troop. Eleventh and twelfth graders will see the performance in fifth period."

"Guess who gets to go watch the dance team perform at an assembly?" I send to Trey.

Trey snorts in my mind. *"I speak from experience when I say that little show's gonna be less than riveting."*

"These people are gonna think it's sooo cooool."

He chuckles. *"I've got a meeting with the CSUN coach in fifteen minutes. Apparently, he's looking to recruit me, so maybe that'll save Mabel a little tuition. I'm shutting down our connection until it's over."*

I return a love bubble. *"I'm headed to the auditorium. Don't forget that we have Rich's Emmy win party at my house tonight."*

"I'll be there. Catch you on the flip side."

Joining the orderly line, I follow the class out the door. We work our way through the full hallway and reach the auditorium. Inside, there's no exciting music playing like I'm accustomed to hearing before an assembly at Hollywood High. Everyone looks bored.

Our class is assigned to the first seat-bank on the left side. I'm last in the line, and as I take my seat next to a mousy girl named Natalie, it's apparent she's about to cry. She leans away from me, her hands shaking.

When I empathically pick up that she's crying about having to sit next to me, I sigh.

Mr. Wilcox, our grizzled teacher, says, "You're being ridiculous, Natalie. Melanie's a nice girl."

I look his way, and he offers a fatherly grin.

"The rumors are a bunch of hogwash, I'm sure," he tells me. "But even if they're not, I've been paying attention. You've caught a bad rap."

Gratefully, I smile. "Mr. Wilcox, I've already seen these dance pieces, and I've got homework to do. Think anyone will care if I sit by myself at that table in the corner and get caught up on my assignments?"

He gestures to the table. "That works." He winks. "If anyone asks, I'll tell them you're in detention and can't watch the show."

"They'd believe it," I say with a laugh. "I'm always in trouble around here."

I cross to my personal isolation table, pull out the chair, and unzip my backpack to retrieve my homework folder. The moment I toss my backpack under the table, my intuition blazes to life at excruciatingly full power. I double over, gasping around the pain in my chest. I try to reach Trey, but our connection line's shut down tight on his side.

Of all the times for him to be busy!

I fight to think around the pain in my chest. I close my eyes, willing my intuition to pick up whatever memory I need from the crowd in the auditorium. My eyes snap open, and I watch as Principal McGregor crosses to center stage. A memory blasts in with such ferocity that it almost knocks me off my feet. I sit down in the chair and watch the memory on fast-forward in my mind. Principal McGregor's in a meeting with the district's planning and budget people.

Why is this relevant?

I hear his thoughts in the memory. *"They've put this off for eight years. We're one good shake from catastrophe, and they don't care."*

I pause the memory so I can examine the image of the paper in Principal McGregor's hand. Infrastructure . . . Retrofit . . . Unviable . . . Failing supports . . .

Just as the dance team takes the stage in their matching shorts and tank tops, I hear a roar that sounds like it's coming from far away. It takes a moment to place why it's so familiar. A clip from a documentary on the 1906 San Francisco earthquake soars up from my memories. An elderly survivor, who was a little boy at the time of the disaster, describes the sound of a thousand raging bulls running alongside a speeding freight train. The old man on the documentary memory stares back at me in my mind, clear as day, and I break into a panicked sweat.

The roar becomes deafening just as the floor under me bucks hard and I'm thrown onto the table. I pitch and slosh as the sound of everything evil screeches and grinds, crashes, and moans all at once.

There's nothing still to hold on to!

The room bounces violently as people scream and chaos ensues.

Don't run with the crowd!

My intuition is tossing specific information at me in a way it never has before. I usually have to play *Where's Waldo?* for clues.

The lighting rig above the stage crashes down, smashing into the dance team. Realization that a dozen girls are likely dead drops me into a frozen panic. I'm brought back to reality as debris starts crashing around me.

The building's coming down!

I dive under the table, realizing that it's a big, heavy industrial piece of old metal furniture. *Please let this thing be well built!* I grab my backpack, unzip it, and pull out my hoodie. I press the hoodie over my face as the world around me goes black and dust fills every inch of breathable air.

I scream as I feel weight pressing steadily heavier on top of me. The sound is demonic, and the shaking seems like it has lasted a lifetime. My body goes numb, and the world suddenly stops rattling.

The silence is ominous. I try to remove the hoodie and look around, but I can't move anything except for a few fingers and one foot.

My claustrophobia rages.

I'M TRAAAPPED!

I feel the mental scream boom from me on a massive energetic blast like I've never experienced before. Mentally, I watch it flow out of me. It gets to my stepfather first. His head snaps up.

The message reaches Bear and Darren next, and I see that they're under their desks with the rest of their class.

The wave hits Trey, and smashes through the blockage. *"Hang on, baby!"* he sends.

It hits Demitri next. I feel his heart seize. Panic rips through him.

The wave hits Adam last. My connection with Adam is blocked off by Bear and Darren. I shouldn't be able to reach him. He hunkers lower over Valerie, who's on the floor in what I assume is their bedroom.

I've never been able to reach anyone but Trey and Adam through our soulmate connections before, but apparently my terror allowed my energy wave to reach most of the energy workers in my life.

As fascinating as all that is, I must deal with my crippling reality. I'm claustrophobic to the point that it's paralyzing. Bear thinks I was crushed to death in a past life, and it's left me with soul-deep trauma.

I hope that my claustrophobia was a sign from the past, and not a warning for the present.

I don't have time to panic further about that, because a deafening rumble explodes, and the table over me makes a cracking sound and presses down harder against me.

My world goes black . . .

CHAPTER 33

I wake slowly, sluggish and confused, as an aftershock jolts and rocks under me. The shaking stops, and an excruciating weight bears down on me, jarring me out of my mental fog. I remember what happened. I try to take stock of my body, but I'm in an odd combination of pain and numbness that's confusing. I blink, trying to see, but there's nothing but darkness.

Panic fills me. My heart races. My breathing is raspy. Tears pour as I desperately try to move.

I mentally reach for Trey, but I'm blocked by something I can't quite place. I try the other guys, but it's to no avail.

Another aftershock hits, and the ground bucks violently. I scream, and it feels like sharp knives are stabbing me all over my body. It's like I'm being run through a compactor. Panic swells in me, meeting with resistance that freezes my mind in terror. I feel like I'm going to explode, even as the ground eats me alive. A painful energetic explosion fires out of me. I go limp as the jagged heaviness presses harder.

I feel Zane startle, and suddenly, he's in my mind.

"Melanie? What's happening?"

This has never happened between Zane and me, but now isn't the time for pondering how I've managed to reach him.

I moan as the pain becomes excruciating on my back. I feel Zane panic so severely that his legs collapse. With his mouth hanging open, he tries to wrap his mind around what I'm experiencing. He can't figure it out, but he knows it's bad.

I gather my terror into a finely honed energy ball, and load it with the message, *"I love you. I'm sorry the last time I saw you was horrible. Let it all go."* I launch it with every bit of my metaphysical ability, unsure what it will take to get the thought to him. I watch through his eyes as it hits him, knocking him flat on his back. He's on set and is surrounded by his concerned coworkers. He lies there with tears in his eyes, realizing I'm in serious trouble.

My world goes black . . .

I'm jarred. The more aware I become, the more pain I'm in. I test the possibilities of moving but can't. Getting a full breath is impossible. My claustrophobic panic surges violently. I've never felt anything like this. Tears well as my throat constricts.

"Please help me!"

Awareness opens in my mind, and Zane's eyes snap wide, revealing the ceiling above him. He says aloud, "Melanie!"

Relief that he can hear me in his mind makes him feel sick. I can feel that he thought I was dead.

He bolts upright and throws up in a wastebasket next to him.

Through his ears, I can hear a TV newscaster say, "The epicenter of the earthquake is in Canoga Park, California. The entire area is decimated. Rescue crews can't get to the area due to blocked roads and gas fires."

"Look to the TV," I attempt to send.

Like a miracle, Zane's gaze switches to the TV. I watch aerial footage of the destruction. It looks like a third-world war zone.

I moan as the shaking starts again. Excruciating pain rebounds up my arm as the meat grinder starts rolling and pressing. I pull my arm toward me, and figure out that when the world shakes, I can move my arm through the rolling pain. My arm feels like it's being torn apart. I get it to me and curl my hand at my collarbone. I open and close my hand, and my panic slows a little now that I've regained control of at least one part of my body.

I freeze as the shaking stops. Unbearable weight settles, and I try to whimper but can't. I attempt a breath, and discover that there's only enough room for shallow gasps. I send desperation across my connection with Zane.

He whispers in my mind, *"Baby! Oh my God. You have to breathe."*

It takes a moment to settle in before I laugh a little in my mind. *I've gone completely nuts. Zane is on a movie set in New York, oblivious to what's happening. Enough, Melanie. Deal with reality.*

"I'm in your head!" Zane barks in my mind. *"It's real."* His terror rolls in waves down his connection to me.

I swear I can feel him, but it's ridiculous! Zane is a Normal, with no metaphysical abilities.

"Melanie, please. Focus."

I watch through his eyes as Molly walks in. "I'm checking on you," she says with a sultry pout.

"Out!" he screams. "Now."

"Zane, I told you that I'm sorry," she says, sounding exasperated. "I'm sure she's fine. The phone lines are down. That's why she's not answering."

"Get OUT!" he rages.

Molly tears up and leaves.

Zane focuses on me again. *"Talk to me, Melanie."*

So typical. I can't even escape Bimbo Bingo while I'm dying.

Zane attempts to gasp, but his panic is unbearable. "I'm so sorry, Melanie," he whimpers aloud.

This isn't real, I tell myself. *You're delusional. Get it together, girl. You're Melanie fucking Slate. Act like it.*

I pull a massive energy wave, attempting to use my panic to get somewhere productive in this nightmare. I bubble around myself and try to push. The effort makes me vibrate hard. My energetic swell is met with unbelievable resistance, and I give up before the effort kills me in a rebound blast.

"Damn it, Melanie!" I hear Zane say in my head *"You can do this. Try again."*

"I can't get out!" I mentally scream, as terror gets the best of me again.

"Please try again," he begs.

My lungs scream for air. My tomb starts shaking again, but this time is different. Instead of sifting, or rolling, the world bounces hard, over and over. One of the bounces lightens a bit of the weight for a moment, and I manage a full breath even as I yank my other arm to my chest. With each new bouncing slam, fresh pain seers through me.

"Melanie!" Zane screams in my mind.

One last jolt hits, and then the world settles with a strange creaking sound. The air is knocked out of me, and a fresh round of panic thrums in my core. I groan in my mind as immense pressure descends.

Zane's voice says in my head, *"I need you to stay hyperfocused on something. You can do this, baby."*

I replay my last memory with him. Ms. Alice yells, and I cower. *"Not that memory!"*

I switch to just after the meeting, and Trey is pulling me to his chest as I sob. In the memory, he cradles my face and starts his "fuck this" list of people who can kiss my ass. I smile a little. *Damn, that man is at his best when it all crashes down.*

I attempt to get through to Trey but can't. All mental routes are blocked, except for one. I study it, and it actually does seem to lead to Zane.

Weird. I'm clearly losing it.

"If I hadn't done this with Molly, Melanie would be here right now," I hear Zane thinking.

It takes me a moment to realize that I can hear his thoughts, but it still doesn't register as real because Zane and I have no connection.

"You heard my thoughts?" Zane says in my mind.

Uninterested in hearing about Molly, my thoughts slip to the ocean. I'm swirled and rolled in the water just as another aftershock starts. The feeling of drowning overtakes me, and my body jerks in the ocean of the memory. I smile a little to myself. I know this one.

Pierre and Zane are going to save me.

I sigh in my mind and let myself drown. In the next part of the memory, there is Pierre, telling me to throw up the salt water. Seeing him suddenly helps me recover my emotional state. I can feel his hand on my back. I can feel the salt water come up as I violently hurl. I'm there, on the beach in Hawaii. The rain is a relief on my skin. It helps wash away the pain.

In the memory, Zane grabs me from Pierre. Zane's arm wraps around my stomach, and he squeezes, forcing another rush of salt water to come up. When the next round of shaking starts, I curl a little around his arm, and I swear I can feel it in reality. Extreme relief overcomes me.

"I'll hold you while you go through this," Zane says in my head. He's sobbing desperately. *"I can see the memory."*

I swear *I can hear him in my mind.*

"You can," he insists.

I smile a little. *If he holds me, I can die, and it'll be okay.*

"*I'm so sorry, Melanie.*"

I can't inhale much again. My lungs burn, and I distance my mind from the lung pain, focusing instead on Zane's arm. I see white flashes in the dark and realize I'm seeing stars as my oxygen-deprived body starts shutting down. I can no longer feel my hands or feet. My arms go numb next, and I sigh again in my mind. Each part that goes numb brings immense relief.

No pain. Thank God.

"*I love you, Melanie,*" Zane gasps out through earthshattering heartbreak.

An explosive pop explodes just before unbelievable pain blisters through me. Then, the pressure releases in my head. I lie, limp, and the bizarre connection with Zane seems to dissolve.

Everything disappears.

CHAPTER 34

"I don't even know where to start!"

The words drift through.

"I can feel her," Trey bellows.

"Get us to her, Trey!" Mabel orders. Apparently, Trey brought everyone who's anyone.

I try to move but can't. *Where . . . I?*

My thoughts are choppy and distant.

Muscles detached and exhausted.

"Something is very wrong," I hear through Trey.

"Explain," someone else demands.

"Her thoughts are garbled in a weird way." Dread and panic fills Trey.

I groan, unable to comprehend. I do the only thing I can make sense of, and swell my energy, pulsing the intensity level up and down.

"Yes, Melanie! Do it again, honey."

After I send more pulses, he says to our group, "She's energy pulsing. I can find her. That way."

I watch through his eyes as he runs. He reaches a massive mountain of rubble.

Through Trey, I hear Marcus say, "Oh. My. God. What do we do? We'll never get through this."

"Pulse again, Melanie," Trey sends. *"I need to pinpoint your location."*

I do as he asks.

Trey skirts the edge of the biggest side of the rubble mound, then runs to the other side of the disaster. A few disheveled students pass him, but no one appears to be doing anything to rescue people.

"Again, Melanie. I think I'm in the right place." I pulse again, and he says, "She's right there, around twelve feet down."

Through Trey, I watch and hear all my friends scampering partway up the rubble mound. They grab debris and toss it away. In a matter of minutes, I hear a metallic scraping sound above me. Without warning, debris falls from the rubble mountain, covering the flattened table on top of me with a fresh mound of weight.

"ST . . . OP!"

"Everyone, stop!" Trey yells, and he's close enough now that I can hear him even without our connection. "I think that's what she said." He swallows hard. "She's right under here. Take it slow." I watch through his eyes as everyone starts slowly pulling up debris.

"I've got a motorcycle boot over here!" someone informs.

A moment later, Demitri says, "Those are Melanie's!"

I feel some of the weight lifted, bringing a fresh round of pain.

Now that my body is revealed, I can see through Trey's eyes that I'm in deadly shape. He falls to his knees, and Tanner puts a hand on his shoulder.

Everyone is frozen in place, staring at me as I lie on my stomach in the rubble.

"Everyone, gut up," Arch manages to get out. It's the first time I've heard him sound as if the world is ending.

I watch through Trey's eyes as Bear looks to Demitri, who takes a massive breath and stares down at my crushed, pulpy, oozing body. I've been minced.

"What I'm about to do never gets discussed outside of our group," Demitri orders in a gravelly tone.

"Can you help her?" Bear asks desperately.

"I'm going to try, but . . ." Demitri shakes his head before pulling it together. "I'm a healer," he informs. "I don't tell anyone that. I've never attempted anything like this."

"Do anything you can," Finley gasps. "We won't say anything."

Demitri just stares at me blankly.

I watch through Trey's eyes as Arch rushes to Demitri and grabs him by the shoulders. "It's Melanie. For her, you always can, and you always do."

Demitri's shocked gaze slides to Arch, who guides him over to my destroyed body. "Demitri, *that's* Melanie. I want you to be a magical beast, because none of us are going to be okay if we lose her."

As the reality of my condition sinks in, Demitri lets out an animalistic moan. His knees buckle, but Arch isn't having it.

"NO YOU DON'T, Demitri Cantrell!" Arch drags him to his feet before shaking him hard. "Come on, pretty boy! Gut the FUCK UP! Suck it up, face the impossible, get those angelic hands dirty, and fix her!"

With new determination in his eyes, Demitri rushes the last few feet to my body before plunging to his knees. "When I crater, feed energy into me," he says to the others. "This is going to take all of us."

He closes his eyes and puts hands on what used to be my back. I don't feel his hands, but I can see him touching me by looking through Trey's eyes. I try to blink but can't see anything.

I watch through Trey as Demitri's head drops.

"Her core is crushed," he says mournfully. "Her skull is severely fractured. Her brain is damaged. Somehow, her heart and lungs are still functioning."

I watch through Trey as Demitri leans and lifts my hair away from my cheek so he can see my face. Even though my eyes are open, I can't see him in the natural way. Demitri gags and puts my hair back over my cheek. He turns his back to me and throws up on the rubble.

"What is it?" Trey asks with dread. Demitri won't answer, and Trey screams, "What? *Tell* me!"

Demitri squeezes his eyes closed, trying to get it together. "I need everyone with a weak stomach to go where they have no view. Tanner, you need to stay with them. Don't let them over here."

Tanner tips his head suspiciously. "What are you hiding, D?" When he gets no answer, he marches my way and carefully moves my hair to look at my face. I feel my hair move, but still see nothing.

I watch through Trey's eyes as Tanner starts to hyperventilate. He turns in a rush and grabs Trey by the cheeks. "I need you to come with me."

"Tell me!"

Tanner shakes his head before his eyes glaze and he gets a far-off look. He turns in shock and looks at Big Joe. "If Demitri can't heal her, can you handle ending this, so she doesn't suffer?"

Big Joe swallows hard. "Richard is one of my closest friends. You want me to kill his stepdaughter?"

Mercury, the toughest of the Hellhounds, stands from his kneeling spot at the edge of the group. "I'll look at what has everyone so rattled," he says with a dead expression. He makes eye contact with Trey from across the group. "I'll tell you what I see."

I watch through Trey's eyes as Mercury crosses to me. He kneels with surprising grace, given his size. He gently lifts my hair from my cheek and instantly tears up. Everyone's eyes widen. None of us has ever seen Mercury fall apart like this.

Big Joe rushes to Mercury as the tough guy stands up. Mercury collapses at the waist with his hands on his knees. Big Joe starts to kneel to look at my face, but Mercury stops him by barking, "Don't. No one else look." It takes Mercury a long moment before he collects himself enough to stand upright. He rubs his face hard before hitting everyone with a stoic expression. "The weight was too much," he explains. "Her right eye ruptured from the socket. The other side of her face is crushed."

Mouths drop open. Finley makes a keening sound. All eyes slide to me. I see through Trey that my back is barely rising and falling as I struggle to breathe. I don't even have it together enough to emotionally register what Mercury said.

Mercury turns to Demitri, who's on his hands and knees with his head hanging. "I need to know if you think you have a shot at this miracle."

Demitri shakes his head slightly.

All hell breaks loose as Trey screams, "Yes you do! You DO HAVE A SHOT!" He starts to lunge at Demitri, and it takes Arch, Bear, and Tanner to hold him back. Trey collapses to his knees and bursts into uncontrollable tears. "Damn it, Demitri, PLEASE!" he begs.

"I'm going to end this," Mercury says softly. "All of you need to go away." He starts to kneel by my prone body.

"She's in my head!" Trey screams. "She can see through me! She can hear through me! STOP!"

Mercury looks to Trey with a mournful expression. "She can't live like this, seeing and experiencing through you."

A wave of terror washes through me at the prospect.

"Give this a minute," Trey sobs out. "Just hang on!"

Mercury shakes his head. "We must have compassion for her. I can't just leave Melanie like this."

"Everyone, stop," Big Joe orders. How he can be so calm is beyond me, but the man is remarkable that way. He kneels and puts a hand on Demitri's shoulder. "Son, I need you to look at me." Demitri looks to Big Joe, who asks, "Do you have any chance at this?"

Demitri opens and closes his mouth, but no sound comes out. Big Joe sits cross-legged. Demitri shifts to match, and Big Joe smiles softly.

"I'm going to say something, and I apologize to everyone for it, but I have to." He takes one of Demitri's hands and squeezes it. "When I met all of you, I was positive that one day Melanie would be Melanie Cantrell."

Demitri's face crumples.

Big Joe nods. "I know you're scared, but let's work through this for Melanie's sake. Can you handle the broken bones?"

Demitri nods.

"Good," Big Joe says with a supportive lilt. "Good, Demitri. Now, can you handle her brain damage?"

Demitri nods again.

Hope starts to shine a little in Big Joe's eyes. "Can you handle the organs in her gut?"

Demitri swallows hard. "I think so."

Big Joe smiles wider. "Can you fix her eyeball?"

Demitri nods. "I think I can."

Big Joe beams. "I know this is a lot, but I'll talk you through each injury. I'll be with you through all of it."

When Demitri starts to look my way, Big Joe shakes his head.

"Look at me, son." Demitri stares into Big Joe's eyes. "Good." He glances to Mercury. "Will you put your jacket over Melanie's upper body, please?"

I feel the jacket cover me. It's warm.

Demitri swallows hard and scoots to me.

Big Joe takes the place on my other side. "Okay," Big Joe coaches. "From here down." He gestures to my legs. "Name an injury you can fix."

"Broken tibia," Demitri rushes to say. Now that he's decided to do this, he seems to be chomping at the bit to get to it.

"Then I want to see you fix that tibia," Big Joe says.

Demitri slides frightened eyes up my leather-jacket-covered upper body, and Big Joe steers his chin back to focus on my legs.

"Nope. We're not focusing on the whole problem. We're focusing on one little tibia."

"It's Melanie's tibia," Demitri whimpers.

Big Joe shakes his head. "It's a random tibia."

I feel hands on my leg, and quickly, they heat up. After an indecipherable amount of time, some of the pain dissipates. I groan.

"Immense relief from her, Demitri," Trey says softly.

"Tibia is done," Demitri says.

"Good," Big Joe says. "What's next?"

This coaching and healing dynamic goes on for a long stretch. The only interruption is from Darren, who says in disbelief, "I can't BELIEVE help hasn't arrived yet!"

"It's a good thing," Mercury says. "It's giving Demitri time to focus."

After another long while, Demitri breathes out, "Legs are done." He sounds exhausted.

I send a bubble to Trey, who says, "Melanie's worried you're going to quit."

"I'm not quitting," Demitri says with conviction.

"Okay," Big Joe coaches, and I feel the jacket scooted off my back. Only my head is covered now. "Let's start low and work our way up. Who's going to boost Demitri?"

Suddenly, an aftershock roars beneath us, and I feel something heavy hit me.

"Stop the debris," Marcus screams.

I watch through Trey's eyes as many of our people attempt to block the debris by circling us. With the debris handled, Bear yelps, "Use the earthquake energy to boost D!"

Trey, Bear, and Darren grab onto Demitri, and their eyes close, cutting off my view. I feel Trey channel the earth's unsettled aftershock energy into Demitri. I hear someone gasp, and then hands land on me, radiating fire into my lower back. I groan again.

"I've got this," Demitri snarls with sudden clarity. Every new place that he moves to heats up and then stops hurting.

Something wet keeps falling on my back. *"Rain?"* I try to send to Trey.

"No, baby," he answers aloud. "Demitri's pouring sweat."

The moment hands land on my ribcage, I attempt to scream. It comes out a horrifically garbled sound. A new set of hands land on my hips, and Trey says, "Do it, D. I'm going to pull the pain."

The pain is more bearable now as Demitri's hands land on my back again. I hear Trey groan, but he's blocked off our connection to try keep me from feeling the pain he's pulling.

"Hang in there, Trey," Bear coaches.

"Oh my God," Trey moans out.

"I know," Bear says. "I can't imagine how bad Melanie is hurting. You're doing good, Trey."

Time stretches into infinity, but the pain keeps lessening.

"Are you ready for her skull?" Big Joe asks.

"No. I need a breather. I'm going to handle her shredded arms. Skin is easy, and the only broken bones are her fingers." Demitri sounds past the point of exhaustion.

Another aftershock rumbles.

"Fill me up again," he begs of our friends.

A moment later, hands land on my shoulders, and stinging pain is quickly alleviated as the hands slide closer and closer to my elbows.

"Keep feeding that aftershock energy!" Demitri gravels out.

I hear moans but can't make sense of it. Demitri's hands get to my fingers just as the aftershock quiets. My hands heat up, and then the pain is gone. I exhale hard before taking a deep breath. My head feels heavy and foggy, but there's a sudden zing as oxygen fills my body.

"Okay, D, this is it. Time for the final test." There's a fearful whimper, and Big Joe says, "I know you're scared, but I've never seen anything like what you've managed. I'm so proud of you, Demitri."

Desperate crying punctuates the air. I reach out a hand, grasp a leg, and know it's Demitri the moment I feel his energy. *"I'll help,"* I send.

"She's trying to boost you, D," Trey says tearfully. "She meant to say, 'I'll help.'"

"Baby, no," Demitri whispers. "Just give me a second."

Ignoring him, I gather an energy load and send it through my hand and into his leg. I hear a sharp inhale.

"She just juiced me," Demitri says, sounding revived. "Let's do this. I need antiseptic liquid."

"We have none," someone says.

"Water bottle then," Demitri says. "Anything that can clean her eye and face."

"Melanie and I both keep medical kits in our trunks." When I send confusion, Trey chuckles a little. "I put a kit in your trunk, love. It's under the piles of clothes you keep in there."

I send amusement about his typical irritation at the messy state of my car.

"Melanie's backpack is by her left hand," Trey says. "Someone grab her keys, run to her car, and get the medical kit. It's in a black duffel bag in her trunk."

"Also, get something for her to change into," Tanner requests.

"We aren't worried about fashion right now," Big Joe admonishes.

"Like hell we aren't!" Tanner sasses back. I see through Trey's eyes as Tanner cocks a hip. "Melanie Slate is about to get her ass up, and when she does, she's going to rescue people who are dying under this rubble."

"I think Melanie's earned a break," Arch retorts.

"We aren't leaving these people to suffer! *We're* the rescue crew, and SHE is the leader." Tanner points down at me before waving his hands about, indicating the barren expanse of rubble. "Do you see anyone ELSE rushing in to superhero these Canoga Park High assholes to safety?"

Everyone sets in with a determined look.

"Give me the keys," Tanner orders.

Marcus opens my backpack and hands Tanner my car keys.

"If you'll excuse me, my friend is about to look fabulous!" Tanner stalks off, radiating fear, rage, and hope.

"He's clearly gone nuts," Big Joe mutters as he watches Tanner's retreating form.

"Let him be. This is how he processes." Trey gives a nervous laugh. "We're all going to go a little nuts after this."

I watch through Trey's eyes as Rich runs at full bore around the rubble pile. He sees the group and pounds up. Mercury stops him before he can get to me. Rich screams my name, and Mercury calmly says, "We're working on it. Demitri is healing her. She was in bad shape fifteen minutes ago, but we're about to tackle the worst of it."

Arch crosses to Rich. "I need you to come with me. Trust us."

Rich shakes his head adamantly. "Not a shot."

"Rich, you don't want to see this," Arch assures.

"That's my KID," Rich screams.

"I know." Arch sounds tearful. "We're all terrified, but the miracle Demitri has already pulled off is unbelievable."

I hold up a hand and wave it about. "Memory."

"Why does she sound like that?" Rich asks fearfully.

"She has brain damage," Trey informs. "Demitri is about to tackle it. She tried to say, 'Memory.' Take her hand."

Rich grabs my hand, and I send the memory of what I looked like when I was first uncovered. He gasps. "Oh my God."

"Like Bear said, we've come a long way," Big Joe says compassionately. "What's under that jacket isn't for you. I need you to do me the honor of finishing this task."

I watch through Trey as Rich swallows hard.

"I'm scared," Finley says softly. "Will you come with me, Rich?"

Rich's jaw tightens. He gets his papa bear look and puts a hand on Finley's back. "Who else needs to walk away while they finish healing Melanie?"

Marcus, Presley, Drake, Deb, Hiram, and Susan all raise their hands.

"Demitri," Rich says, "are you positive there's nothing I can do to help you?"

"I need to be able to focus," Demitri says. "Getting everyone to a safe place in this mess will help me more than you know."

"Let's walk away," Rich tells the others. "I'll stay with all of you." The ones who need to leave gather by him. He looks to Mama Mabel. "Are you coming?"

She shakes her head with steely resolve. "I can help them." She compassionately gazes at Demitri, who's lying on the rubble with his eyes closed. "Demitri, I've never been prouder of anyone than I am of you."

Demitri looks her way. "I promise I'm going to fix her."

Mama Mabel smiles. "You'll finish the task, my dear. Of that, I'm certain."

Tanner jogs back and hands a duffel bag to Trey. He opens it, and Big Joe surveys the contents.

"You put this kit together, Trey?" he asks.

Trey nods and Big Joe's eyebrows rise.

"Nice work, son. You've got all the supplies we need."

Big Joe looks to Rich. "It's time for all of you to walk away. Tanner, would you like to go with them?"

Tanner shakes his head. "I'm here for Trey."

"I'm staying too," Arch says.

"Bear and I are staying to boost Demitri," Darren says. "He'll need it."

Big Joe looks to Mercury, who replies, "I'm staying to body-guard so you can focus."

The brave few all gather around me while the others move to the other side of the rubble pile, out of sight.

Big Joe pulls a water bottle from the duffel bag. He opens it and pours water over Demitri's hands. Demitri rubs them together until his hands are as clean as they're going to get in this disaster. Arch takes a new bottle from the bag and pours water over Big Joe's hands. Big Joe pulls blue latex gloves from a sealed Ziplock and carefully puts them on. He helps Demitri put on a set as well.

Big Joe takes a deep breath. "My tattoo business has me disinfecting for a living. Let me disinfect her eyes and face. I want Trey, Demitri, Arch, and Tanner to close their eyes while I work."

My view is cut off as Trey's eyes close. I feel slight movement, but it doesn't hurt. Liquid splashes my forehead, chin, and cheek.

"Oh, sweetheart," Mama Mabel breathes out. Apparently, she's watching.

"Okay, Demitri," Big Joe encourages softly. "Here we go."

Trey's eyes open, and I see my ruined face through him. He tears up as he grabs my hand. "I'm going to pull pain."

Demitri takes a huge breath. "Eye first." I feel the side of his hand along the bridge of my nose. There's no pain, only pressure as his hand presses against my eye socket. That's when fire rips through my head. I gasp, and Trey's hand shakes while he pulls the pain. "HURTS," I attempt to scream.

"I know, Melanie," Trey manages to get out through gritted teeth. "Hang on, baby."

I see through Trey's eyes as Demitri's face scrunches. He pours sweat while his upper body collapses around his lungs. Bear and Darren clamp hands on his shoulders. He revives a little with the energy boost. Finally, he exhales hard. He keeps his right hand over my eye. He turns my head, and I see through Trey that my face is crushed on the other side. Big Joe squirts water all over the side of my face and doesn't stop until the dried blood and dust are gone.

Demitri puts his hand over the side of my face, and it heats up. The pain is deep and throbbing this time. An odd reforming feeling starts to trickle over me, and I wait through the strange sensation.

Again, Demitri exhales hard. "Trey, get her in your lap."

"Are you sure we can move her?"

Demitri nods.

I'm shifted and pulled into Trey's lap.

"I'll sit behind you, Trey," Arch offers. "Lean your back against mine."

There's shifting, and then Trey guides my back to lounge against his chest. I feel my face released.

"Open your eyes, Meley," Demitri says fearfully.

I open my eyes and see blurry outlines. I hold a hand to Demitri. He takes it, and I send the memory of what I see.

"Got it," Demitri says before putting both hands over my eyes again.

My sockets heat up, but instead of pain, I experience an enormously pleasant sensation. I sigh with relief.

Demitri's hands release me. "Try again."

I open my eyes, and there he is. I smile. "Hi," I say softly.

Demitri looks to Trey, who clarifies, "She's saying hi to you."

Elated, Demitri breaks into an exhausted smile. "Hi, Meley. How about I fix your confusion?"

"I'm confused?"

Trey laughs a little. "Yes, baby, you're confused. If it weren't for me being able to hear your thoughts, we'd have zero clue what you're saying."

"Tell him that he looks like shit, and I love it."

Trey cracks up. He tells Demitri, who chuckles, the tension breaking a little as everyone softly laughs.

Demitri looks down at his clothes. "It's not as bad as it could be. Just dusty."

"I'm referring to you being all pale, with dark circles under your eyes. You're all sweaty." I waggle a hand his way. "I prefer you like this. Your perfect side is annoying."

Trey snarls a little. "Down, girl."

I giggle at Demitri as Trey relays what I was attempting to say.

Demitri rolls his eyes in a good-natured way. "Only girl on the planet who wants me to look normal," he says before wrapping his hands around my head.

All conversation is cut off as the most excruciating pain I've felt in this lifetime rips through my skull. Convulsions start, and Trey is occupied with my shaking body. Tanner rushes into the fray, steadying me so Trey can pull the pain. I hear a moan a moment after the pain dissipates some, and then Trey's gone from behind me. The pain roars back.

"He's out cold," Tanner yelps.

I'm hefted, shaking, into another lap, just as a fresh aftershock rattles hard.

"Don't let anything hit her," Demitri barks.

The pain gets worse somehow, and my eyes roll into the back of my head. There's a blinding crack, and I scream. The shaking earth, and my shaking body, go still all at once.

I exhale hard and roll off the lap I'm in. With my head hanging, I groan, "Holy SHIT that hurt. Screw you, Demitri Cantrell! Screw you sideways, upside down, right side up, and UNCONSCIOUS!"

"Huzzah!" someone bellows.

I glare at Big Joe. He grins.

"We didn't need a translator," he says. "You're back, Firebird!"

Demitri collapses onto his side. "Upside-down screwing will have to wait. I'm tapped out."

I laugh a little and lie down next to an unconscious Trey. I'm thoroughly exhausted, body, energy, and soul. I smack at Demitri, and he rolls closer to my other side in the rubble. I curl up against him with my head on his chest. He exhales with relief.

"Thank you for saving me, Demitri," I say softly as I lightly scratch my nails on his chest.

"You're welcome," he quietly replies. "I'm sorry I didn't think I could do it."

"In your defense, this wasn't a run-of-the-mill damaged brain stem and broken neck this time."

Demitri laughs a little. "Girl, you sure know how to sustain damage." He puts an arm around me, squeezing me tight.

Rich and the rest of our group return. Cheers and exclamations boil over exuberantly as they survey me.

CHAPTER 35

"**H**ere's the plan," Darren says. "During the next aftershock, the energy workers need to funnel it into Trey, Melanie, and Demitri. Once they're on their feet, we can get to stage two of this day from hell."

"Stage one was a real thrill," Mama Mabel exclaims.

"I'm onstage at least four hundred for the day," I groan.

The earth starts rattling, and Bear gets hands on Trey, while Darren and Mama Mabel grab ahold of Demitri, and Rich grabs my legs. They funnel giant swells of aftershock energy into us, and I feel human again. The aftershock slows to a stop, and Demitri, Trey, and I sit up.

Trey's forehead thumps to my shoulder. "Melanie, you scared me to death."

"So sorry," I apologize, before looking to Rich. "Our house? Mom?"

"Both are standing. I left your mom with a neighbor who's going from house to house checking for gas leaks. She's helping people in the neighborhood."

"Then we get to work. People are buried alive."

When I stand, Tanner hands me a black tank top and artfully shredded black jeans he chose from my trunk collection. I strip off my T-shirt with little concern for my bra state. We're past worrying about that at this stage of disaster. I change out of my destroyed leggings, into the black pants. After I pull on my heeled boots, Tanner grins at me. He sets to clipping my favorite chains on my pants loops. He outfits me in all the accessories he found in my trunk before pulling on my slouchy fingerless gloves.

I raise an eyebrow. "You think this is a practical choice?"

"Sometimes we have to fake it until we make it," Tanner insists cockily.

I hold my gloved hand for everyone to survey. "As you can tell due to my fabulous accessories, I'm not a hot wreck with a ruptured eyeball, ruptured personal life, ruptured career, or ruptured school life."

"And so it is," Bear caws.

Tanner surveys the destruction around us. "This looks bad."

Everyone stares at the massive disaster in disbelief. The gravity of the mission we face leaves them floored.

Big Joe rallies. "What's your plan, Firebird?"

"I'm going to search for memories. Where there are memories, there's someone alive. I pinpoint the area, and we start digging."

"I think we should start with the smaller classroom rubble piles and work back this way," Mama Mabel suggests.

I shake my head. "The entire ninth and tenth grade are in this pile. So is the principal. We start here. We need to find him if he's alive, so there's someone in charge that actually belongs here. Then we can switch gears."

Stubbs points to the area where they threw the rubble that had pinned me down. "Search and rescue crash course. That's our discard pile. The last thing we need is people getting confused and digging where no one is trapped."

I close my eyes and open the part of my psyche that connects with people's memories. The whole disaster site lights up like Christmas. "There are so many people buried alive! We need to work fast. Split into three teams."

Our group divides up.

"There are three under here," I say, pointing to a spot right next to me.

Team One rushes there and starts tossing debris.

I point to another area to my right. "At least ten are there."

Team Two rushes that way and gets to work.

I turn to Team Three. "A huge mass of memories is around this edge." They follow me, and I point out the area.

"Found one!" Arch yells.

Bear and Darren rush to help him, and they carefully lift a girl out of the rubble. Her leg's bent at a crazy angle, but she's alive.

"Everyone's likely to be injured," Tanner says. "What do we do?"

Finley and Jayla step up with Mama Mabel, who grabs the medical kit.

"The three of us will set up a triage area on the grass over there." Mama Mabel points to the edge of the field closest to us.

Bear turns to Demitri. "Do you want to fix any of the issues in triage?"

Demitri shakes his head. "I'm burned out. I can help dig, but I'm done healing for the next few days."

Tanner and Darren carry the girl over to the newly established triage area just as Drake yells, "Located! We've got people over here."

Team Three members start moving people out of the rubble, leaving them lined up on the grass with our makeshift triage team.

"Adult male!" Drake yells.

Drake and Bear pull a man from the rubble, and I exhale, relieved.

"Principal McGregor!"

The principal looks my way and orders, "Put me down."

"There's no rescue crew yet," I explain to him. "We're digging people out." I gesture to my friends, all working like mad. "My friends from Hollywood came to find me. CPH was at the epicenter of the earthquake, and it's leveled, along with every building within a ten-mile radius."

Trey gives me a look. "How do you know that?"

I pretend I don't hear him. I have no interest in discussing the weird Zane connection that happened when I was trapped.

"I *knew* it," Principal McGregor says with a furious tone.

"I know. Right before the earthquake hit, I saw your memory of the meeting where they put off the campus infrastructure project."

His eyes widen. "Are you serious?"

"We don't have time for another round of 'fear the witch.' Bottom line, I can see people's memories and have other abilities. It's how I'm finding people right now."

"Are you hurt?" Bear asks him.

"I think I have a broken arm. I can deal with it later."

Team One comes to me, and Deb asks, "Where to next?"

I close my eyes, scanning for memories, and point to a pile of rubble ten feet from me. "Huge bunch of memories there."

They start tossing rubble.

While they dig, I get Principal McGregor up to speed. "This rubble piles behind us and behind Team Three are our discard piles. Triage area for rescued people is on the edge of the field."

He looks that way and then back at me. "Do you think this will work?"

My answer is interrupted as Hiram yells, "Found them!"

Half of Team Two works together, pulling people from the rubble, while the rest work to clear what threatens to fall on the located survivors.

Big Joe yells out from across the way, "I think we need to split Team Three into two separate groups, and Melanie needs to take them to the opposite side of campus. That group can take on the smaller classroom rubble piles and start working this way. We'll meet in the middle."

Team Three pulls the last of their survivors from under the rubble.

"Melanie," Arch yells, "check this area and make sure we didn't miss anyone."

I circle the debris field with Principal McGregor in tow. I close my eyes and search, announcing after a moment, "You cleared it."

"Let's head the direction Big Joe suggested," Arch says.

I turn to the other two teams and close my eyes, searching. "Team One, you've got two memories six feet diagonally to your right. Team Two, you have at least ten memories on the other side of that concrete pillar that's sticking up from the ground. I'm taking what are now Teams Three and Four to the other side of campus. I'll return shortly."

They keep moving rubble.

We rush to the far end of campus.

"This is devastating," Principal McGregor laments. "Do you have any idea how many people are dead under this catastrophe?"

I stop at our destination and hit him with a frustrated gaze. "THAT is precisely what's wrong with the people at this school! You *must* change your thinking. No. I don't know how many are dead, but I *do* know people are alive. We're going to start focusing on what we CAN do, instead of what we CAN'T do."

"Put that in your pipe and smoke it," Tanner snarks as he sparks a joint that he pulls out of his fancy silver cigarette case.

"You can't smoke pot here!" Principal McGregor scolds sternly. "It's illegal."

Tanner barks out a laugh. "Blow it out your ass." He passes the joint to those who are interested, as I close my eyes and search.

I locate eight memories, and instruct where they are. "I'll be back," I tell the groups.

Principal McGregor and I wind around the massive debris mountain that used to be the cafeteria, and we're met by Rich, Adam, Bear, Stubbs, and Trey.

"I need you two to settle a debate," Rich says.

"We're finding a lot of dead," Stubbs informs. "What do you want to do with them?"

After a moment's thought, I say, "I vote that we leave them where they are and let the official first responders handle them when they arrive."

"Most of us agree," Stubbs says, "but . . ."

"We can't just leave them there, Melanie," Bear insists. "They're someone's kid."

I close my eyes, and the pulse of hundreds of memories is waiting in my mind. I shake my head, overwhelmed. "There are only so many of us. If we take people off the rescue mission and put them on dead-body detail, more could die."

Bear exhales hard and surrenders to my logic. "That makes sense."

A yell interrupts us, and we run around the cafeteria rubble to what used to be the front of the school. At least fifty parents are rushing our way, clearly distraught. We run to meet them.

"This is Melanie," Principal McGregor says. "She's heading the rescue operation. I need you to go to the triage area on the field to search for your children. Anyone who's willing needs to help dig out survivors. It's a long story, but Melanie can locate them."

One of the moms hits me with a snooty look. "Aren't you the witch my daughter told me about?"

I glare at her and mutter to Principal McGregor, "This is ridiculous."

He turns scathing eyes on the mom. "Melanie's already managed to instruct crews who have pulled over fifty living people from the debris."

The mom looks my way and seems unsure.

Principal McGregor says to me, "I'll take these parents to triage to search for their kids. Willing helpers will meet you on the far side of what used to be the auditorium."

I nod and turn to Bear. "Go get Susan. I need her to handle any parents who come this way. Explain to her the triage-then-search plan."

He jogs off.

"I need you to go to Teams Three and Four," I say to Trey. "I can look through your eyes and instruct where to search, instead of running back and forth."

He kisses my forehead before jogging off.

Next, I turn to Stubbs. "Any new people who join the rescue effort need to be put on teams. Make sure our original group is divided up among the new people who join us so that no one digs through pointless piles. You're in charge of organizing them."

Stubbs lopes away with purpose.

Rich follows me, and we pass Susan, who assures, "I've got my part covered. They need new areas to search. Hurry."

We round the auditorium rubble, where new people are being divided up and assigned to search teams.

Big Joe yells out, "Where to next, Firebird? Team One is ready."

I close my eyes and search, locating a mass of memories around the bend. I wave them over and point out the spot. They get to work.

"Melanie!" Drake yells.

I rush his way and close my eyes, finding the next group of people trapped below us. I point it out, and Team Two makes quick work of finding another survivor.

"We're ready," Trey sends. *"We've moved to the next two classroom rubble piles."*

I look through his eyes while simultaneously opening to the memories pulsing all over the campus. *"Heaven help me. I need to be split into four people right now."*

"We can work together. Drop your shields."

I do, and Trey scans the memory pulses.

"Got it. I'll deal with these two teams. Any time we need to find a new area to search, I'll tap into you and pull the information."

I send him a love pulse and am immediately pulled back to Team One to give new instructions.

CHAPTER 36

A second mortuary van is filled to the top with body bags. The coroners close the back doors, and one says, "Another van from Northridge Mortuary is en route."

They drive away. My head hangs.

The lead emergency responder crosses to me. "How are you holding up?"

"I'm okay." The truth is that I'm not okay, but I can't quit now. We've cleared two-thirds of the rubble, and there are still more memory pulses coming from the wreckage. My senses are scrambled from the fear and pain that rolls off of those still buried alive. With my shields dropped to allow Trey memory map access, energy reserves running low, and ever-present exhaustion, I can't block the panic radiating from the unfound.

"I really don't think we could pull this off without you," the first responder says. "We'd get people out, but a lot more would die. I apologize for being skeptical and rude at first, but I've never seen anything like what you can do."

"There's been a lot of skeptical and rude through this nightmare, but most people have eventually come around."

He takes his leave, joining his team to search a new debris field.

"Melanie," Drake calls out exhaustedly. "We need a new area."

I cross to Drake's team and find a new set of memory pulses in the middle of the rubble pile in front of them. I point it out and head to the top of the pile to determine the next spots to send the teams to.

As I get to the top of the mound, another aftershock, stronger this time, rolls and jumps.

"Hunker down and hang on," Stubbs yells to all of us on the top of the pile.

I drop to all fours, head hanging, and wait it out. This has become a frequent occurrence, and we've all learned how to get through it.

After the jolting aftershock stops, Trey, Rich, and Demitri meet across the way and confer with Big Joe.

"Teams Four and Five need assignments," Big Joe yells up to me.

Before I can answer, a parent volunteer screams. The anguished sound sends shivers up my spine, and I know what's wrong before he says it. We've been through this so many times already.

The dad yanks his son's corpse out of the rubble and sets him down on the top of the debris heap. He turns my way and sprints, sending rubble crashing down on rescuers below. "HOW DARE YOU NOT SAVE HIM!" he screams.

Demitri, Rich, and Trey run up the rubble mountain, and Demitri gets to the man just before he attacks me. I'm so exhausted that I don't bother to run or fight. Demitri puts his hand flat on the man's chest. He's secretly calming the father while he holds him back. We're having to use our gifts without permission because things are getting dangerous.

"I'm so sorry for your loss," Trey says calmly to the grieving father. He turns and yells below, "I need Bear, please." He turns back to the man. "We have counselors on-site. I'll introduce you."

He leads the distraught father away.

People need me right now. I can't cry. If I do, I won't be able to stop.

Rich hugs me. "You need to take a break."

"I can't."

Mama Mabel motions us down, and we carefully descend to her. She hands me a bottle of water.

Trey makes his way back to us and puts his arms around me. "Put your shields back up and block your side of our connection," he instructs. "You can send me a mental image of the memory map every time I need information. You can't keep taking in everyone's emotions or you're going to crater."

I snap my shields up and fuzz out my connection with Trey. My hands are shaking against his back.

"Trey and Demitri," Mama Mabel says, "you're doing an incredible job deescalating every situation that arises."

Exhaustedly, they murmur their appreciation.

Mabel turns to me. "I rode here with Bear, and I'm thinking I need to head home and get things coordinated." She gives Rich a no-nonsense look. "You and Carol should stay at my place. It's better if we hunker down."

"Thank you," Rich says. "I'm going to take you up on that."

"I'll put you and Carol in the guest room across from Melanie and Trey," Mabel says warmly.

Rich heads in the direction of the triage area.

Mama Mabel turns to me. "Would it work if I took your car, and you ride home with Trey?"

Trey nods on my behalf. "I don't want Melanie driving. She can hardly stand at this point. This solves the problem of what to do about her car."

"Mabel," Demitri says, "my dad is out of town. Can I stay at your place while this all gets figured out?"

Mama Mabel hugs him. "Of course."

"Thank you."

Mabel hefts my filthy backpack on her shoulder and sets a brisk course for the still-full student parking lot. Luckily, my bright-turquoise car is easy to find.

"That's the third distraught parent who's attacked Melanie." Trey shakes his head, radiating frustration.

Demitri quietly says, "At least this one didn't demand that the 'witch' bring their child back from the dead. Distraught or not, that lady was off."

I rub my face. "I need to go give instructions to the teams."

Trey shakes his head. "I've got it. Stay with Demitri for a few minutes. You really need a break." He turns to Demitri. "I've hit survival mode, and I'm exhausted. Melanie needs a boost, but I can't do it. I'm running on empty. Will you try?"

Demitri nods. "Go do what you need to. I've got her. If she can't handle it, I'll come get you."

I send Trey a mental snapshot of the memory map. He heads up the rubble mountain. Trey being able to receive information has taken some of the pressure off, but we're still struggling to keep up with the demand.

Demitri wraps his arms around me, pulling me in.

I sag against his chest. "Are you holding up okay?"

"Don't worry about me. I need to boost you so you don't crater."

"Are you sure you're up for that?"

"Put your hands on my chest. You'll see."

I put my hands on him, and he drops all his shields. After a moment of studying, I gasp. I have more energy reserves than any of our energy workers. At least I thought I did, but my four reserves are beaten by Demitri's five. His third, fourth, and fifth reserves are still untouched from when he was boosted after healing me.

"I hate needing help," I say, "but I'm worried about things slipping down my connection, unintentionally. I'm tired and that's not good. Trey needs regular access to my memory map."

"Do I have your permission to shield off your memory center, so he doesn't get anything you don't want him to? I promise he can't get through my shield."

I smile. "Yes please, but only if you can handle it. My control is slipping, and you'll have access to all my dirt."

He chuckles.

I drop my shields, leaving my connection fuzzed with Trey while Demitri puts a hand on my forehead. I feel him enter my psyche, and after a moment, he gasps.

"How bad is what you're seeing?" I murmur.

"It's not bad. It's just confirming something I'd wondered but wouldn't ask."

I scoff sarcastically. "Fantastic. That's cryptic and nightmare inducing."

"It's you being in love with Zane. I didn't know if you were, hoped you aren't, and knew it wasn't my business."

He engulfs my memory center, and a calm hum settles in that area of my mind. I sigh and lean my forehead on his chest, relieved to be able to drop my own shields that I was barely holding together.

He extricates himself from my psyche, but the calm remains.

"Hoped I wasn't, huh?"

Demitri laughs a little. "Yeah. I hoped you weren't."

I shake my head. "When I was trapped, I woke up several times. I couldn't get through to any of you. I hallucinated that I got through to Zane, but he's all the way in New York. It felt so real."

"You probably had a fractured skull by then." Demitri clears his throat. "I was terrified when you were in my head, but it means a lot that you connected with me like that. Hearing you in my mind was wild."

I look up at him. "Don't you and Victoria speak mind-to-mind?"

He shakes his head. "We have none of the soulmate perks that the rest of you seem to enjoy. All we have is an undeniable need to stay together so we can continue being miserable."

"Shitty," I commiserate. "I'm surprised she isn't here, bitching about having to help other people."

Demitri rolls his eyes. "I told her not to come with us when we headed this way. I knew you were in trouble, and I didn't want to deal with her. I hate her. I hate the soulmate bond. There's no passion, no fun, no actual love."

I wince. "I'm sorry that you're so drawn to her." I quirk my mouth. "Thank you for healing me after everything we decided."

"We didn't decide anything. I did," Demitri admits. "Every damn time I do that, I wonder later what I was thinking."

"Zane did the same thing," I inform quietly.

Demitri looks at me curiously, and I fill him in on the Molly debacle, and everything that happened with Ms. Alice, and me being fired.

His eyes widen. "Holy crap."

I smile sadly. "Looks like my wish was granted. I have clarity. Adam, you, Pierre, and Zane are gone. My options boil down to Trey."

"You said that Zane was devastated because if he hadn't screwed up with Molly, you'd be safely in New York right now," Demitri says. "Did Trey realize that if he hadn't had an affair with Tiffany, you wouldn't have been crushed to a pulp?"

"The Zane *hallucination* said that. Not real Zane. Also, no, Trey hasn't realized that." I huff. "You're right though."

He puts his hands on my back and sends a steady energy stream into me. His energy is the exact opposite of mine. Where I'm fire and rage, he's calm and healing. It feels so strange that my knees buckle.

He catches me as I crumple. "Whoa, baby girl. What's wrong?"

I laugh quietly. "Sorry. Your calm vibe dropped me. I'm really tired, and my knees didn't hold."

"You keep getting more charming," Demitri says with a chuckle. "But that's a conversation for another day."

After he's refilled me enough to function, my head hangs. "We've got work to do, but the break was nice."

He picks me up, draping me over his chest. "We can rest for a few more minutes. You need to slow down. My healing sessions tend to leave a person exhausted."

"You did an amazing job healing me. I'm not even bruised. I don't know how you did it."

"You'll be bruised tomorrow," Demitri admits. "There's secondary bruising that takes time to pop up. You'll have them everywhere you were injured."

I wince. "So, I'll be a giant head-to-toe bruise?"

Demitri nods. "You're scaring me. You can only take so much, and you burned out an hour ago."

Another anguished scream pierces the air just as another aftershock hits. Demitri locks his knees to hold steady as the ground rattles.

I lift my head from his shoulder, inhaling sharply. "Guess that means our break's over."

When the aftershock ends, Demitri sets me down hesitantly before rushing off in the direction of the traumatized parent.

CHAPTER **37**

As the sun casts its final rays over the horizon, the last survivor is pulled. We stand in the glow of dusk. All the survivors and their parents have been carted off to hospitals. Our group, Principal McGregor, and the first responders are the only people left at the rescue site.

Everyone gathers around.

"I need Melanie to take one more pass over the entire campus debris field to make sure no one is left behind," the lead first responder says. "After she's sure, we're going to cut you guys loose and finish the search for the deceased." He turns to the principal and adds, "You need to head to the hospital and get your arm looked at."

I take another deep breath, something that's become my ritual through all of this. My head sags. I'm running on nothing.

Trey's not in much better shape, but he rallies for me like he has all day. He takes my hand. "Come on, love. Let's do this together."

To conserve what's left of our depleted energy, we haven't been sending mind-to-mind messages. We start a slow walk along the top of the rubble, and I carefully scan the expanse for memories as we pass. Trey double-checks as we go. We make it to the end of the debris field.

"We've found everyone who's alive," I confirm. "I'm not getting anything on my memory scan."

The first responders thank us for everything we did, and rush to set up their floodlights to tackle the rest of the gruesome recovery work through the night. The rest of us turn to each other, filthy, exhausted, and covered in things so horrific that I don't want to think about it.

"I don't know how to even begin to thank you all," Principal Macgregor says.

He's cut off by a maniacal screech coming from the parking lot. Storming our way is Coach Sheila, Trevor's mother.

I roll my eyes. "Why is every coach we deal with bat-crap crazy?"

Everyone gives a gallows chuckle about the reminder of Joel's dad, Coach Stamp, who held Hollywood High hostage.

"I'll deal with her," Principal McGregor offers. "Give me a minute."

I put up a hand. "No. Let her come this way. Big Joe pulled her son, alive, from the rubble. So whatever has her spun out is likely going to be insane but manageable."

Coach Sheila flounces up. "Did you save everyone?" she demands of me.

"We saved everyone we could."

She glares. "Maybe if you had moved quicker, the hospital could have saved my son's leg. It's been amputated."

Trey finally loses what patience he has left. His temper rages as he venomously snaps back, "You need to check yourself! If it weren't for Melanie, your son would be dead! I helped Big Joe load

Trevor into an ambulance and personally held his severed leg that was hanging by one muscle." He holds out his hand that's covered in dried, rust-colored blood and filth. "Blame the earthquake, not my Melanie! You need to learn how to treat people, you maniacal *BITCH*!"

Everyone grins at Trey, eyebrows raised. Trey shakes his head and pulls me in, kissing my filthy forehead.

Tanner waves a flourishing hand at Coach Sheila. "Be gone with you, maniacal hell-bitch!"

Trey glances around, his eyes wild. "I HATE THIS PLACE!"

Suddenly, some form of humanity shines through Sheila's eyes. "You've all been through a lot, and I realize you didn't have to help us. I'm sorry. Thank you, Melanie."

Radiating exhaustion, I look at her. A complete emotional breakdown looms just under my surface, and I fight to keep it in check. We've seen abominable things today that are going to haunt me for several lifetimes, I'm certain. I've still got the remnants of Bethany's brain matter under my nails from when I was helping dig out survivors. She didn't make it, and it hurts my heart. She was one of the good ones around here.

Finally, my tone dead, I explain, "We *did* have to help because that's who we are. My family doesn't lie down on the battlefield. Most of the people from this school are assholes, but they're still people, and we had what it took to save them. With that said, let me be CRYSTAL clear. I don't *ever* want to see you again . . . And you're welcome."

Our group walks together to the parking lot. We stop at Trey's car.

"Hey, Melanie," Arch says. "I didn't get a chance to tell you. Ms. G told me that school district policy states that any student displaced by a disaster can be enrolled at any school in the district."

He smiles. "She expects to see you at Hollywood High bright and early when we reopen. You're back in."

My head drops, relief filling my exhausted psyche, and the tears I've held back all day cascade down my cheeks. I gasp and bend at the waist, trying to breathe.

CHAPTER 38

We walk through the door and step into the sound of a humming generator. Battery-powered lanterns are on every kitchen counter. My mom is happily stirring a pot of soup on a camp stove on the floor. Rich, Mama Mabel, and the four working girls who live here are gathered around Mom.

"Carol's resourceful," Mama Mabel says. "Power's out, and she still puts together a homemade soup."

Trey inhales. "It smells great. Thank you, Mom."

Mom looks up from her stirring. "You're welcome, Trey. But this is nothing compared to what you've done today. I'm just so proud of you kids." Her expression morphs concerned. "Are you all okay?"

We sag, exhausted, and nod.

"Hey, Demitri," Rich says. "I'm glad you're staying here."

Demitri smiles.

Another aftershock hits, and Mom turns off the burner and clamps a lid over the pot. Mama Mabel grabs the big pot with potholders and attempts to hold it steady. Apparently, they're now practiced at this.

"Now you see why I have the burner on the floor," Mom says through the rumble.

My tired legs struggle with the pitching and reeling, and I plop down cross-legged with a bouncing thump before flopping on my side. Everyone cracks up about my plop while the ground continues to heave. Trey and Demitri give in and stretch out next to me, looking nonchalant.

Finally, it finishes.

"Most people fight to stand through earthquakes because they're not going to give in," Sapphire says. "You three flop down and lie there looking bored."

Demitri shakes his head. "We spent hours on top of a mountain of loose debris during these aftershocks. We discovered that if we just lay down on the rubble, we got to have a nice little shaky breaky."

Everyone laughs.

"We've put flashlights in your room," Mama Mabel says to Trey and me. "Don't light candles. We're worried they'll start a fire. I'd say we could put the generator on the lights, but we opted to use it to run the refrigerators, walk in freezer, and water heater instead."

"Good plan," Trey says. "Has the gas line been checked?"

Mama Mabel nods. "We've been checking it after each aftershock. So far, we're good."

"Dumb question, given our life-and-death nightmarish day," Trey says sheepishly, "but would it be okay if Mel and I took one of these battery lanterns to our room after you guys are done in the kitchen? We've been taking turns reading *The Caves of Steel* to each other, and I'm dying to know what happens."

Rich raises an eyebrow. "You're reading Issac Asimov together . . . On purpose?"

Trey chuckles.

"You wild and crazy kids!" Rich jokes, looking to Mom. "This is what we were worried about?"

Mom chuckles. "Don't be offended," she says to Trey and me, "but you two are like old people sometimes."

Everyone laughs.

"Dinner's ready," Mom announces.

"What's your priority, kids?" Mabel asks. "Food or shower?"

Trey, Demitri, and I all say, "Shower," at the same time.

"I'll show Demitri to his room," Destiny offers.

"Grab a change of clothes from my dresser for him," Trey says.

Demitri thanks Trey and follows Destiny.

"We'll get dinner served and be on the back porch where it's not so hot," Mama Mabel says.

Trey nods and helps me up from the floor. We head to our room, where he grabs the flashlight that Mabel left by the door and clicks it on. Our room is only a bit disheveled from the aftershocks. I exhale, relieved to be in a place that's quickly started to feel like home.

"Come on, love. Let's get cleaned up." Trey riffles through the dresser and pulls out shorts and tank tops for each of us.

He guides me into the bathroom with a hand on my shoulder.

"I'm sunburned," I say, wincing away from his touch.

"We all are. It was so hot today." He grabs a tissue and sneezes. "I'm sneezing out concrete sludge."

He starts the shower as I strip down. We slide into the shower in the gloom, and I start working concrete dust and dried chunks of heaven-only-knows-what out of my hair. The soap has an intoxicating sandalwood-and-vanilla scent that makes my tension start to fade away.

"Are you okay?" Trey asks. "Today was a new level of horrific, even for us."

"Tired, a little traumatized, and SO relieved to be home with you." I put my head on his shoulder as the water sluices down our sides.

Trey's leaning against the shower wall with his arms around me as another aftershock hits. He holds me tight with one arm and braces a foot and hand against the tile wall. "It's like being in a damn Slip 'N Slide in here!" he snarls.

The glass door flies open as the ground pitches us harder.

I start to lean to grab the door, and Trey yells over the sound of growling earth, "Leave it. Hang on."

The shaking intensifies. Trey slides quickly down the tile wall and pulls me down, cradling me sideways across his lap.

Finally, the shaking stops. I stand and pull the glass door closed.

Trey stands and starts washing his hair like nothing happened. "I'm looking forward to dinner."

My usual post-trauma hysteria hits.

He looks at me and busts up. "Was I oddly casual just then? It felt oddly casual."

I laugh harder.

He puts a hand on my cheek. "You were remarkable today. Do you realize how many people we pulled out of the rubble because of you?"

I shake my head. "I don't know how many, but everyone else did the heavy lifting. Our group makes a hell of a team."

Trey puts his finger to my lips. "No. You aren't downplaying this like you always do. Five hundred eighty-seven people were pulled out alive because of *you*. The rest of us helped, but without you, we wouldn't have found many of them in time."

"You saved over fifteen hundred during the hostage escape," I remind. "You still have me beat."

He barks a laugh. "Baby, if there were fifteen hundred people alive under that rubble, you would've saved just as many. I'm giving you the *W* on this one."

I smile. "I learned quite a few things today."

As the water cascades over us, he sits on the tile floor and pulls me down to sit across from him, knee-to-knee. It's oddly comforting to be here in the gloom of the bathroom, the space lit only by the flashlight propped up in the sink.

"Tell me," he says.

"I learned that we can use this soulmate connection seamlessly. That we have the BEST friends and family in the world. That this new memory ability is a blessing instead of a curse." I raise an eyebrow. "That people are bat-shit crazy."

He laughs. "Damn, are they ever!" After some thought, he asks, "Should I be worried about you and Demitri? There's something seamless between you two."

I sigh. "He and I are fine. Full disclosure, everyone else bailed on the group outing, and it was just him and me."

Trey closes his eyes. "That makes me nervous. Did you kiss him again?"

"No. Just talked."

He puts his hands on my cheeks. "I don't want to lose you again, Melanie. It helps that Mr. Perfect is looming because I needed a reminder of what I have."

I laugh softly.

"He really is looming, isn't he?"

"You have nothing to worry about," I assure him. "He really is into Victoria."

Trey's expression melts around the edges. He radiates worry. "Are you in love with him?"

I scoff slightly and avoid the question. "The worst thing that happened was me wrapping my legs around him on the dark stage."

"I bet that was eye-opening," Trey goads.

I crinkle up my nose playfully.

Trey rolls his eyes. "Great. Mr. Perfect is locked and loaded."

"Quit worrying about Demitri and his assets."

He helps me up and shuts off the water just as it runs cold. He grabs two towels off the towel rack and hands me one.

CHAPTER 39

Showered and fed, I settle in on my favorite Victorian love seat in the parlor. Trey's in our room, likely pondering our conversation about Demitri's attributes. I'm secretly amused. After everything he put me through with Little Miss Pompom, it's kind of endearing to watch Trey squirm over Demitri.

Demitri comes out from the hall, showered and changed into Trey's clean clothes. He sits down on the love seat and glances my way. "You good if I sit here?"

I nod and lie down with my legs stretched over Demitri's legs and my head on the ornate wooden armrest.

"Nice toddler shirt," I tease him.

He chuckles. "Trey's clothes are a little small on me, but they're clean, so I'll take it."

Mabel's phone rings. Surprised, we all stare at each other. She's picking up the phone when Trey comes in and says, "Apparently we have phone service back."

He looks from me to Demitri, sighs, and sits on a chair across from us. I wiggle my feet, tucking them under Demitri's leg. He smiles. I do this in rehearsals a lot because my feet are always cold.

Mama Mabel says into the phone, "Of course you can, Randall."

Mom and Rich look at me quizzically.

"He's the chef," I inform.

Mabel looks quizzically at the phone. "Phone line's dead again." She hangs up the receiver. "Randall and his husband are on the way. Their neighborhood's been evacuated. He called from his cell. They're almost here."

"This place is incredible, Mabel!" Rich says

She smiles wistfully. "When I was little, this building housed my late father's custom stained-glass window business. All the windows you see are his handcrafted work." She glances around the room. "Those windows inspired everything about my style and life." She clears her throat, a touch misty-eyed. "When I inherited it, the building was renovated into what you see today."

"This place is massive," Mom says.

Mama nods. "It takes a full staff to keep things running, and I hire as many people as possible. Frankly, there's a never-ending stream of money that flows through this place. Sex sells, and I figure, what's the point of sitting on a mountain of money when I can use it to make other people's lives better?"

A few minutes later, in strolls Randall and his husband, Howard.

Randall smiles, but his eyes are lined with strain. "Sorry to dump in on you like this. It was rough getting over here. Like walking through the apocalypse. We didn't even try to drive over. Been trying to get here for an hour." He appears sheepish. "We tried calling the whole walk, and finally got through when we were almost here. I'm sorry we assumed you'd be okay with it, but it's safer here than our house. It's getting wild out there."

"Don't be silly. You're always welcome. I'll show you to your room." Mabel heads down the hall with the guys.

Trey goes to the foyer. I already know that he's checking the door to make sure it's locked. Mama Mabel, Randall, and Howard make their way back to us as Trey returns with a transistor radio Mabel keeps in a cabinet in the foyer. He sets it down on a delicate dark-wood coffee table and turns the dial until an emergency broadcast comes through clearly.

Three disturbing squawks sound before a voice crackles out, "All Los Angeles County residents are under mandatory curfew orders starting at midnight. Please seek shelter. Mandatory curfew lifts at seven a.m. and will resume tomorrow night at seven p.m. Ensure that you have proper supplies to last fourteen days. Critical services will be down for an undetermined time. Streetlights are nonoperational all over the region. Travel is discouraged. Bridges and overpasses are unpassable countywide. Water is not safe to drink. I repeat, water is not safe to drink." Three more loud squawks screech from the radio, and the message loops again.

Trey clicks off the radio.

All eyes shift to me as I gasp and double over around the pain in my chest. My heart's racing, and my eyes are unfocused. An intuitive bubble boils up. I study it in my mind's eye. Panicked, I say, "Babe, tap in."

Trey studies the bubble with me, and our eyes meet across the distance.

Mama Mabel says, "Uh-oh."

With a no-nonsense tone, Trey takes charge. "Randall, how are we looking for supplies?"

"Not good. We're fully stocked on bottled water, but I don't believe in canned shelf-stock. Everything I make is from fresh ingredients. We need to get canned meat, vegetables, fruit, and packaged rice and pasta."

Trey turns to Mabel. "Go get the girls and bring them here. We need to fill them in."

Mabel races down the hall, returning quickly with her four resident girls.

"Can you make a supply run?" Trey asks of Randall. He checks his watch. "We have an hour until curfew."

Randall nods. "I'm going to make a quick list." He moves briskly through the dining room door, headed to the kitchen with Howard.

"What are we up against?" Rich asks.

A loud pounding sounds from the foyer.

Trey glares that way. "Fantastic." He stalks through the parlor with Rich. They come back with Big Joe.

"I was ordered to evacuate," Big Joe says. "After my neighborhood was evacuated, I had myself set up in the little living quarters in the back of my tattoo shop. Officer Striker came by and ordered me to evacuate there too. He said to warn you all that there are looting mobs forming on Sunset, Hollywood Boulevard, and Vine. He's worried they're going to come this way."

"I hate being right," I say quietly.

Trey closes his eyes, exhausted. "Melanie's intuition showed us exactly what we're up against. We're in for a long night."

My eyes un-focus again as someone outside intentionally hurls memories my way. How Adam is doing it is beyond me, what with our soulmate connection shut down and all.

"Head to the door, Trey. Incoming."

Trey leaves through the foyer door and quickly returns with Adam and Valerie.

"We're not safe at our house," Adam explains. "Cars are on fire, and people are losing it out there. The chaos brought out the creepy-crawlies."

Rich rolls his eyes. "Of course it did."

Randall rushes in. "I have my list. Howard and I will hurry back as fast as we can."

"New plan," Trey says, shaking his head. "We'll have to make do with what we have. I'm enabling the perimeter vault system in a few minutes. I'm going to wait and see if any more of our people show up first."

Mama Mabel's eyebrows rise. "Is this really that serious?"

Trey nods. "Looks like I'm getting a trial run as head of security a little sooner than we thought." He looks around at everyone's anxious faces. "Anyone who wants to leave needs to do so now. Once I lock this place down, the doors don't open again until Melanie is positive this madness is over. I don't trust the emergency broadcast system like I trust her intuition."

"Is everyone staying?" Rich asks.

Heads nod all around the circle.

"Anyone with a car in the parking lot needs to move it into the garage as soon as our meeting's over." Trey turns to Randall. "You said we've got fresh food. How long until it spoils?"

"Three days, tops. I was stocked for a big engagement party booked in Mabel's event center, so the walk-in refrigerator's stuffed."

"The freezer and fridge are powered by the generator. Get in the kitchen and make everything you can. We'll freeze it." Trey turns to Rich. "Double-check the gas line again. We're going to turn the gas on long enough for Randall to use the stove and ovens."

Rich rushes to get it turned on.

"I'm going to get busy," Randall says.

"I'll help," Mom offers.

Howard and Destiny volunteer to join them.

There's another knock, and Trey stalks through the foyer. He comes back with Mr. Isley.

"I was stuck at the school with the kids whose parents couldn't get there," the dance teacher explains. "I live in Culver City and can't get home. Can I crash here?"

Mama Mabel nods. "Are you okay if I put you in the guest room with Demitri? There are two beds in that room."

Mr. Isley looks to Demitri, who says, "I'm good with that. He and I need to talk anyway."

"Big Joe, can you take everyone's car keys and move cars into the garage?" Trey asks. "There's room for fourteen if you angle it right. We can fit them all."

Big Joe starts gathering keys. Rich comes back and offers to help. They head out to open the garage door.

Adam, Demitri, Trey, Mr. Isley, and I huddle up.

"Are you okay, Melanie?" they all ask in unison.

I roll my eyes and laugh.

"I see you have all your lion tamers here to deal with you," Mr. Isley quips.

"How fortunate I am," I say with a groan.

"Sorry, Mel," Adam says. "Marcus managed to get a call through while they were headed to rescue you at Canoga Park. I was worried, but I couldn't leave Valerie."

"Rescuing me was the least of it. I used my memory-seeking nonsense to find people in the wreckage. We all spent eight hours digging through, and stepping over, crushed skulls in the rubble." My stomach churns at the thought of Bethany, but I harshly push the memory away. "I still have dried blood under my nails from the survivors we pulled out." I look up at him. "So, just another day in paradise." I intended lighthearted sarcasm, but only managed to achieve childlike fear.

Adam wraps his arms around me. I rest my forehead on his chest, and we inhale and exhale together like we always do. "You need to talk?"

I chuckle mirthlessly. "Definitely not. One more conversation with you boys and I'm going to walk into the impending doom and offer myself as a sacrifice."

All three guys laugh.

"I'm going to check on Valerie." Adam heads to the hall.

Demitri motions to Mr. Isley. "I'll take you to our room." They leave through the hall.

Trey gathers me up in a hug and holds me. I feel dead inside. My usual post-trauma hysteria has been replaced with a flat hum. "You have work to do," I remind.

He sighs. "I do, but we need a minute." He rubs my back lightly. "I love you."

I smile and wrap my arms around his waist. "I love you too."

Someone pounds on the front door. I groan, then follow Trey to the door.

Bear and Darren rush through.

"Lock it," Bear says. "*Now.*"

"Mob on Hollywood Boulevard," Darren informs. "We have fifteen minutes max before they make it this far."

"How many?" Trey asks.

"Thousands," Bear says dejectedly. "The mob is herding down every street in the area, destroying and looting everything in their path. It's mayhem. We were trying to get to my house, but overpasses are collapsed everywhere. We backtracked."

Adam, Rich, and Big Joe are listening by the parlor door.

Big Joe grabs gas canisters from the foyer. "I brought them with me and left them here when I arrived."

Darren and Bear help him, and they head in the direction of the garage.

"What's the plan?" Adam asks.

His question jolts Trey from his frozen state. He rushes past, instructing, "Every door and window lock, checked now. All the windows are open because it's so hot and we don't have electricity.

Hurry." He turns to me. "Mel, go get Mr. Isley and Demitri. Head to the security office."

I race down the hall and knock on the door to Demitri and Mr. Isley's guest room.

Mr. Isley cracks the door and says, "It's Melanie."

"Let her in," Demitri says.

Mr. Isley opens the door just enough for me to scoot in before closing and locking it again. Demitri's sitting on one of the beds with his head in his hands, crying. I side-eye Mr. Isley.

"He just needs a second. We're dealing with it."

"Unfortunately, we have a mob headed this way," I inform. "We're supposed to join everyone in the security office."

Demitri groans.

I run my hands down the back of his hair and pull his head against my chest. He drops his hands from his face and wraps his arms around my waist.

"Is this a new problem, an old problem, or the complicated shitstorm with us?" I ask.

His voice is muffled against me as he says, "Shitstorm."

"He filled me in," Mr. Isley says quietly. "He's spun out."

I can't help but chuckle ironically. "Well, D, when a guy gets spun out over me, the choices are to propose to Valerie or screw a cheerleader. Which is it gonna be?"

Demitri belts surprised laughter. Mr. Isley snorts. I crinkle my nose mischievously at him.

"I'm not into pregnant chicks, and cheerleaders giggle too much," Demitri says. "I'll have to settle for being upset."

"You're smiliiing," I tease.

He laughs through his slowing tears. "That's usually my line."

Mr. Isley raises an eyebrow. "Why is it that every guy who touches you loses his marbles?"

"For the record, Demitri and I have never gone there. All we did was kiss."

Mr. Isley rolls his eyes. "Oh good. When you do, I'm in for an avalanche of disaster."

The earth chooses that moment to buck and heave in another aftershock. Demitri holds on to me so I don't fall.

When it's done, I say to Mr. Isley, "Pump the brakes on the avalanche. One natural disaster at a time." I look at Demitri. "What's wrong?"

"I'm an idiot, Melanie."

I nod jokingly, and he gives me a look, but he's smiling a touch.

"What happened when Pierre threatened to turn the tables at CityWalk has changed everything. So did seeing you crushed to death." Demitri's expression melts. "I swear I'm done running, and I'll handle things much differently."

My heart suddenly hurts. "Umm . . . That's not what I expected to hear."

"I know. Melanie, I'm sorry. I absolutely hate that I didn't figure all of this out in time."

"Are you seriously with Trey again?" Mr. Isley asks, baffled.

"I freaking put a promise ring on my finger and moved in with him after Demitri was like, 'Best-friend category, can you handle it, Victoria's so special, you're a Fraggle.' He bailed from the dinner table, never came back, and I was *done*."

Mr. Isley gives Demitri an exasperated look. "You've been grumbling to me about how you can't handle being without Melanie for how long now?"

Demitri groans. I snap wide eyes Mr. Isley's way.

He nods pointedly at me. "What would you have done if Demitri had told you in the dressing room that he wanted to date you?" Mr. Isley asks.

I laugh. "The dressing room? Demitri had a lot more opportunities than that to get this right. I fell for him a long time ago, but I DO NOT want Trey to know that. I'm working my ass off to shut it down and switch back to adorable sidekick mode in my head."

Demitri inhales sharply and thumps his head against my chest.

Mr. Isley looks at him and demands, "What is WRONG with you?"

His expression is pained. "All I could think about in that moment was that it was wrong to hurt Victoria."

"Seriously?" Mr. Isley squawks. "You were concerned about Victoria's feelings? Does she even *have* feelings?"

I bobble my head comically. "Welcome to my life. This always happens. God forbid a bimbo gets her feelings hurt."

"I swear I was yours, and then Victoria kissed me right before we went in the dressing room to talk with Mr. Isley." Demitri winces. "It's like this soulmate bond flares anytime she touches me." He shakes his head, at a loss. "I don't think it's just the soulmate bond, Melanie. There's something else."

"Sometimes it seems like that," I admit. "The bond is powerful."

"I feel trapped," he whispers.

"You are," I commiserate.

His head drops as a fresh round of tears wells up. "Damn it, Melanie," he whispers. "Please rescue me."

I wipe tears from his cheeks. "Pull it together, love. I promise we'll unpack this once that mob is gone." I hug him and rub his back. "Thank you for saving me. I know how hard that was for you."

He cradles my cheeks in his hands. "You don't understand. Healing you changed everything for me. You were almost gone."

"I know, D. I promise this conversation isn't over, but I have a dark-water vibe shift I need to make."

His expression morphs to concern as I take a few steps back and close my eyes. My dark-water side rises, and I wait until I'm full of the intensity that lives in me. The room is suddenly heavy with a violent energetic thrum.

"Holy crap," Mr. Isley says. "You're a trip, Melanie."

My dark-water side studies Demitri and sends a suggestive pulse through me. "Yeah, yeah," I say to my dark-water side. "He's perfect. Down girl." I inform Demitri, "Sorry. My dark-water side likes you. You don't want to deal with her when she gets like this."

Demitri chuckles.

"Let's go," I snarl.

We leave the room and join everyone in the hall.

Trey passes by and looks in my eyes. "There's my girl," he says with a smile. "I see you're geared up to level a mob."

I nod.

He unlocks the security office door and crosses the room as everyone files in. He unlocks a long metal cover on the wall, swinging it open to reveal an intricate series of buttons. "Hopefully no more of our people show up looking for a place to crash, because they're shit out of luck."

He presses the largest red button, and it glows. A computerized voice that's all too familiar to me says, "Perimeter vault system initiated in ten . . . nine . . ." Trey presses a button labeled *Countdown Override*, and we listen to metal sliding, followed by thumps and clanks that sound out all around the outside of the building.

Most of our friends look at Trey quizzically, and he answers their unspoken question. "We're equipped with a perimeter system. Steel gates just rolled down and locked over every window and door."

Confused, I ask, "Then why did we have to close the windows? We're going to boil in here."

Trey gives me his infamous "Are you serious?" look. "If there's a lock, it gets locked. You've met me, right?"

"How are the security monitors running when the electricity is off?" Bear asks.

"This is a TransitSecurLock system," Trey explains. "It's got its own backup power system that can run for four days on a battery power pack, and Mama Mabel has ten of the packs. I've got them charged and ready. We're secure in here for up to forty days."

"How do you know all this?" Rich asks.

"Mama Mabel offered me the head of security position. I don't officially start until after I graduate in a year and a half, but I've read the manual and just went through an extensive training session on the system."

"Why?" Big Joe asks.

Trey glances away from the monitors to Big Joe. "Melanie's living here part time. I need to know the system to keep her safe."

Big Joe bobbles his head comically. "Why of course. I should have known."

Trey turns back to the monitors. "Here we go." He points to a monitor that shows a view from the roof, aiming up Hollywood Boulevard. A massive wall of people spread the entire length of the wide road, moving our way. Trey zooms in, and we see people crushing together, stretching out of sight.

"There must be thousands," Mama Mabel breathes out fearfully.

Trey leans to the security system wall panel and pushes two buttons. A single beep emits from the panel, and then we listen as steel locks on the security office door slide into place. "I initiated the interior panic room system and overrode the voice warning."

We all watch the monitor again.

"How do we fight that many people?" Adam asks. He looks at Valerie and puts a hand over her pregnant belly.

"I'm so sorry, Valerie," I say when it occurs to me how frightened she must be.

I tap Trey's hip, and he shifts as I pull out the rolling chair that's pushed in under the desk. Bear hands it over to Adam, and Valerie sits.

"Thank you," she says. She's sweating profusely. "This heat is going to drop me."

Mama Mabel grabs a stiff file folder from the desk and fans the back of Valerie's neck.

Without taking his eyes off the monitors, Trey says, "When this is done, we'll figure out a way to run the air-conditioning system off the generator. I know it's hot."

Big Joe thinks for a moment. "I helped Stubbs install it. There are three separate systems. If we run only the system that's attached to the living quarters, we have a chance of not blowing the generator."

A minute later, the mob reaches us, and we hear chaos from outside.

"What's the plan, Trey?" Adam asks nervously. "How do we fight that many people? Even with Melanie as the front line, we're outgunned."

"We don't," Trey quietly responds. "Our job is to be invisible. Due to the illegal nature of the business, Mabel intentionally makes this place as uninteresting as possible from the outside. This mob's going to go after the shiniest prizes. We don't have a fancy storefront."

"How do you know the mob will do that?" Mama Mabel asks him.

"I've been studying urban warfare, de-escalation tactics, hand-to-hand restraint, one-on-one fight tactics, mob psychology." He turns to Mama Mabel. "I have work to do before I take over security here. I'm rusty. My dad shut down his bodyguard business a while back."

Mama Mabel smiles softly. "Trey, I'm putting you on payroll effective immediately. You can work part time so you can still handle school and baseball practice."

Trey smiles. "It means a lot that you trust me."

"It means a lot that you read that boring vault manual," Mama Mabel retorts. "It's the size of a textbook."

We hear screaming, and the sound of something cracking against metal. A clang, clang, clang reverberates ominously through the building, and everyone reacts in their own way. Some cower, others gasp. Big Joe and Adam crack their knuckles. Valerie puts her head on the desk and moans.

Panicked, Mama Mabel gasps, "What do we do?"

"Wait it out." Trey points to one of the monitors. "We're hearing one thug banging on the metal gate with a baseball bat at the street side of the building. He's not getting anywhere. These gates are rated to withstand a head-on truck collision. Short of a tank, they aren't breeching the gates. Mama Mabel's got good taste in security systems."

We watch, hearing the growing sounds of mayhem, but Trey remains calm and contemplative. Panic rises in my chest as the sound of the massive mob we've got no shot against screams and rages.

My voice is dark-water gravelly as I say, "Trey, if I have to take on a power load to deal with the mob, I'm going to kill the generator. With all the lights out, there's no other source."

"I don't think you'll have to. Hang tight."

Footsteps run across the roof above our heads. Trey glances up but doesn't react. My heart starts racing, and I whimper down our connection but keep my dark-water stoic expression in place so no one else panics.

Trey puts his arm out to me. "Come here, love. I'll show you."

I step up next to him, and he points to the monitor showing the roof view down Hollywood Boulevard. He pushes a button on what looks like a big video game controller on the desk. He toggles a joystick, and the camera view pans to show the buildings across the street. He presses two buttons, and the view on the largest monitor shifts from the empty alley main entrance to the view across the street.

He points at the big monitor. "Here it comes. There's a huge electronics store across the street. That's the flashy distraction I'm counting on."

Just like he anticipates, we watch as the mob starts working on the chain gate over the glass front doors of the electronics store. It doesn't take long before the gate is ripped from its track on the right side. People slip through, and someone throws a cinder block through the glass door. A roar emits from the crowd outside as people rush the store. The gate is ripped down completely as the crowd flows in.

"Bingo," Trey says. "Mob mentality. They'll all follow."

Just like he says, people race in and out like ants on an anthill. Everyone who comes out is carrying an armload of stolen goods. Trey pans the camera the other way on Hollywood Boulevard, and the crowd swarms that direction, looting every interesting shop they find.

The sounds of chaos die down as the mob continues down the street. Trey scans all the monitors carefully. Satisfied, he hits a button on the wall control panel. There's a click from the office door.

"The captain has turned off the fasten seat belt sign," he jokes. "You're free to move about the cabin."

Everyone exhales.

CHAPTER 40

I'm jolted from a deep sleep by the bed heaving and bouncing.

"Melanie, get over here!" Trey yells.

The ground jostles sideways and bounces harder. I'm tossed out of the bed and land near Trey by the door.

"You rang?" I yell sarcastically over the sounds of the earthquake.

Mom and Rich laugh from their position braced in the doorjamb across the hall. Trey reaches out a hand and pulls me to the doorjamb. He has his back against the left side, with his feet pressed against the base of the right side. I take a surprisingly complicated step his way and brace my back against the doorjamb opposite him, straddling his legs. I lean forward and grab the doorjamb over his shoulders.

"This is a long one," Rich yells. "Hang tight."

I glance down the hall to see that all the inhabitants are in doorways. "Adam, where's Valerie?"

"I've got her here. She's lying on the floor in the open area where nothing can fall on her. I don't want her standing just in case she accidentally falls."

"We have to get these aftershocks to stop," I send to Trey. *"I can't take any more."*

He cracks up, grabbing the doorjamb harder as a particularly bouncy buck hits. *"You want us to stop earthquakes? We're good, but we ain't that good."*

I laugh. *"Yeah . . . I've clearly lost it."*

Finally, the shaking stops.

Big Joe calls out from the room he's sharing with Darren and Bear. "Everyone okay?"

We all respond in the affirmative and gather in the hall. Valerie sits, and I join her. She looks exhausted. Her face is gaunt, her eyes hollowed out with dark circles under them. I take her hand, and she puts her head on my shoulder.

"We're going to get through this," I quietly say to her.

Val sighs and says to Big Joe, Trey, and Rich, "Thank you for getting the air conditioning running in our rooms. I feel a lot better."

"You're welcome, little mama," Big Joe says. "We can only run it on low, but it's definitely taken the edge off."

Demitri and Mr. Isley sit in the hall by their door.

Rich takes a seat next to my mom, his back leaning against the wall. "I've lived in LA most of my life, and I know earthquakes, but this one's a monster."

Mama Mabel plops down by Bear. "You're not kidding! This is intense."

"For you youngbloods in the group, there's some stuff you need to know," Rich says. "We've had earthquakes during your time spinning around on this big blue globe, but not like this. Some earthquakes bounce. Some roll. Some shake you side to side. I knew we had one coming because the weather kept shifting from hot to cold so rapidly."

Interested, Valerie lifts her head. "What do you mean?"

"People are always talking about earthquake weather, and scientists may disagree, but it's always made perfect sense to me. Earth expands with heat and contracts with cold." Rich puts his fists together, knuckle to knuckle. "My fists are two plates of earth. The space between is a fault line. When it's cold, they contract, giving a little more room between them." He parts his fist slightly, allowing them to shift a bit. "But then it heats up and the earth expands. It puts intense pressure where the two plates meet." He presses his fists against each other, and they buckle up. "Enough pressure and the plates slip. If the pressure of the two plates is pressing together, they move upward, creating mountains and hills. If they are moving the opposite direction . . . now that's when it gets interesting. We're currently experiencing the results."

"When will it stop?" Valerie whimpers.

Rich shrugs. "No telling. The original quake was a whopper. Aftershocks are generally a lower magnitude than the original, but they can be nearly as bad. In my experience, this could go on for a couple of weeks, but the aftershocks will weaken with time. We've got a few more days of this bad shaking, at least. Part of the issue is that with each subsequent rattler, more damage occurs to buildings. They can weaken and eventually collapse."

"When I did the big remodel of this building," Mama Mabel says in a reassuring tone, "I had it reinforced and retrofitted by an earthquake specialty construction company. This building isn't going anywhere."

"I'm more concerned about what *people* are capable of during this disaster than I am about the aftershocks," Big Joe says.

"Me too," Trey says.

"Everyone, sleep in clothes," Rich advises. "Have a pair of shoes by the side of your bed in case we have to evacuate, or there's broken glass."

"I hate to suggest this," Trey says, "but we need to start watching the monitors in the security office full time. The rescue at Canoga Park High was a lot, and I need to sleep at some point." He takes a breath. "So, if I hand out a schedule with two-hour shifts, can you all step up and take over some of the workload each day?"

Everyone agrees.

"Randall and Carol, you can stick to kitchen duty," Trey says. "I'd like to assign Savannah and Daphne to cleanup duty in the common areas. Melanie, can you and Sapphire handle dishes and help with kitchen cleanup after each meal?"

We all agree. Then, hopeful that the ground will cool its tantrums for a few hours, we head back to bed.

CHAPTER *41*

With morning came extreme gratitude to still be alive. After a quick shower and a long cry, I come out of the bathroom in a towel. Trey's putting the finishing touches on his hair.

"I swear, you spend more time getting ready than I do," I point out.

He chuckles. "I need some normalcy, hence doing my hair." He picks up a gray tube from the dresser and waggles it over his shoulder. "Also, Mabel got me hair gel that smells like the kind of heaven only wealthy people are welcome in."

I laugh.

He turns my way, and his mouth drops open.

"What?"

"Oh my God, Melanie," he breathes out. "Have you looked in a mirror?"

I shake my head and cross to the mirrored sliding closet doors. My face is a deep purple. The side that was crushed is swollen. The eye that popped from the socket sports a wicked shiner. I drop the towel, and Trey and I survey my undressed state. The bruising reveals every spot that was damaged. My feet are the only place that isn't discolored.

He wraps me in his arms. "I almost lost you. If it weren't for Demitri . . ." He trails off in fear.

"I'm okay," I say softly. "I woke up really sore but that was expected. Demitri warned me that I'd be terribly bruised. I know it's disturbing."

Trey tips up my chin and looks into my eyes. "I couldn't save you this time."

Someone knocks hard on the door. "Yo, Trey!" Arch sounds harried. "I need permission to open the gate over the front door!"

Trey cracks the door. "Why?"

"Helicopter just landed in the parking lot, bro," Arch reveals. "I'm on security duty. Saw it on the monitors."

"Move, move, move," I bark as I hastily dress and then push past Trey. "Open the gate, Arch."

He looks down at me, unsure. "Yes, ma'am," he sasses.

Trey grabs my arm as I start to run to the parlor. "Don't do this, Melanie!"

I pull my wrist from his grasp. "If Zane is here, I need to talk to him."

"I'm begging you not to."

"Why?"

"Because I want you to focus on us," Trey insists.

I raise my eyebrows. "There's stuff I need to deal with that you don't know about."

"I thought secrets weren't okay!" Trey accuses. Then he winces, clearly recognizing that he has also kept secrets.

"I'm not keeping secrets," I retort. "There hasn't been time to discuss this with you, but I planned to."

"Melanie, please!"

"Welcome," I hear Mama Mabel say from the next room. "What a nice surprise."

I make it to the parlor with a very unhappy Trey following.

"When is the service?" Rocco asks.

"What service?" Mabel asks.

"Melanie's memor—" Rocco trails off as he stares at me.

"Hi," I say quietly.

Rocco looks me up and down with tearful puppy dog eyes. "You're alive?" he breathes. He slowly crosses to me. His eyes are huge. "You're alive, but you look dead."

"You should have seen me yesterday. The bruises are nothing." I hold a hand his way. "Wanna see how bad it was, so you know how good it is?"

He takes my hand, and I send the memory of seeing myself through Trey's eyes. I'm lying on the rubble, my face crushed on one side, a dangling eyeball on the other side. Rocco comes out of the memory. Immediately, he snakes out a hand and grabs Demitri. He yanks D to him, and says with extreme conviction, "Thank you," hugging him tight.

Demitri returns the hug. "You're welcome. Melanie pushed my healing limits this time."

"The eyeball was freaking gross!" Rocco lets him go.

Demitri grins. "I barfed when I saw it."

"I kinda wanna barf now that I've seen it." He gingerly pulls me in for a hug, holding me like I might break. He's so tall that I feel engulfed as he curls around me.

"Not too much," I whisper. "I was trapped for a long time, and I'm scared to be trapped again."

"I know you were," Rocco murmurs for only me to hear. "I heard from Zane."

I snap my gaze up to him. "What?"

"He thinks you're dead, Melanie. That man is working on bribing, begging, or threatening his way onto a military flight to get back here. The only air traffic currently allowed into Southern California is military."

"Then how did you get away with a helicopter flight?"

Rocco laughs a little while he wipes at his drying tears. "I insisted that we not, but after Zane sent us the message about you through goodness only knows what CB channels, Brian raced to the helicopter and was determined to head here." Rocco shrugs. "I'll pay the fine if we get one. Brian's hysterical. May I get him?"

"Of course," Mabel says. "Bring him inside."

Rocco leaves for only a moment before he and Brian rush into the parlor. Brian sees me, doubles over at the waist, and gasps out, "Thank GOD!" He whips around to Rocco. "We have to get word back to Zane before he ends up court-martialed!"

"First, can I have a word with you?" I ask of Brian and Rocco. "In private?"

Eagerly, they nod.

The others stare after us as I lead the way down the hall into the dance studio/gym, closing the door behind us.

Brian gapes at me. "You're so bruised!"

"It's bad, but it could be worse." I sit on the tumbling mats.

Rocco sits next to me, and Brian chooses a spot on the floor facing us.

Settled, I ask, "What did you hear from Zane?"

Rocco takes a slip of paper out of his shorts pocket. He reads, "Melanie somehow got through to me mind-to-mind. She was trapped in the earthquake. I was with her in her mind when she was crushed to death. I need you to get to Mabel's and find out when the memorial is. The parking lot is big enough to land. I'm doing everything I can to get home on a military flight."

I put my face in my hands. "It was real," I whisper.

"How did you do it?" Brian asks.

"I have no idea. You have no clue what it takes to have that kind of range even with a *soulmate*! I thought it was impressive that I can reach Trey from across town. Zane and I shouldn't have that ability. We have no soulmate connection, and he's a Normal."

"Zane must be dying inside," Brian says, worried. He gives me a soft look. "You need to know that he cares deeply about you. He's never like this, but when it comes to his little Melanie, it's a whole different ball game."

I shake my head sadly. "I know what happened with Molly. We aren't what you're thinking." When Brian winces, I rush to add, "I'm okay with that. I'm grateful to have Zane as my friend."

"He was so destroyed about that mess. He was already mortified, and then when you lost your first movie . . ." Brian looks pained. "He was inconsolable. Zane flat doesn't make mistakes. He's so damn irritating. Being his brother sucks. I was always a screwup, and then along would trot Mr. Perfect."

"It hurts me and Brian to see Zane fail like this," Rocco says. "He's so well intentioned. And believe me, he has zero interest in Molly. He came over after he left her apartment that night. He was absolutely devastated."

"I can't help you there," I reply. "What Zane does is on him."

Rocco sighs. "Then, it came out on *Splash TV*, and he died of shame. You'll rarely see him on trash TV shows. When he found out that Molly set him up to gain her spot back in the movie, I thought he was going to kill her."

"That was nothing compared to when he got the news about Melanie from Ms. Alice, though," Brian says. "It was brutal. She called him while we were sitting there the next morning. I could hear her screaming from across the room. He nearly passed out when he heard the news that you were being replaced by the person who manipulated him. Then," Brian dramatically pauses, "Zane *Drell* begged. He doesn't do that."

"He cried during the meeting I had with Ms. Alice," I reveal.

"Holy crap!" Brian barks.

I hold out my hand. "Take a look at that meeting first, then we'll get to the rest of this."

The guys take my hands, and I pass the memory to them. Brian looks stunned but trusts me enough to close his eyes and watch.

When the memory of the meeting with Ms. Alice ends, they open their eyes.

"Zane wasn't thinking, obviously," Brian says, "but he had NO idea how many layers would be affected by him giving into a one-night stand."

I scrunch my face. "Ick."

Brian laughs a little. "It's not like you're an innocent virgin."

"Nope, I'm not. I don't like one-night stands, though. Sex boils down to love for me. There's a reason I've only been with three people, and one of them was a mistake."

"Which one was the mistake?" Rocco asks.

"Adam. That was once, and should have never happened, but he was my first and I didn't understand that he wasn't serious about me."

"He used you?" Rocco asks. "He's one of your soulmates."

"Yes, but he's also Adam. The other two are Trey and Pierre. I loved all three dearly." I shrug a little. "Zane is welcome to do as he pleases."

"Zane's casual dating past is one of his few bad qualities," Brian reveals. "In his defense, he became a household name at seventeen. He's only twenty-one, and he's one of the most famous actors in the world." He shrugs. "Everyone throws themselves at him."

I grimace hugely. "I kissed him. Now I feel gross."

Rocco smiles. "He told me. He didn't think you were one of those girls. Since his career took off, he missed out on being a normal teenage guy who's enamored with a girl. He loves laughing with you and doing normal things. Being invited over to swim at a pretty girl's house, a girl who kissed him in the pool and watched cartoons with him, was his idea of heaven."

"For the record, I'm back with Trey," I inform.

"Uuugh," Brian groans.

I give him a questioning look. "Why are you so caught up in this?"

Brian sighs and glances at Rocco, who says, "You already know that Zane doesn't have casual feelings for you."

"And you already know that I'm too young and this is a moot point," I remind. "What did you expect the guy to do? Sit around and wait for a year and a half while I slog through high school?"

"Yes," Rocco and Brian say in unison.

I laugh a little. "I have a boyfriend. Zane has a hussy. Moving on . . ." My cheeks burn hot, and I feel dizzy. "I need to lie down," I whisper.

Rocco jumps up and goes to the door. I hear him quietly talking with Mama Mabel. A few moments later, Demitri strides in with Mabel. He crosses to me, kneeling.

"Hey, talk to me," Demitri says softly.

"I don't feel good," I whimper.

Demitri smiles a little and puts a hand on my forehead. After a quick scan, he informs, "I think you're just overwhelmed. Your body is fine, other than shock and residual pain from rapid healing. You've been through a lot."

"My head hurts."

"Your face was crushed, and your eye was hanging out," Demitri reminds.

"I feel icky." I squish up my face. "I bounced back to Trey really fast."

Demitri wobbles his head. "It's been a weird year. Everyone but Trey feels icky. He's grateful to have another chance with you."

"I think I moved a little faster than I can handle with the Trey reconnecting," I admit. "I feel like I'm a hamster for being with him again."

Demitri laughs. "You're not. How you keep that dark-water side in check is beyond me. If any of the rest of us had it, we'd have plowed through half the county."

"A lot of you *have*," I say with a pitiful laugh.

"True, but that's just testosterone. Guys are gross."

"Eeew," I reply, sitting up and wringing my hands.

Demitri shrugs. "If it helps, we all feel dirty and tainted because you think we're hoes."

I consider this a moment before giggling. "That does help, actually."

"Adam and I have discussed it. It freaks him out. He and I are used to being seen as the ultimate prize. He said that, with you, he feels like a used vibrator at a thrift store."

We all howl laughter.

"That's exactly the brand of icky I'm talking about!" I squeal. I playfully point at Demitri. "You're Victoria's used buzz-buzz at a thrift store!"

"Uuugh," Demitri groans. "I'm going to go die of shame now."

As he stands, I remind, "You hate being seen as a perfect god by girls." I grin. "See! I'm helping."

He chuckles bashfully and takes his leave.

Mabel comes over to join us. Rocco offers her his spot on the tumbling mat, but Mabel waves him off and sits cross-legged on the floor.

"I can't believe I got through to Zane," I say. "I'm so sorry he thinks I'm dead."

Rocco hands Mabel the slip of paper, and she smiles a little as she reads it. "That guy is so sweet."

I shake my head. "He's Molly's icky."

"Now, now," Mabel says. "Sometimes it takes tragedy for someone to be less icky. When the world crashes down, we learn."

"He's aware, if it helps." Rocco scrunches his nose at me. "You might not want to tell him that he's Molly's thrift store vibrator. I really think he might die of shame."

"Well," Mabel says suggestively, "how would you three like to get a message through to Molly's thrift store accessory?"

We all stare at our hostess.

"Come with me," she says with a smile.

We follow her out to the hall, where we find Trey, Demitri, and Adam engaged in a squawking session.

"I can't believe you told Melanie I said that," we overhear.

Adam focuses on us as we head his way down the hall. "Oooh, field trip," he says as they start to follow.

"Not for you," I chide.

"Ah, come on," Adam whines. "We're bored!"

I wave a dismissive hand. "Go be Valerie's thrift store accommodation."

Adam looks like he smells something foul. "She's all big, and bitchy, and needy."

My mouth drops open. "She's pregnant with your love twins, you jackass!"

"I hate this," Adam says, stomping his feet in frustration.

"You're about to be a father of two. Quit acting like a toddler."

He tosses his hands. "I don't want any of what's happening here."

Mama Mabel purses her lips. "I think you and I need to do some talking, Adam. You need help working through your looming reality."

Everyone watches with compassion as Adam straightens up and suddenly starts to look his age. This is a rare occurrence for him. His senior year, he'd stride through Hollywood High looking like a twenty-five-year-old in a sea of teenagers.

"I don't want babies and a mortgage," Adam says just above a whisper. "I miss sitting on the beach with Melanie, talking about bright futures and possibilities."

I take pity on him and offer an honest admission. "If it helps, Valerie is simpler. The worst she does is complain at you and demand that you take out the trash. Meanwhile, I'm regularly dying, crapping my pants in the hospital, and requiring eyeball repair."

The look Adam gives me hurts my heart. "Your problems are real," he says. "You aren't a privileged brat with first-world complaints and shallow needs."

I furrow my brow. "I'll give you that. There's one good thing that's come of all we've been through, I guess: I don't complain about nonsense like all your other vapid, immature girls." I survey the three. "Valerie, Victoria, and Tiffany are the perfect example of Normal girls, right where they're supposed to be in life. Teenagers who are shallow and learn the slow way. Be glad."

"Pardon," Trey says, "but I'm not with Tiffany. Last I checked, I'm with you, have a ring on your finger, and we live in a room here together part time."

"Yes, dear," I placate. "Sorry for the Tiffany mention." I smile congenially at the gathered group. "We're maturely moving past the indiscretion."

Adam cracks up at my tone. He waves a hand to Trey. "Give Mel a minute. She'll be pissed again."

"I will not!"

"Yeah, right," Adam says. "I know you. Trey will see." He points at me. "You hold a grudge, girl. I remember some of our past-life moments."

Trey gives me a suspicious look that I ignore.

"Right now," I say, "I need to deal with Molly's thrift store appendage. Please give me a minute."

"Can you PLEASE let Zane Drell go?" Trey begs.

"He thinks I'm dead, Trey." I look to Demitri. "It wasn't a hallucination. Zane was with me in my mind while I was trapped. The connection is gone, and the last thing he experienced through it was my skull popping. That's when the connection poofed."

"You have a soulmate connection with ZANE?" Trey yelps. "He's a NORMAL!" He says the last bit with condescension, and I laugh a little.

"I don't have a soulmate connection with Zane. I have no clue what it was, or how it happened." I point at Demitri. "*He* has a soulmate connection with a Normal, though. So it's not unheard of."

Adam pans a slow, horrified look Demitri's way. "You have a soulmate connection with Victoria?"

Demitri nods, his face ashen. "I hate it."

"I'd DIE if I ended up with a soulmate connection with Valerie," Adam blathers before looking like he regrets it.

"Whoa," Mabel says, studying Adam with concern. "Everything okay in marriage-ville?"

"Definitely not," Adam replies quietly.

We exchange looks.

"We really need to talk, Adam," Mabel says. "I'm going to help you."

"I don't think this is . . ." Adam trails off before finally saying, "We can talk." He looks to Demitri. "I'm sorry, D. There's nothing harder than soulmate life because everything is so deep."

Mama Mabel looks at Adam like he's insane. "Isn't that the goal? Deep connection? True love?"

Adam nods. "Yes, but I couldn't imagine a deep connection with frivolous Victoria. It must be hell. The problem with soulmate love is that it eats you alive with its depth. Soulmate bonds are the ultimate perfect prison. Trey and I talk about that all the time."

I turn a pained expression at Brian.

"Damn it, Adam," Trey breathes.

"I'm sorry, Melanie," Adam says softly. "I shouldn't have said that."

I stare at Trey, blazingly uncomfortable that he thinks of me as his prison.

"I never wanted you to hear that," Trey rushes to say. "You know how Adam's just *so* hilarious. He says stuff; we all laugh."

"I know life with me has been challenging," I say sheepishly. "I'm glad you have someone to commiserate with."

Trey clenches his jaw. "I don't really feel that way. It was all just guy talk."

I take a slow breath. Knowing I have other things to handle than some flippant comment, I start walking again. Mabel puts an arm around me and guides me down the hall. Brian and Rocco follow.

CHAPTER *42*

"All right," Mabel says as she flips a few switches on a contraption she pulled from her storage closet in her office. It's unlike anything I've ever seen before. "How did you get this message?" She reads the paper in her hand for the second time.

"My friend Malibu Joseph is an air traffic controller," Brian explains. "He got the message and CB'd it to the lifeguard headquarters by the pier."

"Okay, I think that makes sense. We're going to backtrack through those routes." Mabel pushes a series of buttons on the complicated contraption. She refers to a typed list before flicking a few more switches and pressing the CB button. "Good morning. I'm searching for the route to reach Zane Drell. Over."

The speaker crackles a moment before a man asks, "Who is this?"

"Mama Mabel, godmother of Melanie Slate."

Brief crackle, and then, "I'm so incredibly sorry, Mabel."

"You won't be in a minute," Mabel joyfully replies. "Say hi, Melanie."

"Hi," I say awkwardly into the CB.

"NO WAY," is screamed through the CB, followed by raucous cheering.

I laugh a little.

"Hang tight. I'm connecting with Joseph." There's more crackle followed by, "You're on the line with her, Malibu J."

"Melanie?"

"Hi, Joseph," I say. "Can you get me through to Zane, please?"

"Holy crap! Yes, I caaan," Joseph says with bubbling excitement. "When he couldn't get through to you, he bought a military-grade CB." He chuckles through the speakers. "Gotta love a rich man on a mission." There's crackling static, and then Joseph says, "Zaney Mania, I've got news."

Zane's tearful voice comes through. "Did you find out when the memorial is?"

"There isn't going to be one," Joseph informs.

"WHAT?" Zane blisters. "YES there is. I'll pay for it."

Joseph chuckles. "Get your barf bucket ready, Zaney."

"Ugh," Zane replies. "All I've done is throw up and cry."

"Yeah, I know. You keep that damn CB button pushed every time you hurl." I can hear Joseph grinning as he says, "I've got someone on the line."

"Who?" Zane asks dejectedly.

"Me," I say timidly as Mabel holds the button down.

When she releases the button, we're met with crackling silence. I look up at Mabel with big eyes.

"Melanie?" finally comes through, and I've never heard someone use my name in a tone so mixed with hope and disbelief.

"What's up, Helicopter Hottie?"

The sound of Zane hurling roars, then slops, loudly through the speakers. I crack up.

"Damn, Zane," Joseph says. "You've got to quit holding down the button when you yak, brother."

"Sorry," Zane says. "Melanie, you're alive?"

"Yup," I reply. "Lucky for us, Demitri did what Demitri does. Now, quit working on getting court-martialed, and stop making your brother helicopter around during no-fly restrictions." My heart flutters. "Also, thank you for almost getting court-martialed, and for making your brother helicopter around during no-fly restrictions."

Zane groans. "I never . . ." He trails off, and the static crackles.

"I know," I reply softly. "You didn't think you'd hear from me again. I'm so sorry about that bizarre connection we shared while I was trapped. I have no explanation for it."

"I'm glad it happened," he says. "You didn't have to go through that alone."

"What you felt was me being pulverized under the CPH auditorium," I explain. "The Hollywood crew dug me out. I have no idea how I was still alive. I came to when Trey was trying to find me. My soulmate connection with him was blocked the whole time you and I were chattering. I'm sorry I didn't think it was real, but it really is strange that we were able to do that at all, let alone while we're three thousand miles away from each other."

"In your defense, you were in a very bad situation," Zane says softly. "I knew it was real, though."

My eyes tear up. "Thank you for helping me."

"Aaaw," comes through the CB. "They're so cute!"

Zane's laughter rings out. "That we are. All right, here's the plan. I need Brian to fly you to me."

"No can do, Zane-a-roo," I inform. "There's rioting, chaos, and general fuckery out here."

"That right there is why I love your quirky ass." He sighs.

"Molly has proven to be a royal pain. She's demanding and beyond difficult. Considering that I can't stand her, extra super a *lot*, I'm half-assing all our scenes. If I have to kiss that disgusting abomination one more time, I'm going to hurl up another round. The director is regretting his choice and has been beside himself because you should have been here instead of dying in the earthquake. Now that you're alive, I think it's time to bulldoze your way in, wow them, and get Molly canned."

"That's tacky," I say sheepishly.

"It's how this industry works," Zane encourages. "Melanie, she sucks. The footage is trash. You know how some people look good until they try to be sexy, and then it's all awkward and disconnected?"

"Yeah . . ."

"That's Molly. They tested her reading lines, and dancing, but didn't test her body language. It's weird." He chuckles. "In one scene, when she was supposed to rush down a hall and leap into my arms, she looked like an ostrich on the run from a predator."

"Eww," I say. I look to Mabel. "Thrift store vibrator."

"You bought a vibrator from a thrift store?" Zane breathes out, aghast. "I'll have my assistant buy you a proper vibrator."

I giggle. "I don't want a vibrator. I'm saying that YOU'RE Molly's thrift store vibrator."

Laughter howls from the speakers. It's all garbled, as the Malibu Joseph air control location and lifeguard headquarters apparently have their buttons pushed at once.

"Sorry," I say, blanching. "I forgot we have an audience."

"You listen here, little miss," Zane blisters. "I'm not Molly's thrift store vibrator! Who even says that?"

"Adam," I chirp.

More laughter ripples from our CB audience.

"That makes sense," Zane says. "Tell Adam I said hello."

"Can I tell Trey also? He's THRILLED that I'm in here talking to you."

"Oh definitely," Zane says, sounding amused. "Tell him I'm sending high fives, big hugs, and secret handshakes."

"Who's Trey?" someone asks.

"Her ex-boyfriend," someone else replies.

"Wrong. We're back together."

"Excuse YOU?" Zane snarls. "I don't think so."

"You're with MOLLY. I'm so *thrilled* about THAT," I bark defensively. I wince and let go of the button, muttering, "Well, that sounded insane."

Brian and Rocco spurt laughter.

I slump and grimace at Mama Mabel. "I think I'm moving off the Richter scale fast." I rub my face with my free hand, scolding myself with a groaned, "I can't believe I had sex with Trey again. I need to have Demitri check me for cooties. God only knows what he contracted from Tiffany."

Mama Mabel laughs as Rocco takes the CB from me. He pushes the button, announcing, "Melanie's humping Trey."

"Right now?" comes the excited gossipy reply from Malibu Joseph.

Rocco busts up. "No, you moron. She's humping him in general."

"Oh eeew," comes Zane's response.

"You humped Molly," I accuse back.

Zane groans. "Don't remind me."

"She's got awesome cans dude," comes through the speakers from an unknown male.

I hack.

"No, she doesn't. She got a HORRIBLE boob job."

"Lumps and bumps," someone says through the speakers. "Sometimes you have to ride the waves, even when they're eh."

With a horrified expression on my face, I push the CB button. "Boys are nasty!"

"Shut up, Joseph," Zane bellows. "Don't remind her that I'm nasty."

"You've done so much worse than Molly, my dude," Malibu Joseph says. His proclamation is met with boisterous agreement through the speaker.

I whimper through the CB, "Can I please have brain damage again?"

Mama Mabel takes the CB and presses the button. "My goddaughter isn't coming to New York, Zane! You have cooties."

"I swear I don't," Zane whimpers.

"I'm not hunching, Zane," I bark. "Good GRAVY! What do you think I am? A carnival ride?"

Laughter howls from the speaker.

I sigh. "All right, Helicopter Hottie and company, I'm going to let you go. I have bored hiding in a fortress to do. Maybe I'll try to get to New York when I can."

"Thank God you're alive," Zane says.

"Thank you for barfing because you care," I reply softly.

"I dropped eight pounds," Zane admits.

"Go eat then. And film another humpy humpy scene with Lumpy Boobs."

Laughter peels.

"Ugh. If I have to see those again, I'm going to scream. She rubs them on me, and I gag."

"Sexy," I say, disgusted.

"So sexy," he replies sarcastically. Then, he changes tack. "Bring your gummy bear hoodie when you come out."

"Check. One gummy bear hoodie and two lumpless, boringly real boobs coming right up."

Zane groans again. "You're perfect."

"And you're an icky thrift store vibrator. I need a script for this movie. Just in case I decide to take you up on this plan. Have one ready so I can wow them."

"Done, and I'm not a vibrator!" Zane chortles out, offended.

"That's a shame," I flirt, against my better judgment.

"DAAAMN!" bellows from the speakers.

Zane laughs. "Now you see why I can't leave her alone."

I giggle. "Bye, boys. Love you, Zane."

"Love you, too, gorgeous."

Mabel shuts off the machine, and I stand there reeling beside her, with Brian and Rocco gawking at me.

"Well, all right," I say, a little baffled. "I'm alive. Molly has lumpy boobs. Zane is icky but adorable. Everyone in Malibu knows my business. I'm apparently thinking about going to New York, and I just might be a carnival ride. Sounds like a Melanie mess."

CHAPTER 43

The next morning, we're standing in the kitchen at Mabel's, talking about all my troubles with the Three Stooges, and my desire to take Zane up on his offer to storm into New York and take my movie role back. Mom and Rich, like always, are completely understanding, and like always, are making some really solid points about where my loyalties should lie right now. Still, I'm a little surprised that they seem to favor the idea of me going to New York.

Half the city is rubble, while the other half is facing riots and looting. Maybe they just want to get me out of here. Maybe they're right.

My intuition twinges before it starts roaring insistently. I look inward, gathering the intuitive information and spinning it like a top to view it on all sides. The intuitive bubble rotates rapidly in my mind.

"Damn it!"

I run to the parlor with Mom, Rich, and Mabel following. We've hooked one TV up to the straining generator so we can follow the news updates, and my intuition is confirmed.

"Everyone! Family meeting!" I bellow.

Trey skids around the corner from the hall with everyone quick on his heels. "What's wrong?"

I point to the TV. A local reporter is speaking over aerial helicopter coverage. "Tension mounts as Los Angeles area residents find themselves in desperate circumstances. We've been informed by the mayor that residents should expect another two weeks where travel, services, and supplies will be limited. Unable to get supplies through collapsed overpasses and bridges, gas stations are already out of fuel, and shoppers are facing empty shelves. As desperation mounts, home invasions are on the rise."

"Okay . . . What does this have to do with us?" Trey asks. "We have plenty of supplies, and we're safely locked in here."

My breathing is labored from the intuition pain in my chest. "Do you remember Mack?"

"Who?" Trey asks.

His confusion is shared by most.

"My old security specialist?" Mabel says in a dark tone.

I nod, radiating concern.

"You already dealt with Mack," Trey reminds. "Melted his brain and all. What the hell does that asshole have to do with anything?"

"It appears that his brain is functional enough to realize he has no supplies, and we do," I inform.

Demitri whimpers, "We haven't been through enough? Now this?"

"What does he have planned, Melanie?" Trey asks. He studies the intuition bubble I fling down our connection. His eyes widen after a moment, and he snaps his head Mama Mabel's way. "How well does Mack know the security system?"

"He was my head of security for a year," she says. "He knows it well."

Trey turns to me. "Take Valerie, Mama Mabel, her girls, Howard, Randall, and your mom. Lock yourselves in the security office."

I shake my head. "That won't work. Mack plans to cut the system somehow. If he does that, we're vulnerable to all the chaos outside of Mama Mabel's fortress. We need to turn off the vault system, lure him in, deal with him, and then enable the system again."

Bear clears his throat. "Can we talk you into filling us in? We don't know what you two saw in Melanie's intuition."

"Mack and some of his buddies are on the way with a plan to raid Mama Mabel's place," Trey explains. "They're apparently desperate for supplies, and she's always fully stocked. He knows how to cut power to the vault system." He gestures toward the TV, and adds, "Given the report we just saw, we don't want to be vulnerable to the outside world right now."

Trey turns to me. "I can feel that you have a plan. Tell us."

I take a breath, attempting to ground out my nerves. "Mack doesn't expect anyone but Mabel's previous residents to be here. He seems to think he can easily subdue Mabel and her four girls. We're all here, and that gives us the element of surprise. There's no way Mack's planning to bring many allies. We can take them. Shut down the vault and leave the parking lot door open so they can get in without having to destroy the system. Everyone who isn't an energy worker should hole up in the security office, and then you enable the panic room interior system. The rest of us need to be ready for Mack's home invasion."

Trey shakes his head. "I don't want you involved in this."

"Sorry, Trey, but I've got an ax to grind." I shrug. "He's trying to harm Mabel. That won't fly."

"We'll deal with him," Trey insists, gesturing to the guys. "I want you to take a knee."

My intuition nags at me. I stand opposite him, my feet wide and hands on my hips. He matches my aggressive stance. Darren whistles the showdown tune from every Western movie ever.

Everyone laughs pensively.

"I'll compromise," I say.

"What are the conditions?"

"I won't be on the front lines, but I'm not willing to be locked in the panic room."

Trey's eyes narrow, and he nods once. "I'll take it."

I don't hesitate to spring to action. "Everyone who's getting locked in the security office needs to head there now. Hurry. Everyone else, be ready."

Trey rushes to the security office, and I follow. "Do you know what buttons to push?" he asks Mama Mabel.

She nods.

"Melanie, I'd prefer you stay in here," Mom implores.

"I know, but I'm the most dangerous person in this building." I cross to her and quietly whisper, just for her to hear, "I'm hiding some stuff from Trey. I need to be out there."

She looks at me with terror in her eyes. I hug her and leave just as Trey pulls the door closed. We hear the door lock click as Mama Mabel enables the panic room system.

Trey and I walk with purpose to the parlor, where Adam, Big Joe, Bear, Darren, Mr. Isley, Demitri, and Rich turn to us. We all stare at each other as the metallic slide of the perimeter steel gates roll up with a series of wooshes and clangs. We're exposed to the outside world.

"Anything new from your intuition?" Trey asks.

"Nothing new," I lie. "Open the foyer door, giving Mack easy access. He'll come straight through that door. Be ready."

Mr. Isley motions me to join him and Demitri across the room. "Hand it over, Melanie," he says quietly.

"Hand what over?"

"What you're hiding," Mr. Isley clarifies.

"If you want everyone to live, you can't tell anyone what I know."

Mr. Isley nods. I grab his hand and give him the memory of my second intuition bubble. He studies it and stares at me in shock.

Demitri's watching Mr. Isley and me suspiciously.

"We might as well have a smoke by the door while we wait," Darren says from across the room.

A smoke sounds good, so I head that way, leaving Demitri to panic with Mr. Isley.

Hesitantly, Trey unlocks the door. "I should have checked the monitors first."

"There's no going back now," I tell him. "Just do it."

Trey opens the door, and we step out into the warm night air. Darren, Big Joe, and Adam pass out smokes. We light up.

"Battle tactic," Adam says. "I vote we lure them in and deal with them from the foyer. It's a narrow bottleneck, and we can hold them off from behind the parlor door. If they pour in, we might find ourselves outnumbered."

Demitri and Mr. Isley step outside and interrupt our tactical preparation.

"Melanie," Demitri says, "you're hiding something. I want to know what it is, and Mr. Isley won't tell me."

I take a drag from my cigarette. "No time to be gossipy girls, D. I'm currently smoking what could be my last cigarette and making a plan with the Hellcats over here."

"Please put that out," Demitri insists, gesturing to my cigarette.

Trey and Adam look Demitri's way, baffled.

"Isn't it sweet when the good guys try to regulate us?" Adam quips. "You see, we're the bad seeds." He waves his hand flippantly at me, Trey, and himself. "We smoke. We drink. We cuss. We get into deadly altercations. Why do we do all of that, you ask? Two reasons. First, it's a good time, and second, to save all your soft asses. Melanie's a beast, and if she needs a smoke before this, then Trey and I are giving her a smoke." He puts his arms out wide and smiles at Demitri. "Welcome to the dark side, Peter Pan!"

Bear and Darren chuckle.

"Whatever she's up against could get her killed," Demitri says.

Adam rattles his head, baffled. "Are you new? EVERYTHING she's faced already SHOULD have killed her. It hasn't because this particular Hellcat has nine lives." He gestures his head my way, and I smile at him. "Let's play your hypothetical game, though! What if it does kill her? Then she'll hang tight for a few, wait for me and Trey to die and enter the next life, and she'll come back as a hot blond bombshell the two of us fight over YET AGAIN." He shrugs. "Same old shit, different dance, Peter Pan."

Rich looks Adam's way. "That's actually how this goes, isn't it?"

We nod.

Bear switches back to our tactical planning. "Any clue how many we're up against?"

I shake my head.

"Mack's joined the Reapers," Big Joe says. "They're a small biker club. Worst case, there are only eighteen members that I know of."

"Nine against eighteen." Darren scoffs. "Realistically, we've faced worse odds and won."

Bear snorts. "Sure, against *teenagers*. These are bikers."

"Nah. They're out of shape middle-aged guys with beer bellies. We've got this." Adam turns to Big Joe, adding, "No offense."

Big Joe raises an eyebrow Adam's way. "Don't underestimate these guys. They fight dirty."

I smirk.

Trey narrows his eyes at me. "You obviously know something more than you're telling us, based on Peter Pan's effort to rescue you. Spill it."

His eyes narrow a touch, just like they always do when he tries to search my mind. I throw up a rock-solid wall on my side of our connection.

A slight smile graces my lips. "Huh-uh-uh. You have to buy a ticket to this show and wait for the theater doors to open, like everyone else."

Trey glares at me.

"How much do I get to fight in this thing?" Rich asks me. "Or am I supposed to worry sick and just stay by you?"

"You have a good time," I tell him with a smile. "I've got my part down in spades."

"It's intense when Melanie lets loose, Rich," Adam warns.

Trey picks up the thread. "You've never seen what she can do when she attacks with energy. She won't even look like herself. No matter what, don't jump in during the heat of the moment. If I rush in, that's when you need to join. Because of our soulmate connection, I'll know if we need to assist her."

Rich nods and turns to me. "Kick ass and take names. I've got your back, Firebird."

"You can't be serious, Rich!" Demitri exclaims. "She's your stepdaughter and you plan to stand back and watch her fight these guys?"

Rich hits Demitri with a hard gaze. "Let me tell you a few things about my kid. If she says she can do something, she can do it. Is it unfortunate that my tiny kid is on the front lines? Yeah, it is, but this is what she does, and I respect her enough to let her be who she is. PERIOD. My WIFE is in that building. Adam's wife and unborn babies are in that building. I'll personally kill everyone I have to if it means keeping those two women safe. If you aren't up for this, that's okay, but stay the hell out of the way because the rest of us plan to crack skulls."

Everyone's eyebrows rise. I smile appreciatively at Rich, but deep down, I wonder if I can really pull this off. I've hidden my second wave of intuition because I know better than to fill Trey in. If I'm not careful, he'll make a wrong decision that costs us the vault system and tosses us into a worse situation than what we currently face.

Before Trey can argue with me, we hear the rumble of motor-cycles coming this way in the quiet.

"I guarantee that's them," I say. "All of you get in place at the door from the foyer into the parlor. When I rush in, let me through. I'm going to be behind you."

Demitri hesitates as the others rush through the door.

Adam comes back, grabbing Demitri by the elbow. "She's rarely wrong. Come on."

Demitri gives me a desperately worried look before Adam pulls him through the open door.

I hope he doesn't step into my firing range when this gets live.

One foot propped up, I lean against the wall outside Mama Mabel's door and take another drag from my cigarette. Motorcycles pull into the alley, and I count them as they park. Through the dark, I can pinpoint exactly which one of them is Mack because he's currently replaying the memory of me leveling him.

The last of the bikers cuts his engine.

I rush inside the building and push through the guys' tight formation at the parlor doorway. "We're up against only twelve of them," I say. "And it's definitely Mack leading them."

They steel up.

"You guys get to have some fun, but I'm cleanup crew," I instruct. "When I tell you to move, I need you to scatter quick to the far side of the parlor. When I give the signal, whatever you do, just don't get caught in the middle of the Reapers."

They don't have a chance to ask for further details, because the Reapers come through the door into the tight foyer.

"I saw that she-devil outside smoking," Mack says. "Where is she?"

"Oooh, I like that," Adam quips. "I'm stealing it. Melanie's DEFINITELY a she-devil."

Our guys all laugh, the sound tinged with evil. I can feel the energy workers in the pack amp up in preparation for an all-out brawl.

Big Joe and Bear have taken point, figuring they're the biggest guys and most likely to effectively block the doorway into the parlor. Unfortunately, it quickly proves to be a bad plan because Big Joe's a hothead with a rough history with the Reapers. He rushes the guy closest to him, shoving him halfway down the foyer hall. That clears room for others to push through on the Reapers' side.

Adam steps up in Big Joe's place and coldcocks one of the bikers. Bear gets another biker pinned against the wall, but it clears another gap. Two of the Reapers push up, and Darren fights to shove them back, to no avail. Mr. Isley moves into the fray and backs one of the guys up by sheer presence alone.

I glance to the side, and Demitri's standing near me. "You don't want to be there when I take over," I tell him. "It's going to get ugly."

Back in the fight, Rich gut-punches one of the Reapers while Trey knees another in his family jewels. Both Reapers drop to their knees.

"Yes YOU DID, Rich!" I proudly exclaim.

"The old guy's still got it," he says over the mayhem. I can feel him radiating his love for a good fight as he rushes further into the foyer, giving me a clear view.

Our guys have been swallowed into a giant ball of swinging fists, screams, snarls, slung curse words, and flying legs. It's like a cartoon catfight, all hissing and slashing claws.

"You don't need to worry about all of this," I say when I notice Demitri is still next to me. "Everyone's loving it. You just aren't made like we are."

"I can't handle you having to live like this," he says.

Trey chooses that moment to toss a thug through the door. The guy lands at my feet. He looks up to find me smirking down at him. "Damn, girl," he exclaims. "You're PURPLE!"

I crack him in the face with my combat boot. He gets up, staggers, and stumbles backward toward Trey, who spins him around and hits him with a right hook.

"Having fun, babe?"

He grins at me as he grabs the guy by the shirt and tosses him back into the foyer scrum.

"I have to let the boys play or they'll get mad at me for taking out all the bad guys on my own," I joke to Demitri.

Before he can reply, we're interrupted as a wall of a man gets through our guys and rushes me. I hit the guy as hard as I can, and he falls.

He looks up at me, shocked, and says, "Screw this," before heading back to the fight with the guys.

The two biggest of the Reapers create a wall at the outside door and start bulldozing their way in, pushing everyone with them. Big Joe and Bear push back, trapping all the guys in the middle of the tight space.

One of the big bikers on the outside of the crush reaches over the battling men and swings, connecting with Big Joe's temple. Big Joe drops, and Adam grabs his arm, dragging him into the parlor, out cold.

Adam and Big Joe's departure leaves our guys at terrible odds. Darren's head is slammed into the wall, and he doubles over, clearly seeing stars. He stumbles into the parlor just as Adam pushes back into the chaotic mix. Adam takes an uppercut that rattles his teeth. He flies through the door and lands at my feet. He's slow to get up. I do the mental math and realize that this leaves only Trey, Rich, Mr. Isley, and Bear up against any of the Reapers who are still standing.

"Playtime's over!" I yell. "CLEAR!"

Rich, Bear, Mr. Isley, and Trey rush through the door into the parlor. They get to the others and pull them out of my peripheral vision. I'm hoping Mr. Isley got Demitri back with them, because I'm left no choice but to just trust that everyone is out of my line of fire.

All the Reapers, beaten and unharmed alike, pour through the parlor door. I expand my energy in a flash of heat that causes pain to radiate down my spine. I hold the image of water vapor in my mind as the energy bubble expands. The moment the bubble surrounds all twelve Reapers, I switch the energy image from vapor to hard steel.

I shake from the effort, my teeth gritting as my energy reserves dredge to nothing.

Realizing that I need a huge source of power to make this work, I send out a searching tendril and find a traveling mob of looters coming down Hollywood Boulevard. I tap into their energy, creating a line from them to me, and pull with ferocity. I feel their shock and fear as one after the other drops with no explanation.

For a flickering moment, I experience guilt about doing this to someone unsuspecting. But then, a thought occurs to me. *They're out doing harm during this catastrophe, and this is their Karmic punishment.*

The energy of hundreds of people pours into me, and I'm suddenly full to the point of nearly exploding. My entire body rattles as I reinforce my invisible steel bubble around the Reapers.

The Reapers are all staring at me in shock. My dark-water side roars up, and I allow the fullest extent of the evil that lives in me to shine viciously through my eyes. Mack blanches, turning sheet white. He whips around, attempting to flee out the foyer door in terror.

Let's see what happens. At least in the way I'm attempting to use it, this energy bubble ability is new and largely untested. But if I was able to affect everyone on the dance team in a positive way, why not the opposite?

Mack crashes into my invisible steel barrier at full speed. He thuds to the ground and rattles his head, trying to clear it. I smile viciously, elated that my invisible barrier is solid enough to contain them.

"Holy crap!" Demitri exclaims.

"You ain't seen nothing yet, D." Trey's watching my plan in my mind, and he sends fear down the line.

I ignore it.

The Reapers watch what happens to Mack, and all descend into full-scale panic. Some test the barrier. Others stare at me, frozen in place with terror in their eyes. One drops to his knees, begging in Spanish with his hands in a prayer position.

"What's he saying?" I snarl in Trey's direction. My voice is deep and gravelly. I don't sound like myself as I ride the wave of energy from hundreds of people. Those people, a mob until a minute ago, are all lying unconscious in the middle of Hollywood Boulevard.

"He's begging you not to harm him because he's got a wife and children," Trey says, running pale. "He also called you a demon."

"Right now, he's not wrong." I hit the begging man with my dark-water gaze. "Switch gears, asshole, and start praying HARD to your God."

Tears slip down the man's cheeks as he screeches, "LA DIABLA!"

Not needing help translating that one, I grin evilly at the man. "Call me what you want. The devil works fine."

"BIG JOE!" the largest Reaper cries. "If you call off La Diabla, we'll leave and NEVER come back. I promise on mutual club edict!"

"He just invoked a clause among biker clubs," Big Joe says, sounding a little woozy still after being knocked out. "If they go back on their word, we have the right to off them. You achieved our goal. You can stop."

"Excellent, but I'm not done yet." I clench my teeth. "I need added insurance that I've driven home my point."

At my command, the steel energy bubble starts to constrict, forcing the guys into a tighter and tighter space. Finally, when they're all mashed together like a bunch of sardines in a can, I start mentally shoving the bubble through the door into the foyer. The effort of moving twelve grown men should be impossible, but I'm riding a soul-bending wave of borrowed energy.

The men skid backward through the foyer and out the door to the parking lot. They're all screaming and trying desperately to break free, to no avail. I hear my friends' footsteps behind me.

"Baby, you can stop now," Trey says. "Holy shit!" I keep pushing, and Trey insists, "MELANIE, they get it!"

"The last time we thought Joel 'got it,' he nearly killed me," I snarl. "We're not making that mistake again."

I continue to push, knowing exactly what I'm doing. When we get halfway through the parking lot, I turn up the heat inside the bubble. The men's screams rise higher as the heat intensifies. I wait until they're writhing and pressing against the invisible barrier in desperation before I drop the temperature down all at once.

They're left panting, gasping, and crying. Sheer terror radiates from them.

I tip my head, one hip cocked, and purr, "Did I make my point, or do you want to go another round?" The look on my face sends them all into another writhing, panicked fit. *"That was fun!"* I send audibly into the bubble. It bounces around inside the barrier and echoes so loud we can all hear even from a distance.

From behind me, Bear gasps.

"If you EVER come back here, threaten my family, or attempt to harm us again, I WILL END YOU."

As they quiver and quake, I clamp down on my dark-water side, leaving my more pleasant side in the driver's seat.

I smile sweetly, widening my eyes into my most innocent teenage expression. "Are you sure we have an understanding?" I ask politely.

The sudden shift in my demeanor pushes some of the guys into mindless panic. One of them passes out cold, and another pees his pants.

"Looks like we do," I chirp.

One final hard push sends their bubble prison tumbling into the row of their motorcycles. The bikes all crash on their sides as the Reapers' bodies plow them over.

I brace, getting a handle on what's left of the raging energy I've borrowed from the looters. My spine boils and seers as I send the energy to the base of the bubble and push as hard as I can.

"Oh my God!" Trey says. "She's not . . ."

Straining to the point that I might combust from the inside, I lift the bubble and hold it six feet off the ground while the bikers lose what's left of their marbles. Finally, when the strain threatens to break me, I burst the bubble in a shower of energy that radiates like an atomic blast across the parking lot. I hear my friends gasp behind me as the invisible energy wave passes through them. The Reapers drop, crashing down on top of their fallen motorcycles just as the last of my borrowed energy drags out.

My knees buckle, and I hit the pavement.

One more boost and this will be over.

I tap into the terrified bikers, syphoning a little energy from each of them, refilling my energy stores enough that I can function. Rejuvenated, I stand and announce, "I left you alive because you're going to pass the word that NO ONE messes with the Hellhounds and Hellcats."

I strut across the parking lot toward my guys, who are all radiating shock and awe. I sashay through the door with everyone following behind me. Trey, the last one through, closes and locks the door.

CHAPTER 44

I storm down the hall to the security room, where I knock on the door. "It's Melanie," I say as I push the intercom button. "Disarm the panic room system."

The door clicks and swings open.

Valerie's on the other side. Panicked, she asks, "What happened? We were watching through the monitors, and then they suddenly went black when Melanie was faced off against the biker guys in the parlor. The monitors came back on a few minutes later, and all the biker guys were lying on their motorcycles."

My battle-weary crew follows me into the security office.

"Melanie happened," Trey says. "She must have shorted out the monitor system for a bit."

"I don't even know where to start." Adam turns to me and sputters, "How? Where? When?"

"You forgot who, what, and why," I tease.

The tension drops, and my fellow Hellcats laugh.

Trey weaves through the crowded office to the control panel on the wall. He pushes the perimeter system button and silences the countdown. We hear the gates crash into place around the exterior perimeter windows and doors.

"We're safe," Trey says. "I guarantee that by morning, every troublemaker within a hundred-mile radius will know not to come here. The gates are in place. Everyone needs to get some sleep. The only thing we should fear tonight are the aftershocks."

Big Joe, Randall, Howard, and Mabel's girls all leave the security office, clearly ready to get some rest.

Rich turns to my mom and says, "I'll fill you in. It's a doozie."

Mom gives me a hug. "I love you, Melanie."

"Love you too, Mom."

Rich grins my way. "Night, La Diabla."

I laugh. "Night, Pops. Ice that hand. Love you."

"Love you too," he says.

Mom inspects his swelling knuckles as he ushers her out the door.

"I'm exhausted, but the three of us are going to discuss that sparkling display tomorrow." Darren gestures to himself, me, and Bear before the two of them clear out, headed to bed.

Demitri and Mr. Isley exchange a look.

"I can't WAIT to head to the studio and choreograph a solo for Melanie," Mr. Isley says. "That was wild!"

The two guys leave the security office.

"Is everyone okay?" Mama Mabel asks the rest of us.

Trey stares at me, baffled. "We're all fine. There are about a hundred people currently out cold on Hollywood Boulevard, though. Melanie energy drained the mob. There are also twelve urine-soaked bikers in your parking lot who may be mentally and spiritually damaged."

Mama Mabel raises an eyebrow. "Sounds like Melanie strikes again."

Adam laughs and Trey snorts.

"Goodnight, Mabel," I say sweetly.

"Goodnight, dears. Get some rest."

Adam, Trey, Val, and I are left staring at each other.

"How did you do that?" Adam asks.

I shrug. "You know how this shit works. I don't know I can, then I do, and we're all surprised."

"Ready for bed?" Trey asks.

"My dark-water side is still thrumming. I'm going to sleep on the couch in the parlor."

"I can handle your dark-water side," Trey reminds.

"I'd rather avoid that."

He looks disappointed. "Why?"

"Because I refuse to be a hormonal mess. It's a bad look. I'm more than a slave to my carnal core."

Trey closes his eyes.

"We're headed to bed," Adam says tactfully. "Goodnight, you two."

"Night," I reply.

Alone with me now, Trey says, "We have a home at Mabel's. We're reconnecting. I need time with you."

With a sigh, I tell him, "I need things to slow down, Trey. I don't even have my birth control pills here."

"Shit," he says intensely.

"We're fine. I took them up until this earthquake mess hit. I just don't want to take any chances right now."

Trey swallows awkwardly. "Melanie, I just want to spend time with you. This wasn't about sex."

"I get it, but my dark-water side makes things uninhibited. I need some space tonight."

"Hey." Trey grabs my wrist as I start to pass by. "Did you sleep with Zane? I know you said you didn't, but the way you rushed to talk to him on that CB . . ."

"I didn't sleep with him," I reply.

He sighs. "I'm incredibly insecure about him."

I give Trey a look. "I promise not to do him any more than twenty-two times."

Trey squeezes his eyes tight. "The thought of you with someone else even *one* time breaks me."

"Yeah, Trey," I say quietly. "It sucks. I'm really working on letting it go. I promise."

He opens his eyes, and they're shiny with emotion. "I would do anything to take it back," he says sincerely.

"I know." I clear my throat. "Thank you for fighting for me out there."

"You didn't need my help." His head drops. "I'm realizing all the excuses I leaned on to convince myself you'd stick with me. You needing me to battle evil with you was one of them. So was our friend group. You can fight on your own now, and our friend group abandoned you."

I nod. "True. Good thing for you that I love you."

"I love you too, Melanie." He pulls me in, hugging me.

"Prove it, Trey," I softly say while I stare into his golden-brown eyes. "Please resolve whatever lived in you that made Tiffany an option. You and me. Soulmates with all the connection and depth."

Something deepens in Trey's eyes. His expression shifts vulnerably, but he's got me blocked off and I can't tell what he's thinking. "It's all changed now. I promise."

"Are you sure?" I question with a tone of warning. "I'm taking Ms. G up on the offer of being a student at Hollywood High again."

Trey looks quizzical. "Of course. I knew you would. Why the reminder?"

"Because Tiffany will be there every day. Can you handle that?"

He nods emphatically. "I won't even notice her. I just want a solid chance with you again."

"Thank you." I squeeze his hand and reluctantly back to the door without letting go. Our arms stretch long while I hold on. I want to stay with him, but I'm so unsettled. *Slower is better, Melanie. Make him show you that he can be trusted. That takes time.*

"The door to our room will be unlocked in case you decide to come to bed," Trey says.

With a grateful smile, I take my leave.

CHAPTER 45

Trey sends through our connection, *"The Hellhounds are here. You might want to come out and explain this."*

I sigh and head out the bedroom door, walking with purpose into the crowded parlor. All my housemates have been fetched, and the room's nearly busting with people.

Fists on his hips, Stubbs stands wide-legged and gives me a *disappointed dad* kind of look. "Did you REALLY try to boil the Reapers to death, lift them up, and drop them on their Harleys?"

Sheepishly, I say, "Maybe," and scrunch up my shoulders.

Stealth and Mercury crow with laughter, saving me from Stubbs's disapproval.

I grin at Stealth and Mercury, the two most lethal members of the Hellhounds. "You two would have LOVED it!"

They smile from ear to ear at me, and it looks a little strange on their usually tough faces.

"Get over here, you little troublemaker," Mercury crows. "We owe you a hug. The Reapers are a bunch of asswads, and I couldn't be prouder of you!"

I practically skip to them. They wrap me in fatherly hugs.

"I'd give my right ARM to see what happened," Stealth says.

Trey grins conspiratorially. "If you guys have a minute, I'll show you."

He's interrupted by a pounding on the foyer door. Big Joe heads through the foyer and ushers in the rest of my group of friends.

"Sounds like we missed a hell of a show," Arch says. "Thanks for leaving me out of the fun, jackasses."

We all laugh.

"So you guys want to see what happened or what?" Trey asks, holding up a VHS tape.

"How?" Valerie asks. "I thought Melanie drained the power to the system during the fight."

Trey shakes his head. "She temporarily drained the monitors' ability to broadcast, but apparently the VHS recorders kept running. We're equipped with an editing machine, and I couldn't sleep, so I took the liberty of cutting together a tape that shows everything in real time from the foyer, parlor, and parking lot cameras. Anyone up for a premier showing of the wildest short film you'll ever see?"

Everyone nods enthusiastically.

"I'll be right back." Trey heads through the hall door, Hiram in tow.

Everyone takes a seat on the couches and floor. Others lean against the wall. We hear the metallic slide of the gate closing over the door, and I exhale, feeling safer. In the next breath, I realize how silly it was to have felt unsafe to begin with. Even if I hadn't just single-handedly caused a whole biker gang to wet themselves, I'm surrounded by an incredibly dangerous crowd.

Trey comes back in and pops the tape into the machine. He pushes play, and in black-and-white security footage that's surprisingly clear, our battle crew enjoys a cigarette break out front while we wait for the Reapers.

Mom huffs from her spot across the room on my favorite love seat. "You have to quit smoking, Melanie."

I roll my eyes. "I know. I know. It's my one bad habit."

"Riiight," Mom says, raising an eyebrow at me. "You only have *one* bad habit."

"Fine. It's *one* of my bad habits. I promise I'll work on it."

Satisfied, she turns her attention back to the footage. We watch the Reapers pull into the parking lot, and our group heads inside. The whole first half of the video is a standard fistfight.

We get to the exciting part, and Trey says, "Buckle up. Here we go."

Everyone leans forward and watches the TV without blinking.

We get to the part where the squashed pack of Reaper sardines are shoved into the motorcycles, and the Hellhounds all wince as the bikes crash to their sides.

"Damn, Firebird!" Stubbs says. "Not the hogs!"

My internal horror is growing as I watch the reality of what I did last night. The Reapers are yanked off their feet and into the air. They hang suspended for longer than I'd thought. The sound of grown men whimpering, terrified, begging and pleading, makes the hair on the back of my neck stand on end.

Suddenly, the suspended Reapers crash to the ground, landing haphazardly on top of their fallen motorcycles.

"You can do THAT?" Victoria screeches, her voice full of fear.

"Apparently," I reply with little emotion.

Everyone turns and stares at me in disbelief. Trey pushes the pause button just in time to capture my face frozen in a seductively evil smile.

The sight drives my fear the rest of the way home. *There's a fine line between light and dark, and I've crossed it.* "I need a minute," I announce.

They all watch me blankly as I head to the hall door.

Mama Mabel steps in front of me. "No, you don't."

I stop, with my head dropped in shame.

"We're going to deal with this right now, so you don't spiral for a week." Mama Mabel pauses, but I don't look up. She says sternly, "Look at me, Melanie."

I do what she says.

"What we just watched was one of the evilest things I've ever seen," Mabel says. "But YOU are not evil. Those men came into our home and threatened your family and friends. Our guys were outnumbered. They did a hell of a job, but the Reapers would've eventually bested them with their greater numbers. You made a choice to do what was in your ability, and I'm thrilled because we could've been planning funerals today instead of being shocked by your nifty display."

She gestures to the TV, and my gaze flicks to the image of my evil expression frozen on the screen.

"You didn't kill any of them," Mabel says. "Hellfire, you barely even *hurt* them. At least not physically. They likely have bumps and bruises from the six-foot fall, but they'll be fine. What you did was *flex*. They're terrified, but they've also learned a hard lesson that I'm chalking up to tough love. Much like a mom scolding a pack of naughty toddlers, you put the Reapers in time-out and set boundaries."

Demitri's in my line of sight, and it looks like he agrees.

I consider what Mabel's saying.

Movement catches my attention out of the corner of my eye. I turn to see Hiram scurrying here and there, turning on power strips.

"Mom lectures make me nervous," he says bashfully. "I decided to stay busy while Mabel gives you a talking-to."

With that, he puts a pair of plugs together and the stereo clicks on, revealing the first haunting notes of the CD that must have been playing when the power went out. The song is familiar, yet different, and I turn curious eyes Mama Mabel's way.

"You and your music," she says appreciatively. "It's the demo reel for an upcoming rehash of 'Livin' on a Prayer.' It's titled 'Prayer '94.' The original is my favorite song, and I have a friend who's involved with the Bon Jovi remake. It's an amazing version. You'll like it."

I listen as the drum kicks rhythmically and a bell chimes. A voice speaks hauntingly through the speakers as Trey and I make eye contact from opposite sides of the room. Neither of us try to speak mind-to-mind. Instead, we stand, staring at each other, our expressions a touch haunted.

Trey taps into our connection and starts syphoning off the nervous energy that's got me spun out. I smile softly at him.

"I'm proud of you," Trey says.

"You sure?"

He nods. "Yeah, Melanie. I'm sure."

"Thank you."

Trey strides my way and wraps his arms around me. I exhale, feeling a little better about the new "me" I'm struggling to understand. Every new ability comes with a fresh set of regret, it seems.

Mabel winks at me. "How about we go to the banquet hall where we've got more room?"

"We have a banquet hall?" I ask.

Trey rolls his eyes. "This place has everything. I was hoping you wouldn't find out about this particular room, though."

"Why?"

"You'll see."

We all follow Mama Mabel through the kitchen and down a hallway I've never been in. She flips on a few light switches as we wind and weave past storage closets and butlers' pantries that I never knew existed. We get to a door, and she takes out her key ring, unlocking it. She flips a switch to her right, and a giant room with a shiny wood floor is revealed.

We all step in, and Rich says, "This room is HUGE."

"This space and the garage make up half of the square footage of the original warehouse," Mama says. "I use it for events, rentals, and philanthropy banquets."

Hiram points across the room. "Is that a deejay booth?"

Mabel laughs. "It is, but you might be disappointed. The system is outdated, and there's only a few turntables and a bunch of old disco records behind the booth."

Excited, Hiram rushes across the room to check it out. Our group lives for music from all decades, and he clearly can't wait to play as much of it as he can.

"Why didn't you update the system for your current events?" Arch asks.

Mama shrugs. "When I hire deejays, they always have their own gear, so I didn't bother."

"What was the original booth for then?" I ask.

"You'll see." Mabel yells across the room to Hiram, "Did you get it running?"

Lighting up with enthusiasm, Hiram pulls a record from its sleeve. "Kick ass!" He points across the room at me and proclaims, "This one's for you, La Diabla!"

Mama Mabel grins and flips a bank of light switches just as "I Will Survive" pumps from the blasting speakers hanging from the ceiling. Flashing lights blaze to life on the ceiling, casting in a starburst pattern. A disco ball turns in the center, sending mirrored flashes around the suddenly festive room.

Mama flips another light switch, and a counter with row after row of roller skates on shelves is revealed.

I jump up and down, clapping. "It's a ROLLER-SKATING rink!" I leap at Trey, enthusiastically blathering, "Can we skate, babe? Let's SKATE!" I wiggle from head to toe like an excited puppy.

He drops his head and mutters, "Shit." He turns to Mama Mabel. "You just HAD to show her, didn't you?" He looks to me and pointedly says, "I have work to do in my office. You have fun."

Mama Mabel blocks his exit. "Oh no you don't. Don't reject her! You get over there and strap on some skates. Melanie's earned some fun, and I can't wait to watch you fall ass over teakettle."

Trey huffs as I drag him to the counter. In no time, everyone's ready to roll, even the Hellhounds.

My parents skate by, holding hands. The Hellhounds all take turns comically flying into walls, falling over, and crashing into each other. Their slapstick shenanigans have me in stitches. The dancers from the Hellcats, Mama Mabel, and her girls all whip and zip, glide and turn around the rink with grace. Everyone else is a mixed bag of talent, but all are having a blast. The only one not skating is our pregnant Valerie, but she's enjoying the show from a chair on the edge of the rink. Actually, that's not true. Victoria and Trey have also ducked out of the fun. They're quietly talking on the far side of the skating rink. I send a little curiosity pulse his way, and he skates away from Victoria, headed toward me.

Trey surprises me by taking my hand and whipping me ahead of him. I squeal happily and race past Big Joe.

I reach for Big Joe's hand as I pass. "Come on!"

"No, no, NOOO!" he exclaims, losing his balance and falling on his keister.

This earns loud guffaws and taunts from his Hellhound buddies, who aren't doing much better.

Demitri glides up next to me. "Are you actually okay?"

"I'm legit good."

"You're remarkable."

I smile at him. "Thanks, D."

Victoria skates up and grabs his hand, pulling him away.

Trey rolls up next to me and pulls me to the center of the roller rink, under the disco ball. He grabs my hands, and we start circling to the right, picking up speed.

Suddenly, an aftershock hits. Everyone falls as the angry ground protests and snarls, bucks and violently shakes.

The power goes out mid-rattle, and when the shaking stops, Marcus says in the dark, "Awww! There will be no more fun!"

We all crack up.

A colossal sound whip-whip-whips from outside. A moment later, everything goes eerily quiet.

"Anyone know what that is?" I ask.

"Your ride is here," Mabel informs cryptically.

"My WHAT?" I ask.

In the dark, Rich announces, "Sorry Melanie but I couldn't let it go. I CB'd Zane and we had a talk. You need to get your role back. I'm not letting you get manipulated and shoved aside. Our family aren't pushovers."

"Oh shit," I mutter while my heart races. A combination of nerves, insecurity, and excitement race through me.

"You have to be kidding," Trey mutters next to me.

There's pounding on the door. We all grapple to stand, bumping into each other in the pitch black.

"No damn lights," Trey snarls. "No damn security monitor."

"Melanie!" someone bellows from outside the door.

"That must have been Brian landing Drell Two," I say.

"Drell Two?" Marcus asks from somewhere on the other side of the darkness.

"Zane's helicopter."

"Then what's Drell One?"

"I'm not sure, but my money's on a private jet."

"Damn, it must be nice to be loaded like that," Tanner says wistfully.

"Necessary privileges of a very complicated life."

From behind the skate booth, Mabel clicks on a flashlight she found. She grins in the beam. "I got you packed up in secret."

"You were in on this?" I ask.

"Naturally," Mabel replies. "I'll grab your bags." She clicks on a second flashlight that she hands to Rich, who heads to answer the door.

After boisterously greeting Rich, Brian strides in. He looks me over with a chuckle. "You decided to roller-skate before hopping in a helicopter to snag back your role in a questionable movie?"

I shrug a little. "I didn't know I was hopping a helicopter." I grin, gesturing around. "A girl has to have fun in this topsy-turvy madhouse."

Brian shakes his head adoringly. "You and Zane are the same person, I swear."

Trey gives a nasty look that Brian ignores.

"You ready to go, gorgeous?" Brian asks.

"I guess." Worry chills me as I take off my skates and slip into my flip-flops. "Are we taking the helicopter all the way to New York?"

"Of course not," Brian says with a grin. "We'll take the helicopter to the airfield, where a private jet is fueled and waiting."

The power comes back on as Mama Mabel wheels in a massive suitcase. Arch has several hanging bags and another suitcase.

Worry suddenly turning to fear, I take a deep breath. "Okay, here goes nothing," I say as my stomach bubbles.

Mom and Rich step up and hug me tight.

"Take no prisoners," Rich says. "Go get your part back."

Feeling insecure, I look up at him. "Are you positive it's okay to do all those sexy scenes?"

Rich looks to my mom, who says, "We're going to figure it out," as she takes the handle of a suitcase and cocks a confident hip.

"You're coming with me?" I ask. I'm a little more bolstered by that possibility.

"Someone needs to." My mom grins. "I'll be nice . . . to everyone but Molly, that is."

Anticipatory chuckles punctuate the room. My mom is a sweetheart with the death chomp of a great white.

"I'm going to face scrutiny for this movie at school." I grimace.

My mother laughs. "Is that new?" She gestures to my friends. "You couldn't even escape scrutiny from the people who claim to be your friends." She shrugs. "You're damned if you do and damned if you don't. If you do though—" she smirks—"you're damned to the tune of a possible dream career." Mom smiles endearingly at me. "It's my job as your mother to help guide you. You want this, and I think you've got what it takes. I'm not letting you slink away with your tail between your legs because some bimbo bullied you. Let's give your dreams a shot."

"Thank you," I breathe in disbelief. This is huge and scary, but I want the opportunity badly.

Mabel steps in and hugs me. "People are going to find stuff to talk about whether you do this movie or not. When we secretly CB'd Zane, he seemed certain you've got a shot. Apparently, Molly's 'performance' got worse, not better. The director knows you're alive, and he asked Zane to get you down there."

"I'm hoping they *do* talk shit at school," Presley interjects. "I'm looking forward to another brawl." She grins at me. "Get to New York and shake your ass."

"Quit worrying about what other people think." Mom offers a sad smile. "You're already hated, Melanie. It is what it is."

My friends all have mournful eyes.

"We've all got your back," Bear says. "We'll never ditch you like that again. You need to do this."

Heads nod from all the misfits. I smile, but it's a little unsure. Their ditching of me was a difficult thing I've had to work hard to forgive.

"I don't want you to do this," Trey admits.

"I'm sorry you feel that way, Trey." I take a grounding breath. "I have to take my shot. Mom and I will take this moment by moment and get it worked out. You need to trust us."

Trey looks from Mom to me. He nods but has clearly caged down. I guess it's understandable. Ms. Alice was clear that the movie is of a suggestive nature, but realistically, so am I. Considering that he dated both Victoria and Tiffany, who are the school hoebags, he's no stranger to suggestive natures.

My eyes narrow as I contemplate this. *He was willing to accept both of them. Why not me?*

Trey was apparently studying my thoughts because he sends, *"Because you're better than them, I don't expect them to be above all that. I just don't want you to compromise yourself for a paycheck."*

I meet Trey's vulnerable gaze. *"Thank you for that. I need to follow my path, though. Suddenly that path holds more than having to be constantly attacked and tortured, both socially and by evil people. I deserve to grow in other ways now."*

Trey lights up a little. *"Then go get 'em."*

A smile warms my face, and I'm surprised to see Trey's eyes tearing up.

He rushes to me and hugs me tight, saying, "You're going to be amazing."

"*That's* my best friend," Tanner pridefully says as Trey lets me go. Tanner hugs me next, encouraging, "Take no prisoners, Mel."

Everyone takes turns hugging me. Demitri and Victoria maintain their distance. As usual, the moment Victoria is here, Demitri shuts down.

"See you later, Mel," Demitri says from across the group.

"See you later," I reply stoically.

Trey wraps me up in a hug one more time. "Please be safe," he murmurs.

"I will, I promise. I'll see you when I get back."

"Will you call me?" Trey asks, clearly insecure.

"Of course I will." I smile up at him.

"Ready, ladies?" Brian asks, already gathering up our luggage.

Mabel hands me my backpack and purse. "Go get your job back. Love you, Mel."

"I love you too. Thank you for packing for me."

Rich hugs Mom tight and murmurs just for her and me to hear, "No hesitation. Edgy is okay. We're edgy people."

I take a sharp breath and grin at him with hope shining in my eyes. He smiles back ferociously.

We head outside, and Brian helps us get in the helicopter before closing the door. The propellers whip before we lift into the air. I look out the window as all my people stare up at me from the parking lot.

Once we're clear of Mabel's compound, I survey the streets below. Because of the news helicopters, it's not the first time I've seen the destruction that has hit Los Angeles, but to see it firsthand changes my sense of the scale. It's completely unimaginable how much damage the city has taken.

Brian flips several switches before grabbing his CB. "Zaney?"

"Talk to me, big brother."

"I've got your girl. We're headed to the airport."

"Yes! Thank you, Brian." Zane sounds like a little kid when he gets like this. "Melanie?"

"Hi, babe."

"Hi. I want you to settle in on Drell One and enjoy every moment."

"I'm so excited," I bubble.

"Me too," he says. "Get her here safe, Brian. Are you sure you can handle a red-eye flight?"

"I slept all day in preparation. Nothing's going to happen to her."

"Keep me posted," Zane says nervously.

"I'll be fine," I assure. "Quit worrying, Zane. A few days ago, I was trapped under a massive building. I think I can handle cat-napping in your fancy-ass plane."

Zane chuckles. "I'll see you in the morning. Get rest. You head straight to set. We've got one shot at this."

"Done, and thank you."

Brian turns off the CB and grins back at me. "He's bonkers, I swear. The kid has been a loon since he was a baby."

I laugh and watch out the window as my thoughts take me away. The humiliation I've endured has taught me a great deal, and I'm suddenly grateful for it. What Zane and I went through in the hospital was grossly horrific, but it set the stage for me to learn how to trust. Sometimes we need help. Sometimes we're not at the top of the heap. Being little, broken, and helpless wasn't a life sentence—for me or for anyone. It was a stage of life that makes me more resilient.

I scoff silently to myself. Being a part of the Normals at Canoga Park High drove home how different I am. It was good, though. I needed the realization that my circle will be small. I belong with the misfits from Hollywood. Maybe they needed the break from me to realize their own loyalties and shortcomings.

My thoughts drift to Trey. I'm a little unsure still, but trying with him feels right. I always thought I'd have a zero-tolerance policy on cheating. With that said, we all deserve a second chance. The idea that we worked through the Tiffany mess battles with my feelings about him keeping the extent of the affair from me. He hid it out of love. That's a quandary because I'm big on open honesty. I guess sometimes we have to bend the tight constraints of our moral code. I smirk to myself at the thought that I'll be pushing Trey's own morality boundaries with this edgy movie role. Maybe it's his turn to flex his constraints out of compassion for his partner. Karma's a funny one that way.

So . . . How did it go? Well . . .

One last glance in the full-length wardrobe mirror revealed perfection. My usual insecurity had no shot against the woman staring back at me. Considering how small I am, the head of costuming didn't have an evening gown ready for me. Fortunately, it turned out Mabel packed my gold dress, along with the stunning jeweled shoes.

Thank God for Mabel, I thought.

I looked like a million bucks at this pivotal moment because of the loving efforts of Mabel, my mother, and of course, Demitri. Another wave of appreciation wafted as I thought about how, once he was restored enough energetically to handle the monumental task, Demitri healed my bruising. I wouldn't have been able to do this without him.

Next, gratitude for my mother streamed through me. Mom woke me up from a power nap two hours before we landed and proved to be the best glam squad I could have ever dreamed of. She did my hair and makeup while coaching me on how to approach this unconventional audition.

As I headed out of the dressing room and made my way down the hall to the ballroom, I could already hear Molly squawking in protest. Everyone was so consumed with her tantrum that my entrance went unnoticed. Finally, mid-rage, Molly whipped around and spotted me. I stared back from across the ballroom, aiming for neutral. Considering that she was thoroughly losing her shit, she made me look pretty damn good.

"You already put her through hair and makeup?" she screamed maniacally.

"I showed up with hair and makeup done," I replied as I slowly took in her sweatpants, greasy hair, and shiny, unwashed face.

"You showed up looking like THAT?"

I raised an eyebrow. "I'm a professional actress. Not a spicy ferret."

"What did you call me?" Molly screamed over the laughter spurting from everyone in the room.

"A spicy ferret," I repeated matter-of-factly before looking to Jack Griffin. "Sir, I'm ready."

Jack grinned. "I can see that. It's good to see you again, Melanie."

"You as well," I charmed back.

I was introduced to the director of photography, and I greeted him just as Zane stepped up next to me.

Jack said, "Roll it," and we watched footage of Molly and Zane on a monitor. I got the gist, but my head tipped and my face Fraggle-scrunched. The Molly on the monitor was all gangly, her movements weird. The whole scene felt disconnected—more like two people *trying* to be sexy instead of actually being sexy. The scene differed vastly from what was called for in the script.

When the footage ended, all I could say was, "Huh . . ."

"What's so funny?" Molly barked at the sound of Zane's laughter.

"Is that what you were after?" I asked the director as professionally as I could manage.

His mouth twitched as he fought amusement.

"I mean, damn," I said. "That was a thing."

Everyone in the room cracked up. Molly huffed before dramatically thrusting a sassy hip.

"Would you like to see the script?" the director asked.

"No sir," I replied. "We read it on the plane." *It's a lot.*

The director looked to my mother. "What are your thoughts about what you read?"

Mom's eyebrows rose, her gorgeous face taking on a regal quality. "I think it's spectacular."

Mouths fell open all around the room.

"We can make adjustments based on Melanie's age," Mr. Griffon offered.

"No need," Mom replied stoically. At the director's gobsmacked silence, she added, "My daughter is here to do a job, not pretzel this cast and crew to her bidding."

The director looked to a stunned Zane before staring at my mother.

"How much of this can she do, given her age?" Mom inquired.

Jack was clearly befuddled by her calm lack of pushback. "All of it, if we get the camera angles right and have parental approval."

"Granted," Mom said as she slid steely eyes toward a gaping Molly. As much as Mom can be the ultimate southern lady, she's also a brass-balls bitch.

"That script is filthy," Molly said, disgusted. "No lady would do what's in there without changes."

Mom smirked. "That script is a true depiction of life, love, heartbreak, and dejection."

"It's nothing but trashy porn," Molly retorted in disbelief.

Sinister laughter bubbled from my mother. "Maybe how *you'd* do it." Mom slid rock-solid certainty to the director. "My daughter is young, but no one understands the character of Layanette like she does. We thoroughly analyzed the script together. I assure you that if you want *this* movie," she gave the script a little shake, "then you need *that* girl." She gestured to me.

The director's eyes lit, and he slowly started to smile as his hopeful gaze panned to me.

My nervousness was washed away by my mother's belief in me. *Screw it. We go for big air.* "Work out the angles," I requested.

The director's eyes widened. "You're sure?"

I nodded. "I wouldn't be here if I wasn't. I don't toy with people or waste their time." I fought not to give Molly the look she deserved.

Zane rapidly blinked before rubbing his face hard.

"I get one shot, right?" I said to him with a hard edge.

He exhaled. "That's the theory."

"Then I'm taking my shot."

"Get everything set," the director ordered.

Everyone started scurrying about. Zane was whisked away to wardrobe, and I was left to contend with what I was about to do.

Taking the script with me, I headed out to the veranda. My mother joined me, holding a pack of smokes and a lighter.

My eyebrows rose.

Mom popped open the pack and handed me one. "Take a breather and get your head on straight. Talk to me about anything you're unsure of. Now's the time."

I took a drag. "There's this thing about being Melanie Slate," I said quietly. "What lives in me ensures that I'll never fit in. I'm nothing like kids my age. My friends try, but I stretch their boundaries." I side-eyed my mother. "My dark-water side is the tool they need to get this movie done." I turned and leaned my back against the railing. "I'm not only comfortable with the material, but I'll smoke this scene."

"I agree," Mom said.

"What makes me uncomfortable is people seeing, and then judging, the reality of what I am."

"Can you handle that?"

"I'm already judged." I shrugged. "If you and Rich are good with me after this, then I can handle it." I looked to her. "He hasn't seen the script. Should we call and discuss this with him?"

"No," she said with finality.

"Dads and moms don't think the same," I reminded.

"Your stepfather is the most open-minded, movie-industry-savvy, realistic man I know."

Just then, Zane rushed onto the veranda in a tuxedo. Before I could put out my cigarette, he snagged it and took a huge drag.

"Are you positive about this?" Zane asked.

"Rock solid. Just do your part."

Zane leveled my mother with serious eyes. "I've never even

kissed your daughter. I need to hear that you understand and approve of the reality of what's about to happen. The director intentionally picked the most heated scene so he could truly test Melanie."

Mom smiled with a touch of arrogance. "I'm fully aware of what I'm permitting. I'm not naïve, and I did a lot of thinking as we read and discussed the script on the plane." She shifted, her arms crossing over her chest. "The real question, Zane Drell, is if you truly understand the nature of Melanie's dark-water side."

"I think I do," Zane said, glancing from me to my mom. "I'm a little surprised that *you* seem to understand it."

Mom quietly scoffed before leveling me with a serious gaze that sent chills up my spine. "If you unleash just enough of it, it'll get captured in the film. Every movie watcher will feel just a breath of it. The movie will hit number one."

"How do you know that?" I asked suspiciously.

"Focus," Mom said evasively. "Just enough to be captured on film, but not enough to kill him. Remember that Zane is a Normal. Got it?"

"You're not an energy worker," I insisted. "Tell me how you knew that!"

Without another word, Mom walked away.

Gaping after her, I asked Zane, "What do you think that was about?"

It seemed Zane was caught in a different suspicion tornado. "Your dark-water side can *kill* me?"

"I won't let that happen," I answered absently, my mind still stuck on the strangeness of everything Mom seemed to know.

"I'll be damned if I die by simulated orgasm on a movie set," Zane insisted to his brother, who chose that moment to join us.

I laughed, coming back to reality. "It'll be fine. I've got this."

Zane morphed serious. "You do realize that once that footage is on film, it lives forever."

I hit him with a bright smile. "Reputation be damned. I'm already a five-alarm disaster. It can't get any worse."

"Melanie, we're ready for you," a production assistant called out.

I smirked up at Zane. "We're about to see how much control you have. Keep your shit in check through this, or it'll get messy."

His eyes widened.

Brian howled laughter before clapping his brother on the shoulder. "You think you got this, Movie Star?"

"I feel fifteen in the back seat of a car with a girl for the first time," Zane admitted bashfully.

"I'm not called La Diabla for nothing," I chortled.

As I sauntered inside, hips swaying, I could feel Brian and Zane's gazes on my back.

— —

"Quiet on set," someone bellowed.

Everyone got into place.

"Roll film . . . Action."

I leaned on the bar. The bartender flirted with me. Per the script, I turned my back on him, uninterested. I panned the mingling partygoers, stopping as my gaze met Zane's across the room. He gave me a hopeful look. This scene was from the middle of the movie, and our characters had been through a lot by that point—most of it related to Zane's character, Rex Kendall, having an affair.

Madonna's "Erotica" came on, and I let my vibe shift seductively. A touch of evil wafted up within me, my expression reflecting that my character was pissed and yet in the mood. Zane smirked before turning with perfect musical timing and sauntering to the hallway, where the set split into a hotel room.

Internally, I winced because we didn't discuss the timing with the music, but I still believed we could pull this off. I sauntered through the ballroom with a camera following me, stopping as I turned into the hall. Zane was opening a door at the far end. He smoldered at me. I waited until he held a hand my way. He looked breathtaking in his tuxedo. I smirked before running my hands down my gold satin-clad hips. Working with the song, I took hip-swaying steps while reaching for my zipper behind me. I unzipped the dress and gave the spaghetti straps a flick. Camera B's light went off to avoid filming something it wasn't legally allowed to show. We now depended on the camera following me as the gorgeous dress drifted to the floor. I stepped out of it and slowly continued down the hall in my heels and underwear while Zane gave me the most attractive look I've ever seen from a man. He fully faced me with his head cocked as I unhooked my strapless bra and let it drop to the carpeted hallway.

I got to him, my steps perfectly timed to the music. *So far, so good.* I reached up, gripping his throat, and thudded his back against the wall. I put my fingertips on his forehead before running them lightly down his face. His eyes closed as he gasped. He spun me around and pressed my back against the wall. Strategically, he placed his hand on the wall, blocking the camera's view of my chest.

He leaned into me, kissing my neck. My eyes fluttered closed, and my brain rattled. I gave into it enough that I revealed how suddenly spun out I was, but my focus was on keeping my dark-water side from launching into the stratosphere. Zane and I had never worked through anything like this, and . . . well, HOLY CRAP!

Unfortunately, he chose to kiss my neck while I was a rattling mess. Vanilla woohoo filled his senses, and he moaned, melting against me. He picked me up and whipped us around, opening the door. He backed into the hotel room set, which was equipped with more cameras. The door slammed shut, and camera operators, who were only just now getting to know the vibe, watched us with slack jaws.

The room was barely lit. Zane got us to our mark on the floor, offering the perfect camera angle somehow, and I was grateful that he knew what he was doing, because by that point, I couldn't think worth a damn.

We stared at each other, eye to eye. Per the script, I ran my thumb delicately along his cheekbone before kissing him. We had so much built-up tension between us that neither of us could function. As far as first kisses go . . . Let's just say it was the kiss to end all first kisses. It started off slow, and then things heated while I unbuttoned his dress shirt. I lost my careful hold over my dark-water side as his shirt fell to the floor, and it blew sky-high as a seductive sonic boom detonated from me. Everyone in the room silently gasped, and two people hit their knees.

Panic shot through me. What I released threatened to actually *kill* most Normals. I looked down at Zane as we fell to the bed.

His expression turned animalistic as this masculine growl escaped him.

Oh yeeesss, blazed through my thoughts. *He can handle me.* I smirked at him.

He rolled, pinning me to the bed with my arms stretched over my head.

I managed to keep enough of my mind intact to remember that I was supposed to unzip his slacks as he let go of one of my hands. I undid them, but had to grab the covers and yank them over us as he rolled me on top of him. To say he was locked and loaded would have been an understatement, so this was the only way to hide it from the cameras.

Lying on him, covered to my tush, I kissed him again as Madonna continued moaning and purring her way through "Erotica." I ran a hand up his arm before grabbing the headboard. I started to sit up, and Zane ran his hands up my abs, sliding over my chest to block the view as I straddled him and tipped my head back on the last whispered word of the song.

"Cut," someone called.

I looked the director's way, and his mouth was hanging open.

A quick survey of the crew revealed similar reactions. One guy started fanning his face with his clipboard.

My mother's bawdy laugh was the only sound.

Zane sat up, wrapping his arms around me to block the view of my chest from the enrapt crew and spectators. His breathing was uneven, and I secretly loved it. I also secretly loved the destroyed vibe that rolled off of Molly. I don't usually revel in someone else's pain, but Molly was an exception.

"Where did that come from?" the director breathed on a wave of disbelief. "Who *are* you?"

An evil laugh bubbled up and slunk from me as my head tipped back. I took my time, enjoying my dark-water thrum before sliding a sultry gaze to the director.

"Perhaps we need a fresh introduction," I purred. "I'm Melanie Slate. Nice to meet you."

Special thanks to the incredible team of models that keep pulling through for me over and over. Thank you to Deidre Michelle for her endless ability to find the right people to depict these characters. Thank you to Anna Hall, Kyle Fager, and Stephen Knezovich for making this series magic. Thank you to Jordan, Bear, and Carol for their endless conceptual support.

MELISSA VELASCO is a true explorer of the arts. With a well-rounded background as a choreographer, professor, dance teacher, stage manager, author, and Crystal Grid teacher, she thrives in creation. At her core, she believes that the arts save lives and provide a route for passion and connection. The artistic ride makes life a whole lot brighter.

With a quick wit, often edgy mouth, and loud laugh, Melissa exuberantly embraces life. To find balance from the mental cacophony in her head, she enjoys expansive views in her mountain home. Her ideal day involves a mug of hot tea, music playing, and a whole day to write. Her greatest loves are her three children and husband. The four pillars of her ultimate happiness include her family, friends, dance, and laughter.

Sometimes we forget Melanie Slate is a teenager, and then circumstances smack us back to reality. When a critical mistake leads to a series of life changing battles, we see what these kids are made of. When it's Melanie who needs saving, do her Misfits have the superhero stones to step up?

www.ingramcontent.com/pod-product-compliance
Lightning Source LLC
Chambersburg PA
CBHW022257310726
48973CB00001B/111